REALM-LORDS
DALE LUCAS

BLACK LIBRARY

A BLACK LIBRARY PUBLICATION

First published in 2020.
This edition published in Great Britain in 2021 by
Black Library, Games Workshop Ltd., Willow Road,
Nottingham, NG7 2WS, UK.

Repr

Real
Realm-l
Warham
logos
locati
thereo

A CIP record for this book is available from the British Library.

ISBN 13: 978-1-78999-310-3

See Black Library on the internet at

blacklibrary.com

Find out more about Games Workshop
and the worlds of Warhammer at

games-workshop.com

Printed and bound by CPI Group (UK) Ltd, Croydon, CR0 4YY

For dad, who was always willing to wait.

30p

REALM-LORDS

Beastgrave
C L Werner

Neferata: The Dominion of Bones
David Annandale

The Court of the Blind King
David Guymer

Lady of Sorrows
C L Werner

Realm-Lords
Dale Lucas

Warcry Catacombs: Blood of
the Everchosen
Richard Strachan

Covens of Blood
Anna Stephens, Liane Merciel
and Jamie Crisalli

Stormvault
Andy Clark

The End of Enlightenment
Richard Strachan

Cursed City
C L Werner

A Dynasty of Monsters
David Annandale

Novellas

City of Secrets
Nick Horth

Bonereapers
David Guymer

Audio Dramas

• REALMSLAYER: A GOTREK
GURNISSON SERIES •
David Guymer

BOXED SET ONE: Realmslayer
BOXED SET TWO: Blood of the
Old World

The Beasts of Cartha
David Guymer

Fist of Mork, Fist of Gork
David Guymer

Great Red
David Guymer

Only the Faithful
David Guymer

The Prisoner of the Black Sun
Josh Reynolds

Sands of Blood
Josh Reynolds

The Lords of Helstone
Josh Reynolds

The Bridge of Seven Sorrows
Josh Reynolds

War-Claw
Josh Reynolds

Shadespire: The Darkness in
the Glass
Various authors

The Imprecations of Daemons
Nick Kyme

The Palace of Memory and
Other Stories
Various authors

Sons of Behemat
Graeme Lyon

Heirs of Grimnir
David Guymer

Also available

Realmslayer: The Script Book
David Guymer

From the maelstrom of a sundered world, the
Eight Realms were born. The formless and the divine
exploded into life.

Strange new worlds appeared in the firmament, each one
gilded with spirits, gods and men. Noblest of the gods was
Sigmar. For years beyond reckoning he illuminated the realms,
wreathed in light and majesty as he carved out his reign. His
strength was the power of thunder. His wisdom was infinite.
Mortal and immortal alike kneeled before his lofty throne.
Great empires rose and, for a while, treachery was banished.
Sigmar claimed the land and sky as his own and ruled over a
glorious age of myth.

But cruelty is tenacious. As had been foreseen, the great
alliance of gods and men tore itself apart. Myth and legend
crumbled into Chaos. Darkness flooded the realms. Torture,
slavery and fear replaced the glory that came before. Sigmar
turned his back on the mortal kingdoms, disgusted by their
fate. He fixed his gaze instead on the remains of the world he
had lost long ago, brooding over its charred core, searching
endlessly for a sign of hope. And then, in the dark heat of
his rage, he caught a glimpse of something magnificent. He
pictured a weapon born of the heavens. A beacon powerful
enough to pierce the endless night. An army hewn from
everything he had lost.

Sigmar set his artisans to work and for long ages they toiled,
striving to harness the power of the stars. As Sigmar's great
work neared completion, he turned back to the realms and saw
that the dominion of Chaos was almost complete. The hour
for vengeance had come. Finally, with lightning blazing across
his brow, he stepped forth to unleash his creations.

The Age of Sigmar had begun.

CHAPTER ONE

Ferendir stumbled on loose rock resting in dry soil. He first fell forward, overcompensated by shifting his weight backwards, then felt gravity – sure and inexorable – seize him. There would be no course correction – he was falling, and the steep, thinly wooded slope was about to thrust him away from its cold, sere face as though disgusted by him. In desperation, Ferendir whirled his arms, hoping to save himself from a painful impact and a merciless slide back down the steep incline. Further on, ahead and above him, he saw his master, Serath, turn back to stare.

Surely that was the worst – not the slip, not the fall, not even the impact to come, but Serath's cold, appraising glare and silent disapproval.

Then a gentle pressure upon Ferendir's back steadied him. His fall was arrested, his humiliation postponed. His other master, Desriel, had stopped his backward fall with an outstretched hand. Regaining his balance and planting his feet widely to stabilise himself, Ferendir lowered his eyes. Deep within him, buried beneath layers of physical conditioning and mental inculcation gained throughout his years as a supplicant to the mountain temple, he felt the seething, roiling forces of his emotions, like subterranean waters warmed by geothermal vents, made turbulent by a sudden underground tremor. Embarrassment, relief, fear, self-loathing – all were so close in that horrible instant, so present just beneath the mask of calm he fought to project to his mentors, that he could almost taste them.

Breathe, he ordered himself inwardly. *Just as they taught you. Regain your composure. Centre yourself. It was just a misstep... an understandable accident.*

But was it? He raised his eyes to Serath again, further up the slope.

Serath makes no such missteps, does he? That is why he looks upon me with such disdain, such disappointment. Nothing I do will ever be good enough for him.

And Desriel. Quiet, compassionate, supportive Desriel. He makes a good show of believing in me, maintaining his patience no matter how often I make mistakes, but he is probably ashamed of me on some level, as well... certain that I'm unequal to what's ahead.

The trial. My final *trial.*

Perhaps my final anything.

Stop, that cold, quiet voice within him said again. *Fear will destroy you. First things first, now – just get up the mountain without another fall.*

Ferendir forced himself to follow the voice's command. He continued to breathe evenly, consciously, to count slowly backwards as he did so, inhaling on the even numbers, exhaling with the odd.

Inhale. Exhale.

His heart rate slowed. The subtle tremors in his hands disappeared and the sweat upon them began to evaporate.

'Shall we continue?' Desriel asked quietly.

Ferendir opened his eyes. Looked up the steep incline of the mountainside. Saw Serath up ahead, silently impatient, still watching, radiating a vaguely disdainful air.

'Onwards,' Ferendir said, and resumed his climb.

Today, he faced his final initiation rite as a supplicant and acolyte of his Alarith temple. He could not afford to let a single misstep, a single, foolish mistake, ruin the calm and confidence he had worked so hard to cultivate within himself in preparation for this final, harrowing rite. He must be present, mindful, ready for anything yet expecting nothing.

Today, he would suborn himself to the mountain's will and beg its blessed sanction.

Today, he would be buried alive.

If the mountain accepted him, he would survive the ordeal. If, on the other hand, it found him unworthy...

'We linger too long,' Serath said from above.

Ferendir forced himself not to raise his eyes or meet Serath's disapproving gaze. From behind him, Desriel answered.

'Patience, Serath,' his master said. 'Our young supplicant was simply recomposing himself.'

Serath persisted. 'Had he stepped carefully, noted all possible impediments to his passage and skilfully avoided them, he would not have slipped, or fallen, or lost his composure.'

He could hide no longer. Trudging on, never breaking stride, Ferendir raised his eyes to meet Serath's, however difficult doing so might prove.

'I beg pardons of both of you, my masters,' the supplicant said. 'Please, let us continue.'

He lowered his eyes to the path, set one foot before the other and said no more. He leaned into the steep slope and chose his footholds swiftly but carefully.

The terrain they moved through – deep in the Ymetrican mountains of the realm of Hysh – was sparsely wooded and dreary, slate-grey knobs of cold stone and dry, subalpine soil scattered with towering sentinel trees and blanketed here and there with cushions of moss and islands of sedge. Hand- and footholds were not hard to find – there always seemed to be some jutting stone, the gnarl of a tree root or a narrow shelf of tightly packed earth awaiting his employ. Ferendir concentrated on finding the best of these, determined not to slip again simply because he had failed to closely examine where he planted his feet. As he trudged onwards, he sometimes used his small, delicate hands to assist in his ascent. He could still hear the burbling rush of the last stream they had crossed before beginning their climb, far below them, because the wind-wracked forest around them was so deathly silent, so funereally still.

Ferendir stole a glance upwards at Serath, to see if his stoic mentor yet lingered above him. To his chagrin, Serath had not moved. His master stood, bedecked in his shining white plate armour chased in gold, leaning upon his long-handled stone mallet. One of Serath's booted feet was braced upon a bleached-white tangle of deadfall wedged between two thin, sickly trees, and the stoic Stoneguard stared down at his long-time apprentice with his familiar reproachful glare. Ferendir could not tell if that expression – so subtle, so inscrutable – was a sign of complete disdain or simple pity. Serath held Ferendir's upturned eyes for only an instant, then turned his back and began to climb again.

Behind him, Ferendir heard Desriel begin to hum quietly – a slow, melancholy tune. Ferendir recognised the sombre melody at once as one of the temple's hymns, a wordless song taught to all the servants of the mountain. Its dolorous melody and slow, lilting cadence were designed to sharpen one's senses, to suppress one's conscious thoughts and widen one's consciousness – a sort of musical state of meditation, useful when undertaking laborious physical tasks such as a slow climb up a steep, wind-scoured mountainside. Ferendir was tempted to join Desriel in humming the old hymn – he had always loved the sense of plaintive peace that it stirred within him – but a part of him was reticent.

It was Serath. Though Ferendir now bore down upon his master with his senses and struggled to listen closely, he could not hear Serath humming. Serath, apparently, was centred, focused and fully present without the benefit of the hymn's quiet, hypnotic power. Therefore, Ferendir, determined to earn Serath's respect if not his affection, would do as *he* did, and remain silent, no matter how much he wanted to join Desriel in his song.

They had set off in the early hours of the morning, when the dim Hyshian twilight that constituted night was yet upon them and most of the temple Stoneguard and acolytes yet slept. His masters were each fully armoured and carried their personal weapons – an elegant diamondpick hammer for Desriel, a massive, long-hafted stone mallet for Serath – while Ferendir himself, facing a trial, wore a supplicant's tunic and had only been permitted to bring along his well-worn yew staff and a small dagger. Their path led them north-west, along one of the many narrow hiking trails that criss-crossed the rolling ridgelines and deep valleys of the mountain, taking them far from the lovely, well-hidden, tree-packed dell in which their temple resided towards the thick, shadowy forests that blanketed the mountain's western slopes. After hours of following the hill-hugging trail, they finally came to a rocky stream tumbling down out of the woods. At the stream, they left the path and followed the wending waters deeper and deeper into the shady hollows and rough-hewn gullies that formed the uneven geography of the mountain. Just as the full light of day began to bleed back into the world – Ulgu's darkness waning at last before the imminent glow of the Perimeter Inimical – they finally came to the lower edge of the thinning subalpine forest that marked the beginning of the end of the mountain's life-sustaining lower slopes. Whereas before the rolling, climbing landscape had been thick with intertwined, leafy decidua and tall, needly dreampines shading banks of shaggy verdibrush and beds of sprouting toadstools, the world above the stream suddenly exhibited signs of weariness and surrender. The spaces between the trees widened. Green turf and fronded ferns were replaced by dry soil, bald stone and isolated beds of spongy moss or obdurate sedge.

Hour by hour they climbed, the light invading the thinning woodlands growing brighter and brighter, even as the gusts blowing down from the mountain's heights grew colder and more insistent. The world stirred little, only a few lonely birds offering sad songs while from the last clinging shadows beneath the thinning trees they heard the rattle of tiny claws on stone and the soughing, subtle passage of small, fleet bodies. The moribund forest, the steepening mountainside, the air above and around them – everything, no matter how austere and faded it appeared, showed signs that it was alive, awake, hungry. This was one of the most basic lessons imparted to young supplicants of the mountain temple – or any temple, for that matter.

There is life in everything, desire in everything, will in everything. One forgets that fact at great personal peril.

Around them, the pines fell away. The only trees remaining upon the mountainside as they climbed, higher and higher, were stunted, pale and permanently bent by the hitching winds that raced down in gusting squalls from above. Those trees – spread far and wide, no hope of creating anything like a true canopy – hunched and curled against the slope, leafless and ragged as sun-bleached banners frozen forever in a wind-whipped frenzy.

Here, even that which grew slowly and stood impassively against the elements was bent into submission, subject to the implacable will of the mountain and its cold, furious winds. Seeing before him the evidence of just how merciless and unrelenting the mountain's will could prove to be, Ferendir was suddenly filled with a mingling of both awe and dread at what he was about to undergo.

Seeking the desires of the mountain, testing the will of the mountain that he called his aelemental master, was the sole aim of Ferendir's trial that day. Per the immutable laws of holy Teclis and the aelementiri principles held sacred by his temple, Ferendir would, like hundreds before him, be taken by his masters to a place of solitude and reflection – a place close to the heart of the mountain, in the direct path of the rushing, invisible pathways of deep and ancient energy that its sublime soul radiated. There, he would dig what was, essentially, his own grave. In that deep burrow, his masters would bury him alive. And there, beneath cold, arid soil and rock, slowly, inexorably crushed by the physical presence of the mountain's will and desire, Ferendir would dare asphyxiation and a slow, panic-stricken, forsaken death in the close darkness, in order to earn the mountain's approval for his lifelong service. If he was found worthy, the mountain would not allow his expiration. It would, instead, feed him the air required to survive, so that he could rise again transformed and sanctified – no longer an eager supplicant but a hallowed and holy acolyte, warranted, transformed, devoted evermore to the mountain's service and maintenance.

If it found any part of his mind, body or spirit unworthy, however, he would die.

No amount of preparation, no words from his mentors or the high priests and Stoneguard he served at the temple, could penetrate the mystery of what the mountain had in store for him. The trial, he had been assured, was his only path to enlightenment, and, likewise, the only means of proving his potential worth. To become what he hoped to become, he must dare the nullification of his very existence. Only courting death in so direct and terrifying a fashion would galvanise his spirit, assure his worthiness and empower him to carry on – to begin to lead the life of usefulness and service that he had always hoped to lead.

Behind him, Desriel spoke.

'Do you see the end of the shoulder above us?' his master asked.

Ferendir raised his eyes. He saw a place, fifty yards ahead and above them, where the sparse, bent trees simply disappeared, leaving only broad, bald rock pocked with sickly, sere moss and even more stunted furrows of sedge. Though the sun shone brightly upon that vast, empty expanse, he knew it would be cold there, for the gales blown down from the mountain were strong, and there, upon the tundra, there was no shelter, not even so much as a clump of low scrub to break the wind's cold, crashing force.

'I see it, Master Desriel.'

'We are almost at our destination,' his master said easily. 'The place of your trial lies just beyond the lower barrens, over that shelf and deep into a box canyon cut into the mountainside. You can almost see the cleft from here, though the colours of the stone hide it well.'

Ferendir stared as he climbed. He thought, squinting and half imagining what the colours visible on the far side of the treeline suggested, that he could see what his master described, but he could not be certain.

'Must he be entertained?' Serath called from above. He had pulled far ahead, now almost to the rocky shoulder. 'The boy is a supplicant, Desriel. Let him make his own discoveries and draw his own conclusions.'

'There is nothing indulgent in being informative,' Desriel called back amiably. 'Ferendir can draw his own conclusions – I was merely imparting information.'

Serath gave a short, swift glance backwards, but never broke stride. 'You coddle him.' It was spoken flatly, baldly – a simple fact. It sounded neither like an indictment nor a recrimination.

'Perhaps,' Desriel said, so quietly that it might have been only to himself. Again, there was no feeling in the statement – no indicator of shame or embarrassment – only quiet, assured agreement. Perhaps he did… or did not.

Ferendir kept climbing.

Part of him wanted to look back at Desriel, to see his sharp-featured face, his kind brown eyes, the vague ghost of a smile haunting his usually implacable expression. But he would not. If Serath saw him looking to Desriel for comfort, for encouragement, he might take that as a sign of weakness, an indicator – however subtle – of Ferendir's unworthiness to undertake the final trial.

I need nothing, Ferendir told himself. *I desire nothing. I expect nothing. I go to meet my trial willingly, fearlessly, begging only that the mountain will know my heart and find me worthy of being taken into its service and confidence.*

Those were the words he told himself, inwardly, silently, ever eager to settle the emotions that stirred and seethed deep, deep in the darkest centres of his consciousness.

Desriel was as encouraging as Serath was dismissive, as supportive as Serath was challenging. Though Ferendir had always drawn a great deal of his strength and confidence from Desriel's serene, unwavering support, some impulse inside him always strove to impress Serath, to earn his respect and admiration, to draw even a single word of praise from him, however subdued such praise might be. Ferendir knew it was foolish to feel such things, but some dim, deeply buried part of him always seemed to regard his desire for one master's praise or support as a subtle betrayal of the other, even though their particular temple made it clear that every supplicant had two masters for a very pointed purpose.

This is Hysh, the High Stonemage had said all those years before, when Ferendir was just a young aelf, presented to the temple for training as a supplicant. *This realm – the realm that gave birth to*

*our kind – is a place of balance... a place of harmony... a place of
reconciled opposites. Just as our twin gods, Tyrion and Teclis, embody
warring impulses yoked to the same divine ends, just as the two halves
of the Great Mandala express those warring and reconciled opposites,
so your masters will push and pull each of you to the very extremes
of your own, still-under-formation natures. They will be the warring
forces that help each of you to reconcile the war inside yourselves.*

Thus, from the start, Ferendir knew precisely why his two masters were so different, and how their differences should have helped
him to reconcile the conflicting halves of his own nature. What he
had not anticipated was the strange sense of impatience and jeal-
ousy that often gripped him when under their tutelage – how he
maintained his will to go on, his desire to try just one more time,
because of Desriel's subtle, artful teachings, yet how he craved – all
but demanded – even the smallest acknowledgement of his excel-
lence from Serath. One gave a great deal, yet Ferendir felt he'd had
enough and required no more from him, while the other gave him
nothing, made him scratch and claw and struggle and humiliate
himself for even the smallest, most underwhelming compliment –
and still, from that master, the one who withheld, Ferendir wanted
more. He strove to be like Serath, to be worthy of Serath, even to
someday best Serath, yet he constantly found himself circling back
to Desriel for some sense of his worth, his potential, his true value.

No matter how hard he tried to be independent and unshakeable
like the one, he could not help but seek support and encouragement from the other.

And so, now he would not look back. Nor would he look up
again to see if Serath watched him. He would simply climb. He
would make that shelf above the treeline. He would follow his
masters into that box canyon where his destiny awaited, and there,
sheltered from the world and at the mercy of the mountain, he
would face his final trial.

And he would not, under any circumstances, let Serath know how truly, deeply frightened he was of what that trial might reveal.

Foolish, he knew, to let his emotions assail him. He was reasonably sure that outwardly he revealed nothing. Nonetheless, the storm raging within him was impossible to deny. He'd come a very long way since his early years as a young supplicant, told time and again that his feelings – and his failure to control them – would be his undoing. He had struggled all through childhood and adolescence, always winning praise and high marks for his understanding, his spellcraft and his physical capabilities, yet also always falling short in the realm of suppressing his emotions and robbing them of their latent power to manipulate and sway him. Now, he found himself on the cusp of maturity, the threshold of adulthood, the very precipice of his initiation to become a committed and invested Stoneguard of the Alarith temple. And yet, for all the prowess and confidence and insight that his many years of study, toil and struggle had given him, there was still a small, isolated part of Ferendir – a part buried deep within him, yet still burning bright with some stirring, combustible force – that constantly assailed his sense of self-worth.

All the Lumineth of Hysh were trained, by the means most useful to their various tribes, to suppress their emotions, to always seek solutions that were, first and foremost, best for the realm itself and all the people who inhabited it – never to put their own desires, their own fears, their own petty preferences ahead of necessity and the maintenance of life and balance.

Emotions, they were taught, were anathema to rational thought, the bane of right and beneficial action.

They were taught to suppress their emotions, to ignore them or to redirect them... but they could not be entirely *free* of them, could they? That, it seemed, was Ferendir's eternal struggle – to suppress the powerful, contradictory, wholly unconscious forces that roiled and raged inside him, so that he could do his duty and be of service.

Emotions such as his fear of failure, and dying within the mountain.

Emotions such as his abiding desire to please Serath and earn his respect, while simultaneously hating and resenting him for never granting even a modicum of that respect or praise he so desperately sought.

It was as if no matter how many times he proved himself equal to a task, worthy of a responsibility, he was still, inexorably, assailed by the sense that he was an imposter – a place-holder for some unnamed champion who had yet to arrive upon the scene, to take the place that he'd kept warm and ready for him.

Why should he feel that way, he wondered during his meditations, or in his loneliest hours, alone and unable to sleep. Why, after so many accomplishments, should he still suspect – however subtly, however quietly – that he was unworthy of trust, unequal to challenge?

Was it because he did not *trust* Desriel's confidence in him? No. That was foolish. Desriel was the most trustworthy, the most dependable person that Ferendir had ever known. He would not be such a well-respected Stoneguard if his skills and character were not of the utmost strength and purity.

Was it, perhaps, because Serath always seemed so disappointed in him? So dismissive of his achievements and doubtful of his successes yet to come? Perhaps... but that still seemed unequal to birthing and cultivating his many, ever-swirling doubts and their adamant hold upon him. Ferendir's fears and misgivings were far more intrinsic than anything the actions of any person – even his masters – could inflict upon him, buried so deep inside him, so far beneath his seemingly calm exterior that he could barely imagine Serath's outward attitudes having anything to do with their creation and sustenance.

Eliminating those two possibilities left a third one, far more disturbing – Ferendir, despite all of his strengths and capabilities, lacked the great, final component that would elevate and distinguish him, that special alchemy of character that made the difference between being merely a talented supplicant, and truly earning his place as a fully fledged, wholly empowered Stoneguard.

He was not unworthy in essence. But because he doubted himself, he would *prove* unworthy... because the worthy never doubted themselves or their worthiness.

Did they?

A paradox. And a maddening one, at that.

Ferendir glanced upwards. Serath had reached the rocky ledge above. There he stood, just beyond the ragged edge of the sere alpine grass that faded against the mountain's stony shoulder, his silent impatience subtly palpable even though his face was as stony and unreadable as a sheer cliff. Ferendir forced himself to move swiftly over the last uneven span of ground between where he climbed and where his master waited. He scrambled over the ledge and took his place beside Serath, Desriel following quickly behind.

They stood upon a broad, bare rocky shoulder that receded from the steep slope towards a more sheer, vertiginous cliff wall a few more yards behind them. For a moment, the three aelves – masters and student – stood silent and exultant, the rising cliff at their backs, the sparsely forested slope falling away sharply beneath them. They drank in the stunning vista that sprawled before them: widely scattered spruce and pines, sickly and stunted beside bent, curling birch and giving way to bare alpine rock; the thicker, darker forest lying like a green blanket on the slopes and hills beneath, a broad green valley bounded by the declining spurs of the mountain's roots, tumbling away below until the land once more rose towards the peak of a neighbouring mountain some great distance away. In the great gulf separating them from the nearest peak, they saw raptors whirling lazily on the thermals rising out of the valley below and heard the echoing screech of a bird of prey carried on the breeze to their waiting ears.

Ferendir studied the sublime scene, awed and reassured by it in the same breath. Birds in flight. Balmy, upswept breezes intertwined with fierce, chill gusts from the heights, the whole of the world before him burnished with gentle golden Hyshian sunlight. Far away, on the far side of the ridgeline to the east of them, lay their home temple nestled warmly into a beautiful, shady dell on a misty promontory beside falling waters. They had set out from that place mere hours before, but now it felt a world away.

Desriel dared a subtle, satisfied smile as he studied the view.

'Ennobling,' he said.

'It's beautiful,' Ferendir agreed.

'It simply *is*,' Serath added flatly. 'It can be nothing else. Come, we're wasting light.'

He turned from the ledge and began a steady march up the shallow stony slope towards the cliff face. Now that they were out of the forest, Ferendir could finally see their destination – a high, narrow cleft in the slate-grey stone of the mountainside, barely visible because the pattern of light and shadow upon the cliff face painted the sharp rent in a sort of camouflage. Somewhere, deep within the mountainside, his fate awaited him.

Ferendir looked to Desriel. His master only swept his arm sideways, as if to say, *After you, supplicant.*

Ferendir fell in behind Serath, following his stone-faced master up the sweep of the grassy sward towards the beckoning shadows of the canyon.

The cleft gave the appearance of allowing only narrow passage, but as they entered, it broadened beyond. Though the canyon floor was wide enough for three Dawnriders to gallop abreast, it was nonetheless strewn with fallen boulders of various sizes and mounds of rocky scree deposited by old wash-outs and landslides. A shallow, snaking brook burbled along the canyon floor, under large rocks and over smaller ones, really little more than a steady seep. The walls of the canyon climbed high on either side, angling outwards to a certain height then ominously contracting inwards again, looming precipitously, as though threatening at any moment to collapse. Because the canyon was so narrow and uneven, little light penetrated. As a consequence, the air was still and cool, the silence oppressive. Worse, the meandering path of the canyon meant that Ferendir could not see more than a few dozen yards ahead of him. However deep their destination lay in this accursed place, it was not readily visible.

Ferendir forced himself to stand still, performing a sort of silent appraisal of the place where he now found himself. The presence of all that scree and the absence of plant life suggested it was a young formation, but a hundred thousand geological epochs were clearly visible in the layered regolith.

Serath led the way, picking out the most direct path along the canyon floor, over mounds of fallen scree and past boulders that might have hindered the progress of lesser beings without such nimble feet. Here and there, the little stream would find deeper depressions in the rock and seem to flow for a few metres as a proper body of water before the stone beneath it once more shallowed and it turned thereafter into a vaguely running wet stain along the canyon floor.

At intervals, sharp winds cut through the narrow alley, compressed and solidified by the rock walls on either side of them. Ferendir clearly heard the voice of the mountain itself in that wind, the narrow breezeway giving the cool, driving air a voice of its own, one moment a moan, the next a plaintive sigh. It seemed a strange road they now traversed – working their way at a slow, steady pace towards the mountain's interior via such a strangled aperture – but Ferendir knew better than to question the route.

His place was not to question. Only to follow.

'I would be remiss,' Serath suddenly said, marching ahead of him, 'if I did not ask you, for a final time, if you feel equal to the trial before you, young supplicant.'

Serath was uncanny. Even wholly unemotional and speaking in even tones, he managed to impart a vague sense of dismissal and condescension. Ferendir fought the urge to be overwhelmed by shame or anger in answer. He only sought the appropriate response to the prompt within himself.

'The mountain has called to me, master,' Ferendir said, 'bid me come to the place of trial and submit myself to its reckoning. Such has been my only aspiration for all my years of education and service. So called, I come.'

'A worthy outlook,' Desriel said from behind him. Somewhere, a small stone fell from a great height. It rattled down the throat of the cleft, clicking and clacking in noisy echoes as it did so. 'I predict success for you, supplicant. Not only in today's trial but in the years yet before you.'

'Predict nothing,' Serath said. Though cutting a path over uneven ground, ground frequently littered with obstacles and obstructions, he yet maintained a swift pace that even young Ferendir struggled to match.

'Weigh probabilities and analyse all possible outcomes to anticipate that which is most likely,' Serath continued. 'Prediction is a fool's game – the province of non-aelven scryers and fortune tellers. Analysis requires a combination of both knowledge and discernment – clear senses assessing hard facts, nothing more.'

'Just so,' Desriel said. 'And yet, there *is* a diaphanous membrane connecting the two, would you not agree? A web, if you will–'

'A web?' Serath asked.

'Between knowledge, discernment and rational analysis lies the web of intuition, Serath – the understanding that leads to true seeing, true knowing, even when what is seen and known defies what is rational.'

Serath was silent for a long time, pressing on, never looking back. He skipped up a rockfall and over a rocky incline in order to cut a track past a massive boulder blocking their primary path. Finally, just as he was about to disappear on the far side of the rockfall: 'I would call your intuition a false and personalised mask placed upon rational analysis. It is not a web at all, but a line, moving from each object to the next in an unbroken pathway of causation and effect. Nothing more.'

'We shall agree to disagree,' Desriel said. 'As we so often do.' Ferendir thought he heard a smile in his master's voice, though he wagered that if he dared look back at him he would see no such smile.

Serath said nothing in answer.

As Ferendir mounted the same rockfall his master had just clambered over, a cold, stiff mistral whipped suddenly, mercilessly, through the narrow rocky pass. It raised a terrible howling sound in Ferendir's ears and assailed him for an unnerving instant with a bone-numbing cold that made him shudder reflexively and halt his forward progress. He smelled something on that wind, as well... something foul and unnatural. Though he could not immediately identify that scent, the subtle, wind-borne clue yet seemed to stir Ferendir's whole body to nervous excitement. The beating of his heart increased unbidden, and he sensed a tautness and tremulous energy shooting through all his limbs from the centre of his being to his extremities.

Farther ahead of him, on the canyon floor, Serath stood rigid, his lithe, muscular body squared and ready for violence. His master's head was tilted slightly to the left and his chin subtly raised, as though he were listening for something and sniffing the scents on the wind the same instant.

Ferendir heard the subtle crunch of Desriel's soft leather boots on the loose shale of the rockfall. Heaving up beside his supplicant, Desriel drew a deep breath of his own, then slowly blew it out.

Ferendir dared a look at his master. Desriel's eyes were slowly rolling about in their sockets, studying the narrow confines of the meandering canyon as though in search of something hiding among the ledges and precipitous overhangs.

'Master?' Ferendir asked.

Desriel said nothing. He only nodded forward, towards Serath.

Ferendir looked to his other master. Serath stared back at them, gaze steady but narrowed. Clearly he sensed something of import ahead... something unexpected.

'Slowly,' Serath said, then led the way. As he progressed, he drew his sunsteel longhammer from where it bumped and jostled, strapped across his back. The brutal spike protruding opposite its flat, terrible head caught the dim grey light in the canyon and glinted.

Desriel had drawn his hammer as well. Ferendir, wishing at that moment that his trial was already passed and that he held such a weapon in his own hands, tightened his grip on his yew staff. Part of him wanted to ask what that strange, unnatural smell portended – what now had both his masters so tense, so on edge – but he knew better.

Follow their lead, he reminded himself. *Their actions tell you all you need to know at the moment. Waste no words on idle conjecture...*

They pressed on.

In short order, the canyon took a sudden bend to the left. Just past that bend, they emerged from the narrow throat of the canyon into its broad, boxy terminus. The space before them, though bounded by the stony cliff walls, was wide open, large enough to accommodate a great phalanx of Auralan sentinels, forty wide and two hundred deep. At the far end of the box canyon, meltwater from the mountain peaks above trickled or fanned down along the sheer rock walls, collecting in a wide, shallow pool at the back end of the gulf and flowing forth out of the canyon as that persistent trickle that meandered along the path they'd just threaded. High above, where the cliffs receded, mists hung low and obscured their view of the reclining mountainside and snowy peaks that loomed far above them. Streamers of dripping moss and sagging saplings drooped precipitously from the canyon walls, the only signs of life in the otherwise damp and desolate slag heap.

Serath stood at the mouth of the gorge, surveying the canyon before them, still on edge about something. Ferendir sniffed, but could no longer detect that foulness that had assailed him when they'd been mounting the rockfall just moments before. Now, there was only the fresh, mineral scent of the fanning waters from the mountain heights, the vague, distant perfume of pines and loamy soil mingling with the pure, strong scent of wet stone and damp gravel.

Finally, Serath seemed satisfied. He jerked his head sideways, in the direction of the waterfall.

'This way,' he said, and led them up the slow, easy incline towards the great pool of dark water at the canyon's far end.

As they went, Ferendir studied the bare grey landscape surrounding them. He could see no wildlife, but he still sensed it – small, furtive souls threading the dark shadows under the looming rock, tiny claws scrabbling eagerly along narrow cliff ledges, birds making nests in the cracks and crevices far above them, staring down with dark, implacable eyes, wondering just what these trespassing strangers might be doing in their normally quiet, out of the way canyon home. In short, everywhere, life – teeming, edgy, eager.

'Is this everyone's place of trial?' Ferendir asked as they trudged on. 'Or only mine? Do all come here to seek the mountain's anointing, or was this place chosen for me?'

'Immaterial, in either case,' Serath said over his shoulder without breaking stride.

'It's a fair question,' Desriel said. 'The boy only wishes to know the how and the why of what he's about to undergo. He may, after all, someday have to perform the same function for another young supplicant as we perform today for him.'

'I have a question of my own, then,' Serath countered, still not looking back. 'Tell me, Ferendir – how does this place *feel* to you?'

'How does it feel, master?'

'Must I repeat myself?'

Ferendir frowned. 'Honestly, it feels... anxious,' he said after a moment, answering intuitively rather than logically. 'Restive and on edge, as though expecting something unpleasant in the next instant. Whatever we smelled back in the cleft–'

Serath froze. Turned. He speared Ferendir with a probing gaze. 'You noted it as well?'

'Of course,' Ferendir said, vaguely insulted that his master would think him so obtuse.

'What about now?' Serath asked.

Ferendir sniffed the air. For the most part, he could only smell the myriad scents of the canyon: cool water, washed stone, damp moss, sandy soil and the vague, musty under scent of sprouting fungi. But there was something else, wasn't there? Something foul... bitter...

Something that did not belong.

'We're not alone here,' Ferendir said suddenly.

Serath made no reply. He only looked to Desriel, just over Ferendir's shoulder.

'Do you concur, old friend?' Serath asked.

Ferendir turned to Desriel. His other master nodded slowly, eyes darting about, searching the bright heights and dark shadows of the world around him.

'I concur, Serath. I suggest we be on our way.'

'No!' Ferendir said emphatically, instantly ashamed of his emotional reaction to his master's order. Desriel and Serath both stared at him, seemingly just as shocked by his outburst as he was.

'We cannot,' Ferendir said slowly, quietly. 'I came here to be tested. I *will* be tested.'

'Be careful what you wish for, supplicant,' Serath said, eyes narrowing again. 'The realms have a way of giving us the things we most desire in ways we never imagined – ways we are often wholly unprepared for.'

'He's right,' Desriel said. 'This has nothing to do with your trial, Ferendir. Something is very *wrong* here. Your trial will be tainted by it. Our only option is to go. Come on.'

Desriel turned to lead the way back along their track… but their retreat was already blocked.

Three strange figures stood in a broad skirmish line, obstructing the entrance to the narrow gorge that allowed them access to the canyon.

Ferendir stared, trying to make sense of what he saw, or thought he saw. Their forms were vaguely anthropoid – two arms, two legs, heads and torsos – and yet they were wrong, *all wrong*. He saw pale skin; black, unnatural eyes; curled flesh and pins and wires; bright, colourful silks stained by soil and sweat and the damp air; the glint of bright jewels and baubles on the clothing and the wearers themselves.

And yet, for all their apparent humanity there was something beastly about the trio. Hands that were not hands. Feet that more resembled hooves. A swishing tail. Faces, twisted and transformed by some blasphemous art that Ferendir could not identify, let alone imagine the ultimate purpose of.

Serath moved up beside Ferendir, shoulder to shoulder with Desriel.

'Get behind us, supplicant,' Serath whispered.

The three figures at the mouth of the canyon advanced slowly, casually. The closer they drew, the more terrible they seemed to Ferendir. The young aelf was overwhelmed by a sense of dread and terrible wonder.

'Well, now,' one of the creatures drawled, 'what have we here?'

Movement. Boot heels and hooves on bare stone. Ferendir and his masters turned, surveying the great gorge behind them.

There were more than just the three blocking their egress.

They were surrounded.

It troubled Ezarhad Fatesbane that his minions could not cheer for him, sing praises to him, exalt him when he marched through their massed ranks to the overlook. They were trying to surprise their quarry, after all. Undue noise – even for such a justified reason as the celebration of his own person by his servants – would do little to help them achieve his ultimate aim. Just this once, he decided to let the issue lie. They could sing his praises to their vile hearts' desire later, after the victory was won.

Still, he enjoyed the sight of them – an entire invader host, hundreds of eager daemonettes, stamping fiends and hunkered hellstriders, all pressed close and tight in among the shadows of the tall pines, doing their best to remain quiet, patient and out of sight. Their quarry was just across the little tributary valley they found themselves in, an Alarith temple facing the dawn of a new Hyshian day with not the slightest inkling that its utter destruction lay just around the corner. If all went according to Ezarhad's plan – and he had no reason to believe that it would not – that temple would be smoking ruins in just an hour or two, and he would be swiftly away with his prize.

His minions bent in silent worship as he passed among them, all bowing their heads in respect or raising their twisted, mutated arms and inhuman hands in supplication. Knowing they could not sing for him or cheer for him, they hissed and gnashed their teeth and grinned horridly in the twilit half-light of the dim glade where they gathered. Tails swished and swooped in joyful adoration. Inhuman feet stamped, skipped and danced. Ezarhad even saw tears of joy and ecstasy on a few of their pale, twisted, wire-pierced cheeks.

I fill them with ecstasy, he thought, with no small amount of satisfaction. *I am wondrous to behold – their very reason for being!*

And why shouldn't I be? Am I not Ezarhad Fatesbane, scourge of the Mortal Realms, the one true chosen heir to the Vile Throne of our lord and master, immortal Slaanesh?

He was… at least, in his own mind. His foul comrades, Meigant and Astoriss, both had their own designs on the dread lord's title and throne – poor, misguided souls. In truth, Ezarhad was convinced that he could bury both of them – he just needed one strong, undeniable advantage.

And that's what had brought him here, to the temple.

That advantage – the first requirement of his ultimate victory and salvation – lay within.

He raised his four muscular arms, the bangles and tattoos and many-coloured silk scarves adorning those arms making subtle music in the near silence of the forest. As he displayed himself – almost three metres of beautiful pale flesh, pierced with a thousand tiny flashing ringlets, painted with the foul symbols of ancient sorceries and blasphemies from head to foot, his black, marble-like eyes wide and bright for his many supplicants – Ezarhad felt a sense of real satisfaction. How could they help but worship him. Was he not a thing of exquisite beauty? A thing of glory?

'Soon,' he promised them all in a quiet voice that only the nearest could hear. 'Soon, my children, my servants, my lackeys, all of our foul appetites shall be gorged. The time draws near.'

More hisses, strangled laughter and bodies trembling in anticipation. Like children. How he loved and loathed them all at once.

They had been moving into position all night long – at least, what passed for night in this accursed place. It never grew dark, precisely, only yielded to a sort of wan twilight as the realm's own inherent luminescence waned and the darkness of Ulgu asserted itself for a few short hours. Perhaps once he had taken his place as supreme potentate of Chaos in this realm and claimed it as his own, Ezarhad could do something about that. Draw Ulgu closer to impose a longer twilight, and shorter hours of full daylight from the Bright Periphery. If today's raid played out as Ezarhad hoped, he knew that there would be very little he would be unable to do. If he could just lay hands upon that gem…

A tall, broad form in armour encrusted with flayed skins and human bones moved into Ezarhad's path – Kraygorn, Ezarhad's warlord supreme. The enormous Slaaneshi warrior – nearly as tall as Ezarhad himself, his visage twisted into a form still vaguely human yet also somehow reminiscent of a mountain ram, crowned by a pair of curling horns – bowed low in obsequity.

'Good morning, my lord,' Kraygorn said in his low, sonorous voice. 'I trust you are well rested?'

Ezarhad gave a curt nod, and Kraygorn raised his head. 'Well enough,' Ezarhad said quietly. 'Are the other hosts in place?'

Kraygorn nodded. 'Hordes poised on three sides of the temple, my lord. Fiends and daemonettes up the slopes at the temple's rear, hellstriders and invader forces on the flanks, while your best troops are here, at the fore, ready to charge.'

'And our duardin?' Ezarhad asked.

'The sappers have been digging all night, my lord. At last report, they were in position under the curtain wall.'

Perfect.

Ezarhad nodded, satisfied, and kept walking, his jewel-encrusted greatsword jouncing against his hip in its gem-spangled, filigreed scabbard. Kraygorn's monstrous size and ominous bearing made him a natural leader among the Chaotic hordes enthralled to Ezarhad's beauty and exquisite wickedness, but there was also something in the creature that made Ezarhad distrust him. A sense of self, perhaps? Some small, lingering measure of confidence and free will? He would have to keep a close eye on him.

The overlook was just up ahead, through a screen of thick pines. Stepping forward through the needles and low-hanging boughs, Ezarhad was suddenly presented with a stunning view from a great height. Beneath him lay a slanting tributary valley folded between two soaring ridgelines of the great mountain that hosted them. Opposite and above where he now stood, foaming water sluiced from a sheer, vertiginous cliff face, plunging over the mountainside towards a broad, roiling pool on a promontory below. There, in a rocky, long-eroded bowl, the waters swirled and churned before cascading over a series of massive stone tiers down the gently sloping valley floor to the tributary river far below.

It was on a rocky, mist-shrouded outcropping above the promontory where the waters stirred that the Alarith temple awaited them, quiet and oblivious in the soft early-morning light. From a distance, it looked peaceful, stately – and wholly unequal to repelling an assault from Ezarhad's savage forces. Its high, peaked roofs and towers were huddled behind a thick, stout curtain wall, with only a single gate allowing entry via a narrow road that approached the gate under the auspices of the wall itself.

Two thousand, Ezarhad thought, casually assessing the losses likely on that narrow approach. *Perhaps three. No matter. I can spare them. I need what waits inside...*

'Have we any clear indication of the number of defenders within?' Ezarhad asked, assuming that Kraygorn still lingered at his elbow.

His major-domo had no opportunity to answer. Instead, a shadowy figure seemed to melt from the darkness beneath the trees – a slender, black-swathed form slinking cat-like from its place of hiding into Ezarhad's proud and glorious presence. This was Tyrirra, his primary seeker, scout and spy. Her movements were lithe, smooth and wholly inhuman, as though she were made of swirling smoke, like some nighthaunt from the plains of Shyish. She wore shadows like most of his troops wore flashing jewels or decadent silks, and her knack for appearing out of nowhere – even when Ezarhad himself was not aware of her presence – both troubled and amazed him. He needed to find some means of knowing when she was present, preferably one that she could not counter or circumvent.

One must always keep one's subordinates in line, after all.

'Two dozen, my lord,' Tyrirra said, her voice a feline whisper. 'Certainly no more than thirty. At least half of those are supplicants, still untested and seeking full initiation into the Alarith Stoneguard ranks. It almost seems beneath the concern of one so great, so ambitious, as yourself.'

Flattery. Ezarhad smiled. He certainly welcomed it, but he could never entirely trust it. Nonetheless, she was both useful and effective. He would do his best to resist the urge to flay and skin her before he'd found some evidence of her possible disloyalty.

'Under normal circumstances,' Ezarhad said, 'such a pitiful little encampment might be beneath my contempt. But these Stone-worshipping fools have something in their possession which could prove useful to me. I shall have it, no matter how many of them – or all of you – have to die for me to acquire it.'

Tyrirra nodded and slowly backed out of his peripheral vision. Ezarhad studied the scene before him, weighing the variables of the strategy he had already set in motion. He would be at the rear of the party charging the main gate and seeking to breach the forward wall. The rest of his forces would engage the temple from the other three sides, knowing full well that their task was not to breach the walls or climb over them but to simply keep the defenders busy while the main force, at the fore, could batter their way inside. He would spend a great many mortal and daemonette lives in the effort, he knew – the Alarith were renowned for their ferocity as fighters, for how sternly and stoutly they could hold even the most indefensible position. But he also knew that he could penetrate their defences if only he had sufficient time to do so. He had more than a few surprises held in readiness for the assault. When the moment was right, he would happily deploy them.

'Sound the horns,' Ezarhad said at last.

Kraygorn nodded. 'As you wish, my lord.'

'Send the rear and flanks in first – then we'll charge the main gate. Soon enough, we'll be through that wall, I promise you.'

Kraygorn had already given the orders. In the distance, from the hills beside and around the Alarith temple, Ezarhad heard the foul horns of his phalanx commanders sounding.

Music to my ears, he thought. *Soon, this realm – all the Mortal Realms and all the forces of Chaos – will be mine.*

Ferendir had heard tales of the minions of Chaos from the time he was a toddling child to the day before the trial he had come to the canyon to submit himself to. Only once or twice had he seen the minions of Chaos up close – usually as corpses after an already-won victory by his fellow Lumineth over the vile invaders. He'd heard of the treacherous Disciples of Tzeentch, the cruel, mad Bloodbound of Khorne, the foul Rotbringers of Nurgle and, especially, the Hedonites of Slaanesh, the most hated and despised of all servants of the Chaos gods to threaten and infect his beautiful home realm of Hysh. Staring at the creatures loping or swaying out of the stony shadows to slowly surround them, he could not say what god they served, let alone whether they were human or daemon in origin. All he saw was a ravening pack of demi-human anthropoid abominations – sick, twisted facsimiles of personhood adorned with appendages that did not belong on their bodies, sporting decadent silks and bright jewels and precious gold and silver even as their horrid faces and sickly skins made it clear they were anything but aristocratic in origin.

The figures directly before them, blocking their exit, were tall, willowy and pale, projecting a strange sort of strength and formidableness despite an underlying inkling of sickness and decay. Each wore scraps of leather and silk, baubles, bangles and chains of gold and silver, jewels upon their wrists, their ankles, or hanging from piercings in their flesh. And though they gave the vague impression of having once been human, Ferendir would not swear on the Great Mandala that they remained so now. Clearly they had undergone myriad changes – sorcerous, blasphemous changes – in the course of dedicating themselves to whichever foul deity they called master.

The male at the fore – the one who had spoken to them – sported ears splayed in great, fan-like patterns, the flesh and cartilage split and skewered on a framework of thin needles anchored into the outer curve of its skull. The final impression given by those flayed and framed ears was of dreadful sails protruding from either side of its head. Its eyes were a horrible deep red that was almost black, like ebony spheres dipped in blood, rolling about salaciously in the creature's deep-set sockets and glinting with a terrible, malign light. Its thin purple lips were curled back, revealing a wall of purple-black gums housing interlocked rows of needle-sharp teeth. Those teeth gnashed together in an expression that was either a rictus grin or a threatening snarl – it was impossible to tell precisely which. Its companions were no prettier.

Ferendir turned and glanced over his shoulder. Half a dozen more of the strange beings – twisted, malevolent, even foppish – had emerged from the shadows under the looming canyon walls, clearly having lain in wait for the three of them, only revealing their presence when Ferendir and his masters moved to retreat. They made for a bizarre conglomeration of vaguely anthropoid forms sporting decidedly non-anthropoid features, such as snapping pincers, two-thumbed, six-fingered hands with long black claws, or whipping, forked tails that swung and snapped behind them like eager serpents. One of the foul creatures even seemed to have a scorpion tail, rising from the base of its back and arcing over its shoulder, some foul venom hanging as a pendulous, cloudy drop on its curling barb.

Nine Hedonites. Three aelves. Ferendir tried to convince himself those were good odds.

Desriel's face was slack, impassive, as though what now presented itself to them was nothing more than a mild annoyance rather than a grave existential threat. Serath's face was harder – brows furrowed, mouth set sharply – but offered no more clear indication of what he thought of the situation than Desriel's expression did. Ferendir noted – with little relief – that his masters had positioned themselves on either side of him, sheltering him with their bodies from whatever attack the daemons might launch. His masters were prepared for a fight – both armed and fully armoured – but Ferendir himself was dressed only in an everyday tunic, armed with little more than a long stick and a knife barely large enough to gut a fish. Staring at the monstrous enemies now surrounding them, the supplicant felt horribly exposed and helpless.

'Three little willows, bending in the breeze,' the fan-eared leader recited, 'hack through every bough and you'll have them on their knees.'

The half-dozen creatures that had emerged from the cliffside shadows made strange noises now, some cackling like hungry hyenas, others panting like overheated wolves.

'You should go,' Desriel said. 'This gorge is sacred, and no place for you.'

'Oh, on the contrary,' the fan-eared leader said, his purple-black lips widening to reveal an awful-to-behold grin. 'This is precisely where we belong. Such stark, pristine beauty here… such desolate, untouched purity and harmony. This place cries out for us.'

One of the creatures behind the leader laughed and nodded its foul, bald head. Its eyes were sewn shut, but it wore a mad grin, as though it relished every word from its commander and could clearly see what unfolded before it despite its apparent blindness. The third invader blocking their escape had vicious eyes and tapered, pointed ears – almost like those of an aelf – but no mouth. The aperture was not even sewn or clamped shut – it simply wasn't there. Where it should have been was an obscenely smooth, unblemished plane of tightly stretched skin.

'You will not be warned again,' Serath said darkly. 'Go now and there will be no need to kill every one of you.' Ferendir could see that his master was appraising the adversaries now creeping closer from all sides, assessing each in turn, rapidly running through each and every iteration of the possible fight to come and choosing the best courses of action even before the first blow had been struck. Ferendir tried to do the same, but found his fevered mind, unbalanced by shock and panic, unequal to the task of sorting probabilities and variables on such short notice.

The foul creatures hissed and laughed, as though Serath's threat were a jest to them.

Ferendir knew now that these few fleeting moments – the last before chaos ensued – were all that might be afforded him to prepare himself. Violence was eminent, unavoidable. Using every ounce of his willpower, he struggled to slow his breathing, recalling his many hours drilling with the staff as his only offensive weapon, every lesson ever taught to him by Desriel or Serath or one of the other Stoneguard of the temple regarding the seizure and arrestation of time, even in moments of shock and panic.

This is the Lumineth way, they had reiterated, time and again. *Time is fluid. It cannot be stopped, but it can be slowed, if only in our own minds. Use every fleeting moment to your advantage.*

Ferendir slid into the proper defensive stance, eyes swinging back and forth between the three monsters before them and the six behind. He was about to defend himself – to the death, more than likely. Not precisely the trial he'd left the temple expecting that morning.

The laughing leader took two steps forward.

'Tell us, aelf – how would you like your remains displayed? Shall we nail your carcass to the canyon walls with iron spikes while there's still a little life left in you? Let the birds come and pick at you, day after day, until the life remaining ebbs away and you're nothing but rotten, listless meat? Or shall we simply split you limb from limb and toss all the separate pieces about in a great, haphazard mandala? We'll give you just that much, as a courtesy – a choice of where you end up. But how you get that way? That'll be up to us...'

Desriel caught Ferendir's eye. He spoke low, so that only his student would hear him.

'Stay between us.'

Then, swift as a mountain zephyr, he struck.

Desriel's movements were fluid and quick, like a fox bounding through choked underbrush without stirring a single leaf. One moment he stood beside Ferendir, between his student and the foul daemons looming across the narrow entryway to the gorge. In the next instant, Desriel bounded forward, spun three times like a whirlwind, then struck with his whistling pick hammer. He smashed the skull of the nearest of the Chaos servants – that foul creature without a mouth – and the monstrosity fell, trailing a glut of thick black ichor and diseased brain matter. Before the corpse even touched the ground, the eyeless monstrosity charged, levelling its matching pincers at Desriel. As Ferendir watched – wide-eyed, amazed – the eyeless beast thrust, swiped, stabbed, those pincers slicing the air like a pair of foul shears – yet not a single stroke touched Desriel. His master's strong, ropy body curved, bent and darted in perfect counterpoint to the death strokes of his adversary. The moment the attacker's defences were spent, its confusion and frustration mounting as it failed even to draw a small drop of blood, Desriel thrust out the head of his pick hammer and the blunt weapon struck home. It cracked the eyeless monstrosity's teeth and sent the creature reeling back, stunned and stumbling. Without skipping a beat, Desriel spun in a full circle, using his movement to build momentum. The pick hammer struck the creature's head, crushing its skull, and it hit the stone, heavy and limp, beside its dead companion.

Ferendir was eager to see how Desriel might now meet the fan-eared leader of the trio, but already he sensed movement and imminent danger closing from behind. He whirled, staff ready to repel any comers. Briefly, he caught sight of Serath, standing fast and immovable, swinging and thrusting with his massive stone mallet as the beasts from the cliffs charged and attacked. Serath swept their foul feet from beneath them, putting a few on their backs before crushing one hapless skull then caving in another's bare barrel chest. By the time the first three – downed with non-lethal force – could overcome their shock and agony to even attempt to rise and attack again, Serath had already laid out two more of their sinister companions.

That left only one – the monster now charging Ferendir. It was a frenzied, fully bedecked jester of sorts, its long, trailing hair dyed several colours of the rainbow, its half-torn motley checked and striped in clashing colours and bedecked with tiny tinkling bells. Though seemingly human from the waist up, the foul thing's lower half seemed more goat-like, its thin, skeletal form capering about nimbly on small cloven hooves at the ends of furry, backward-bent legs. One hand bore impossibly long fingers not unlike the long, bald legs of some mutated spider, while the other hand had been replaced by a strange metal apparatus resembling a barbed and sharpened hook.

The beast cackled and hooted as it came, the sound maniacal and blood-chilling.

Ferendir recalled his quarterstaff drills and began a series of defensive swipes – side to side, low, high. He struck twice, deflecting two haphazard blows from the terrifying jester's hooked extremity, then saw an opening. It was only for an instant, but – just as he'd been instructed on numerous occasions by his teachers – a strange sort of calm came over him. Time seemed to slow, allowing him an eternal instant to clearly recognise and exploit his enemy's point of weakness. He lunged, thrusting the end of his walking staff towards the jester, and stabbed it square in its skinny, bobbing throat. The strike sent the beast reeling backwards, choking and sputtering, allowing Ferendir another instant's opportunity. The young supplicant charged, swinging the staff in a broad arc towards the jester's rainbow-crowned head. Just as he expected to feel the yew wood connect with his adversary's skull, to hear the satisfying, sickening crack that would accompany a palpable hit, something went wrong.

The jester threw up its hook hand, blocking the strike. The sharp inner edge of the barbed hook bit into Ferendir's yew staff and held fast. Ferendir tried to draw back, to prepare himself for another attack, but his staff would not move. The barbs and serrations of the hook were set into his staff's grain like a spring-loaded trap holding unwary prey.

The jester smiled, a forked purple tongue darting salaciously from between its pointed teeth. In the next instant it lunged forward, reaching for Ferendir with that foul, spidery hand, its long, multi-jointed fingers spreading wide as it sought to draw the young aelf into its embrace.

Ferendir acted on instinct – dangerous, he knew, but the present situation left him little alternative. Still holding his arrested staff in one hand, his other hand dove to his belt, snatched his sheathed dagger and swept the short blade upwards, right into the path of the grasping hand. The blade bit deep, black ichor glutted forth, and the jester howled in pain. As the creature's shock overtook its reason, Ferendir yanked. This time, his staff was freed. He swung the yew sideways in a sloppy, single-handed strike. This time, he felt the impact and heard the satisfying crack he'd hoped for the first time. The jester fell to the rocky floor of the canyon. Not allowing himself time to think – let alone to hesitate – Ferendir bent and drove the point of his dagger deep into the jester's corpse where its heart hopefully lay. The fiend howled and bucked for an instant, then fell silent, its whole foul form twitching as it expired.

He rose, yanking the dagger free, and tried to take a step back. He wanted – needed – to remove himself from the chaos – from imminent danger – for even the briefest of moments. To breathe. To appraise. To formulate. For an instant, he saw Desriel engaged in a desperate fight against the leader of the daemon horde, while Serath held off three more adversaries all at once. But that instant was all he managed to snatch.

Too late. Another of the monsters – this one tall and muscular, sporting four sinewy arms each ending in massive, thick, six-fingered fists – lumbered out of the fray towards him. The stomping brute lowed and roared like some daemonic bull, and its enormous fists began to swipe and pummel the air, seeking Ferendir's fleet, graceful form. The young aelf danced backwards, as fast as his feet could carry him, trying to come up with some means of overpowering or at least slipping away from the sudden onslaught. His adversary was enormous, towering, blotting out the world before him, those seeking, slashing fists like hurled boulders.

Something caught Ferendir's boot heel. Before he could recover, he was falling. Down he went again, reliving his humiliation from earlier in the day – *You fell! You fool! What would Serath say to that? You'll never know because you'll be dead!* – before finally landing on his back. The impact was on rocky, uneven ground, and more than a few pieces of shattered stone cut deep into him. There was no time to indulge the pain, however – there was only the mandate of the moment: to avoid those fists, those enormous, thundering feet, that thing looming over him and blotting out the light of the sun itself.

Ferendir used his legs to kick himself upright and followed through into a forward somersault. Just as the looming monster bore down on him and drove its four fists in quick succession into the stone that he had lain on just moments before, he tumbled between its planted feet and came out on the far side, now behind his adversary, still feeling the ache in his muscles and bones from when he'd hit the ground so mercilessly. Ignoring the pain, Ferendir scrambled to his feet, turned and drove his staff between the four-armed monster's legs. He planned to lay all his weight on the staff and try to trip the creature – but, miraculously, it did the work for him. The beast tried to turn, got its legs tangled on his staff and immediately plunged face first towards the rocky floor of the canyon. The moment the brute's face hit the stone and it roared in pain, Ferendir was upon it. He brought his staff down once, twice, three times, with all the strength he could summon. The brute grunted and groaned with each strike. But on the third, his weapon failed him.

The staff snapped with a sickening crack. Suddenly, Ferendir held only half the length of wood he had the moment before. His opponent was stunned, but would not stay down for long. Already he saw the great muscles under its taut, pale skin rippling, its back arching as it sought to lift itself once more.

Ferendir considered drawing his knife, but the small blade seemed paltry, wholly incapable of dealing his huge opponent a painful wound, let alone a fatal one.

But there, protruding from his opponent's belt – a massive sheathed scimitar, handgrip tilting tantalisingly towards Ferendir. With no other options, Ferendir went for the blade. As his adversary managed to get its knees underneath it and rise up onto all fours, Ferendir snatched the big, curved sabre from its sheath. Its weight was uneven and ill distributed, but he corrected quickly and took the only action likely to save his life.

He brought the blade down, hard and fast.

The four-armed brute's head separated from its shoulders and went rolling away in a jet of black, foul blood. Its body lost all rigidity and collapsed upon the stone.

A nasty gout of the monster's blood splashed Ferendir and he reeled back, gagging and spitting, hoping that nothing had got in his mouth. Savagely wiping the ichor away, he spun, still gripping the overlarge, heavy sabre, and surveyed the scene before him.

Every other minion of Chaos was dead, save two crippled survivors.

One was the fan-eared leader, now lying in a horridly twisted position, at least two of its limbs shattered and crushed. Desriel was keeping the crippled alpha pinned in place with the blunt head of his pick hammer.

The other was the scorpion-tailed creature – said tail now lopped off and bleeding a thick, sticky substance that looked like cloudy honey onto the stone. That beast had been crippled and immobilised by Serath's martial prowess, and now thrashed defiantly, impaled on the ferule spike of Serath's stone mallet.

Ferendir barely knew what to do with himself. Nervous energy pulsed through him, sending his heart into a thrumming storm and making his small, delicate hands shake. He made fists at his sides, lowered his head and all but willed himself to calm down, to restore his serenity, to regain his composure.

The danger has passed, for the moment. Dispel your nerves. Dispel your fears. Find yourself again, the conscious you, the purposeful you, not simply the instinctive, reactive you...

'Fools,' the leader spat from where it lay. 'This is but a small reprieve for you – a misleading calm before the storm that will lay you to waste before it.'

Ferendir's concentration broke. He could not complete his calming meditations while that foul beast thrashed and cursed so close by. The scorpion-tailed abomination pinned by Serath snarled and spat curses as well, but they were not in a tongue Ferendir knew to speak – thus it was easier to marginalise its speech, to pretend it was just some background noise like the roaring fall of water or the whisper of trees combed by a cold east wind. But the other... He could not block it out, for it spoke in words he understood, and what it said...

Desriel leaned on the pick hammer, using his weight to apply pressure to one of the immobilised Hedonite's broken bones. The creature howled in agony, but then, a moment later, shocked Ferendir by breaking into raucous, almost exultant laughter.

'Blind,' it sing-songed, 'unknowing, unseeing, unready, unworthy, all of you...'

Its companion, held immobile by Serath, began to sing its own taunt in its own vile tongue to the one who held it down upon the stone. Ferendir, standing exactly between his masters, saw both of them exchange dread-filled, mordant looks. Then, without warning, Serath raised his stone mallet and brought it down in a swift, cruel arc upon his quarry. The scorpion-tailed Hedonite died mid-guffaw, its skull crushed, its foul voice silenced forever. Serath then moved to stand beside Desriel, the two of them now looking down upon the broken-limbed, fan-eared Hedonite with cold, inhuman indifference.

Ferendir edged closer, though something within him did not want to. He was still shaking inwardly, still feeling raw and exposed by what had unfolded around them, the violence that had met them and drawn them in and forced their hands...

'How did you find this place?' Serath demanded of the creature.

The monster smiled vilely and shrugged. 'Just a morning stroll, eh? Combing the countryside for a nice, quiet place, is all.'

Desriel leaned on his pick hammer. Ferendir thought he heard cracked bone creak against itself. The Hedonite howled but still managed to force out a cackle at the end of its long, agonised scream.

'Is that all you can manage?' it taunted.

Serath started to lift his own enormous hammer. Desriel stopped him by raising a single hand.

'This place is sacred,' Desriel said calmly, 'and out of the way. What brought you here?'

'Sacred!' the Hedonite spat. 'It's a pile of dead, wet rock and scree! What a pitiful people you are, holding such a slag pit as this scar upon the mountainside sacred!'

Desriel calmly applied pressure to his pick hammer again. He did so slowly, this time, subtly. The pressure caused the Hedonite a great deal of pain. It seemed to well up slowly but surely, once more dragging a scream out of it and making its broken, barely human body shake beneath the weight of its captor's weapon.

'To the fires with all three of you!' the Hedonite snapped. 'There will be others! More will come, I promise! Our master makes no demands if he sets us free, only that we follow our noses and do his good work where we find untouched canvas in want of pigment.'

'Untouched canvas,' Ferendir muttered, barely understanding the metaphor.

The vile creature turned its red-black eyes upon him. 'All the Mortal Realms are surfaces in want of colour and shade,' it said, as though explaining a very simple concept to the lowest of dullards. 'The blood we spill, the havoc we wreak – all is our art, expressed and created to serve our god in the making! The one whom we serve!'

Then, without warning, Serath swung his stone mallet low. The spike opposite the blunt head bit deep into the Hedonite's brain, and it said no more. Once more, the gorge was quiet, still, the only sounds the distant hitch and moan of the mountain winds and the water falling down the cliffside, burbling over stone and scree as a seeping, seeking stream.

For a long, silent moment, Serath and Desriel studied one another, seeming to communicate silently without any words passing between them. What they each seemed to clearly recognise and convey towards the other as the danger now presenting itself was a mystery to Ferendir, but he yet saw how gravely they met one another's gazes, what a terrible weight and oppression now lay on both of them. After a moment, Serath broke away and took off at a swift, steady trot towards the narrow canyon that had led them into the hidden gorge.

Desriel looked to Ferendir. 'Do you know who these vile creatures belonged to? What power they serve?'

Ferendir nodded. 'Slaanesh, the god of excess,' Ferendir said, hoping that was the right answer. That had been his first assumption, given the bizarre extremity of their body modifications and the colourful, haphazard nature of their raiment.

'Just so,' Desriel said. Miraculous. Even now, after fighting for his life and killing a slew of adversaries, with danger clearly at their doorstep, he would not stop teaching his student lessons. 'We have to go now, quickly. We'll follow Serath back through the canyon to the mountainside.'

Desriel moved away from the strewn corpses of their enemies, backing away while never taking his eyes off Ferendir. When he saw that the young aelf was still rooted where he stood – by shock, by ignorance, by simple failure to understand what was happening – he gently urged him along.

'Come, supplicant,' Desriel said. 'There's no time to waste. We must away.'

'But, master–'

'Come now,' Desriel snapped, as insistent and forceful as Ferendir had ever heard him. 'Questions can come later. Just follow me.'

He turned and broke into a run, following in Serath's wake. Ferendir, completely at a loss and unable to make sense of what was unfolding, fell in behind his master, struggling to catch up but keeping pace easily once he did so.

Threading the narrow canyon seemed to take no time at all, a strange phenomenon, since following it upon their entry had struck Ferendir as a long, meandering stroll into the back of beyond. Clearly it was only his misgivings, his wariness and lack of surety, that had made the time spent seem to stretch so interminably. In short order, they were once more emerging from the narrow ravine through which they'd entered and jogging down the gentle slope of yellowed grass and bare rock towards the place where the mountainside grew suddenly steep and gave way to forest shadows and jostling trees.

Serath was far out in front of them, already standing at the place where the slope dropped precipitously into the forest below when Desriel and Ferendir emerged from the canyon's mouth. His feet were planted wide, and he stood staring out across the wooded valley beneath them towards the great, rolling ridgeline that separated their current position from their place of origin. Ferendir knew that on the far side of that huge, curving ridge lay the shadowy vale where their temple waited, folded into a misty cleft between untrod forests and the shoulders of the mountain's south-western slopes.

Before he'd even reached the drop-off to stand beside his two masters, Ferendir saw the horrible sign that so transfixed Serath: a small, subtle indication against a vast, unchanging natural back-drop that something very horrible – very wrong – was currently unfolding at the sanctified site they all called home.

Smoke.

It rose in three thin tendrils, white, grey and black, drifting lazily up from the mountainside before the buffeting winds caught it in their currents and blew it forcefully southwards, turning the three distinct twisting columns into a single feathered, half-effaced smudge of soot and vapour. Worse, a bevy of small black forms were already wheeling and bobbing on the thermals rising from the valley beneath the smoke columns, forms so small at this dis-tance they almost appeared to be gnats.

But Ferendir realised quickly just what they were, and what they portended.

Scavenger birds, smelling death, eagerly awaiting the cessation of hostilities before swooping in to break their fast on carrion and corpses.

Something terrible – unspeakable – was unfolding back at home.

Serath leapt over the ledge and began a rapid descent of the steep, forested slope.

'No time to waste,' he said absently, more to himself than to either of his companions.

Ferendir looked to Desriel. Desriel, for the first time in the whole of Ferendir's memory, looked genuinely worried. His eyes were wide, his brow furrowed – if only in the slightest – indicating that, for all his training and mental conditioning, he could not hide his fear and anxiety. Ferendir opened his mouth to ask a question, but his master spoke before words could tumble out.

'No more questions,' Desriel said with finality. 'We need to move, and quickly. Keep up, now.'

He set off behind Serath. Ferendir, knowing that there was nothing left for him but to obey, to follow and to stay with them, did as he'd been commanded.

CHAPTER TWO

Ezarhad had heard of the immovable might and serene ferocity of the Alarith Stoneguard, and his enemies did not disappoint. For the first hour of the siege, a small, close-ranked unit of hammer-wielding Alarith had blocked the ground approach to the main gate, using their mountain-derived magic to repel every onslaught as if they were literally made of stone. Massed charges of daemonettes, galloping fiends and charging hellstriders with blades and lances all broke upon the line of Stoneguard like ocean waves upon implacable cliffs.

But if Ezarhad had found himself amazed by the aelven defenders as they repelled his troops, he was positively awed by them when they finally broke ranks and waded into the forward lines of his recovering minions, their flashing diamondpick hammers and long-handled stone mallets wielded with swift and deadly efficiency.

As he anticipated, it was slaughter. In a span so short he barely need measure it, almost a thousand of the mixed forces in his vanguard had been broken, crushed and pulverised by those hammers. When reserves were ordered forward to meet the blood-thirsty aelves, they fell back into formation, once more presenting an impenetrable barrier, and the whole frustrating mummer's show started over again.

No matter, he reminded himself. *I was prepared for this. Planned for it. Be impressed if you must, Ezarhad... but know that you still retain the upper hand.*

Having spent a massive amount of ground troops, Ezarhad ordered the next wave unleashed – everything in his arsenal that could be called artillery, from bolt-firing scorpions to incendiary-lobbing catapults to the thunderwaves and warp storms conjured by his deadliest war mages.

The Alarith, true to form, were unfazed. They responded with potent spells of their own – storms of deadly sharp rock shards summoned out of the earth itself; living fissures that split the rock of the hillside and sent scores of his troops crashing down from their high positions to the promontory below, sudden recesses opening from the stone like living mouths to swallow and crush his swarming troops, even shining, impenetrable domes of light and energy that protected the ramparts and inner wards of the temple from falling missiles and raining sorceries.

And still the Stoneguard below the gate held the narrow approach. Still his foot soldiers charged and crashed and were broken upon the impenetrable barrier those hammer-wielders presented. For a short time, he knew a flash of hope, for when the Alarith defenders broke ranks to wade once more among his troops and strike them down, he could detect, even at a distance, subtle signs of wear and fatigue among them. For the first time since the siege began, Alar-ith fell to his minions' talons and blades. At last, miraculously, the Stoneguard betrayed some small measure of their inherent fragil-ity, their mortality.

But that had been a short-lived victory as well. A second unit burst forth from the sally port beside the main gate and took up the familiar massed ranks across the road, allowing their injured – often carrying their dead – to retreat behind the curtain walls.

Keep pressing them, he'd reminded himself, always so eager – so impatient – to spring his trap, even as he knew that the longer he could wait, the more effective his surprise would be.

The scene was repeated. Infantry broke upon the Stoneguard ranks. Hammers reduced his soldiers to shattered bones and bloodied pulp. The wizards sacrificed scores of daemonettes in order to summon more powerful daemon champions who charged the walls and drew the full force of the Alarith Stonemages' spellcraft. He relented when pressed by his chief mage and signalled for the conjuring of the wheels of excruciation, a storm of swiftly moving razor-sharp blades that flitted and whirled hungrily among the Alarith when they broke ranks, leaving more than a few dead – slashed by a thousand bloody cuts – on the now-littered field before the temple walls.

Still, the Alarith held them. Still, their Stoneguard stood fast and the walls of their temple could not be scaled or breached.

The Alarith, it seemed, would hold them off indefinitely.

But Ezarhad was no fool. He had heard the stories, considered all the possible means by which he could use the adamant will of his enemies against them – and their repeated employ of magical defences to both shield themselves from aerial bombardment and mount their own ranged counter-attacks was part of his plan. He would let them drain their energies, their resources, protecting their temple from falling incendiaries and magical missiles while their adamant Stoneguard kept his ground troops from scaling or penetrating the walls – his real coup was beneath them.

Before dawn ever came, Ezarhad's duardin sappers were in place, dug in deep under the south and east walls of the monastery, preparing for the shocking, spectacular killing blow that would finally break the stalemate and grant him access to the great temple and reliquary within.

After hours of siege, when the fighting was at its fiercest and most unrelenting, Ezarhad gave the signal. His sappers ignited the explosives they'd installed beneath the temple walls, and, all at once, it looked as if the whole of the promontory upon which the monastery stood was convulsing. A massive spume of pulverised stone, soil and shattered granite leapt high into the air – first beneath the south wall, just beside the main gate, then beneath the defensive tower at the south-east corner. The great, smoky geysers struck Ezarhad as oddly beautiful when they tore the walls asunder and flew high into the sky, explosive and celebratory, and he shuddered with ecstasy at the sight. Sweetening the experience was a chorus of screams and cheers from his own forces – some of whom were snatched up in the explosive up-rush and blown to bits in the destruction.

When the debris crashed earthwards again and the smoke began to disappear, their path was clear – two massive, appalling rents in the thick curtain wall, each wide enough for half a dozen four-legged fiends to charge through, shoulder to shoulder. Beyond the shattered walls, through masses of swirling smoke, Ezarhad imagined he saw the slender, pale forms of the Alarith defenders who'd survived the blast scurrying to and fro, taking stock of the damage, rushing to save any injured survivors and fall back behind the walls that enclosed the monastery's inner ward containing the great temple and twin shrines that acted as the locus for their worship and daily meditations.

Mundane chemistry and simple misdirection, he thought with no small amount of satisfaction. *There is no better means of surprising a proud, powerful, magically engaged enemy than a well-aimed, unexpected fist to the gut.*

'Call up the hellstriders,' Ezarhad told Kraygorn when he saw the way clear and his forces streaming through the breach to overwhelm and slaughter the last hold-outs. 'They can accompany me as I claim my prize.'

Kraygorn, his warlord, nodded in the affirmative and cracked his enormous whip over his horned head, calling for the hellstriders to come forth at once.

Most of the resistance remaining was neutralised by the time Ezarhad travelled up the hill and past the mounds of his slaughtered and scattered minions to enter the monastery himself. He strode fearlessly up and over the enormous piles of pulverised stone and scorched earth choking the breaches and stood for a time in the outer ward, surveying the beautiful desolation that his servants had wrought.

Scores of dead Lumineth lay hacked to pieces, their riven extremities arranged in strange geometries, while others, still whole in death, had been posed in stirring and blasphemous postures. The death artistry of his minions was most satisfying to behold, but that satisfaction was undercut by the massive expenditure of resources also on display. For every dead Lumineth, the corpses of a dozen or more of Ezarhad's own servants were scattered about in kind. The Alarith Stoneguard had clearly made Ezarhad pay dearly for the day's victory. Everywhere he looked – in the courtyard, upon the ramparts, in yawning doorways, beside ruined arches and still-burning structures threatening to collapse – he saw death, dismemberment, slaughter, catastrophe.

But what did he care for a few spent lives in the service of his own desires? The joy, the ecstasy, of the slaughter around him was yet so moving that it nearly brought tears to his foul black eyes.

Kraygorn and a small knot of mounted hellstriders haunted Ezarhad's vicinity, affording him a wide berth so that he could enjoy this well-earned reward but also enclosing him in a cordon to assure his safety. There still might be Lumineth about, skulking in the shadows or hiding in unburnt dormitories or storehouses, just waiting for the opportunity to strike at him. It might not save their home, their temples or their precious, venerated relics, but it would allow that survivor some measure of solace, finally expiring knowing that the great and glorious leader of the warhost that had destroyed his or her home was dead.

Ezarhad smiled. Let them try. The success of his plan to destroy the walls and breach the temple precincts was only the prelude to his ultimate victory this day.

He strode on, tall and proud, letting Kraygorn and the fiends scurry along behind him to deal with any lingering threats.

The inner ward had been penetrated as well, one of the small portals in the wall watched over by a knot of heavily armed invaders still toying with a Lumineth female who, despite the horrid pain she must have been enduring under their pincers and thorny skin spikes, yet maintained a stoic, silent defiance, even as the life slowly ebbed from her. Ezarhad gave her a nod of approving admiration as he marched by, then ducked and passed through the doorway – too low to comfortably accommodate his unusually tall frame.

Beyond, he entered the inner ward that enclosed the Alarith's most holy shrines and their primary temple. Already, his forces were heaving some of their favoured enemy dead up from the littered ground to nail their corpses to the lintels of the temple entryways or bind them with thorn-vines to the pillars looming in the holy porticos. At the periphery, Ezarhad saw a few hold-outs fighting on against overwhelming numbers of his servants, but deigned not to waste his time bearing witness to their dying struggles. They were already dead, the lot of them – they simply did not know it yet.

Ahead stood the great temple – the place where these mountain-loving fools sought their greatest and holiest insights, raised their voices in solemn hymns to the aelementiri spirits that attended and empowered them, meditated alone or in small groups to seek the will of the mountain and the realm of Hysh itself. Therein lay his quarry – the inner sanctum, beyond the pillared peristyle and the primary sanctuaries, where the venerated relics and most powerful artefacts possessed by these pointy-eared rock-worshippers waited. Everything within the sanctum was held there in solemnity and secrecy, their isolation and disuse precisely the point, for none but the most senior members of the Alarith guarding this shrine even knew the whole of the inventory held there. They reckoned that by hiding their most powerful and terrible secrets in a dark and silent place, time would erase their memory, and the Mortal Realms' collective ignorance to their very existence would keep them safe.

A sound plan... but it had failed. For Ezarhad Fatesbane, secret knowledge was the only currency. The fate and location of their holy lord, Slaanesh, was yet a mystery, was it not? If the fate of their god was itself an impenetrable mystery, then, Ezarhad reasoned, only impenetrable mysteries and their exploitation could ultimately lead an ambitious pretender and usurper like Ezarhad to claim the throne of Slaanesh. That had been his guiding principle for centuries now – if there was something to be learned that *could* be learned, and that secret knowledge would aid him in his quest for ultimate power and exaltation, then Ezarhad would find it, no matter what stood in his way.

That was how he found the Eidolith.

He mounted the broad stairs that climbed from the yard up to the looming, dark entrance of the temple. Smoke already poured from within, the interior lit only by a few crackling fires feasting on still corpses or torn-down curtains and banners. Ezarhad would have to remember to instruct his servants to fire the remains of the temple once his prize was claimed – he wanted nothing to remain once the Eidolith itself was safely in his hands.

He stepped over the threshold. In the vestibule of the temple, the bodies of elderly Stoneguard and young acolytes were strewn about in equal measure. Once more, his own dead minions outnumbered the defenders – but what of that? He'd begun the day with almost five thousand in his warhost. He would end the day with a respectable three thousand remaining. For his purposes, that would suffice. Once the Eidolith was in hand and he had ferried it through the mountains to his ultimate destination – his ultimate destiny – his warhost would grow exponentially. Claiming the weapon he sought – the weapon that the Eidolith would allow him to control – would make the servants of his rivals and the forces arrayed against him decry the objects of their loyalty without hesitation and join him.

And so he would spend as many lives as necessary to bring himself to that point – to claim the Eidolith, to brave the mountains, to awaken Kaethraxis…

A lone figure materialised out of the smoky darkness directly ahead of Ezarhad, the entryway that led from the main sanctuary into the secret reliquary beyond. For a moment, Ezarhad stared, his eyes refusing to focus or make sense of the form now emerging from the Stygian gloom. Off to his right, one of Kraygorn's still-mounted hellstriders spurred his two-legged mount forward and toppled a flickering iron brazier with his lance, spilling its coals upon the stone floor and causing a sudden flare of gold-red light that illuminated the newcomer.

It was a Stoneguard of the temple, face and hands deeply carved by age and experience, yet still possessed of a strong, taut body and ropy, powerful muscles. He was covered in soot, streaks of drying black ichor from slain daemonettes and fiends, as well as gobbets of rent Slaaneshi flesh. His own blood – red and tacky – clung to him in places, for he had suffered a number of horrible if not fatal wounds. His eyes were a haunting red-brown, like firelit garnets, and he carried with him a long, graceful diamondpick hammer that Ezarhad admired instantly for the artistry of its craft and the luscious film of bloody tissue yet clinging to its spiked head.

The Stoneguard planted his feet and raised the hammer.

'Turn around,' he said softly. 'Leave this place.' The velvety whisper of his voice belied the fire burning in those red-brown eyes and the unmistakable determination in his stance.

Ezarhad smiled, feeling a sort of pride for the poor, misguided old aelf. *Well done*, he thought. *I salute your bravery, you pointy-eared old zealot... but my admiration will not stop the inevitable.*

Ezarhad said, 'Kraygorn, remove this old fool from my path.'

Kraygorn lumbered forward. 'As you command, my lord.'

The aelf's gnarled old hands tightened on the longhammer.

Ezarhad crossed his arms patiently. He had fiends, hellstriders, daemonettes and mortal Hedonites unnumbered. Surely he would not have to spend an exorbitant number of them to move one determined Stoneguard...

Their fast march homewards took half the time that their slow march to Ferendir's trial site had that morning, and when they reached their destination, what they found was worse than Ferendir had imagined.

Firstly, the perpetrators were still on hand, though in the process of making a steady, orderly withdrawal. If the sight of those nine Hedonites in the trial gorge had unsettled Ferendir, the wholly unwanted, and unimaginable, spectacle of a whole army of such abominable, misshapen monsters swarming away from the smoking rubble and still-burning ruins of his home positively shattered him. He felt the urge to burst from their hiding place when the columns of the warhost tramped by down the winding forest road that led out of their little vale, but Desriel and Serath ordered him to secrete himself and keep silent. They were three; the legions of their enemies were seemingly numberless. There was absolutely nothing they could do until the Hedonites were gone.

After watching for a time from some underbrush near the road, they quietly withdrew to a small, shallow cave in the hillside, out of sight of the road but within listening distance. There, secreted in the airless, sunken space beneath a slab of stone and a pyramid of fallen, half-rotted old trees, they could hear the marching feet, the rattle of weaponry and armour, the terrible, bone-chilling songs sung by the Hedonites as they marched out of the valley. Because the road was narrow and their numbers were great, most of the day passed as they waited for their enemies and would-be destroyers to be away from the vale. More than once, Ferendir began to speak, to ask – as quietly as possible – what they were waiting for, or how long they might have to wait before seeing to the ruins of their home temple. Every single time he drew breath and opened his mouth, Serath speared him with a silent glare. Every time he saw his master's burning, warning gaze, Ferendir closed his mouth and kept his questions to himself.

Finally, late in the day, when the shadows grew long and the light began to slowly redden towards the lingering, persistent twilight that would signify Hyshian night, Serath ventured forth from their little grotto to scout the road and ensure that the way was clear. He returned a short while later, said that the Hedonites seemed to have all gone, at last, then turned and set off – without waiting for his companion and their supplicant to follow.

Desriel looked to Ferendir in the gloom of the little cave.

'What we're likely to find… It will hurt. It will shake you.'

Ferendir nodded. 'I am ready, master. I won't be controlled by my fear.'

Desriel leaned forward. When he spoke, it was softly, and with the utmost gravity and compassion. 'You cannot be ready,' Desriel said. 'I am not ready. Serath – despite what he shows you – is not ready. No one is ready to see their whole world torn down and destroyed by an act of malign will. But… that is what awaits us. Just… be ready. Inwardly. Be ready for it to hurt.'

He set out then, without another word. Ferendir, dreading what awaited them at the end of their trek, followed in silent obedience.

What they found at the top of the forest road, on the promontory overlooking the cascading falls, sheltered by the looming cliffs and close-gathered ridgelines of the vale, surpassed his worst expectations.

He was not sure what was more horrifying, the sight – the living fact – of his home, his whole world, now sundered and broken and reduced to rocky fragments and still-smouldering fires and haphazard mounds of earthen debris and mutilated corpses, or the fact that all the ruin now before him had been perpetrated since that very morning. Twelve hours, perhaps fourteen, since they set out to undertake his final trial. Now, in that short blink of an eye, everything he had known and cherished for most of his life was utterly destroyed.

Clearly, the Stoneguard of his temple – along with their eager supplicants – had made the servants of Slaanesh pay dearly. The narrow road that climbed the escarpment and the landscape surrounding the temple walls had been churned, shattered and broken into upending fragments by geomantic magic of great complexity and power. There were enormous swathes of the rocky mountainside now levelled and transmogrified to volcanic glass by more sorceries of the most destructive sort, while large portions of the regolith and landscape had been crushed, flash-burned and turned to smoking slag. Strewn like falling leaves among the ruined landscape were the bodies of thousands of Slaaneshi Hedonites, their many body modifications and strange, repugnant faces largely pulverised, shredded, blackened to a crisp, or crushed into a foul, bloody pulp. As they picked a path over the uneven, sundered ground, amid all those dead monsters and marauders, Ferendir tried to imagine the mindset of his teachers and keepers – how they must have tried to hold off the onslaught at first with the simplest, most reliable tools in their martial and geomantic skill sets, only gradually seeing the necessity for using the most destructive weapons and magicks at their disposal to try and stem the never-ending tide of monstrous invaders that broke upon their massive walls in wave after corrupted wave. For the wisest and most patient Stoneguard of the Alarith to stoop to the use of their most destructive and disruptive weaponry after a siege lasting only a few hours bespoke just how determined, how merciless, the enemy's attack must have been.

And look at them, Ferendir thought, scanning the littered ground all around them. *There are hundreds... thousands... and we saw still thousands more marching out of the dell. If they spent so many in the attempt yet retained so many upon withdrawal... how many might there be in all?*

How could any force, anywhere, stand against such an enemy?

One of the half-charred corpses nearby gurgled and twitched – apparently not so dead as they had supposed. Desriel, with blinding speed, spun upon the creature and used the ferule spike of his stone mallet to finish it. Without so much as a pause or a grimace, Ferendir's master withdrew the spike and carried on his meandering way across the ruined battlefield.

Ferendir forced himself to raise his eyes and take in the sight of the temple compound itself. This morning, when they left in the early-hour twilight, the high, thick walls that surrounded the temple compound had loomed above them, strong and sure, as enduring and immovable as the mountain they called home. Now, those walls were half-collapsed, the entire front span crushed and rent by some unknown, immeasurable force that seemed to have cloven the curtain wall in two then torn every bit of cyclopean stone and mortar down, block by enormous block. It was as if a creature from a nightmare – something as enormous and unstopp-able as the mountain itself – had simply risen up and crushed the forward wall with a single blow. Beyond, through a lingering haze of swirling dust and still-billowing smoke, Ferendir could barely make out the outline of the barracks, temples and archives that had once been the full extent of his world and his ambition. He had thought to spend the rest of his long life in this place, serv-ing the mountain's will, seeking its insights and wisdoms, never venturing forth beyond its protective walls and the surrounding rolling, mountainous landscape except on specific errands and limited pilgrimages to other temples in search of knowledge that he could absorb and bring home for the betterment of his order.

But it was all gone now. Destroyed.

Desriel suddenly raised his diamondpick hammer and brought it down in a powerful arc. Something soft and squidgy splattered among the strewn dead. Ferendir shuddered inwardly.

The sight of his ruined home. The inherent wrongness radi-ating from the rent and scarred earth beneath them. The horrid smell of all these slain and half-burnt bodies. He had never, ever been in such a terrible place... and he was on his own threshold.

Up ahead, Serath had entered the colony proper via the great riven gap in the curtain wall. After only a few steps, he was swal-lowed in the lingering whorls of smoke billowing from within the compound.

'Serath!' Desriel called. 'Do not be overeager. We should not separate.'

Desriel turned to search for Ferendir. He found his student fol-lowing a few long paces behind him, shuffling along aimlessly because the terrible sights stretching as far as he could see robbed any desire he had to reach any meaningful destination. Ferendir had no idea where they were going now, or what they were doing.

He could simply place one booted foot in front of the other and try not to step on any bodies. What was left for them now? What could they possibly do with themselves when all that they served had been so unceremoniously destroyed?

'How fare you, supplicant?' Desriel asked. His eyes betrayed his concern. Though his tone was easy, he clearly knew what a heart-rending experience this must be for Ferendir.

'I am...' Ferendir had no answer. He wanted to offer some affirmation, some simple statement to let his master know that, come what may, he could navigate through it. But what could he say? Were there any words?

'I am at a loss,' Ferendir finally said. They were the only words that made any sense, in the midst of all the senselessness.

Desriel nodded and carried on without a word. His silence was his own affirmation.

More than anything, Ferendir wanted to be strong now – not only for himself but for his masters. Whatever grief he felt deep within him, tearing at the fabric of him, clawing and gnashing at his spiritual essence, how much worse must it be for them? True, as master Stoneguard, well advanced up the Teclian ladder, they were masterful when it came to hiding what they felt. They could be suffering the most profound trauma of their lives and Ferendir would be none the wiser. That was what strong Stoneguard – wise Stoneguard – did: they suppressed their emotion, suppressed their desires, suppressed everything within them that could cloud their thinking or muddy the waters of their reason and understanding. They did this not because they did not feel, or could not feel, but because they knew the inherent power that feelings had. They felt sorrow, they felt fear, they felt hatred, they felt love, they felt pity – but they were too wise, too well versed in the myriad ways that emotions could amplify and complicate the needs of the moment, the simple necessities of any given situation, to give those feelings excess power over them.

Thus, even now, Ferendir wagered his masters' hearts were breaking – shattered and rent and upturned, like the rock and soil around them. But they would not show him their pain. Instead, they would concentrate on what the larger exigencies of the situation might be, what they might salvage, how they might still be of use, how best to put their skills and insights to work for some greater, loftier purpose.

But what was that purpose? That was what prodded Ferendir now. He knew that his masters – grieving or no – must have a purpose in the present moment. If they did not, they would not be advancing so confidently, acting as if there were some greater mandate guiding their actions. But whatever that purpose might be, neither had deigned to yet make Ferendir aware of it. Even now, as Desriel stared at him, waiting for his response to that simple question – *How fare you, supplicant?* – Ferendir knew that if he asked a similar question in return, no answer would be forthcoming.

I must wait, then, he thought. *When they want me to know, they will tell me. Until then, I must do what I was already sworn to do. I must listen, I must learn, and I must serve.*

A figure appeared from the smoke and mounted the fallen stones of the curtain wall. Serath again.

'What do you see, brother?' Desriel called, increasing his pace to reach his counterpart more quickly. 'Did you find survivors?'

Ferendir quickened his own pace, more than anything to keep from being left alone with the mountains of dead surrounding him.

Serath offered no response. He simply stood there atop a massive pile of toppled stone, a small, pale figure framed against the still-billowing black smoke that curled and drifted from behind the curtain wall as the mountain winds skated down from the passes high above. As they neared, Ferendir tried to read his master's face. Though at first assuming he could read nothing – because Serath was a master of suppressing his own feelings, his own anxieties and desires – Ferendir found himself shaken to the core a moment later when he realised that the look of loss and desolation now apparent on his master's normally unreadable face was wholly alien and unprecedented. Ferendir could recall three times that he had seen traces of anger in Serath's expression, four or five times when he had read the barest hint of true satisfaction and perhaps once when he was able to note clear and unmistakable contentment and pride.

But what he saw now was something new entirely. Serath's expression was blank, wholly abstract and wanting.

It was the complete absence of understanding.

It was desolation.

'Everything,' Serath said when they drew closer to the great pile of debris that he stood atop.

Desriel began to swiftly climb the stones, never once looking down for the right foothold, as though he could not possibly make a misstep.

'Everything, you say?' Desriel asked. 'What do you mean, brother?'

Ferendir began to clamber up the fallen stones. He erred on the side of caution and used both his hands and feet.

'They destroyed everything,' Serath said quietly. 'And everyone.'

Ferendir froze mid-climb and raised his eyes. He studied his master. Serath was not even looking at him or Desriel. His eyes were raised to the edge of the vale and the horizon, as though he were searching for some compass point to fix upon, some sense that the world he'd known for all of his aelven-long life still, in some sense, existed.

Desriel reached the summit of the rock pile. He stood for a moment, eyes searching, trying to snap Serath out of his reverie with minimal effort or intrusiveness. Serath finally lowered his eyes, concentrating at last on the broken stones beneath his feet. When he spoke to Desriel, he spoke quietly, his voice barely a whisper.

'Go,' he said. 'See for yourself.'

Desriel descended the far side of the stone pile. Just as his master's feet once more touched soil below, Ferendir made the summit. Before turning his gaze inwards – past the breached walls and outer towers towards the temple and living spaces that had housed and protected him for so many years – he stood beside his master, Serath, and studied him.

After a long, pregnant silence, Serath raised his eyes to Ferendir. He had a new look about him now – a quiet, unspoken desperation and desire, the deep, burning force of which threatened to incinerate Ferendir where he stood. He could not put a name to what he saw in Serath's eyes, precisely, for it seemed to be not one desire – not one impulse – but several, all at once. Rage. Grief. Loss. A failure of conscious understanding. The small ember that starts a raging wildfire.

'It would appear,' Serath said at last, 'that this is your trial, supplicant.'

Ferendir, sensing the import in Serath's words, turned and descended the great mound of fallen stone. When he finally reached the bottom and stood once more upon the bare soil of the inner ward, he raised his eyes and forced himself to drink in the bitter scene before him.

The bodies outside had been bad enough, even being those of the enemy. Here, now, he saw hundreds more, but most of them – to his grief – were not strangers or twisted alien simulacra at all: they were his friends; his fellow supplicants; his teachers – for all intents and purposes, the only family he'd known since childhood.

There, Stoneguard Valacra, bent and unmoving atop a pair of slain Slaaneshi adversaries, her pale hands still clutching the spear she'd used to defend herself in her last battle.

Off to his right, the huddled form of Stoneguard Myanvelis, shielding two of the younger supplicants of the temple against some long-completed attack. It looked as if the Hedonites had doused her and the apprentices she protected in some horrid incendiary, for their bodies were burned to a crisp and frozen for all eternity in a terrible, bounded instant of fear, pain and suffering.

Across the yard, Stonemage Aidolyn, cloven and rent by a hundred enemy blades, even though she lay atop a veritable mountain of her slain enemies. She had died with her staff of the high peaks in her hands, and the evidence of her deadly prowess lay strewn about her on all sides. In the end, there had been too many, and she had succumbed to their deadly, filthy weapons – but she had taken many with her into the waiting darkness.

Desriel moved slowly, almost idly, from grim tableau to grim tableau. Ferendir imagined his master taking stock of those he found, performing a sort of mental roll call in an effort to record – in the simplest terms – the price of this unprovoked and merciless attack. Desriel's mind – like Ferendir's own – was well conditioned to making and memorising lists. Now, as he surveyed the loss and carnage, Desriel was compiling the longest and most terrible he would ever create – a list of all those lost to evil, spite and cruelty, on a day like any other when no trouble should have been expected.

Ferendir's eyes sought the temple. Normally, it dominated the inner ward of the compound, towering and sprawling behind its own inner wall, a magnificent edifice of perfectly etched stone blocks fitted together so precisely that not even a sheet of parchment could be slipped between them, its tall, peaked roof standing above all the other structures of the compound like a mountain in miniature, the perfect, hand-built evocation of the aelemental force that they had all come here to worship and study and serve. For a moment, Ferendir could not find the temple, and that simple fact – its apparent absence when it should have been unmistakable, even amid the chaos – made him skirt the edge of panic.

Then he realised he was looking right at it. The gate that normally separated the inner ward where the temple stood from the outer ward of the colony had been torn asunder and collapsed, a small redux of the massive ruin dominating the outer wall. The temple itself seemed to have been blasted from within. Its high, peaked roof was no more. Its walls were broken and strewn about as massive debris. Black smoke still whorled and rose from its broken, burning bones, the corpse of a massive saurian beast now slain and left to rot under a setting sun, its stone-and-terracotta carcass set afire to assure the impossibility of its salvage.

'No,' Ferendir heard himself say. His feet began to move, unbidden. He raced forward, closer and closer to all that ruination and destruction, sickened by the thought of studying it up close yet wholly incapable of resisting the urge.

You fool, a voice within him hissed. *This is not our way! Impulse! Emotion! The satisfaction of small, animal urges, however fearful or desperate! Get hold of yourself, supplicant! You are not Alarith yet! You still have much to prove!*

And yet, was this not his home? His family? He might be younger than both Desriel and Serath… but had he not lost just as much as they had?

And yet, they did not grieve. Not so irresponsibly. Not so feebly.

Very well, then, he thought, feeling the sting of tears and having no strength to choke them back. *Let them practise self-control. Let them swallow their grief. Let them suppress their horror and fury. I will grieve for all of us… and for all those we've lost. In this moment, untried as I am, purposeless as I am, my grief is all I have to give. Let me give it, freely.*

He stared into the black and broken maw of the fallen temple, drinking in the sight of the whirling smoke, the still-flickering flames lost deep in the gloom of the ruins, the dozens of bodies of his comrades and mentors lying hacked or burned or broken all about the courtyard before the temple's debris-littered steps.

The tears came.

He made no effort to stop them, even as he forced himself to put one foot in front of the other and mount the littered steps to survey the damage done to the peristyle and sanctuary.

Serath and Desriel did not hesitate. One after the other, they disappeared into the temple's half-exposed, smoke-filled interior. In moments, both had been reduced to thin, wandering ghosts, moving slowly and aimlessly through the permanent shroud of lingering haze and black fog. Here and there, a few fires yet burned amid the inky darkness, smudging the whirlpools and eddied tides of smoke, casting strange shadows across the inner walls of the ruined shrine.

Ferendir wanted to join them, to explore the interior, to punish himself with the scarring sight of the familiar dead, the ruined artefacts and holy sanctums, to bathe in the vile smells and stunned silence that seemed to rule the world around him. Given all the fear and grief and revulsion now working within him, he knew that his only salvation – his only strength – was immersion. To see. To let all of it burn deep into the fabric of his heart and soul and linger there, forever. He could not afford to be timid, or anxious, or reticent. He must bear witness.

And yet, just across the threshold, he felt as if he could not take another step... as though the mountain itself had willed that he should be rooted to the spot he found himself standing upon. Whether he would stand there until moved to turn and depart or whether the stone itself might slide up his feet and legs and turn his own body to unmoving shale and make of him a statue, he could not say. He only knew that every attempt he made to will himself onwards failed. No amount of strength – physical or mental – could move him.

His eyes were burning from the smoke, the tears of grief he'd been unable to hold back now flowing more freely for the interference of the charred and foetid air around him. He could feel it working on his lungs, as well – burning, drying, making them seem less like repositories for sacred breath and more like old bellows beside a smith's forge, full of the dust and soot of untold ages, being worked after a long season idle.

He was about to try a new tack, to attempt to turn and leave that place and venture back outside, into the yard of the inner ward, when one of the corpses lying curled on the stone floor of the temple reached out and touched him.

He moved, practically leaping from where he stood and stumbling backwards in a terrified, wholly instinctive gesture that immediately shamed him. He almost fell backwards, but his arched back bumped hard against a piece of protruding, half-ruined wall, and Ferendir knew he could retreat no further. Gulping scorched air, shaking all over, he stared at what had just reached out for him from beyond death.

It was old Merinoth, the most senior Stoneguard of the shrine, the wisest and most advanced – in terms of the Teclian ladder – of any who served their patron mountain. He lay in a foetal ball on the floor of the ruined temple, a spear entangled with one arm, still skewering a Slaaneshi Hedonite just a stone's throw away. Half of his ropy, muscular frame was charred by fire. The other half was torn and rent by the vicious slash marks of alien talons and the cruel ministrations of dozens of blade wounds. He was a hundred shades of charred black and charnel red, with only his one remaining garnet-coloured eye providing icy counterpoint to his horrid condition.

And yet, he was still alive. Ferendir knew this because that single garnet-brown eye all but skewered him with a desperate, beseeching glare, while the hand not scorched and fused to Merinoth's body reached out for him, desperate, seeking, clutching at the air.

'Ferendir,' the old aelf wheezed.

'Masters!' Ferendir screamed, then broke from where he stood and dove to old Merinoth's side. 'Masters, I've found someone alive!'

Ferendir took Merinoth's good hand. Two of his fingers had

been lopped off, but the wounds were now scabbed and crusted. He held that hand close, as though he could hold the old mystic in the state of existence itself simply by not letting go of him. How could he have survived such terrible wounds? The pain he must be in! The agony!

Boots on stone, and two bodies came hurtling out of the fire and smoke from opposite directions almost in the same instant – Desriel and Serath, answering Ferendir's desperate call. Though their faces bore expressions of grim, stony determination, the swiftness of their movements and their headlong rush towards Ferendir told him just how desperate and relieved they were to find even one alive among so much carnage.

Merinoth was shaking now, his body suffering terrible seizures and tremors – no doubt a function of all the damage done. Ferendir held his hand tighter, praying that the mountain might help the old teacher pull through, if only for long enough to tell them what had happened.

No, Ferendir thought with sudden clarity. *Do not pray for his survival. Look at him. He's maimed, crippled, in terrible, inhuman pain. Pray for his release. Pray for an end to his suffering.*

His masters were beside him now, both kneeling over the crumpled, half-immolated form of the old teacher. Serath cradled the old aelf in his arms, gently, so that he would no longer have to lie alone and lost on the cold, sooty stone. Desriel laid one hand gently on Merinoth's taut, bony cheek. Ferendir marvelled at the tenderness shown by his mentors – two of the strongest, surest, most formidable warriors he'd ever known, also two of the gentlest, most loving souls when the suffering of their fellows presented itself.

'Peace, Merinoth,' Serath said softly. 'We will ease your way on.'

'Teacher,' Desriel said, and Ferendir thought he saw the barest glint of tears in his master's eyes. He had never realised it before, but Merinoth must have been Desriel's mentor in his own youth. Tyrion and Teclis, what this must feel like for him…

'Short,' the old aelf managed to say, his voice like a gentle breeze on rough parchment. 'Time.'

'Aye,' Serath said. 'We're here with you now. It won't be long.'

'No,' Merinoth managed, head bobbing as he tried to shake it and failed. 'No… my time… short. Harken. It's gone…'

Ferendir did not understand what the old Stoneguard was trying to say. The sharp, penetrating gazes of his masters suggested that they were just as mystified.

'What?' Serath said. 'What's gone?'

'The stone,' Merinoth said. 'The stone. They took it. They took the stone.'

Ferendir had no idea what the old Stoneguard was alluding to, though he could tell it had some great import. If Merinoth's own determination to spit those words out with his dying breaths were not proof enough, all he needed to do was study the faces of his masters. The moment the stone was mentioned, both their brows furrowed in dismay, just as both their mouths turned down in worried grimaces.

'*Which* stone?' Desriel asked.

'The Eidolith,' Merinoth said, then began choking and coughing, a terrible, wet rattling sounding out of his chest and throwing his whole half-burnt, wizened old form into painful spasms.

Serath cradled him.

Desriel tried to turn his head sideways, to help him breathe more easily.

But even as both sought to comfort and assist him, Ferendir noted that their gazes were locked. Desriel and Serath were staring at one another, silently mulling the import of what Merinoth had just told them. Clearly, whatever this stone – this Eidolith – was, it was valuable.

When the coughing subsided and Merinoth returned to something like regular breathing – however laboured, however shallow – Desriel bent in close. He met the old Stoneguard's single-eyed gaze.

'The Eidolith? From the inner sanctum? There is no mistake?'

'He knew,' Merinoth gasped, his eye growing wide in disbelief. 'He knew where... what... must know... why...'

Once more, Ferendir's masters traded ominous glares. They had only a moment, however, because Merinoth launched into another wracking, deadly coughing fit. Serath cradled him, trying to turn him to some position that might help him breathe. Concurrently, Desriel did his best to catch his old teacher's one remaining eye, to help him concentrate, to help him regain control of his breathing and his body, even as its vitality slipped away from him.

But there was no assistance remaining for the old aelf now. Merinoth coughed, and coughed, and coughed, hacking up blood and black phlegm, his body wracked by tremors and spasms from the pain assailing him, inside and out. The coughing continued for what seemed, to Ferendir at least, a veritable eternity. Each hack made Ferendir wince. Each hard-won breath made him pray it would be old Merinoth's last.

Mercy, he begged in silence. *Mercy, please. Let him go. Let him go. Let him go.*

It took longer than any of them would have liked – longer than Ferendir thought he could stand – but finally, mercifully, Merinoth exhaled for the final time, and the life left him. In an instant, his ruined body relaxed in the arms of his old students, and he was no more.

The three of them knelt there beside his still, silent form for a long time. They said nothing. They did not move.

Ferendir was still holding old Merinoth's half-ruined hand. Gently, he let go of it and laid it down firmly upon the old aelf's chest. That small, subtle movement seemed to snap his masters out of their silent meditations.

'Can it be?' Desriel asked.

'It *must* be,' Serath answered. 'He chose his words carefully.'

'But if the leader of this, this… *horde* knew of the Eidolith – and its ultimate purpose–'

'Then he is cunning as well as bloodthirsty,' Serath said with finality. Then he rose. 'There's no time to waste. We should gather what we can carry – armour for the supplicant, extra weapons, provisions – then be on our way. A host that large will travel slowly – slower than the three of us, at any rate.'

Desriel rose, nodding. 'Aye. A good plan.'

He turned to Ferendir. 'We'll scour the temple precinct. You need to raid the larder and the armoury. If there is anything remaining that might be of use, that we can easily carry, take it.'

'Masters,' Ferendir said, 'what *is* the Eidolith?'

'You dare waste precious moments with questions?' Serath snarled. 'You were given an order, supplicant! Yours is to obey, not to question!'

'Serath,' Desriel said softly. 'He is only–'

'He is only a supplicant,' Serath spat back, more forcefully than Ferendir had ever heard him speak to Desriel before. 'Untried, unproven, unequal to *all of this*.' He made a desperate, expansive gesture with his open hands, suggesting the carnage and ruin that lay all around them. 'We have a hard road and deadly work ahead of us, Desriel. We cannot do it with him slowing our progress or questioning our motives!'

'I question nothing,' Ferendir spat, and was instantly ashamed of himself. He took a deep, calming breath. 'I only sought to understand–'

Serath leaned close to him, spearing him with a bitter, accusatory gaze. 'Yours is not to understand, supplicant. Yours is to obey. Now, to it!'

With that, Serath turned and stalked back into the temple, swallowed in moments by the lingering smoke.

Ferendir looked to Desriel. He wanted to find words but could not. Was that what Desriel thought of him as well? That he was only a supplicant? Their pack animal? A burden to be endured and driven in support of whatever their unspoken agenda might be?

Untried, unproven, unequal to all of this.

'Calm yourself,' Desriel said softly. 'All your questions will be answered, but Serath is right. There is no time here or now. Do as I asked. We'll discuss what lies ahead on the road, and not before.'

Ferendir could only accept his master's order. Away he went, to find the larder and the armoury, all the while wondering just what it was they now set out to recover.

And the identity of the ruthless monster who had taken it from them…

CHAPTER THREE

The path of the Slaaneshi warhost was wide and impossible to miss. Unlike a more disciplined army on the march that might churn up the ground they trod upon and leave intermittent signs of camp or forage, the Slaaneshi seemed to scour the earth before and around them like swarming locusts. For miles, the only sign of their passage might be masses of footprints and trodden earth, then, suddenly, they would infect the forests hemming in the winding track down the mountainside. Trees would be felled and hacked to pieces for no discernible purpose; arrows would skewer birds, large and small, to wide boughs and tree trunks, as though the Slaaneshi simply could not resist the urge to undertake some in-transit target practice; more than once, Ferendir and his masters found dead members of the Hedonite host left dismembered or mutilated by the roadside, some arranged in grotesque geometries upon the bare earth, others tied to trees like horrid scarecrows or nailed to low-hanging branches strong enough to bear their weight. What caused these unlucky victims to be suddenly chosen for murder and display by their comrades remained a mystery. There was only the apparent fact of the warhost's need, at intervals, to invade the world around it and produce mayhem, or to offer up some of its own as rote sacrifices to primitive impulse.

There was no reason for it – for any of it – which left Ferendir particularly disturbed.

'What are they hoping to accomplish?' he asked after coming upon the third or fourth of such signs of the Slaaneshi Hedonites' self-devouring psychoses. 'They slash and burn the forest when there is nothing to gain from it. They fell trees and slaughter wildlife when they have no apparent use for them. They even turn on their own and leave them like ugly trophies in their wake. Why? I just don't understand.'

'You cannot understand them,' Serath said grimly. 'And give thanks for that fact. To understand such madness is to court it oneself.'

They all stood, staring sullenly at the dead Slaaneshi invader hanging upside down before them, its goat-like hoofed feet nailed above, its trunk slashed up and its innards hanging in bloody, ropy ruin over its torso and slack, dead face.

'It's not so hard to understand, really,' Desriel said. Ferendir thought he detected a hint of sadness in his master's voice. 'They are beings of pure impulse. Their only desire is the satisfaction of their appetites and the teasing of their senses. If interrupting their mass march to ruin the landscape around them or slay one of their own for sport stimulates some fleeting pleasure for them, they do it.'

He turned and looked at Ferendir, eyes sober and serious, yet also penetrating and compassionate, as though he were about to impart some numinous insight and wanted his student to listen and understand.

'This is why we do as we do,' Desriel said. 'This is why Teclis gave to us the ladder of ascension. This is why we work, so very hard, from our childhoods to the ends of our long lives, to wrest control of our emotions and sensual impulses. Our people, in the past, were capable of just such atrocities, just such excesses – all because we convinced ourselves that we were superlative and that to be superlative meant to be free of constraint, free of limitation.'

'When in fact,' Serath interjected, 'it means the very opposite. Superiority is only proven by self-control – nay, self-mastery. If one cannot master one's own impulses – from the basest to the highest – and suborn one's skills and desires towards lofty goals existing outside of oneself, then one courts corruption, ruin and disaster. Weakness is death – it is just that simple. Do you not remember all you were taught regarding the Ocari Dara?'

Ferendir nodded. Spirefall, called the Ocari Dara in their own tongue. Every Lumineth child knew the stories. 'I remember, master.'

'Arrogance,' Serath continued coldly, 'ambition, competition, the quest for power and dominion... These impulses – these emotions – were, in that season, the ruin of our people. All our lofty ambitions, all our sense of mastery and majesty, crumbled overnight because we allowed *emotion* to fuel our enquiries and industry instead of reason, purpose and the collective good. Your feelings can give you power and might, Ferendir, but in the end, they are beasts in need of taming, aelemental forces in need of mastery and direction. Remember that, for it is the doom of our people if we ever forget it.'

Ferendir heard what his master said, and understood the wisdom of it – it was a familiar litany from Serath, a well-known proscription. But he still had a hard time reconciling the waste and evil he'd seen perpetrated on the road that day with anything their kind – even in the distant past – might be capable of. It seemed impossible that the Lumineth could have anything in common with such beasts as these servants of Slaanesh.

'Come,' Desriel said at last. 'We must continue before night sets in.'

Ferendir knew not why night should stop them, when night in Hysh was only a dim twilight, still softly illuminated and free of the oppressive darkness that other realms knew as their nocturnal state. But he also knew better than to ask too many questions.

The three of them set off again, carrying on along the well-beaten path of the Slaaneshi warhost as it meandered through the forest and down the sloping mountainside, hour after hour. As the light in Hysh's sky began to ebb towards the gloaming time that preceded night, the land began to rise and fall in rolling waves, for they had now reached the foothills that skirted the mountains on all sides before joining the flat plains in the distance. Following the warhost remained easy enough, for they chose the easiest path that snaked through the rolling hills, always moving west and south-west, clearly on the most direct path afforded to them towards the lowlands.

Serath insisted that the three of them could better close the distance between them and the warhost by taking a winding path over and through the hills, braving more uneven terrain and following on an indirect line, but making up for obstacles and indirectness by maintaining a pace only a small party could, compared to a massive horde on the march. By the time the Hyshian night was full upon them, the twilight a grey-purple dimness softening all the shadows beneath the trees and making of the world a dreamy scrim, Ferendir felt as if they'd traversed a hundred leagues, bounding up hillsides and back down into gullies both shallow and deep, snaking through tight groves of forest trees and splashing through small babbling streams that cut easy paths between the ground-swells.

It was Desriel who finally ordered a halt for the night.

'We can go no further,' he said calmly, peering into the distance for some sign of their quarry. 'Nor should we.'

'You're wrong, old friend,' Serath countered. 'I can smell them. We're right on their tails now.'

'We are exhausted,' Desriel said. 'We need rest if we are to keep pace with them for as long as might be required.'

So far as Ferendir could see, his master did not evidence even slight weariness, let alone exhaustion. Ferendir, however, felt as though he might collapse. He could not remember ever keeping such a mad, frantic pace over such a vast, trying distance in his life. He hoped he would never have to undertake such a trial again, but he supposed that tomorrow would probably bring more of the same.

'We could overtake them tonight,' Serath insisted, 'if we push on.'

'But do we want to?' Desriel asked. 'Consider, old friend – if we suddenly run into their rear guard, or even some wandering band of outriders tearing up the wilderness in their wake, we could suddenly find ourselves in dire straits without enough strength to mount a defence.'

'But the Eidolith!' Serath hissed.

Then something strange and shocking happened, something Ferendir had never, ever seen in his many years as supplicant under Serath and Desriel. Desriel suddenly scowled and raised a single finger to his partner – a peremptory and unmistakable command for silence. Serath, to Ferendir's great shock, snapped his mouth shut and obeyed.

'Ferendir,' Desriel broke in, his gaze never wavering from Serath. 'Take our gourds and waterskins and fill them at the stream in the hill's lee. Serath and I will make camp.'

They had gathered a number of gourds and waterskins – as many as the three of them could easily carry – to make sure they had sufficient water for their journey. There were victuals as well, light and easily transported – dried meat and fruit, smoked and salted fish, nuts and flat, hard-baked loaves of biscuit capable of providing solid, if bland, sustenance. They had barely touched those rations during the day. Perhaps now that they were stopping for the night, they would allow themselves larger portions – at least enough to satisfy the aching hunger in Ferendir's empty belly.

'You were given an order,' Serath said to Ferendir, still staring at Desriel. 'Go, now.'

Ferendir nodded, gathered up the gourds and skins and hurried on his way. He found a clear path down the wooded hillside into a gully that hosted a swift stream burbling over a sandy bed and smooth stones, and there he replenished their water supply. It took him a good deal of time, for the waterskins had to be pressed and expanded to draw the water into their small openings. Worse, balancing all those full containers on his lone person while making an uphill climb was no small feat. More than once, he dropped a gourd here, a skin there, and had to stop and determine how best to arrange them all, whether at his belt, or slung over his shoulders, or embraced in his arms, before carrying on again. By the time he returned to where he'd left his masters, he found them sitting on logs opposite one another, speaking in low, whispered tones that indicated they did not want to be overheard.

Ferendir froze some distance from the makeshift camp. He tried to still his breathing, both to better hear his masters and to keep them from realising he was there, eavesdropping on them.

'…impossible,' Serath said. 'He cannot know of Kaethraxis, or its resting place. Only a handful of our own Stoneguard know the tale, and even fewer know its true–'

'What are we to assume, then?' Desriel asked. 'That raid upon the monastery was not a crime of opportunity. Whoever commands that warhost knew what they were after, and how best to breach our defences.'

'But can he or she truly understand what their ambition might cost them?' Serath asked. 'Nothing can control Kaethraxis. Even the Eidolith was forged as a contingency that's never been tested–'

'Who are we dealing with?' Desriel countered. 'Slaaneshi Hedon-ites are not to be underestimated, but long-term thinking and the assessment of consequences are never their strong suit. The leader of that warhost could simply be overestimating their own capabil-ities. And now that they have the Eidolith, they have no reason to doubt what they might be capable of.'

A long, sober silence fell. The two seemed to be contemplat-ing something.

'What of the boy?' Desriel finally asked.

'He cannot continue,' Serath said without hesitation. 'If we're forced to try and go up against these Slaaneshi beasts to recover the gem–'

Ferendir felt a strange heat moving through him. Was that humil-iation? Shock? Serath wanted to leave him behind! He didn't think him prepared for such a dangerous undertaking! It took all of Fer-endir's self-control to keep from stomping out of the woods to make his own voice heard.

'He's no child,' Desriel said. 'And he's good in a fight.'

'He was lucky,' Serath countered. 'He may not continue to be.'

'You underestimate him.'

'I am fulfilling my purpose,' Serath said, a little too forcefully, Ferendir thought. 'Our task, as his teachers, was to prepare him for his trial, to give him every advantage and tool in our arsenal so that, supplicating himself alone before the power of the moun-tain, he could be found worthy and made one of us. While that trial remains unfinished, he remains unready. I will not risk his safety if it is not of the utmost necessity.'

'What do you recommend, then?' Desriel asked. 'We simply leave him behind?'

'Of course not,' Serath snapped. 'We wait until… until some opportunity presents itself. A safe place. Another group. We must go on, no matter what it costs us, but he – he *cannot*. That is all I will say on the subject.'

Something scurried through the underbrush, deep in the woods behind Ferendir. The movement caused his masters to turn and peer in his direction, and Ferendir hastily set one foot in front of the other, hoping that they believed he was just approaching them, not that he had been lingering in the semi-darkness listening to their conversation.

'It took you long enough,' Serath said icily.

Ferendir set down the gourds and waterskins. 'They were… awkward.'

'You found your way readily enough?' Desriel asked.

Ferendir nodded and sat between the gnarled roots of a nearby tree. 'I know my way,' he said, throwing a glare at Serath. 'I'm not a child, after all.'

Serath glared back.

Desriel began rooting around in one of the provision bags. 'Very well, then,' he said, drawing forth some biscuit and dried meat. 'Enjoy a portion for one not a child. Eat well. You've earned it.'

Food was portioned out evenly and stingily among them. They ate in silence, with only the sounds of the forest and the soughing breeze in the trees to entertain them. After eating, they each drank deeply from the waterskins, slaking their thirst. Finally, Desriel settled in against the log he'd been sitting on, now reclining against it. He began to sing, an old hymn of the temple, sad and mournful, the melody stirring Ferendir's memories of his now-destroyed home so poignantly that he felt tears stinging his eyes and the desire to break into sobs overtake him.

But he would not relent. He would not give Serath the satisfaction. He had to prove to his master that he was no longer a child, trial or no trial.

He would not be left behind while Desriel and Serath carried on to track down the monsters that had murdered their friends and family and peers. He would not be denied a role to play in the vengeance to come, the justice to be served.

And so, Ferendir simply smothered all the feelings roiling inside him – the fear, the grief, the hunger, the frustration – and tried simply to concentrate on the soft, plaintive sound of Desriel's voice. He tried to use the hymn as it was intended – as a meditation, a call homewards when lost in the wide world, a spiritual conduit through any and all obstacles back to the place that had shaped and moulded him.

He was, as Desriel had said, exhausted.

Soon enough, sleep swallowed him like warm waters closing over his head.

Ferendir opened his eyes. The world was darker than he recalled – Hyshian twilight seemingly having subsided to something almost resembling a mundane night. There was no moon, no stars, only a dark blue velvety dome vaulting above his world and the many trees of the woodlands blanketing the foothills. His masters were both gone.

They've left me, he thought, a stir of fury and panic rising within him. *I slept as they left me!*

He rose, spinning this way and that on his heels, searching. The shadows under the trees were deep and dark – darker than any shadows he'd ever seen under the Hyshian sky – and the silence lying heavily upon the benighted world struck him as something oppressive and unnatural: a silence that was not a stillness, nor an absence, but a presence... and a very malignant presence at that.

'Desriel?' he said, careful not to raise his voice too loudly for fear of what he might rouse. No answer came.

He turned, still searching. Something small and bright winked out of existence off in the distance, beyond a stand of elms – like tiny eyes suddenly darting under cover to avoid being seen.

'Serath?' he said. A moment later, he forced himself to raise his voice.

'Master Serath?'

A cold wind stirred the trees, skating through the grove and the surrounding woods like a sliding, curling serpent. It seemed to twist around his body as it passed – clammy, sentient, probing – forcing a shudder to run through his whole body and his sense of panic and abandonment to deepen.

Was he alone? Really all alone?

Could he not be in danger, even now? The Hedonites were still about, weren't they? A small band of wandering invaders could happen along at any moment, and if they found him here, all by himself–

Ferendir searched for the diamondpick hammer that Desriel had presented to him when they departed the ruined temple. There was no sign of the weapon. He had also claimed two mid-length daggers of ancient and elegant make, and he'd worn those daggers sheathed on his hip all the way from home. But even those two blades were gone – their sheaths as well – as though stolen in his sleep.

Is this how they would treat me? Abandon me? Leave me without food, without weapons, without so much as a goodbye or good luck?

'Masters!' Ferendir shouted, determined to summon them with as much force – as much assertiveness – as he could muster. He would not show fear. He would not show them just how hurt and frightened he was at that moment.

'Masters, show yourselves! Desriel? Serath?'

The ground suddenly convulsed beneath him. It was a strange, unnatural feeling. He'd felt earth tremors and the early shivers that preceded a volcanic eruption, but this was different – more pointed, more deliberate. It was as if the earth had stifled a cruel laugh in answer to his cries.

Ferendir looked about him. *Think. Think hard. Where might they be? What might have drawn them away? Perhaps they haven't abandoned you. Perhaps they went to investigate something? Perhaps they saw signs of nearing Hedonites? Perhaps–*

He broke into a run, his body demanding action before his mind had even formulated a plan. He barrelled on through low-hanging boughs and widely spaced underbrush, feeling the whip and tear of a hundred small, sharp twigs and leaves and pine needles. He kept his eyes down, searching the path before him, determined not to fall, but that left him vulnerable to what whipped by at eye and shoulder level, made his progress hitching and haphazard.

'Master Desriel! Master Serath!'

Once more the earth bucked beneath him, a sudden, violent movement so pronounced that Ferendir was literally thrown off his feet. He hit the ground hard, rolled and landed on his back. Above and around him, the world seemed to spin, a cold whip tugging at the looming trees and the thin wisps of cloud in the night sky skating by with strange, steady insistence. As he lay there, staring up, trying to make sense of what he was seeing, everything seemed to come alive. The wind all but danced among the trees, a living thing, one moment moaning, the next sighing, the next seeming to laugh with terrible, malign intent. The trees themselves bent to the pressing wind's ministrations and murmured in answer, their boughs rising and falling, sweeping forward and back in a strange sort of dance that looked, to Ferendir's knowing eyes, wholly unnatural. Beneath him, meanwhile, the earth was once more straining and trembling, the soil stirring as fallen logs and strewn stones and scattered gravel all skated and danced across the ground, moved by some impossible, deeply entrenched force beneath them.

Ferendir struggled to his feet. The trees were swaying so wildly now that he could often see miles beyond them, through the gaps made by their shuddering movements. Rising up in the distance, back the way they'd come, the mountain that they called home – and master – loomed tall and broad against the blue-black night sky. As Ferendir watched, amazed and alarmed, he saw cracks forming in the mountain's surface, thin, radiating cracks that gradually widened to reveal pulsing, red-hot reservoirs of roiling magma and geomantic heat.

What is happening? he wondered, terrified and awe-struck. *What am I seeing?*

The cracks lengthened, radiated, multiplied. Rivulets of lava poured forth and made glowing thermal tracks down the sloping mountainsides like red-hot tears. Slowly, ponderously, the ridge-lines descending from the lateral flanks of the mountain began to shrug and rise, pulling away from the earth that they clung to.

The mountain was awakening.

The mountain was rising.

The mountain was angry.

Ferendir wanted to turn, to run, to fly in the face of the horrible, looming sight that filled the world before him, but he could not. Something akin to wonder had rooted him to the place where he stood. Could he really be bearing witness to such a miracle? The mountain, once more, after centuries of dormancy, walking? He'd heard tales of such things but never imagined he might see it, experience it. The beauty! The terror!

Up and up it rose, a great, broad swathe of rock and earth and small, prickling trees tearing itself away from the ground soil that had so long rooted it. Ferendir saw tiny fragments of soil fall away that he knew to be massive boulders and time-scoured megaliths as vast as his now-ruined home temple. He saw islands of woodland tumble and crash to the rent earth, saw more and more burning, devouring rivers of lava and molten rock pouring forth as though the mountain were a scab and the magma the blood beneath, now exposed and flowing freely.

All at once, he realised that the enormous being tearing itself free of the earth, blotting out the horizon and sky before him, its peak-crowned head rising thousands of metres into the sky, had a face. That face had been carved by the magma now flowing out of its rocky carapace, burned into the regolith of its slopes and valleys – two enormous burning eyes, the great, sloping ridgeline of a nose, a vast, fire-belching scar that served as its godlike mouth.

The mountain rose against the sky and roared. The world beneath and around Ferendir shook, as though in a hurricane wind. He almost feared the cyclone stirred by the giant's open maw might blast him away, like a leaf on the wind, yet still he stood rooted to the spot. Nonetheless, in answer to the mountain's cry, Ferendir sounded a small, high scream of his own. All thought of controlling his fear, of seeking serenity even in his panic, had evaporated. It was simply too large not to be terrified by, too enormous not to feel dread at the very sight of.

Then the mountain raised one vast foot and began to walk. It took one ponderous step towards Ferendir, and the world around him shook as if quaking with its footfall. It raised its back foot and shifted its weight forward to take another step.

Ferendir realised what was about to happen as the great foot left the ground. The mountain was walking, and its next step would bring its tread down upon him. There was nowhere to run, or hide. Its heel was so vast it blotted out the sky.

Ferendir screamed, raising his arms in helpless resistance, wondering idly what it would feel like to be crushed when all that vast bulk came down atop him–

And then he woke.

There was light in the world again – something between night's dimness and morning's brightness. How long had he slept? Minutes? Hours?

Stranger still, he felt a subtle but unmistakable vibration in the earth beneath him. It was not the tread of a mountain or a simple ground-quake, but something far more attenuated – more like the quavering of a plucked harp string, or the way a bell reverberated in the wake of a hammer strike.

To his great relief, both Desriel and Serath were nearby. Both were awake and wide-eyed. Each had an ear pressed to the ground.

Ferendir sat upright. 'What's happening?' he asked. He blinked and studied the lit world around them. No looming mountains. No massive feet blotting out the sky. No faces carved from roiling magma.

Desriel laid one hand flat upon the earth and patted it lightly.

'Press your ear down again, supplicant. Listen.'

Ferendir was puzzled for a moment, but then he remembered that strange vibration he'd sensed upon waking. In the moment, he'd dismissed it as some deep and subtle tremor caused by natural phenomena – an underground river, perhaps, or a stirring of the latent geomantic energies that coursed through the plain's deep recesses like blood through living veins. Slowly, swallowing his panic and confusion, he lay down again and pressed his ear to the ground. It was cool to the touch, but strangely soothing.

Sure enough, something was reverberating through Hysh's crust. It was manifold and rhythmic, as regular as it was indistinct. Then, like a lightning bolt of inspiration, Ferendir realised what he was sensing through the earth itself.

'Marching feet?' he asked Desriel. 'Formations, moving in unison?'

Desriel nodded. 'Many, many feet, meaning–'

'Vast formations,' Ferendir finished. 'The entire warhost!'

'Not just our quarry,' Serath said, listening, 'but another as well.'

'Another?' Ferendir repeated.

Serath rose into a crouching position. 'Two distinct warhosts, with separate treads and patterns of movements.'

Ferendir also rose, still staring. He looked to Desriel.

Desriel got to his feet. 'A battle, supplicant – we've happened upon a battle.'

Since the age of seven, Ferendir had lived at the mountain temple, trained in the ways of the Alarith, learning everything from how to quietly meditate for untold hours in the same position to how, theoretically, an Alarith Stoneguard commanding multiple phalanxes of Vanari troops could hold off a much larger and more aggressive enemy force. He had read the treatises, memorised the maxims and heard untold lectures on the value of this gambit or that stratagem, the proven effectiveness of one warmaster's triad of maxims over another's eighteen immutable commandments of combat and deployment. He had seen numerous representations of the dozens upon dozens of tried and tested battle formations utilised and honed by the greatest martial minds of their race over the course of a thousand years, even seen fully animate living re-enactments of those battles played out in miniature via spells and psychic simulacra. Even at his present, relatively young age, Ferendir had learned and internalised so many military lessons and insights that he almost imagined he was a seasoned warrior, if not a proven combat commander. He liked to imagine that if suddenly thrust into a position of danger and desperation, he could readily call upon the many principles he'd learned through his years as a supplicant and keep a small body of troops alive for at least a reasonable amount of time.

But he had never truly imagined that he would be standing on a tree-dotted headland, staring out across rolling hills, bearing witness to a battle under way between a massive, thousands-strong Slaaneshi warhost and an equally vast, brightly shining contingent of his own kind, streaming up from the broad fields below. At first sight, what Ferendir saw could barely be reasoned or accepted – there were tens of thousands of moving bodies swarming over the hills and fields below them, their ranks dissolving into mobile masses of brilliant, angelic light as the swarming Slaaneshi streamed down from the foothills in massive chaotic waves, like water rushing over the ruins of a burst dam. Meeting the teeming Slaaneshi horde at the foot of the hills or on the shallow slopes where the heights met the plain, the massed Vanari forces fought, as orderly and graceful as their enemies were wild and unruly.

'Tyrion, Teclis and Celennar,' Ferendir breathed, drinking in the overwhelming sight that filled his vision. 'Perfect form. Perfect synchronicity!'

His masters said nothing.

Form, synchronicity – he could think of no better words to describe what he saw. At the forward lines, tight, massed phalanxes of Auralan wardens forty troops wide and a hundred deep interlaced their graceful shields and presented the enemy with a bristling wall of long, flashing pikes, each individual warrior thrusting their spear tip rhythmically in answer to an intermittent call from their marshals. As each line of pikes thrust and withdrew, the next line did the same, followed by the next, in perfect, interlocking unison, creating the effect of some massive, destructive threshing machine seeking any and all grist to be skewered, cut and felled by its steady, unbroken forward advance. More frightening still were the intense magical energies that made all their broad-bladed spear tips glow white-hot, even under a midday sun. As the Slaaneshi enemy charged and collided with the warden phalanxes, the Hedonites were not simply sliced and skewered – they were frequently burned alive, from the inside out, by the sun-bright fire emanating out of those glowing spear tips.

Spaced just behind the pike-wielding wardens, arrayed in sharp diamond formations, were hundreds of Auralan sentinels – the greatest archers in all the Mortal Realms – loosing massed volley after massed volley of arrows upon the charging foe, the clouds of missiles so tight and synchronised that they all but blotted the sun from the sky as they arced over the front ranks of the spear-wielding wardens then came crashing down with murderous, withering lethality on the many reinforcements swarming forward from the rear to replace the Slaaneshi invaders dying on the Auralan lance tips. As Ferendir watched, mouth agape and thoroughly amazed, he saw that there was a strange, arpeggiated rhythm emerging as each phalanx of sentinels, spread in perfect interspersed distances behind the warden lines, loosed their arrows in a pattern that began on the outer wings of their formations then moved towards the centre and back out again. It was terrifyingly effective and strangely beautiful all at once.

But even as awe-inspiring and thrilling as the sight of all those massed troops at the centre of the lines was, the element Ferendir found most stirring – most amazing – were the wings of Dawnrider cavalry thundering in great squadrons up and down the ragged, bleeding flanks of the Slaaneshi warhost. As the wardens and sentinels thinned the Chaos troops at the retinue's roiling centre, those seeking to outflank or outmanoeuvre their Lumineth enemies were cut down, trampled flat or slashed to bits by the fast-moving Dawnriders. No matter how many of the grotesque mortal Hedonites or scampering four-legged fiends or hissing, scuttling daemonettes charged forth, the Dawnriders on their swift, terrible steeds were always on hand to trample them under hoof, cut them down or run them through with lowered lances.

But it did not stop there. Even from farther back – beyond the wardens, beyond the sentinels, beyond the circling outriders awaiting their chance to relieve their deadly comrades on the flanks – the Lumineth warhost still assailed the enemy. Artillery was massed at some distance behind the lines – great, graceful hulks of wood, rope and steel, frozen symphonies of physics and engineering hurtling massive stones, enormous sharp-tipped bolts or fiery incendiaries that exploded when they crashed amid the Chaotic hordes.

Ferendir stared, drinking it all in, almost wishing he could be a lone hawk riding the thermals above the field. He wanted to see that battle as the wind might, as the clouds might, as gods might – from above, to better appreciate the gorgeous, symmetrical precision of the Vanari ranks against the helter-skelter insanity of the Slaaneshi Hedonites, seemingly caught unawares as they emerged from the woods in a mad dash towards the lowlands.

And yet, Ferendir could not exalt, could not celebrate, because as he watched, he realised that no matter how many Hedonites were run through or skewered by arrows or cut to pieces by the swift-moving Dawnriders, their numbers never truly seemed to be reduced. No matter how many died, there always seemed to be more, and more, and more…

Suddenly, he felt rhythmic movement beneath his feet, thundering up the hillside towards them, getting closer – louder, more intense – with each passing moment. Ferendir turned to investigate and realised that his masters were already standing on guard, Serath raising his stone mallet as Desriel took up his diamondpick. Ferendir joined his masters, standing beside them at the ready and raising his own diamondpick hammer, just as–

A quartet of figures broke from the trees, coming up the hillside. Dawnriders, their bright, gold-chased armour flashing gloriously even as their drawn swords dripped with black Slaaneshi blood. Without stopping, the four riders reined their mounts into a slow, steady canter in a circle around the three of them, all parties – the masters and their wary supplicant, the hot-blooded, battle-weary Dawnriders – appraising and studying one another for a moment as they allowed their readiness for violence to subside.

A moment later, as the cantering Dawnriders slowed their circling, Ferendir realised more newcomers had joined them – armoured aelven infantry bearing stone mallets and diamondpicks not unlike those wielded by him and his masters.

Alarith! Clearly they hailed from another temple – some redoubt farther to the north, perhaps – but their weapons and kit made it clear they were both military allies and spiritual comrades.

'Identify yourselves,' a female Dawnrider called from atop her circling mount.

'Alarith Stoneguard and a supplicant,' Serath answered without hesitation. 'All of the mountain temple to the south-east of here, the last survivors of a terrible raid by the very monsters you're now busy slaughtering.'

'Well met, then,' the Dawnrider said. 'It pleases us to know the reaping we now bestow upon these ravening wolves comes in answer to their violence.'

Ferendir wished the rider would rein in her mount. He was tired of turning round and craning his neck, trying to track the speaker's position.

'When did they engage you?' Desriel asked. 'We heard the commotion and came to investigate–'

'We engaged *them*,' the rider said. 'Our scouts saw the horde coming down the slopes, through the foothills, and we drew up our lines where the ground levelled, ready to prevent their escape. They walked right into our trap.'

'And yet so many still remain,' Ferendir said. 'It's like more spring up for each one struck down.'

'Appearances can be deceiving, boy,' the rider said, her voice prickly, clearly indicating that Ferendir's words had offended her. 'They'll be dead or routed soon enough.'

'Steedmaster!' one of the newly arrived Alarith troops shouted. 'Enemy troops, coming up the hillside!'

The Dawnrider broke from the circling formation and drew her mount up to the edge of the nearest slope. Ferendir and his masters rushed forward to see what had suddenly alerted the scout. He was right to be eager – a massive horde of the Slaaneshi invaders had peeled away from the main force on the fields below. They were rushing up the slope towards where they all now stood. Whether they were affecting a determined charge or simply fleeing the battle-field, Ferendir could not say. He only knew that their terrible faces and misshapen bodies were already too close for his comfort, and getting closer with every breath.

One of the hammer-wielding Alarith stepped forward and appraised Ferendir and his masters. 'Can you stand? Will you fight?'

Desriel nodded. 'At your command.'

Serath planted himself. 'Let them come.'

The Alarith fanned out around them and created a broad battle line along the ridge, twenty troops wide and three deep. Though these were strangers – wholly unknown to Ferendir, servants of another mountain and another temple – their presence around him was welcoming. He recognised their formation, felt the quiet assurance and silent strength that each soldier imparted to the other.

Ferendir, not sure what part he could play in the skirmish to come, fell in between his masters on the front line and prepared himself. All at once, his hands were shaking, his palms sweaty and slick on the leather-wound grip of the pick hammer he carried, and the salvaged armour he wore felt strangely ill-fitted.

'Step back,' Desriel said quietly. 'Into the second rank. Let us take the brunt of what's to come.'

'Master, I–'

'Let them break upon the greathammers at the fore. You and I and the rest of these behind will take those that slip by.'

Ferendir did as he was told. Desriel stood calmly beside him. On either side of them, the Alarith Stoneguard closed ranks to solidify their battle line. Ferendir sensed movement in his peripheral vision. When he turned, he saw a tall, elegant Alarith Stonemage standing above the troops that surrounded him – perched upon a boulder or fallen tree, perhaps. Already, the Stonemage's staff glowed eagerly with the bright, pure light of Hyshian magic, preparing for the battle to come. Far on their flanks, the Dawnriders – bolstered by half a dozen more of their mounted comrades – had withdrawn to prepare for concerted charges into the enemy ranks.

'On guard!' the Alarith commander called, and the soldiers in his squad adopted what every Alarith warrior knew as the first position – left leg forward, right leg back, hammer clutched two-handed and held vertically, close to their right side. Ferendir knew the position and followed suit. Broad stone mallets and diamondpick spikes caught the sunlight, glinting hungrily.

The enemy closed, boiling up the hillside.

On the wings, the steedmaster exhorted her squadron and the Dawnriders lined up their strong, elegant mounts along the slope's edge.

'Mountain stance!' the Alarith commander shouted.

Ferendir felt the change in an instant. Though the magic at work resided largely in each of the soldiers now amassed before and around him – even in one so humble as himself – he wagered the Stonemage at the rear was using her own arts to focus their individual energies and weave their separate abilities into a single, unified energetic tapestry.

All at once, Ferendir felt rooted to the ground beneath him. Likewise, his body became hard and heavy – as if truly made of stone – even though his ability to move or strike never once came into question. They were one now – planted, impenetrable, a wall that the enemy would break upon.

Then, like a cresting wave rushing in from a roaring, storm-wracked ocean, the enemy was upon them.

Ferendir's world became a riot of kinetic force, a torrent of swirling activity. The Alarith lines buckled under the weight of the horde's massed impact. Ferendir caught a fleeting glimpse of Alarith on either side of him suddenly dug into the soil of the hilltop, forced backwards a grudging finger length by the force of the enemy's collision. Hedonites struck at their forward ranks – slashed, thrust, leapt, bit, tore – and every single attacker was thrown backwards and crushed in the press from behind them.

The Slaaneshi were an unstoppable force... but the Alarith in mountain stance were a truly immovable object.

The effect, experienced from within, was strange, terrifying, exhilarating – the enemy was there, an arm's length from him, charging, crashing, repelled by his and his companions' collective adamant will. He felt not like a standing soldier in an army but like a single stone in a well-made wall. The enemy battered them, broke upon them, but they, the Alarith, children of the mountain, felt nothing.

Then, miraculously, there came a sudden pause. It was as if the Hedonites had lost the will to press their attack, or saw the need to toss the dead and broken bodies of their repelled brothers and sisters aside, or were hastily searching their addled intellects for a new tactic, another means of advancing. It was only an instant, no longer than a held breath between inhalation and exhalation.

But that instant was all the Alarith required.

'Strike!' the commander shouted.

The impenetrable field created by their bodies, their wills, vanished. As one, the front line – Serath among them – took a unified step forward and brought all their greathammers crashing down, almost in unison, upon the front ranks of the servants of Slaanesh. Bones broke. Skulls collapsed. Blood and ichor flew in warm, wet gouts. As the first slain enemies still fell towards the ground, broken and lifeless, the Alarith struck once more. A score of massive stone mallets smashed another line of Slaaneshi daemonettes and Hedonites. Rose. Smashed down again. Rose. Smashed down again. Skulls collapsed. Brains and foul blood stained the air. Bodies fell.

And yet more bodies – alive, wriggling, savage and vengeful – charged forward.

'Stay close!' Desriel shouted.

Ferendir felt the formation press forward around him: not a charge, not even a surge – those terms were far too vulgar for these cold-blooded sons and daughters of Ymetrica. It was simply a slide, an advance. They were no longer a wall but a field of scattered boulders… and the enemy would flow between them, to be trapped and pulverised.

Out on the flanks, the Dawnriders plunged over the hillside and rode right into the enemy ranks, swords sweeping and slashing, mounts wheeling and kicking with their hooves, throwing Hedonite bodies this way and that.

A monstrous Hedonite trailing a long, serpentine tail and possessed of a low-slung draconian head broke through the front rank of Alarith and leapt towards Ferendir. Hissing and spitting, it raised its long, scaled arms and taloned, grasping fingers to seize him.

Ferendir struck, first thrusting forward with his pick hammer to send the monster reeling backwards, drawing back and arcing the weapon over his head. He brought it down with merciless force upon the serpentine skull. The snake-thing bled, screamed and thrashed. It was stunned, stumbling about, but it did not fall. Ferendir struck again and again. He heard bones break, saw flesh tear, felt the hot sting of blood. Something sharp and rough – the beast's foul talons – dug deep into his side, then raked across his thigh. He shrugged off the flaring pain and struck yet again, battering his adversary. Finally, thankfully, the snake-thing hit the ground in a bloody heap, twitching but no longer a threat. Ferendir stumbled backwards, gulping air and struggling to control the tremors now wracking his body top to toe.

The battle raged around him. He was not only at the fore but right in the thick of it.

Ahead, Serath dealt killing blow after killing blow with inhuman composure, leaning into the oncoming horde as he might lean into a strong, battering headwind. Glancing down, Ferendir saw his master's feet dig into the earth – rooted, immobile, no matter how many enemies beset him. For a moment – just a moment – Ferendir was amazed, disbelieving. Then he recalled that both of his masters were experienced Stoneguard with magical knacks of their own. Foul, grotesque Hedonite bodies slammed hard into Serath's forward-leaning form, eager to tear him down with pure forward momentum, but all those who thought force alone could move him were sorely disappointed. He shrugged many aside, deflected direct attacks with his hammer's haft and met the rest with a blinding-fast storm of deadly blows.

Off to Ferendir's left, Desriel moved forward and back, meeting Hedonite attackers with bloody efficiency and grace. He used their own clumsy attacks against them, in one instance dancing sideways to redirect the hurtling form of a charging daemonette towards one of its foul comrades, then striking both dead when they collided and became entangled. In the breath following the killing blows, he spun on his heels and met a third attacker, one on one, bending it double with a series of bone-shattering hammer strikes to its body before finally breaking its legs and sending it crashing to the ground in a screaming heap.

Movement. More Hedonites had broken through. Ferendir counted two now hurtling towards him, their tooth-filled mouths gaping, a long, slithering forked tongue lolling from one open maw. The creature at the fore moved on a quartet of strange, carapaced insectile legs, while the second bore four arms, each capped with a deadly iron weapon fused to its wrists. More bodies roiled and writhed behind them – more adversaries, more to kill or be killed – but Ferendir could not be concerned with what came next. There was only what lay right in front of him.

He struck with his pick hammer and crushed one of the trundling insectile legs on the first charging Hedonite. As the creature dipped sideways, its balance ruined, it struck with the chained flail in its hand, and Ferendir barely ducked in time to miss being brained by the sweeping ball of spiked iron. Hunkered low in self-defence, he thrust his pick hammer forward with all his might, hoping to punch through the bug-thing's soft middle with sheer force. The creature felt the thrust and shrank from it, screaming, but Ferendir had not penetrated anything. Already, his would-be killer was raising its flail again for another strike.

And here came the four-armed brute, iron fists bearing down like detritus borne by a cyclone – a blunt iron sphere, a notched, half-rusted axe blade, a two-headed spike, a crown of twisted iron thorns. Ferendir had no notion of how to meet all four of those deadly limbs, to redirect or deflect them as each rose and fell towards him in concert.

And so he did all that he could – he scuttled sideways, clearing the space between the charging monster and his insectile adversary.

His gambit worked. Two of the brute's iron-capped arms slammed hard into its insectile comrade and tore through its thin, bent body. As the insectile Hedonite screamed and thrashed and the brute tried to disentangle its striking arms, both bodies fell to the earth and began a strange, rolling dance, each trying to extricate itself from the other.

Ferendir did not think. He saw his way clear and acted, wholly unconcerned for how he was opening himself to hazard. He skittered quickly up the prone form of the four-armed killer, planted himself on the giant's bent shoulders and brought his diamond-pick hammer down three times in rapid succession. Each strike drove the sharp diamond spike protruding from his hammer into the monster's skull. The monstrosity's massive body went limp atop the insectile creature pinned beneath it, now unable to move.

And still, more came. More grotesqueries, more freaks, more monsters, more killers. They filled the world with noise, movement, terror. Ferendir resigned himself to death, his mind suddenly – miraculously – adopting an isolated, blunted sense of both time and space wherein there was no past, no future, no hope, no despair – only the moment and its exigencies. His pick hammer swooped and clanged, rose and fell. Foul black blood painted him, making his grip slippery and his body sticky. He felt strikes here, there, above, below – sharp blades, the bite of seeking pincers, the tear of foul, diseased claws, blunt force from inhuman fists or makeshift bludgeons. But the pain never deterred him. Fear never took him. No adversary could put him on his knees, let along on his back.

And suddenly, blessedly, the chaos began to subside. Ferendir fought his way through half a dozen – nine, ten – adversaries, before realising that their advances were slowing, their numbers thinning. Blinking, spitting out a mouthful of saliva and the blood of his enemies, he surveyed the scene before him.

The Hedonites withdrew, swarming down the hillside as quickly as they'd climbed it. They seemed to scatter in every direction, fleeing into the trees and the shady folds between the ridgelines like scuttling insects scattering before a bright lantern light. Even as they fled, Ferendir saw Dawnriders on their heels, cutting them down in their flight, overtaking the slow or the injured to finish them, leaving their foul bodies rotting beside their already slain companions. Before and around him, the Alarith and his masters finished a few last enemies as well – fallen adversaries still refusing to surrender to death, crippled monsters still trying to escape though their limbs were crushed, broken or severed.

Ferendir felt a strange wave of coldness washing over him, as though he'd been dunked in the waters of a mountain lake. As he surveyed the scene around him, small tremors began to wrack his blood-caked body. They were subtle at first, starting in his extremities, but gradually they crept inwards, towards his torso and the core of him, until at last it seemed that every part of his body was shaking.

He surveyed the world around him. It was a litter of bodies, hacked limbs and ground soaked with the foul ichor that those Hedonites called blood. He counted two dozen enemies lying within a stone's throw of where he stood, then lost count altogether.

The shaking continued. It made him light-headed, robbed him of his strength.

Suddenly, Ferendir was on his knees.

'Masters,' he said, though he was not sure anyone could hear him. He could barely hear himself.

Then they were there. Serath and Desriel each at his side, their arms enfolding him, their level gazes seeking his own, demanding his attention, his concentration.

'Breathe, supplicant,' Desriel said softly, and demonstrated how best to inhale, then to exhale. 'Come now, do as I do.'

Ferendir tried, knowing that breathing in such a manner would in time calm him and stop the infernal shakes that had seized him.

'Concentrate, boy,' Serath hissed. 'Your body is yours to control, to command.'

Desriel continued breathing. Ferendir struggled to synchronise his own breaths with those of his master. Moment by moment, he was failing.

Serath suddenly seized him, his strong, rough hands on either side of Ferendir's head. He forced the young aelf to look into his cold, level gaze, to look deep into his eyes, as if in challenge.

All at once, Ferendir was terrified, exposed. His master was not simply trying to gain his attention but to peer into him, to penetrate his psyche in order to help stabilise it…

'Breathe,' Serath commanded, and demonstrated.

Ferendir, miraculously, breathed in perfect unison with Serath. Inhale. Exhale. Inhale. Exhale.

'Breathe,' his master said again, this time through gritted teeth. Inhale. Exhale. Inhale. Exhale.

Ferendir breathed. The tremors subsided, albeit slowly. Before he realised it, his masters held him in a paired embrace, his young, slim body enfolded between the two of them, the shakes gradually, thankfully, subsiding towards peace and serenity.

Inhale. Exhale.

The sound of hooves on soft, loamy earth. A shadow gliding between Ferendir and the sun. The snort of something large and powerful.

Ferendir opened his eyes. The Dawnrider steedmaster sat astride her mount above the three of them, her beautifully tooled bone-white armour spattered and slashed with the red-black blood of their enemies, along with clods of churned earth and gobbets of viscera. Strangely, for all the blood and flesh clinging to her, she still seemed somehow bright and resplendent, a creature of light, not of the Mortal Realms at all. Her great mount's scale-armoured flanks rose and fell like a smith's bellows, the horse's dark eyes trained upon the ground as it, too, sought to regain its sense of peace after thundering through hell incarnate.

Serath stood, an unmistakably protective gesture that caused Ferendir to feel vindicated and vaguely unworthy all at once.

The Dawnrider still held her long, graceful sword in her hands. The blade was streaked with gore.

'You fought well,' she said, appraising them coolly, then let her gaze linger on Ferendir himself. 'All three of you.'

'And you,' Desriel said. 'Only riders of the greatest skill and daring would chance a downhill charge over uneven ground.'

'Sufficient skill eliminates the need for daring,' the Dawnrider replied, betraying the barest hint of a smile. 'What brings you to this place at such an inopportune time?'

'We are refugees,' Desriel said. 'These Slaaneshi invaders destroyed our home temple yesterday morning. We were away. They left none alive.'

'Refugees,' Serath spat, as if the word offended him. 'We have business of our own with the Hedonites – business that is no concern of yours.'

Ferendir blinked. Was Serath really prepared to be so belligerent as to rebuff idle questions from a warrior not their enemy?

The Dawnrider was nonplussed. 'You shall be free to attend that business,' she said, 'but I have received word from the lady regent, the commander of my warhost. She is Hirva, called Windstrider, and she would like to speak with the three of you.'

Ferendir looked to his masters. His masters looked to one another. There seemed to be a moment's hesitation shared between them – a sense of mutual incredulity and suspicion – that passed in an instant when Desriel gave a small, subtle gesture – one eyebrow raised inquisitively.

Could it hurt? that gesture seemed to ask.

Serath's eyes narrowed. He sighed.

Desriel turned to the Dawnrider. 'Very well, then. Take us to her.'

CHAPTER FOUR

They were each invited to mount the tall, strong steeds of the Dawnriders so that they could be ridden down to Hirva's camp on the plains with all speed. Doubled up on their mounts, they wound down through the folded hills, past thousands of enemy dead and the barbarous, bloodied detritus of the day's campaign. After a short while, they broke from the hump-backed hills out onto the plains that stretched away westwards from the foot of the mountains, and there saw even more of the enemy dead – as well as their own casualties – strewn in an endless charnel carpet upon the ruined, blood-soaked grasses and torn turf. As they passed, Ferendir noted dozens of Lumineth search parties moving slowly but surely across the killing fields, looking for wounded aelves to be extricated and sped to the healers' pavilions or lurking survivors from the enemy camp in need of final dispatch. More than once, as the riders bore them onwards towards their appointment with the warhost commander, he saw movement among the Hedonite corpses and the sudden action of a single aelven warden or champion from among the searchers, rushing forward to deliver a killing blow.

Their actions were sure and merciless. Not a single Hedonite could be allowed to survive the day.

At last, they arrived at the great camp, a sprawling collection of tents and pavilions on the north side of the primary battleground, alive with activity as the day's survivors tended to the wounded or gathered their slaughtered brethren for cleaning and immolation so that their spirits could be returned to the realm that bore them. The day's light was waning, dimming towards twilit night, and cookfires burned among the tents as provisions were drawn out and prepared – a memorial meal for the dead, a celebratory repast for the survivors.

Finally, the Dawnriders delivered them to a pavilion larger and grander than all the rest, seemingly the size of their refectory back at the mountain temple. They all dismounted and the lead Dawnrider – whose name, they had learned, was Veloryn – led the three homeless Alarith and the remainder of her Dawnriders out of the waning daylight and into the cool shadows of the pavilion.

Though the fabric that made up the pavilion appeared thick and opaque from the outside, it seemed to admit a great deal of light within, as well as fresh, moving air, so that the interior was not so stifling and close as some such constructions could be. Aetherquartz lamps glowed softly from tree-like stands or on small, functional tables, illuminating the dim interior along with what light penetrated the membrane of the pavilion silks, making the inner spaces bright, airy and surprisingly welcoming. Immediately upon entering the great tent, Ferendir smelled sweet mead, fresh-baked bread and candied fruits.

The high commander of the warhost, Hirva Windstrider, was instantly apparent – a tall, handsome aelven female wearing magnificently wrought armour of shining sunsteel. Though the armour bore evidence of having seen action that day – a few scuffs and greasy streaks, as well as spatters of Hedonite blood – its overall sheen and purity were still wondrous to behold. Hirva's hair, honey gold and tied back in a long, thick braid, had barely a displaced strand or lock to speak of. Clearly, she had joined the battle and claimed lives that day, yet there she stood before them, bent over a great conference table studying maps of the surrounding countryside and conferring in soft, cool whispers with her subordinates.

The Dawnrider, Veloryn, came to an abrupt halt just a short distance from where Hirva studied her geographies.

'The Alarith, lady regent,' Veloryn said. 'As you requested.'

Hirva raised her eyes. They were deep blue, the colour of melted glacial ice. The moment her gaze fell upon the three of them, Ferendir felt a strange frisson move through him. She was beautiful, yet intimidating as well, her features as sublime and severe as a windswept mountainside scoured smooth by millennia of steady winds, its desolation as moving and breathtaking as any forest teeming with life. Ferendir had the strange sense that the warhost commander did not simply study him but surveyed him, as though he were a small, nondescript parcel of land that she now weighed for its possible usefulness in a coming military action. That same cold appraisal was applied to Serath and Desriel in turn, but the effect of it never entirely left Ferendir.

Finally, the lady regent stood straight and gave a curt nod. 'Welcome,' she said easily. 'You're among friends.'

'Our kind, at the very least,' Serath muttered.

Ferendir saw Desriel shoot his partner a subtle, shaming look.

Hirva rounded the great table. 'I am told you fought bravely and slew many of our enemies this day. For that, you have my thanks. Now, I must ask what brought you to this place… and why there were not more of you. A phalanx of Alarith Stoneguard would have served our needs most nobly.'

'Firstly,' Serath answered, 'we came to this place by accident, and uninvited. This mountain and its foothills are our home. I should remind you that you – your entire warhost – are the trespassers here.'

Desriel leapt in. 'What my companion fails to add is that our home temple was destroyed only yesterday, torn asunder by the very same Hedonites you just routed upon this plain. They shattered our walls, burned our temples and slaughtered every one of the temple's mage-priests and acolytes. The fact that we were away during the siege is all that spared us.'

Hirva studied them, as if weighing their words. For an instant, she looked to Ferendir, as if awaiting his own take on the words of his masters. Ferendir, intimidated by the woman's cold gaze, said nothing.

'In truth, we had not expected to meet them or engage them here,' she finally said. 'The Slaaneshi warhost had already swept across the plain and into the mountains. We've been tracking them for weeks. We expected to only catch up to them beyond the foothills, upon the mountain itself. Imagine our surprise when we found them already retreating from something, heading right back towards us. We had thought that someone – or something – repelled them, driving them back down the mountain towards our waiting spears.'

'They were not repelled,' Serath said bitterly, 'merely finished with the dark business they came to transact.'

Hirva's head tilted slightly. 'And what was that dark business, Stoneguard?'

'If you would address me, lady regent,' Serath said, 'I have a name.'

Ferendir looked to Desriel. Neither could believe Serath's prickly rebuff.

'Tell me your names, then,' Hirva replied, without skipping a beat, 'so that I can extract the information I need to command my host.'

'This is Serath,' Desriel said, indicating his counterpart. 'I am Desriel. We are tried and committed Stoneguard of the mountain temple and invested members of the Stoneguard. This' – he indicated Ferendir –'is our student and charge, Ferendir. He is a supplicant seeking initiation but, as yet, has not passed his final trial.'

Ferendir felt a vague sense of embarrassment. Was it really necessary for his master to so humble him – to so dismiss him – under the gaze of this proud and formidable warrior queen?

'Very well,' Hirva said, gaze swinging back to Serath. 'You were saying, Stoneguard?'

Ferendir felt his body stiffen. Clearly, nothing would intimidate this woman.

Serath hesitated for only a moment before he offered a reply. 'Clearly,' he said, 'they came to our temple in search of something. Once they had penetrated the defences and claimed what they came for, they withdrew.'

'You talk in circles,' Hirva said, 'around some unnamed object. What was it these Hedonite monsters came in search of? What did they take from you?'

Serath's eyes narrowed. 'What did they take? Commander... they took *everything*.'

Desriel intervened, eager to de-escalate the rising tension. 'Forgive our reticence,' he said, 'but may we ask questions of our own before we tell you more?'

'You may *not*,' Dawnrider Veloryn broke in. 'The lady regent asked you a question, Stoneguard. I suggest you answer it.'

Ferendir noted that Veloryn's right hand had fallen to the grip of her sheathed sword.

Worse, Serath saw the gesture as well. His eyes had narrowed – a familiar look, precursor to the employ of his quiet, simmering ferocity. Ferendir felt every muscle in his body start to tense and tighten in answer to Serath's preparation for action.

'Remove your hand from your sword,' Serath said coldly, 'or we shall be forced to assume you wish us ill.'

The Dawnrider stepped forward. 'You are guests here, Stoneguard. Behave so.'

'We are guests in this pavilion,' Desriel said calmly, 'but you are guests of the mountain. You stand in its shadow, and we are its emissaries and humble servants. If you would learn what it has to offer you – and what those Slaaneshi dogs have taken from it – I suggest you bear us the same courtesy you demand in return.'

Veloryn looked to Hirva. Hirva took a long, slow moment to consider. Finally, she gave a subtle nod. Veloryn let her hand fall from her sword and stepped back, clearly making an effort to disperse the gathered tension.

'My apologies,' the Dawnrider said, though Ferendir was not entirely sure she meant it.

'Ask your questions,' Hirva said, addressing Desriel.

'You said you've been tracking them for weeks,' Desriel said. 'Describe their course, and what they've left in their wake.'

'They left in their wake what they left for you,' Hirva said. 'Destruction. Complete and utter destruction. Worse, there are more of them – two more warhosts that we know of, possibly more, ravaging Ymetrica even as we speak.'

'Three warhosts?' Serath asked. 'Is it an invasion?'

Hirva made a strange face at those words – that suggestion of a smile again, though it had a strange, sad cast to it.

'Not a concerted invasion, precisely,' she said at last. 'So far as we can tell, it's a contest.'

'A contest?' Desriel asked.

Hirva broke from them, moving towards a sideboard laid with food and drink.

'Let's eat as we talk,' the lady regent said. 'I don't know about the three of you, but I'm famished, and there is much to discuss...'

The food was simple but filling, and there was, thankfully, plenty of it. Ferendir fought the urge to gorge himself – internally, his hunger was pressing him to near hysteria – but he knew that neither of his masters, Serath especially, would approve of such an indecent indulgence of his appetites. Thus, Ferendir watched Desriel and Serath carefully and resolved to eat and drink only as much as they did, and not a crumb more.

Hirva, bearing her plate and cup, led them to her great command table, strewn with maps and carved wooden markers symbolising her own host or the horde of Slaaneshi Hedonites they had so recently routed. A great many of the Slaaneshi markers had been removed from the map and piled to the side, presumably an estimate of the number she and her host had slain that day. If Ferendir understood the system, a great many yet remained.

Hirva indicated the map but did not single out any particular formation.

'The raids began three weeks ago,' she said, 'here on the continent of Ymetrica. They were not only fast and gathered in large numbers, but there seemed to be more than one warhost at work, for they could strike multiple targets on the same day in vastly different regions.'

She casually indicated the western coast and the plains, nearer the mountains, as well as the space separating them.

'We activated an enormous warhost to meet them, but discovered that even when we found and engaged them, there were still always actions elsewhere – as if two or even three separate armies were at work.'

'A stratagem,' Serath said, studying the map, 'to separate your forces and work slowly towards a particular goal?'

Hirva raised one elegant eyebrow. 'So we thought. After the pattern of their movements failed to reveal itself, we realised it was because there was no pattern. We weren't dealing with a single warhost broken into pieces to work towards a common goal – we were dealing with separate entities, with separate – sometimes competing – interests.'

Ferendir studied his masters. They seemed equally puzzled by that revelation.

'How did they even arrive?' Desriel asked finally. 'For such a massive host to reach the continent–'

'There had to be another Realmgate,' Hirva finished. 'We know not where, but that is the only explanation. They did not come to Hysh and travel cross-realm to Ymetrica – somehow, they arrived here, upon Ymetrica, without our realising it.'

Serath shook his head. 'But separate hosts...'

'Troubling, to be sure. For the first ten days, we ran hither and yon trying to contain the separate forces or win a decisive victory. We routed them at every turn, but they would simply retreat, lick their foul wounds and strike elsewhere a day or two later. Nothing seems to deter them. At best, they can only be slowed. But gradually, one pattern amidst the chaos did emerge.'

She indicated a number of wooden markers all painted in the same shade of sickly pale purple – the same markers that had been diminished by that day's military action.

'One particular host kept pressing east, towards the mountains – towards your home – while the other two kept sweeping aimlessly over the land, going where the targets were most plentiful, or most unequal to repelling them. Only that one warhost seemed determined to get somewhere, to accomplish something, and they used the activities of their competition brilliantly to waylay our efforts to overtake them.'

'Who are they, then?' Desriel asked. 'What do they want? Have you learned anything?'

Hirva looked to the captain of the Dawnriders, who'd been standing in obedient silence at the table's far end. 'Captain Veloryn?' she asked by way of invitation.

Veloryn, whose silence up until that moment had bordered on the funereal, raised her head and nodded curtly.

'As you wish, lady regent.'

Then she took up the tale.

'During our campaign to contain the threat of these vile invaders, we've set our scryers to work, seeking answers in the aether and through the psychometric analysis of prisoners and objects taken in battle. We yielded a few clues, which led us to send operatives far and wide throughout Hysh – from Haixiah to Oultrai, Iliatha to Helon – in search of corroborating evidence to support the magically derived information we gleaned.

'Our realisation that we were dealing with separate, competing warhosts turned out to be correct. As best we could piece together, each host is subject to a powerful Slaaneshi mage whose separate obsessions and desires prompt them to sometimes work in concert, at other times in direct competition. These foul wizards, we learned, have made among themselves a tacit agreement to wage war here, in Hysh, and to prosecute their separate campaigns mercilessly, without withdrawal, until one of them has subjugated the whole of Ymetrica or the three of them – along with their armies – are wiped out.'

Serath and Desriel exchanged worried glances. The gestures were subtle, their expressions barely readable, yet Ferendir knew what he was seeing. Clearly, they were as disturbed by the Dawnrider's words and explanation for their present predicament as she and Lady Regent Hirva had been disturbed to learn it. A stunned silence persisted for a short time, and in that interval, Ferendir studied the map. Knowing the story, he could now see clearly that each Slaaneshi warhost was represented by different markers – that sickly purple for the warhost that had ravaged their home, the other two in shades of decadent yellow-gold or burn-scar pink. The other two hosts were farther to the west or north, separated by great spans but still uncomfortably close to Ferendir's own homelands in the great, craggy mountains at the continent's centre.

'The leaders of the warhosts,' Veloryn continued, 'are not idle strivers, either. Each has a long, terrible history, leaving trails of destruction in their separate wakes in all the Mortal Realms. Though evidence was uncovered of past associations between all three, it seems that their current association is some sort of strange wager. However mad it may sound, their effectiveness just in the past weeks, stretching our resources thin and swarming far and wide over Ymetrica, has proven they are not fools.

'This host,' she said, indicating the pink markers, 'belongs to a sorceress known as Astoriss, the Mother of Calamities, a self-described seeker after her absent Lord Slaanesh. Dedicated to learning the whereabouts of her dread lord and freeing him, she has gathered to her five thousand followers who are as fanatical as they are subtle. Subtle for Slaaneshi sorts, at any rate. Capable of more ambitious undertakings and displaying more depraved modes of slaughter and torture, we consider them the most dangerous of the three warhosts. However, they also seem to be the *least* ambitious, for they regularly strike small targets and withdraw to an unknown lair before we even have the opportunity to meet them or winnow their numbers. It is our belief that if we can eradicate the other two, the children of Astoriss will be our greatest foe.

'This,' she said, indicating the yellow markers, 'is the warhost of Meigant Aelvenbane, a monstrous, bloodthirsty brute whose bellicose nature and excess savagery would seemingly mark him as a follower of Khorne, not Slaanesh. And yet there is no doubt, seeing the host of daemonettes and misshapen mutants that slither and crawl in his wake, that the god of excess can be his only master.

Meigant's warhost are invaders, pure and simple – fast-moving reavers whose only joy is death, depravity and suffering. We've met Meigant's host on several occasions, and thinned them each time, but at great cost. Though disorganised, they are savage and tenacious, always willing to spend dozens of their own lives to take even one of ours. And they have many, many lives yet to expend.'

She stopped. Sighed. Stared at the map for a moment, tight-lipped and pensive. Ferendir suddenly realised that she was moved by a memory – and an unpleasant one, at that. Clearly, someone she cared for – perhaps several someones – had fallen in the battles against Meigant's forces.

'Finally,' she said, 'there is the host we met today – the same host that destroyed your home.' She indicated the purple markers. 'They were the ones we watched most carefully, for they were the only ones who seemed to have a destination, a goal. If only we could have determined that goal before they struck and wiped it out…'

'After our last engagement with the Aelvenbane's forces on the plain,' the lady regent broke in, 'and given new information revealed by deep scryings and expeditions into the depths of the aether, I deemed it vital to pick up Ezarhad's trail and stop him.'

'Ezarhad?' Serath asked, immediately seizing upon the casually dropped name.

Hirva Windstrider nodded gravely. 'Aye. Ezarhad Fatesbane, he's called. The youngest of these three Slaaneshi mage-lords, so far as we can tell, only having dedicated himself to Slaanesh a few centuries ago. His ego and appetites have grown exponentially ever since, to the point that he now fancies himself a pretender – a true and likely heir to Slaanesh's foul throne. Ezarhad, we learned, possesses an abiding hunger for secret knowledge, especially when it comes wrapped in the guise of a rare or much sought-after tome of magic. He has a vast personal library hidden somewhere in the folds of the aether, and he seeks, at all times, to increase his holdings, believing that the accumulation of such knowledge is what will ultimately allow him to surpass Slaanesh in power and supplant the absent god once and for all. We learned that he has a habit of seeking these tomes that he desires with the utmost determination, letting no one stand in his way, readily slaughtering hundreds, or even thousands, if it will put a sought-after folio in his hands. If he thinks other copies of the work in question exist elsewhere, he will hunt those down as well and spare no effort or expense to destroy them.'

Desriel seemed puzzled by that revelation. He looked to Serath, then to Veloryn.

'He wants his possessions to be unique,' the steedmaster clarified. 'One of a kind, solely his.'

Ferendir felt a small shudder pass through him. The willpower! *The naked desire!* To hunger for knowledge and rare collectibles so fiercely that you were willing to kill to either acquire them or increase their value. What sort of a diseased mind was capable of such wastefulness?

'It was that knowledge,' Hirva said, 'that forced us to re-evaluate Ezarhad's relative importance to what was unfolding here. Given his peculiar interests and desires, it seemed unlikely that he would press for the mountains so steadily if he did not have some object in his sights – some ultimate object of obsession.'

Ferendir studied his masters. Desriel and Serath were staring at one another now, their gazes sober and sickly all at once – horrifying revelation coupled with perfect, undesired understanding.

Hirva saw it as well. 'What? What do you know?'

'Clearly,' Desriel said, 'he knew precisely what he sought, and where to find it.'

'Impossible,' Serath spat. 'Our temple has possessed the Eidolith for centuries, and we have done everything possible to eradicate knowledge of its power and purpose from all the records of the Mortal Realms.'

'Apparently,' Desriel said, lowering his eyes, 'we failed.'

'Speak,' Hirva pressed. 'What do you know?'

'We know what this Ezarhad Fatesbane was after,' Serath said bitterly.

'Worse,' Desriel added, 'we know that he acquired it.'

Hirva stood tall and met both of their gazes. Ferendir felt the air in the pavilion change, as though it had grown suddenly colder. The lady regent's transformed mood was unmistakable.

Worse, Ferendir himself felt a terrible dread stir inside him.

What are they hiding? he wondered. *What could possibly be so terrible?*

Desriel sighed. 'Once, in the quiet years preceding the Ocari Dara and the Age of Chaos, there was one of our kind – an Alarith Stoneguard named Lariel – who saw his Hyshian homeland and all the Mortal Realms endangered by creeping corruption and the shadow of coming ruin. The cause, by his reckoning, excess. Be it excesses of pride or emotion or desire – usually compounded by too much power and not enough control – always, *always*, the world's pain was born of excess. Knowing that weakness and excess could pave the way for the growth and dominion of Chaos in this realm and elsewhere, Lariel sought a means of combatting the plague of excess wherever he found it – a panacea to cure all the peoples of the Mortal Realms of their most destructive impulses.'

Serath took over. 'After years of investigation and experiment, Lariel believed he had found the answer – an aelemental cosmic force that he named Kaethraxis. According to him, Kaethraxis – in its most abstract form – was the natural impulse of an environment towards destructive self-correction – chokingly dense forests purged by fire, weakening, half-eroded hillsides smoothed by avalanches or mudslides, droughts or diseases that culled the unchecked growth of populations and the rampant abuse of resources. It was the natural world's corrective impulse made manifest – Creation deploying Destruction to save itself from ruin.'

Hirva Windstrider had barely moved since the tale began. 'He courted apocalypse – sought to enslave catastrophe itself.'

Desriel gave a slight shrug. 'He was convinced that harnessing Kaethraxis – actualising it, controlling it – would allow him to aid all the peoples of the Mortal Realms in abolishing their worst, most excessive impulses. And so, after years of struggling to isolate and manifest this terrible power – without success – Lariel finally attempted to give Kaethraxis form by giving it a host – to be its avatar, its high priest and its most humble acolyte. To aid him in this magical communion – a dangerous magical operation, to be sure – he enlisted a group of his most trusted teachers, peers and students.

'Unfortunately, they underestimated the mindless, impulsive power Kaethraxis would possess once incarnated, and likewise overestimated Lariel's own ability to harness or control it.'

Desriel paused. Breathed. It was as if the very telling of the tale freighted his heart with sorrow and shame – as though the sin of this long-ago mage called Lariel was Desriel's own. Ferendir did not understand his master's depth of feeling, but he could not deny the fact of it. Part of him wanted to offer solace. He knew that if his master showed any outward signs of emotion – hurt, shame, regret – no matter how subtle, then the forces moving within him must have been infinitely more powerful. Such a reality now presented itself, subtle signs that there was a storm raging inside Desriel.

Serath seemed to grow impatient. He carried on with the recollection. 'Lariel took Kaethraxis into himself, tried to contain it, to control it. It overwhelmed all the natural and magical defences arrayed against it almost immediately. An eruption of raw, destructive power instantly consumed his friends and companions, destroying them utterly. Realising what he had done, Lariel was seized by a grief so deep, so scarring, that he was consumed by the aelemental urges of the entity he'd created, unable to reconcile his rational mind with the rash, destructive passions embodied by the creature.

'Thus, Lariel, subsumed by Kaethraxis, became a blight upon Hysh – a looming disaster threatening all the realm with sudden, impetuous outpourings of destructive force driven by a shattered psyche – a cyclical storm that could lie dormant for years before bursting forth without warning to torment the very place it was summoned to protect and purge.'

'But it did lie dormant for a time?' Hirva asked. 'It was capable of withdrawal? Of being contained?'

'It was,' Desriel said, 'but as time went on, each cycle of activity and inactivity shortened. Its destructive power and propensity to roam grew larger, while its periods of hibernation grew shorter. All the good and wise of Hysh knew that if something could not be done to contain it, the whole realm might be destroyed.'

'I cannot believe it,' Steedmaster Veloryn broke in. 'Such a force as you describe, and the havoc wrought by it – I've never heard of it, never even in passing. How can such things simply be wiped from the great record? From collective memory itself?'

It was Lady Regent Hirva who answered the question, though it had not been posed to her. 'All things can be forgotten if they can first be concealed. All that is required is the collective will to forget.'

Ferendir felt a strange sense of shame and abomination at such a suggestion – that the Lumineth, a people dedicated to knowledge, to enlightenment, would wilfully forget or suppress any crumb of knowledge. It seemed almost blasphemous to even suggest it.

And yet… was it truly outside the realm of possibility? Could a perfect storm of fear and shame not move a people to collectively, wilfully forget that such terrible power was once within their grasp?

Desriel nodded. 'Aye, and our ancestors certainly had that collective will, for they realised what a monster had been created by their attempts to control forces that could not be controlled. All the Lumineth of the Ten Paradises were eager to tame the blight that Lariel had become. They sent many powers against Kaethraxis to try and contain it. Soldiers, mages, scientists – all failed to stop its mad, convulsive rampages. All failed to ferret out a great weakness to exploit.'

'All except the forebears of our temple,' Serath added. 'It was, in the end, a trio of Alarith Stoneguard who volunteered to track Kaethraxis to its lair, deep in the Vertiginous Mountains, to make a last-ditch attempt to either tame it or imprison it.

'It was they who ventured through the most treacherous regions of the mountains, to the very threshold of the hidden valley where Kaethraxis slept during its dormant seasons. And there, in the monster's lair, the Alarith attempted to become one with Kaethraxis itself – just as Lariel had. But the difference was their collective spiritual nature, as well as the forces that moved and shaped their psyches. They were already bonded, partnered – a trio of peers and comrades capable of acting as a single unit, a single entity, when necessary. Likewise, they thought to employ their knowledge of the soul of the mountain, of its patience, its understanding of slow change and cyclical growth, to pacify and restrain the destructive aelemental that Lariel had unleashed.'

'Were they successful?' Hirva Windstrider asked.

'No,' Desriel said. 'Not entirely, at any rate. Two of the three were destroyed in the attempt. But their sacrifices laid the foundation for the third member of their party to finally break through the aelemental's psychic defences, to find Lariel's broken, aggrieved soul lodged in the heart of Kaethraxis like a splinter spreading an infection, and to drag it into a state of dormancy and suspended consciousness. If that last, lone Stoneguard could not truly heal Kaethraxis, she would at least put it to sleep, and keep it so until the knowledge and wisdom of the Lumineth finally caught up with our desperate need to control or destroy the beast.

'And so the last Stoneguard of that brave trio remained in the secret vale, in what came to be known as the Kaethraxine Blight, surrendering her life and freedom to the ongoing, age-long task of using her mind, her will and her heart to keep Kaethraxis pacified in an aeons-long hibernation, from which it could not wake to wreak its havoc upon Hysh.'

'But her sacrifice was only half of the solution,' Hirva said pointedly. 'Where was the promised means of controlling or destroying the creature? Is this poor, burdened Stoneguard still dwelling in the mountains, even now, her sole purpose to keep Kaethraxis sleeping and neutralised?'

'Our temple accepted the responsibility for finding that solution,' Serath said, seemingly insulted by Hirva's intimation that the Alarith had somehow failed in their guardianship. 'From the time of Kaethraxis' imprisonment to the present, our most potent minds have sought a means of relieving that last guardian from her eternal vigilance, whether it meant controlling the creature or simply destroying it.'

'We thought we had found the key,' Desriel said, 'though it had not yet been attempted. The greatest minds of our temple had fashioned – after decades of study and experimentation – a large aetherquartz gem containing the power necessary to keep Kaethraxis dormant indefinitely or to control it if it ever reawakened. Experiments were conducted with less powerful aelementals and rogue spirit constructs, but no one had as yet ventured back to the lost valley to see if the gem would work upon the being it was created to control. Whenever the time came to make the attempt, it was decided that Kaethraxis yet remained dormant and we should leave it be, for fear of rousing a force we could not contain.'

'Because you do not know if the gem works,' Hirva said. It was not a question.

Desriel nodded.

Serath added, 'There is little doubt it can awaken the creature. There is considerable conjecture, however, as to whether it can control it.'

Hirva Windstrider bent over her map table, hung her head and sighed. A long, pregnant silence fell upon them as they each tried to digest what the other had divulged. Ferendir, for his part, did not know what to think. He'd had no inkling that his home temple held within it weapons or artefacts of such immense power. For that matter, he'd also had no idea that such creatures as this Kaethraxis could even exist. He knew all about the aelementals – the spirits of the land and wind and water of Hysh whose power and understanding of the inherent symmetries of creation and existence provided conceptual frameworks and spiritual guidance for his kind. He knew that, in theory, there were other spirits – even malevolent sorts – aside from the thousands of aelementals that moved and dreamed behind the material face of the realm they called home. But he had never imagined that, in all the history of the world, anyone of his kind – of any kind professing to serve light and order – could summon such an entity of pure, destructive force and try to contain it within themselves. What had this Lariel been thinking? What had made him so sure that he could control the immense powers and destructive potentiality of one of nature's most fearsome correctives?

Then a new thought occurred to Ferendir, blooming unbidden in his mind like a poisoned flower. If such things as Kaethraxis could be – could exist – and yet remain unknown, what other terrifying destructive entities and treasures yet waited throughout the Mortal Realms for rediscovery? What if this Kaethraxis, far from being rare and unlike any other thing in existence, was actually... common?

At least, as common as such things might be without wholly revealing themselves.

More to the point, what would they now do? If they knew that this Ezarhad Fatesbane possessed the gem stolen from their temple – a gem solely intended for the awakening and controlling of this sleeping aelemental – they could safely assume that Ezarhad's next destination was the secret valley where Kaethraxis slept.

And they would have to stop him.

'We have the advantage,' Hirva suddenly said, standing straight and sweeping one hand over the great map laid out before her. 'We routed Ezarhad's troops and we have them trapped in the hills.'

Veloryn stood straight as well, already showing signs of renewed life, clearly anticipating what her lady regent was about to suggest. 'The Dawnriders could split into two squadrons, supported by Vanari wardens and sentinels. If we can move fast through the night and encircle the Slaaneshi while they're still regrouping–'

'We can smash them before they retreat to higher ground,' Hirva finished. 'If we can keep the host from moving and draw this Ezarhad Fatesbane out, we may yet be able to strike him down before he has the opportunity to go searching for where this Kaethraxis sleeps.'

She looked to Ferendir's masters. 'Does the gem have any other uses? Is it a weapon? Does it, in itself, pose a threat?'

Serath and Desriel both shook their heads.

'No,' Desriel said. 'So far as either of us knows, the Eidolith's only use is as a talisman to commune with and control Kaethraxis. Without the spirit, the gem is just a bauble. Without the gem, the spirit is wholly uncontrollable.'

Or with it, Ferendir thought mordantly. *Hadn't we established that? That no one knows if the gem actually works as it was intended to?*

Hirva, meanwhile, was nodding in answer to Desriel's assurances. 'Good, then,' she said. 'That means we need only worry about the inherent ferocity and power wielded by Ezarhad and his foul servants without having to anticipate a new variable. Steedmaster

Veloryn, prepare your riders and summon the Vanari. The moment night is upon us, I want your forces moving into those hills. We'll encircle them in the night and attack before dawn.'

Steedmaster Veloryn nodded in the affirmative. 'As you wish, lady regent.' She moved away from the table, striding confidently towards the pavilion's entryway. 'I'll report as soon as I–'

The entry flap of the tent was suddenly thrown aside. One of the two sentries posted outside entered with a new arrival in tow, one of the Alarith whose battle line Desriel, Serath and Ferendir had joined on the ridge. His normally silver-white armour was encrusted with enemy blood, mud and soot, his thin, hawkish face criss-crossed by dark smudges that Ferendir supposed were simply dirt or, perhaps, faded camouflage of some sort. Clearly, he had still been bent to some taxing – and bloody – labours, even once the battle had ended.

The Alarith swept past the sentry, marched forward and dropped to one knee a short distance from the map table, making obeisance to his lady regent.

'Lady regent, I come with news of import,' he said.

Hirva Windstrider rounded the table and stood beside the now-frozen Veloryn. 'Report, seneschal.'

'We sent troops into the hills, to trail the invaders and try to deduce their next move. The main force remains, regrouping and eager for another fight, but a smaller detachment – between one and two hundred, no more – broke from the main body and marched out of the hills and up the mountainside, north by north-east.'

'Where is Ezarhad?' Veloryn demanded. 'Did he remain with the bulk of his forces?'

The Alarith seneschal slowly shook his head. He seemed suddenly puzzled, as if the steedmaster's question was more pointed than he had expected.

'No, steedmaster,' he said. 'The pretender, Ezarhad Fatesbane, is leading the splinter company. We thought he perhaps intended to seek a path by which to outflank and encircle us, and so I ordered a small squad of Stoneguard to track him. They broke off when Ezarhad and his company reached the lower slopes of the mountain. He wasn't seeking a path towards our position – he's going somewhere else entirely.'

'Did you engage them?' Hirva asked.

The Alarith shook his head more emphatically. 'No, lady regent. We thought it best to hurry back and report. I left a small team – three Stoneguard – on their trail, leaving signs in their wake that we can follow if we wish to take up the trail again.'

Suddenly, Serath had broken away from the map table. He marched past the lady regent and the Dawnrider and the Alarith seneschal, right towards the entrance to the pavilion.

'We're wasting time,' he said, a faint note of disgust in his voice.

'Stoneguard,' Lady Regent Hirva said, her voice suddenly loud and commanding, 'stop where you are.'

Serath rounded on her. 'I will not. I have a duty. I shall see to it!'

He turned to go again, but Desriel now stepped forward. 'I have that same duty, Serath. You'll go nowhere without me.'

'I will if you don't join me at once,' Serath said over his shoulder, still marching towards the entrance.

'Guards!' Hirva barked. 'Stop him! No one leaves this tent!'

Serath threw back the tent flap and found two armoured Vanari standing in his path. He took a single step back and altered his stance – right foot back, left foot forward, arms rising into a familiar configuration.

He was preparing to fight them.

Ferendir looked to his other master, not sure what was about to unfold. Desriel had already rushed past the lady regent and hurried to Serath's side. He placed himself between his old companion and the armed sentries.

'Serath, stop!' he said sharply, forcefully. It was the closest thing resembling anger Ferendir had ever heard from his master.

'He has the Eidolith,' Serath said. 'We know where he's going. This is our only chance. If anyone tries to stop me–'

'We don't want to stop you,' Hirva said, now stepping forward. 'We want to help you, Stoneguard – now more than ever. But you must be patient.'

'*Patient?*' Serath spat, turning to face her. 'You have a war to win. We have a treasure to recover. Our paths need not be intertwined. Now, tell your guards–'

'This is not the way, Serath,' Desriel said, and Ferendir could hear the plea in his voice – the calm but earnest appeal to Serath's reason. 'The well-placed hammer blow is more deadly than three struck in anger – is that not what we were taught?'

'There is no anger in me,' Serath said quietly, seeming almost insulted by the insinuation. 'I have a task to perform. I mean to perform it.'

'And you shall,' Desriel said. '*We* shall. But with the right preparation. The right tools.'

'And the right comrades,' Lady Regent Hirva said.

Desriel and Serath looked to her. The former seemed appreciative; the latter, suspicious.

'Whom did you have in mind?' Desriel asked.

Ferendir saw the lady regent's hard, stone-set mouth curl into the vaguest ghost of a half-smile.

'I command a warhost,' Hirva Windstrider said. 'I can give you whatever – and whomever – you require.'

CHAPTER FIVE

The sun was dimming and the night's gloaming would soon be upon them. Lady Regent Hirva gave Ferendir and his masters a vacated tent close to her command centre and told them that they could stay there and have their fill of her stores for as long as they required. She knew they were eager to be under way, but until they departed – no matter how soon that might prove to be – they were her guests and would be treated as such.

Ferendir sought to remain close to his masters, to see just who they would gather from among the warhost and how their party would be outfitted, but Serath immediately put him to work with a number of mundane tasks.

'Gather provisions and pack them, equal portions, in three separate packs. Pack as light as possible, but sufficient for three weeks. Bread should be the bulk, rounded out with dried fruit, nuts and salted meat or fish. We will be travelling swiftly over rough terrain. There will be no pack animals.'

Ferendir looked to Serath, knew his master would not brook any argument, then swung his gaze to Desriel. 'Master, I–'

'This is what we require of you presently,' Desriel said softly. 'Pack the provisions, then oil and sharpen the weapons, then prepare us some supper. Something a little heartier than what we'll be carrying. It might be the last satisfying meal we have for some time.'

'But,' Ferendir persisted, 'I want to see who–'

'That is not your task,' Serath said sharply. 'You've been given your task. Leave the rest to us. Say not another word.'

Ferendir fell silent. He nodded sullenly. His masters left him, going off with Steedmaster Veloryn and the Alarith seneschal, presumably in search of new recruits for their little expedition.

As Ferendir saw to his chores, he contemplated what a strange place he found himself in. Only yesterday morning, he'd known precisely what his life would consist of, hour by hour, day by day. He'd awakened early and departed with his masters to climb into the mountains and undertake his trial, not knowing that at that moment, as they all marched out of the main gate of the temple fortress in the dim light of Hyshian night, none of them would ever again return to the place they called home. He'd had friends among the other supplicants, teachers, supporters and masters – even, ashamed as he was to admit it, a few nemeses and enemies. Rivals, he supposed – other young aelves, better at this or that skill than he was, their successes and accolades a constant, bitter reminder that his own seemed humble or unremarkable in every way. Many of them were the best of the best – young protégés already showing infinite promise, advancing swiftly and surely up the Teclian ladder towards lofty achievements and, ultimately, infinite enlightenment.

And now they were all dead. Every last one of them. All that he thought his life would be in the decades to come had been wiped away by cruelty, wanton violence and greed in the short span of a few hours.

Something in that realisation filled Ferendir with a terrifying anxiety. It was not acute fear – the fear one felt upon a narrow ledge or facing a wild beast, or even the fear one felt when undertaking a trial with real, potentially lethal consequences. No, this was far more nebulous... and far more unsettling. Bone-deep, ghostly... like a mist on a meadow, or the vague sense one might have when approaching an open gulf that yawned, black and impenetrable, promising almost anything within.

That feeling, he suddenly realised, had a name. It was dread. He had known it most frequently in his childhood, when still young, untried and without the insight and understanding that growth, maturity and education bestowed. When he was a child, he'd dreaded a great many things – dark forests, the shadows of an unlit corridor at night, the naked feeling of staring into a vast, wide-open sky when crossing level, open ground. Childhood, he recalled, had been filled with dread, because childhood was also marked by ignorance, inexperience, wanton speculation and utter chaos. Maturity brought order, understanding, the subjugation of dread to reason, and so his soul had found a measure of peace, a sense of control and understanding.

Yet now, it seemed that the primal dread of childhood had returned to him. His entire world had been stripped away, turned to blood, ash and memory. If he could not count on the destiny prescribed for him by the gods and the mountain, what could he count on?

What if everything – the whole of the Mortal Realms, all of existence – was constantly balanced upon a knife's edge, threatening to topple into the abyss at any given instant for the smallest, most ridiculous of missteps? What if existence was, at its core – in essence – nothing but constant, unremitting, imminent danger and nothing more?

He shuddered. In an effort to banish his fear, he forced himself to concentrate on packing the provisions.

Ferendir was not sure how long he sat, bent to his duties, struggling to make sure each pack more or less bore an equal weight and contained equal resources. All around him, activity continued in the camp of Hirva Windstrider's warhost, the aelven soldiers bending to their cookfires, preparing their evening meals, scouring mail, sharpening swords or washing and buffing their shining warplate to remove the smeared blood and clods of dirt acquired by the day's murderous activity. Somewhere, someone began singing a song – an old song, not of the mountains but of the plains, vaguely familiar to Ferendir, though he could not specifically identify it. After a time, the melody of the song became implanted in Ferendir's own mind, and he found himself humming it, despite not knowing the words or even what the tune's origins of purpose might be.

He worked. He hummed. Time seemed to have no meaning. Then, all at once, a strange feeling came upon him – the vague, unpleasant sensation of being watched. Ferendir raised his eyes from his task.

Two figures stood nearby, side by side, watching him with heavy, probing gazes. They both wore silver plate possessed of a vague blue-green sheen over coppery-scale mail and silken, saffron-yellow skirts. Their matching helms bore forward-facing horsehair crests dyed the same golden colour as the garments beneath their armour. One bore a multi-stringed longbow that marked her as a sentinel – one of the deadly phalanx of archers that supported the warhost in combat. The other clasped a tall, elegant pike with a long, broad blade at its tip in one hand and a strong, elegantly tooled shield in the other – a warden, one of the front-rankers in the warhost's formidable infantry.

Ferendir shot to his feet. He could not say why – it was a wholly instinctive action, as though he knew these two to be respected officers and he merely a soldier of the line. It simply seemed right, in that instant, to greet them standing straight and tall, in an attitude of respect.

But he had no clue who they might actually be.

The two women – sentinel and warden – exchanged brief glances and removed their crested helms. Though each head of hair was styled differently, the two faces now gazing at Ferendir were identical – the same high, sweeping cheekbones, the same soft, bowed lips, the same penetrating, almond-shaped eyes. They each possessed long, luxurious red-gold hair, but while the warden let her locks fall naturally, the sentinel had hers pulled back and loosely tied.

'Don't stop now,' the warden said. 'You carry a tune well.'

'Can you sing?' the sentinel asked. 'Or is humming the extent of your vocal ability?'

Ferendir's mouth worked for a moment, struggling to find words. Even their voices sounded the same. If Ferendir were to close his eyes, he doubted he would even realise that two different people spoke to him.

'How long have you been standing there?' he managed to ask.

'Long enough,' the warden said, moving forward and surveying the orderly disorder lying around at Ferendir's feet. 'Is that bread? I'm famished.'

She moved around a log that had been hastily thrown down upon the ground before the fire. She laid her shield aside and with practised smoothness sat and shifted her long pike onto one shoulder. Its base was planted a short span before her, deep into the ground so it would not slide, while its weight rested easily upon her shoulder – still at hand, yet conveniently out of the way. With her free hand, she snatched up a piece of the twice-baked biscuit piled on a parcel of oil cloth, took a bite and munched contentedly.

'Now, see here,' Ferendir said. 'Those provisions were given by the lady regent for myself and my masters. I'd be happy to share, if I knew they were mine to share.'

'You just said they were intended for *you* and your masters,' the sentinel said, rounding the log from the other direction and sitting herself down beside her warden doppelganger. 'Sounds to me like they *are* your provisions to share – so long as you're willing to share them. So, I ask, may we help ourselves? Are you *willing* to share?'

Ferendir stared, mouth working again and failing to find words. He began to look around, hoping to see his masters returning from wherever they'd disappeared to, so that he could ask them. He saw no sign of them. Finally, he sighed resignedly.

'Of course,' he said. 'Help yourselves. But please, just one biscuit apiece.'

'Certainly, young Alarith,' the sentinel said. She plucked up her own piece of flatbread and bit off a piece. As she chewed, she looked to her pike-wielding twin, then back to Ferendir. 'Forgive my sister. Her manners are... questionable.'

'How did you know that?' Ferendir asked.

'Know what?' the sentinel asked around a mouthful of the tack.

'That I was Alarith?'

'What else would you be?' the sentinel asked. 'You're dressed like an Alarith, you have the quiet, accommodating nature of an Alarith, and everything around us, from the clasps on these packs to the daggers in those sheaths, bears the mark of Alarith workmanship. Simple deduction, that's all.'

'There are also your masters,' the warden broke in. 'We've already spoken with them. Seeing as *they* are Alarith, and having that fact verified so unequivocally, we assumed you to be as well.'

'My masters?' Ferendir asked, suddenly puzzled.

'The gruff one and the kind one,' the sentinel said. 'Desriel and

Serath. We've already spoken with them. It's our intention to join your little expedition.'

'It was *my* intention,' the warden said irritably. 'You decided to tag along.'

'They made it clear they needed an archer,' the sentinel replied. 'Who better to watch your back than I, eh?'

'There are better archers,' the warden said flatly.

'And better lancers,' the sentinel retorted. 'Yet here we are.'

Ferendir was amazed. Even though their words seemed argumentative, their demeanours remained cool and unruffled. They seemed to be having a quiet, easy discussion, not a disagreement.

'Excuse me,' Ferendir said. 'So… you've met my masters, and you're part of the expedition?'

They both stared at him, as though he'd only now arrived to a supper that began an hour earlier.

'Did I not say that?' the warden asked.

'You did, indeed, say that,' the sentinel replied.

Ferendir found a small boulder nearby, half buried in the earth, and sat upon it. 'You could have told me that from the start,' he said. 'I would have… welcomed you.'

'You have welcomed us,' the warden said, shrugging. 'I'm Phalcea. This is Metorrah.'

'You're sisters,' Ferendir said. 'Twins.'

'In point of fact,' Metorrah said, 'we are the same person in two bodies. Our people sometimes call this process "twinning", but it's more akin to the creation of an exact duplicate from a mould.'

'The same person…' Ferendir said, staring at the two of them.

'Not so uncommon in Iliatha – where we're from,' Phalcea said.

'If you're from Iliatha, what are you doing here in Ymetrica?'

'The Windstrider sent word to all the Paradises when the Slaaneshi scourge appeared here, in Ymetrica,' Metorrah said. 'Many answered the call – the two of us among them.'

'These others who answered the call... are they twins as well?'

Phalcea and Metorrah looked to one another. Shrugged. Phalcea answered.

'Some,' she said. 'But not all. Our elder sagas speak of our greatest mages in past eras creating whole armies of such copies, living several lives simultaneously and switching places from time to time, just to confuse and confound those in their social circles who had not undergone the same process.'

Ferendir could not believe his ears. 'Lumineth, copying themselves?' he asked. 'I've never heard of anything more bizarre.'

'Or fraught with temptation,' Metorrah said. 'Terrible things were born of such profligate replication. It's a practice strictly forbidden at present. Now, only a single copy of any individual soul is allowed.'

'So,' Ferendir said, 'you're identical in every way?'

'We begin that way,' Phalcea said. 'But we soon grow more distinct. The only thing that makes a person a person – an individual – is their experience. And since two people cannot have precisely the same experience under precisely the same circumstances at precisely the same instant – because you can never occupy precisely the same space at the same moment in time – then the ultimate result of one body split into two is that even though we start as the same organism with the same mind and soul, we soon become separate and distinct entities.'

'Who look alike in every way,' Metorrah added.

'Miraculous,' Ferendir said, studying the two of them. He wondered if they were to dress in the same clothes it really would be impossible to tell them apart.

'And what about you, Alarith?' Phalcea asked. 'Have you a name?'

'Ferendir.'

'And have you a story?' Metorrah asked.

Ferendir shrugged. 'I have no story. I am a supplicant – a Stoneguard in training. Yesterday was to be my final trial – my submission to the will of the mountain. But all of this...' He trailed off, indicating the camp around them and the reason that they all found themselves there.

'So you're an orphan?' Metorrah asked.

'Not precisely,' Ferendir said. 'My mother gave me to the temple many years ago, when I was small. I have no ken where she might be now. I have my masters, though. I've lived there since the day she delivered me to them, growing, learning, carving out my path to serve the Stoneguard under the watchful eyes of my teachers.'

'So,' Phalcea said, 'you are not a warrior, you are not a priest, and you are not even a ranking member of the Stoneguard? Are you only a servant to those two others and nothing more?'

'I am not just a servant,' Ferendir said, perhaps too harshly. 'Did you not hear me? I've spent most of my life training to be a member of the Stoneguard. I can fight as well as any soldier in the host–'

'But you are untried,' Metorrah said.

'Uninitiated,' Phalcea added.

Ferendir was about to argue when he suddenly realised that she was perfectly correct. He *was* untried. He had *not yet* been initiated. He might possess a number of skills, have absorbed a great deal of training, be capable of a great many things... but he was, by all practical definitions, a non-entity. Half-formed and insubstantial, like bread that had not finished baking.

'I am willing,' he finally said. 'I should think that is all that matters.'

'I think we offended him,' Metorrah whispered to Phalcea.

'I think *you* offended him,' Phalcea said.

'I simply asked a question,' Metorrah responded. 'Why should he take offence at a simple question?'

'I took no offence,' Ferendir said, suddenly irritated by their verbal sparring. He lowered his eyes to the fire. 'I simply realised... you were right. That realisation makes me feel... less.'

'Less what?' Metorrah asked.

'Simply *less*,' Phalcea offered.

Ferendir raised his eyes and studied her. The warden met his gaze, and she seemed to understand. Though silence persisted between them, Ferendir knew that what he was feeling was clear and evident to her. Finally, he nodded.

'Precisely,' he said.

'Phalcea knows just how you feel,' Metorrah said, 'as she is the copy and I am the original.'

'You were a first attempt,' Phalcea said without a hint of rancour. 'I was a blessed improvement.'

Ferendir smiled a little in spite of himself. So strange, these two – one soul in two bodies, matched and inextricably linked yet constantly chasing one another in circles, fighting and competing, however playfully. There was a truth to be learned in that, he suddenly felt, something meaningful and insightful. But at that moment, he could not discover it, for his own feeling of inadequacy weighed too heavily upon his heart and mind.

A form caught his eye, someone standing straight and tall just beyond the flickering light of their cookfires. Instantly alarmed and intrigued by the strange figure, Ferendir shot to his feet and studied the newcomer. Metorrah and Phalcea followed his gaze and assessed the new arrival as well.

He wore bronze plate covered in finely etched, graceful runes over deep maroon robes. There was a shield slung across his back, a sword sheathed at one hip and an elegantly styled helm cradled in the crook of one arm – also bronze, with a fore-facing fan crest of horsehair bleached to a pale blue and tipped in a rich red that matched his robes. Upon the helm, his breastplate, his gauntlets and grieves, the same beautiful lunar symbols were in evidence. Only after his initial impression was drawn did Ferendir realise the engravings upon the breastplate were stylised images of the archmage Teclis and the incarnate moon, Celennar.

Ferendir forced himself to stop admiring the newcomer's armour and studied his face – narrow, sharply sculpted, with almost feline eyes of a pale, near-silver grey and soft, half-smiling lips. Atop his head was a mop of steel-grey hair that hung just below his pointed chin.

Strange, Ferendir thought. *His face is quite young – almost child-like – while his grey locks and pale, haunting eyes make him look quite old.*

Ferendir stared. Metorrah and Phalcea stared. The newcomer stared back. Silence persisted.

'Can I help you?' Ferendir finally asked.

The newcomer stared. His head cocked a little to the side, as though he were weighing the many possible responses he could offer. Finally, he gave one.

'No,' he said. Then he marched forward, laid down his helmet, unslung his shield and sank to the ground, folding his legs beneath him. Sitting thusly, he stared into the fire and interlaced his hands in his lap.

'The Alarith asked you a question,' Phalcea said.

The newcomer raised his eyes to her, almost surprised to find her there.

'Did I not answer it?' he asked.

'You did,' Ferendir said. 'With a single word.'

The newcomer cocked his head again. 'Why use more than the single word required?'

'Have you a name, then?' Metorrah asked.

The newcomer nodded. 'I do.'

They waited. He did not offer it.

Ferendir stepped forward. 'And your name is…?'

'My sincere apologies,' the stranger said. 'I was lost in thought, contemplating all that is to come and what strange, separate destinies have led us, each and all, to this very place. *Here.* Upon *this* plain. Beneath *this* mountain. Beside *this* fire.' He shook his head in silent wonder. 'What a tapestry is woven of both incidents and exigencies!'

Ferendir looked to Metorrah and Phalcea. The twins each shook their heads. He looked back to the enigmatic new arrival.

'Stranger,' Ferendir said, doing his best to sound patient and accommodating, 'may I ask your name and your place of origin?'

'There,' the fellow said. 'Was that so hard?'

'No harder than a straight answer, apparently,' Metorrah said.

'I,' the stranger carried on, 'am called Luverion. I hail from Zaitrec, but my travels have taken me... well, they've taken me everywhere.'

'Including to *this* plain,' Phalcea mimicked, 'beneath *this* mountain, beside *this* fire.'

The Zaitreci actually smiled a little – not irritated at all, so far as Ferendir could see, but genuinely delighted by Phalcea's humour at his expense.

'Just so!' he said.

'Who sent you?' Ferendir asked.

'Your masters,' Luverion said. 'Celennar whispered to me, in my evening meditation, that they would have need of me, and so I went in search of them. Lo and behold, I found them in search of me. As I said, incidents and exigencies. The random and the requisite, colliding. It shall be my great honour to know you, Ferendir – and you, daughters of Iliatha – in our brief time together.'

'I see you found our camp handily,' a voice said.

Ferendir turned. There stood his masters – Desriel and Serath, finally returned – and they were not alone. With them was yet another aelf – yet another addition to their party – and this fellow was most impressive.

He was taller than any of them – though he only outdid Serath by a few finger-widths – and his shoulders, his entire frame, was broad and strong, closer to muscular human dimensions than the lithe, willowy form of most aelves. He wore iridescent white armour chased with gold over deep purple robes, but it was neither the pearlescent finish of his armour nor the rich colour of his silks that was most impressive. It was, instead, the great quantity of aetherquartz encrusting his armour and clothing from head to toe. The tall, strong warrior positively shone in the twilit night. Everything about him, from his square-shouldered stance to the great, heavy shield in his hands to the bejewelled blade sheathed at his side to the mid-length elegant spear strapped across his broad shoulders, marked him as a warrior through and through – nay, not just a warrior, but a champion. A paragon of strength, courage and virtue.

But there was something else about him, wasn't there? Something else in his square-jawed, powerfully sculpted face and deep brown eyes that made itself evident – even without words – to the perceptive Ferendir. The young aelf simply could not articulate what that inexpressible quality might be.

'Greetings to you all,' the shining champion said. 'For this realm's sake, and your own, you were fortunate to find me before the enemy drew me away.'

Ah, yes. Now Ferendir could name that strange, inexpressible quality he had sensed in the newcomer – it was arrogance.

'This is your squire?' the big aelf asked, stepping towards Ferendir and offering his shield. 'See to that, boy. My hands must be free before I can eat.'

'He is not a squire, but a supplicant,' Desriel said. 'A Stoneguard in training, you might say.'

'That will do,' the champion said, and lifted off his helmet, which he also thrust into Ferendir's grasp. 'Polish those, if you have a moment. The battle today left them horribly soiled.'

'Ferendir,' Serath said. 'This is Taurvalon, born of Syar and eager to join our retinue.'

'The lady regent told me this mission of yours is cloaked in secrecy but steeped in future glory – providing it succeeds. By my blood, by my blade, by my bare hands, I pledge – so long as I live, it shall succeed.'

Ferendir could not quite tell if the Syari champion's self-assurance was a sign of simple confidence or self-importance. Ultimately, he decided to trust his masters' judgement and try to forgive the great fighter a little pride.

Ferendir's study of the newcomer was suddenly interrupted when he noted that Serath was eyeing the half-orderly array of provisions and supplies still strewn about on a large blanket beside the fire, evidence that Ferendir's packing for the journey still had not been completed. His master raised his eyes. His glaring gaze probed into Ferendir and forced him to lower his own eyes in shame.

'You have still not completed the tasks given you?' Serath asked.

Ferendir shook his head. 'No, master. Nearly, though.'

'We interrupted him,' Metorrah offered.

'Blame us,' Phalcea added cheerily. 'It's all our fault.'

'No one can be distracted from a task they are dedicated to completing,' Serath said darkly.

'This will do,' Desriel said. 'It looks as though he's packed these three satchels handily. What remains unpacked can be distributed among the rest of our companions.'

Phalcea and Metorrah rose and introduced themselves.

As his masters and their newly acquired companions all greeted one another, Ferendir stood by, quietly studying them. He could not believe he was in such company: an Iliathan soul twinned into two bodies; a Zaitreci mystic capable of bending reality itself to his will; a Syari champion encrusted with enough aetherquartz to split a mountain in two; and his masters, proven, deadly members of the

Alarith Stoneguard, the very best warriors and the most powerful Stoneguard Ferendir had ever known.

All of these superlative, powerful champions, drawn together to undertake a great quest to save the realm... and he, a no one, trailing alone behind them.

The rest of the evening was a blur. His masters and their companions gathered round the fire and conferred regarding all that was known about the aelemental entity Kaethraxis, the aetherquartz Eidolith and the capabilities and twisted desires of their sworn enemy, Ezarhad Fatesbane. Plans were made regarding the path to be taken into the mountains and the pace they must maintain. After a time, their pointed planning devolved into easy conversation, the champions conferring and comparing experiences, measuring their prowess, each against the other, and telling stories of their travels and personal knowledge.

Throughout, Ferendir saw to his tasks. He finished packing his and his masters' provisions and supplies, oiled and sharpened all their weapons, then distributed the remaining provisions to the packs for their new companions. By the time the dimly lit Hyshian night was fully upon them, all was ready and the conversations were dying down.

'We should retire,' Serath said. 'Sleep for just a few hours, then set out well before dawn.'

All agreed. As everyone withdrew and prepared their bedrolls, Desriel pulled Ferendir aside.

'You have done well tonight. I thank you, supplicant, for all your honest service and hard labour to support us. You are indispensable.'

Ferendir stared into his master's eyes, overcome with gratitude. 'I only seek to be so, master. If I have failed in any way–'

'Never,' Desriel said. 'Let Serath's severity not trouble you. He wants what is best for you, and he appreciates you just as deeply as I do. He is simply less inclined to express it.'

'I have only one desire,' Ferendir said. 'It is to prove to you, before this journey ends, that I am worthy of being your peer and not simply your student. It is to be proven by experience, if not by trial.'

Desriel studied him. His gaze was focused, penetrating. He seemed on the edge of saying something. Finally, though, he only smiled a little and patted Ferendir's shoulder.

'You are worthy, Ferendir,' he said at last. 'Your time of trial will come, as will a long and glorious career as a Stoneguard.'

Ferendir thought his heart would burst. He knew that to give in to sentimentality and the sense of accomplishment he now felt would be foolish, even childish, but he greatly wished he could do so. Desriel's words of encouragement meant everything to him in that instant.

He only wished he could have heard the same from Serath.

'Get some sleep now,' Desriel said. 'We depart well before the light returns.'

Ferendir did as he was told. He found a ready-made place a short distance from the fire and nestled into his bedroll, trying to imagine all of the trials and tribulations that lay ahead of them. This quest they undertook, this enemy they were determined to run down and foil – it was all quite perilous. He soberly reminded himself that it was possible – perhaps even likely – that some or all of them might not survive this expedition.

Ferendir himself could die… die in battle, under enemy knives, before ever having passed his trial beneath the mountain.

Then I'll die, he thought, *and I'll do so bravely, without hesitation or fear. Let that be my trial… my initiation.*

He closed his eyes. Dreamless sleep took him.

He did not wake again until the first light of dawn had begun to seep back into the twilit world.

The fire was dead, nothing but grey, smouldering embers.

To his great horror, his masters and their companions were gone, and they had taken their packs and provisions with them.

CHAPTER SIX

Ferendir fought mightily to contain a sense of panic. All manner of thoughts and fears rushed through his mind as he searched their little camp for signs of what had happened. He had been completely, utterly abandoned. One pack stuffed full of provisions and supplies had been left, right beside the bedroll where Ferendir slept, as had the diamondpick hammer that he'd carried since leaving the ruins of their temple, but there was no note, no sign left as a coded signal, no indication of where his party had gone or why they had left him behind.

In moments, having gathered the pack, the bedroll and the pick hammer, Ferendir abandoned the little camp and went darting among the tents and pavilions of the Lumineth warhost in search of some sign of his vanished party. Maybe they had only left recently? Perhaps he could catch up with them? Perhaps they were not yet even beyond the edge of camp and well under way? There had to be an explanation, a reason for all this.

But soon enough, lost amid the maze of tents, pavilions, cookfires and portable armouries busy with the repair and polishing of weapons and armour, he realised that he had no idea where to begin. He knew they would be heading east-north-east, back into the mountains, to take up the track of Ezarhad Fatesbane's own small party as they climbed into the more remote reaches of the range in search of the place where this Kaethraxis slept. But knowing only a direction helped him not at all. There were a thousand possible tracks they could be taking, and finding the right one and following it might be close to impossible.

They were Lumineth, after all. They would travel swift and light, and they would take great pains not to leave any sign in their wake lest they be followed by someone – or something – that they did not want following them.

Or him.

'Are you lost, supplicant?' a vaguely familiar voice said.

Ferendir turned. It was the grim-faced seneschal of the Alarith battalion, the ropy, heartily sculpted aelf with sun-darkened skin and dark hair woven into a series of small, tight braids. Seeing that one even half-familiar face emerging from the bustling crowds filled Ferendir with a palpable sense of relief. He ran to the seneschal, doing his best to control his probably apparent panic and confusion.

'I seem to have misplaced my party,' Ferendir said.

'No, boy… they left you.'

Ferendir felt his next breath catch in his throat. All at once, he could not breathe.

'Left me,' he said, thankful that the repetition did not come out as a fool's question.

'Your master – the hard-faced one – told me to give you this.'

He handed Ferendir a small, tightly rolled bit of parchment, tied with twine. Ferendir hastily untied the little scrap and unrolled it. The words upon it were written in Serath's familiar cramped hand, the runes and syllabic signs formed with tight, austere elegance.

This is no insult to your capabilities, it said, *but an affirmation of the danger we face, a danger so ardent and perilous we cannot place you in its path in good conscience. Go with this good seneschal. Let the Alarith of his temple to the north complete your training and see you through your final trial. They have already agreed to take you in.*

You have served us well, Ferendir. Go, now, and live the life you were meant to.

Ferendir felt the sting of tears and fought them back. He would *not* give in. He would *not* relent…

'No,' he said quietly.

'He and the other one warned me this might hit you hard,' the seneschal said. 'If it helps, boy, they were clearly only worried about your safety.'

'I am *their* servant!' Ferendir growled through gnashed teeth. '*Their* supplicant! It is their task – *their duty* – to teach me and help me take my place among them!'

'Easy, boy,' the seneschal said softly. 'I understand how you feel, but this is not the way. You should do as your masters asked.'

'I will not,' Ferendir said. 'Show me which way they went.'

The seneschal stared at him. He appeared to be studying Ferendir, carefully appraising just how determined the young aelf was to disobey the orders given him. After a time, the scout cocked his head a little.

'I cannot help you,' he said. 'I have duties of my own here.'

'Just point me in the right direction,' Ferendir said.

The seneschal shook his head. 'It's more complicated than that, and you know it. The path they took skirts the Slaaneshi horde's own camp in the foothills. If you're not careful, you might be caught in transit–'

'I don't care,' Ferendir said forcefully. 'Tell me or don't tell me, help me or don't help me – I'm going either way.'

'Just listen. Wait–'

'I have no time to wait,' Ferendir said, then turned and stalked away from the Alarith seneschal. He was not even sure he was headed in the right direction – he had not oriented himself – but that did not matter. He would get away from this fool, from this moment of humiliation, from this blasted warhost, and reorient himself when he was on the edge of the camp, away from all prying eyes and judgements.

'Stop!' the seneschal shouted.

Ferendir stopped. Turned. He glared, making his impatience clear, all but daring the scout to stop him.

'I have something for you,' the seneschal said. He was not angry. In fact, his normally hard face showed immeasurable patience. 'Just… wait.'

He turned and jogged away. Ferendir half wondered if the aelf might return, moments later, with a large group of his armed companions, ready to drag Ferendir back to their camp and tie him up for a short span, to encourage him to give up on his foolish quest. He supposed the seneschal might be inclined to do something that drastic… but he doubted it. He was a total stranger, after all – what did he care if Ferendir chose to get himself killed running off after his masters and their party?

A short time later, the seneschal returned. He was carrying something small, smooth and shiny. It was barely as big as the palm of one hand and trailed with it a long, light, silver chain.

'This is a geomantic compass,' he said, placing the small, beautifully tooled object in Ferendir's waiting hand.

Ferendir studied it. It was elegant and finely crafted, a thing of rare yet simple beauty – a drifting needle above a round face under a dome of perfectly clear polished crystal. It was a fine gift, and its presentation made Ferendir feel suddenly childish and rude for daring to speak to the scout in such a bullish tone.

'That's very kind of you,' Ferendir said, 'but I can orient myself to the cardinal directions. It's one of the most basic skills required of temple supplicants.'

'This doesn't read cardinal directions,' the seneschal said. 'It follows specific magical markers to guide you on a path laid out by someone who has already walked it. My own Stoneguard left a trail of subtle geomantic markings in the stones and trees of the path along which Ezarhad Fatesbane and his company marched. Your masters will be following that same path. This will help you to find it and stay upon it.'

Ferendir raised his eyes to the seneschal. He could barely believe what he had just been handed.

'I cannot,' he said. 'This is too valuable to you, too precious.'

'Take it,' the seneschal said. 'You need it far more than we do.'

Ferendir wanted to find the perfect words to express his gratitude. Strangely, he could find none.

'I shall never forget this,' he said.

The seneschal managed a very slight smile. 'Just do me one favour, boy.'

Ferendir nodded. 'Anything.'

'Don't tell your masters I gave you that... and try not to get yourself killed.'

The geomantic compass led him out of camp and across the plain, north-east towards the hump-backed forms of the hills huddled at the foot of the mountains. Ferendir knew that those hills and the tree-lined hollows between them hid the roiling hosts of Chaos, the children of Slaanesh, probably even now spoiling for a fight and preparing to swarm forth again in search of bloodletting and fury against the Vanari host camped on the plain. In an effort to remain cautious, Ferendir drifted as far as he could from the forested hills that hid so much danger, keeping instead to the open, rolling hillsides hugging one of the mountain's lower shoulders that loomed on his left as he approached. Open country would expose him, true, but it would also afford him a greater measure of security – without heavy tree or brush cover, he could see anyone or anything approaching from a great distance in all directions. This forced him to leave the path prescribed by the compass, but what of it? He decided that he could remain just off that track for a very long time, until he finally drew closer to the source of the geomantic seal left behind by the earlier scout party. He would not make straight for the marker until he was as close to it as he could be.

To his great amazement, he found evidence along the meandering track he took indicating that his masters and their party had passed that way many, many hours previously. The signs were subtle – a few light aelven footprints in slightly damp mud and some stray crumbs of bread beside a boulder – but they were sufficient to give Ferendir a real sense of accomplishment. He was not only tracking, but employing the same logic that they had in tracking the magical markers while still giving the regions held by their enemies a very wide berth.

He found the first marker at midday, when the sun was at its most brilliant – and most punishing. It was a stone, rounded on its topside, more or less smooth underneath, lying amid a bed of hundreds of others that looked just like it. When he lifted the stone and turned it over, however, he found a painted magical seal – fresh and dark – that could only have been left behind for a specific purpose. Moreover, once he had located the seal and held the compass close to it, the compass needle immediately spun crazily then locked onto another course, some distance ahead, deeper into the mountains. It was as if the needle recognised that one marker had been arrived at, and instantly sought the next closest marker of the same sort. He idly wondered if his masters had been given such a device or if, instead, they had simply attuned themselves to the magical energies of the markers using their own natural, well-honed magical abilities. Ferendir himself knew a number of simple cantrips and light enchantments – all the supplicants of the temple were taught such things – but true magical insight and ability was one of the arts, and gifts, of the vested Stoneguard of the temple. Whereas Ferendir had to use an enchanted device to follow these markers, his masters, no doubt, could simply attune themselves and track the energies radiating from them accordingly.

More than once through the day, Ferendir would imagine he saw movement at the periphery of his vision and scan the rolling horizon on all sides in search of what he'd suspected he'd seen. He would stand, stone-still and silent, gripping the pick hammer his masters had left for him, waiting, waiting, waiting, terrified that at any moment a whole phalanx of ravening, blood-hungry Slaaneshi Hedonites would come charging over the nearest hillside, right towards him, eager to tear him to pieces.

But they never came. All of those fleeting forms he thought he saw at the edge of his vision, all the shadows he imagined, proved to be nothing more than ghosts haunting his imagination. The day wore on, and Ferendir advanced beyond the hills into the lower slopes of the mountains, eventually finding the second marker left by the scouts.

And never once did he face imminent danger or see a sign of their enemies.

Eventually, the open, rolling hills gave way to forest, sparse at first but gradually thickening and darkening until at last he was moving through canopied woodland alive with the song of birds, the scrabble of tiny claws and the burble of swift streams rushing over polished stones from the mountain above. Once the forest began to dominate, the landscape became more uneven and unpredictable, frequently climbing at steep angles for great distances before levelling out or gently rolling again for a time. While woodland dominated, there yet remained a number of empty swathes and mountain meadows, and Ferendir was surprised to find that, after a long first half of his day traipsing through open country and counting the open space as his ally – a means of protecting himself – his mind had already accepted the blessed cover and protective screening of the forest, so that when he now came upon open hillside, he preferred to stay secreted in the woods, skirting the meadows and bald hillside on their canopied periphery when possible.

He had found one more marker and was searching for the fourth when the bright blue sky began to darken, suddenly gloomy with gathering clouds, all pendulous and pregnant with rain. For a long time, he heard the promise of storms in the distance, gathering thunder and the occasional savage arc of lightning, but the rains did not come. Nonetheless, Ferendir could smell them – the promise of it in the crisp mountain air. He knew they would soon burst forth and deluge the world around him. He did not relish that thought, because movement over uneven ground – especially when one was struggling uphill – was never gentled by a storm. With luck, he hoped to find the fourth marker before the skies opened.

His luck did not hold.

He had no ken how far he might be from the fourth marker, but the skies suddenly split and a downpour assailed the mountainside. In moments, Ferendir was soaked. Worse, he could readily see runnels and rivulets of mud rushing down the slope. Soon, he'd be sinking into muddied soil and risk slipping every time he sought a solid foothold. He could go no further. It was time to shelter until the rain stopped. If night fell before the storm abated, he wagered he'd be stuck where he was until morning.

He cast about, looking for some ready place to protect himself. There were no rocky overhangs or signs of a cave nearby, so that meant his only hope for shelter was heavy underbrush at the foot of a strong, shaggy tree that would create a good canopy. Ferendir searched his environs for a time before finally opting for a copse of fern beneath several tall, thickly boughed spruce trees. Wedging himself deep against the slope under the fronds, he found the worst of the pounding rains fettered by the many layers of tree and brush above him. As added proof against the downpour, he wrapped himself tightly in his travelling cloak and sat, huddled and miserable, in the vain hope that the storm now lashing the mountainside would soon blow onwards and leave him behind.

It did not.

Ferendir sat there for what felt like hours, the rain alternately pattering and pounding the forest around him. More than once, he had to shift to the right or left, forward or back, as thin runnels formed themselves in the damp, loamy soil and suddenly swelled to downhill drainage that threatened to half submerge him. Clearly there was a lot of loose soil and rock on this face of the mountain – perfect conditions for a mud- or rockslide.

That gave him no sense of security.

He was contemplating emerging from his barely dry hiding place to carry on in search of a better refuge when he first heard the voices. They were rough, strange and distant, but with each passing moment they grew closer and closer, growing louder and more distinct even as the pattering, insistent sound of the rain beating the forest canopy filled the world around him.

'...telling you, I smelled it, before these infernal rains began! Aelven blood, I'd swear it!'

'Feel it!' another said, exultant and joyful. 'Feel how it smashes down upon your flesh, how it washes over and through you! Silky, soft, wet, sweet and cool...'

'Bah!' another growled. 'Stop preening, you fool! It's only rain!'

Ferendir tried to move in his hiding place. He sought some ready break in the foliage that would allow him a glimpse of who, or what, might be approaching. After a great deal of subtle movement and uncomfortable craning of his neck, he finally found a narrow gap in the fronds that gave an oblique angle laterally down the slope he'd been climbing. Out in the gloomy forest, under the falling rain, he saw several loping, sidling forms moving nearer. Their clothes were a colourful motley, both bright and ruined, bedecked with hundreds of small golden rings and inset jewels. What little he could see of their skins, when they were exposed, suggested pallid, sickly sorts, one a pale, livid pink, another a sickly, bruised purple.

He saw no faces – there was too much scrub in the way. But as the figures struggled to mount the slope and climb higher, he did see that one of them had four arms protruding from its torso, while another, in place of what should have been a hand, sported a long, toothy pincer similar to what one might find on a crab.

Ferendir's heart began to beat hard and insistently.

The servants of Slaanesh had found him!

Worse, with each passing moment, they were coming closer.

Ferendir struggled to keep his breathing even, to stay silent. He could not see with any clarity just how many of them there were, but he was sure there were too many and he knew he'd be outmatched. He could stand against two with some measure of confidence and courage – he'd been trained well, after all, and had always been handy with the pick hammer or a blunt instrument. But he also knew when brave became foolhardy. Three or more of those monsters were most definitely a match for him. He would not last long against so many.

His only hope, then, was to slip away... but there was no cover to be had on the hillside. Once he broke from where he now hid in the shadows under these enormous ferns, he'd be exposed, endangered. His sole advantage was that he was farther up the slope than they, and would, perhaps, be able to give himself a great head start. If he could climb fast, reach some level ground or a strand of denser forest, he might be able to evade them.

Outside, one of the Hedonites slipped, hit the ground face first and cursed.

'Accursed rain!' it barked. 'Accursed mud!'

The others laughed cruelly at their fallen comrade, braying and guffawing at his misstep and fall.

Ferendir blinked, peering out through the dripping fronds. He could see the fallen creature, now splashing about in a runnel of mud and trying to rise again while his companions continued to mock him.

Something shifted beneath him. Ferendir looked down. The shallow depression he was crouching in seemed to be washing away, swift-moving sheets of rainwater sluicing down the hillside and carrying soil and silt with them at an ever more rapid rate. Already his boots were ankle-deep in the cascade.

Teclis! If he did not move soon, he'd be washed out of his hiding place in a sudden glut of mud and rainwater!

He heard a shout, a snarl, a grunt. The fallen Hedonite had launched itself up out of the mud at its closest comrade. The two were now rolling about in the mud and rain, thrusting and punching and slashing, growling and cursing at one another as they brawled. Clearly, that one would not countenance being laughed at.

A few of the Hedonites had run forward at the instant of their collision and now stood in a rough circle around the fighting pair, cheering and exhorting them on. There seemed to be no champion, no favoured combatant – they simply wanted to see blood and ruin. Their tight formation made it far easier for Ferendir to see each individual and count them.

Seven.

Shade of Ulgu… those were terrible odds.

But they were distracted. Now might be his moment…

'Get up, the both of you!' one of the vile creatures shouted. The voice sounded vaguely female, but Ferendir could not be sure.

Hedonites were such twisted, debauched things that distinctions like gender or age or even their race before the onset of their transformations failed to translate into whatever they became once fully tainted by the powers of Chaos.

Now, he thought. *Run. This is your moment.*

He turned, scurried quickly out of the opposite side of the clump of ferns that sheltered him and scrambled for a foothold against the sloping, mud-streaked side of the mountain. He got a false start, his feet wheeling and sliding for a moment in the muck, then finally managed to establish a foothold against a stone bared by the eroding hillside and pushed hard. Off he went, bounding up the slope as fast as he could, never once daring to look back.

He had progressed a good distance, a stone's throw, at least, before he heard the first of them call out.

'There! I told you! One of those accursed Lumineth!'

'Up, you fools!' the Hedonite cried again, apparently addressing the two pugilists on the ground. 'After him!'

Ferendir kept pushing up the hill. There was so much rain, so many looming trees, so many shadows and pockets of glare punching through the canopy above and ahead. As he struggled, still sprinting up the incline, he listened, desperate to have some sense of how far behind him his enemies might be and how fast they were closing, without actually daring to slow himself down by turning to look back. He heard their heavy, irregular footfalls, their cackles and shrieks of delight. They were after him now, moving fast, closing the uphill distance between them with unnatural speed and stamina.

Ferendir tripped, a thick stream of flowing mud washing the soil he clung to right out from under him. He hit the hillside, began to slide, but caught himself between a half-buried rock and a protruding tree root. His slide arrested, he heaved up his body and immediately leapt sideways, climbing along a different track some distance from the treacherous run-off.

He dared a glance backwards, over his left shoulder. One of his pursuers was all but dancing up the hillside, moving swiftly in a strange, crab-like gait back and forth over the incline, making unpleasantly rapid advances on Ferendir's trail. Ferendir did not linger on the sight – he saw only insectile legs, crustacean-like claws and a bobbing, arching scorpion tail – but forced himself to move faster, all but leaping from one protruding knob of rock to another in a desperate effort to put as much distance between his pursuers and himself as possible.

One of them suddenly cursed, and Ferendir heard the hoarse voice receding.

'Get back up here!'

Another casualty of the sheeting mud and rainwater. Having lost its footing, it tumbled backwards down the hillside. Good. That was one less on his trail.

Ferendir stared ahead. Some short distance above him, the semi-steep slope seemed to roll over a ledge. That meant there might be level ground beyond that precipice! If Ferendir could just reach it, he was sure he could pour on more speed and better evade these monsters. If he could just make it up the slope of the mountain-side, a little farther, just a little farther...

Then he heard something. It was a strange sound, rumbling and aelemental, as if the mountain itself were roaring its disapproval of their lethal play, the shattering of its sanctified alpine silence. The strange sound – growing louder, rushing nearer with each passing instant – forced Ferendir to slow his advance for one brief instant, just to search the way before him, the slope above him, to find the source of that terrible sound.

And there it was, sheeting down over the ledge above, blotting out the forest canopy and the choked gobbets of sky in his field of vision, arcing precipitously through the empty air before rushing right down towards him.

It was the mountain… or, at any rate, a large portion of it, torn away by the rainwater and sent hurtling down the incline, borne by liquid force and the inexorability of gravity. A massive portion of the slope seemed to have sheared away and liquefied, and its brown, viscous immensity was now rolling down the slope towards Ferendir.

'Back!' he heard from his pursuers. 'Back, I say!'

Shouts. Curses. Screams.

Ferendir saw nowhere to run, nowhere to shelter. The mudslide was moving too swiftly. Down, down, down it came, filling his field of vision.

Better than by Hedonite hands, he thought briefly.

Then that massive wall of mud and liquefied regolith and shattered stone slammed into him, enfolded him, and a darkness deeper and surer than any he'd ever known swallowed him in an instant.

The world was cold. The world was warm. The world was dark. The world was still and airless.

Ferendir tried to move and could not. Tried to determine which way was up, and failed. Tried to open his eyes but saw only darkness. He was immobilised, blind and deaf, yet he was still, somehow, aware. Alive.

But for how long? he wondered idly. He tried to draw a breath, got only a mouthful of mud. Choked. But even his choking was arrested – it seemed that, like some unlucky insect on a tree trunk, he had been encased in something quick and sticky and all-encompassing. He was literally buried, with no ken of how to dig himself out or which direction to even dig in.

Perhaps this is best, he thought, trying to control the panic now setting in. *My world is shattered – destroyed. Why should I not be a casualty as well? Was I ever so special? So unique that I, alone, should persist when so many others perished?*

He desperately wanted to breathe, but could not. His lungs burned. His mind was starting to swirl, to seemingly grow swollen and feverish inside his skull. He felt his body, unbidden, wholly by instinct, struggling in the mud, seeking some means of extricating itself, locating air, gulping it down in ragged, desperate draughts.

Stop! he thought. *Stop it! Surrender!*

His body still jerked and convulsed.

Stop, he thought again, more softly this time. *Meet your end with some dignity, supplicant… some courage.*

The twitching began to subside – from his conscious will or from the simple impossibility of movement, he could not say. The mud encasing him seemed cool and soft against his skin, damp, but not unpleasantly so. The silence, as well, was quite welcome. A blessed absence… a sanctified abyss for his senses. A place of calm. A place of endings.

I only sought to be of use, he thought, feeling his consciousness drifting now. *I only sought to serve. Perhaps this is the end I always deserved… the end always meant for me.*

I never even undertook my trial, after all. Would it have been so different from this? Buried alive? Fighting the urge to panic and thrash at the end? Seeking the mountain's will? The mountain's peace?

An impulse moved him, somewhere in the murky depths of his slowly contracting, slowly shrinking consciousness.

Seek it now, that still, small voice said.

Seek what?

Seek the mountain's will, it said, the suggestion so casually offered as to sound almost like an afterthought. *You are here, now, at your end, wrapped in the mountain's aelemental embrace. Seek its will. Seek its consciousness. Seek its truth. You will never be nearer to it… never be more attuned.*

And it won't be long now, will it?

Die clinging to the mountain, folding yourself into its embrace, like a babe falling asleep in its mother's loving arms.

Ferendir sought the mountain. He sought some sense of it, some vague, sensory indication of its nearness. To his great amazement, he realised that he need not reach out for it at all. The spirit already encircled him, enfolded him – had consumed him, in fact.

It was not beside him, or near him, or adjacent to him. It was everywhere. It was the mud around him. It was the earth beneath him. It was the soaring trees and the rain-drenched ferns and the rocks and the pebbles and the sedge and the wildflowers. It was the immovable, stony immensity beneath him and the rushing rain-water that skated along its inclined surfaces seeking low ground.

He need not seek it… He was already part of it.

Forgive me, he thought, suddenly realising how great and powerful that abiding, eternal force truly was, and how small and useless he seemed in its presence. *Forgive my ignorance, Mother Mountain. Forgive my failure to see, to truly understand.*

Then, a voice not his own.

There is nothing to forgive.

Ferendir felt a strange sense of both wonder and humiliation in the same instant. That was no voice from his mind. That was the mountain! The great spirit itself! The mountain had addressed him!

Mother, he thought miserably, *I failed.*

You fell, the mountain said. *You have not failed. Not yet.*

Ferendir balked. *Of course I have! Unworthy of my masters! Unworthy of your trust! Incapable of survival in the wild!*

You have not failed, she said again. *Not yet.*

But this is the end, Ferendir said. *I am about to die.*

You should have died already. Why have you not?

Ferendir waited. Gnawed on those words. Batted them around in the dim recesses of his mind and heart. That was true – his air should have already expired. Why hadn't he died? Or was this death?

No. There was air. He drew it in through his nose, blew it out through his mouth. It was close, scant and stale, but it was present. Air, for him to breathe.

Breath... a gift from the mountain.

Mother, he thought, his heart suddenly pounding under the influence of a new motivator – not panic, not fear, not despair... hope.

There was hope.

He breathed. Rather, the mountain breathed for him.

It cannot be, Ferendir thought. *I never passed my trial – never proved my worth!*

Your worth is proven, the mountain said softly, *beyond all doubt. The honour I have now bestowed upon you can never be taken away.*

That was his mother's voice.

Mother?

You are found worthy, Ferendir, that still, small voice said. *You will endure... if you believe you can. Now, go.*

Go?

Go, she said again, firm but still soft, still loving. *Move your right hand. The soil is loose. It will part before you as you climb out.*

He did as he was told. His right hand moved, ever so slightly, sweeping mud and soil aside as it did so. He thought he felt the barest tickle – the smallest suggestion – of dry, open air on one of his knuckles.

Go, she said. *Before I change my mind.*

Ferendir obeyed. In moments, he was clawing his way towards what he hoped to be the open air and the cloudy sky.

His hands broke the surface long before his head ever did.

Miraculously, there were hands waiting to take his own and draw him out.

* * *

The first breath Ferendir drew from the damp, twilit air was like his first draught of cool water after days crossing a desert – sweet, encouraging, so rich and flavourful he almost recoiled from it. The hand that had taken his and helped him complete his extrication belonged to Luverion, the Zaitreci loremaster. As the young aelf emerged into the twilight, the rain yet present but light and easy, he looked up into the haunting grey eyes and young–old face of the foreign mystic and thought, for just a moment, that he saw the ghost of a smile there. As he freed his legs and feet from the mud and came to rest in a heap atop the mountain of newly loosed earth and stone now piled against the slope, he continued to gulp at the cool, mud-free air around him, starving for as much breath, as much life, as he could take into himself.

Luverion was not alone. The Syari champion, Taurvalon, bedecked in his full panoply of aetherquartz-encrusted armour, stood nearby, watching with quiet curiosity.

'How did you find me?' Ferendir managed to ask between deep, desperate breaths.

'I felt you,' the loremaster said quietly, crouching beside him on the great mound. 'Felt the shining, inextinguishable light inside you.'

'Aye, felt the light shining inside him,' Taurvalon offered, minor irritation evident in his deep voice, 'but turned back and wandered off without telling the rest of us. The moon-touched fool had put half a league between himself and the rest of us before we even realised he'd doubled back.'

Ferendir looked to Luverion, not believing what he was hearing.

Luverion's impassive face indicated neither distress nor embarrassment, subtle or otherwise. 'I had faith they would note my absence and come to find me… and thus, help me to find you.'

Ferendir could not make sense of the mystic's words. He could only stare, and gasp for air, and struggle in vain to slow his hammering heartbeat and settle his raw, jangled nerves. On the forested slope beneath and around him, he saw figures moving in the purpled evening light, each of them striding tall and proud, weapon of choice in hand, among a scattered charnel house of death and ruin.

His masters, their companions – they had slaughtered the Slaan-eshi who'd been chasing after him. Every one of the vile creatures now lay dead or twitching their last, crushed, dismembered or feath-ered with arrows from the bow of Metorrah the sentinel, who was already moving among the fallen to collect those arrows for reuse. For a long time, as Ferendir struggled to breathe, the others milled about among the trees and corpses, wholly oblivious – or indiffer-ent – to his presence and survival. Luverion, for his part, took a seat beside Ferendir, crossing his legs lotus-like beneath him and seem-ing to settle in to wait patiently for the inevitable moment when someone would finally see that Ferendir had returned to them.

Ferendir felt the mud still clinging to his skin, the light patter-ing of the rain thinning it and smudging it but doing little to wash it away. Strangely, he felt comforted, even exalted, in the filth that clung to him. It struck him as an anointing, a runic badge of his trial and ascension to a new level of enlightenment and capability.

Down below the mound where Ferendir sat, Serath suddenly turned and caught sight of his newly extricated supplicant. For a long, strange moment, Serath's stare bore such a weight, such gravity, that Ferendir thought it might actually crush him. Only gradually did the others realise that something had drawn the normally remote Stoneguard's attentions and now transfixed him, basilisk-like, where he stood. One by one, they noted his staring eyes, his half-open mouth, his rigid shoulders, and turned to fol-low the line of his gaze.

Soon enough, they were all staring at Ferendir.

'What are you doing here?' Serath finally asked. The edge in his voice was sharp, unmistakable.

Ferendir felt a terrible pang of bitterness coil in the centre of him. That question – so cruel! Why would he enquire thus? Why was his presence so unnerving?

Desriel, thankfully, stepped forward. He, at least, looked genuinely relieved to see his student. 'How?' was all he managed to ask.

Ferendir, still gulping air, waved his hand about, suggesting the now-dead Slaaneshi littering the hillside. 'I was following you. They chased me.'

'You were told to seek the far temple,' Serath said coldly. 'You disobeyed our express command!'

Ferendir could already feel the strange, childish sense of shame and reproach that overtook him whenever Serath disciplined him – the surety that he was a failure, a burden, the worst of a long line of illustrious students who had gone on to great things. But even in the midst of that sickening, rising sense of disgrace, another feeling rose in answer and wrestled the other into easy submission.

It was pride. Pure, unwavering, vulcanised pride. And far from feeling excessive or undeserved or overweening, this feeling rose and took its place in his heart and suffused him not because it was misguided or excessive but precisely because it was in direct proportion to what he had accomplished that day.

He would not lower his eyes and shrink from Serath's reproaches. Not ever again.

'I was climbing this very slope,' Ferendir said, now struggling to his feet and meeting his master's burning gaze with his own. 'Those fiends you slaughtered, lying all around you? They were right behind me. That's when the hill came down upon me – a mudslide, brought on by all this accursed rain. I was buried. I thought I would die.'

'But you did not,' Desriel said, a sense of wonder in his voice. He turned to his counterpart. 'Serath, do you not see? We've been here, in this glade, fighting for a long interval. If Ferendir was buried under that mudfall, he could not have survived for all that time without air.'

'Nor without aid,' Luverion added gently from beside Ferendir. Serath stared at Desriel, then swung his gaze back to Ferendir. 'You suggest the mountain saved you?'

Ferendir nodded. 'I know she did. She spoke to me. She deemed me worthy and she gave me breath when I had none.'

'You passed your trial after all,' Desriel said. Though he maintained his calm, his composure, the muted pride radiating from him was readily apparent to Ferendir, even at the great distance separating them. He imagined it was clear to everyone in the glade.

Except, perhaps, Serath, who still looked as though his supplicant had humiliated him instead of vindicating the efficacy of his training and guidance.

'You are a supplicant no longer,' Serath said slowly.

Ferendir nodded. 'Just so, Serath.' It was the first time he had ever, in all his years of service and training, called his master by his own name, without appending 'Master' before doing so. He prayed it was not overbearing or offensive. He simply knew that if he were to now prove his worth as their peer – their equal – he must begin immediately to shed the trappings of their former association. That began with no longer addressing his long-time teacher as 'master'…

'This is moving, truly,' Taurvalon broke in. 'May I interrupt this touching reunion, however, to point out that night is falling and there still may be Hedonites about? Or, at the very least, a scouting party drawn by the foul stench of those we've here dispatched?'

Desriel looked to the champion. 'You think they were not alone?'

'I think we should act as though they were not,' Taurvalon said. 'We need to be away from here. Get up that slope and find a defensible place for a camp on the level ground above. To stand here conversing as though we were not at all times in imminent danger–'

'I concur,' Serath said with finality, and instantly began a steady trudge up the steep wooded slope. 'Let us push on and make camp for the night. We'll continue this idle talk when we're safe and not a moment sooner.'

He marched up the slope to the right of the great mound of mud and earth that Ferendir and Luverion sat atop. Ferendir dared a single, incredulous glance at Desriel, but his former – and more supportive – master only gave him a small, subtle nod and fell into step behind Serath. As the rest began to take up their own climbs, Luverion unfolded his legs and leapt to his feet beside Ferendir.

'Be not embittered,' he said quietly, 'for the seemingly cruel, intolerant teacher is, perhaps, the one whose lessons we most need to learn.'

Ferendir stared at the mystic. The aelf's pale eyes bored into his own for a few lingering moments, then he turned and joined the others on their climb.

CHAPTER SEVEN

Ezarhad bent closer over the old tome laid open before him, rereading its ancient runic script for the hundredth time, struggling to concentrate, to parse the words and tease out any hidden meanings or implications that had escaped him on previous perusals. In the same instant, a fat, cold drop of rain fell from the sky and splattered unceremoniously on the precious volume's parchment pages. Ezarhad raised his head. There were clouds above. Rain was certainly an imminent possibility. But this… a single, maddening drop. It was as if the sky sought to bait him, to mock him. That single droplet of rain had dashed his concentration and instantly stoked within him the fires of rage.

Ezarhad sat straight-backed in the elaborately carved throne that he forced his minions to shuttle about for him. No doubt he struck a strange sort of figure, sitting alone in a high-backed, cushioned chair on a windswept hillside high in the Vertiginous Mountains, a dusty old grimoire open upon a hastily erected reading desk before him, a tall, beautifully tooled cabinet containing more esoteric volumes standing nearby, furniture in want of a room to occupy. When in transit, he was more than happy to stretch his legs, to stride across the land and claim it as his own, with his retinue of babbling, sycophantic followers trailing far behind him. But when at rest, a fellow needed a place to sit and reflect, did he not? If such a space was required and the environs one moved in would not offer such refuge naturally, it then became necessary to bring it all along.

Another drop of rain. Ezarhad raised his eyes. The sky taunted him now. When he lowered his gaze again, one of his daemonettes was bent over the book, wiping at it with the hem of its dark purple silks.

'My sincerest apologies, my Bright Lord of Decadent Splendour,' the daemonette moaned. 'My Paragon of Beauty and Perfection, oh Pulchritudinous Master of all that is Rich and Living-Giving. I should have been paying closer attention. Your book—'

Ezarhad rolled his eyes. Sighed. So hard to find good help. For a moment, he considered turning back to the text, but it was no use – he might as well put the bloody thing away for the time being and check in with his lieutenants.

'Stop it,' he snapped, and the daemonette scuttled backwards, head still bowed. How dare the creature lay its grubby, blighted hands upon one of his most prized tomes!

Ezarhad rose and kicked the retreating daemonette. The lithe creature went rolling over the dusty earth with a surprised shriek.

'You!' Ezarhad shouted, indicating a small knot of daemonettes milling about nearby – his throne and furniture bearers – each grooming their multi-coloured ridges of hair or using their long, licking tongues to wash themselves like bored housecats. 'Tear this fool to pieces, then break out the mynolope skins. There's rain on the way.'

The fallen daemonette sprang up onto its small, taloned feet. 'My lord?'

The others all tensed, eager for bloody action. Their wide, dark eyes all locked onto their soon-to-be-former comrade. Lolling tongues licked thin, dark purple lips.

'I should be happy to serve you, my lord,' one of the idle pack spat.

'No, I!' another hissed. 'This fool always covers your glorious throne and library inadequately, dread lord!'

'You would call me a fool, and I would tear you to bits!' the first snarled, then lunged.

Ezarhad whistled and indicated the still-cowering daemonette who had dared touch his grimoire to wipe that raindrop away. 'Kill that one first, then you can fight over who shall bear my throne. See to it, now.'

The ravening little pack fell upon the lone daemonette. Ezarhad heard shrieks, howls, grunts and ominous laughter, but he did not bother to watch what unfolded. Instead, he simply took up the volume he'd been reading, crossed to where his cabinet awaited and replaced the book upon its proper shelf within. That done, he closed the stained-wood doors, threaded the fine chains that held the cabinet shut through their mounted rings and closed the padlock that held the contents in safety until he chose to open it once more. The daemonettes were still tearing at their comrade, taking their sweet time about dispatching the creature. Tiresome... but necessary. Heavy was the head that sought to wear a crown. He couldn't simply sit about amusing himself all day by pitting one pack of daemonettes against another. The present situation was simply an exigency of the moment – he couldn't have any of his chosen servants fail him, even a little... not even one of his throne-bearers.

He idly wondered if Astoriss had troubles of this sort. She did, no doubt, though the harridan would never admit it to him. Her pride was the size of the very mountain they trekked upon now, and so she would not countenance even the suggestion that any creature in her retinue – from her most powerful servants to the scrawniest, runtiest daemonette – was anything less than deadly and wholly successful at every task undertaken.

Ezarhad, as he walked among the chaotic array of knotted bodies and milling forms that passed for his camp, contemplated his ages-old rivalry with the godseeker, Lady Astoriss, and the invader, Meigant – how they had all succumbed to the lure of Slaanesh in the same season, bathed their blades with blood on the very same night in three different climes of the Mortal Realms and how, ever since each had ended up in the absent god's vile and soul-stirring palace in the Six Circles, they had been locked in some strange, three-way symbiosis marked by mutual aid alternating with potentially lethal underhandedness and bloody, unending competition.

Now, here they were, the three of them, trying to tear Hysh to pieces and make their mark upon its ugly, bland, symmetrically balanced face. Winner take all…

I should never have agreed to it, he thought bitterly. *Meigant is no threat – he's a blunt instrument, strong but clumsy and unwieldy. I can handle him, if not destroy him. But Astoriss… Astoriss is a dangerous adversary. No doubt she is watching me, spying on me, by some magical means, at this very instant…*

He froze. Looked around. Studied everything he saw. They were deep in the mountains, jagged hilltops and ridgelines dominating the horizon to the north-west and west while high, snowy peaks looming over climbing slopes robed in evergreens and alpine scrub rose to ominous heights to the east and south. All around him in their erstwhile camp was activity: daemonettes cleaning themselves with their tongues or sleeping in curled, scaled bundles, or fighting over the scraps of small forest animals and large birds snatched to fill their ever-hungry bellies; a troupe of four-legged fiends scuttled about at the periphery, alternately charging towards and fighting one another or sparring with their sharp, barbed weapons while grunting at each other in that strange, animal language they spoke that even Ezarhad could not understand without a translation spell; his mounted hellstriders – magically bound atop their two-legged serpentine mounts – cowed lesser Hedonites into helping those mounts find tall, sere grasses to feed upon, then teased and threatened the same Hedonites with being devoured by those mounts; and finally, his lieutenants, his champions, each tending to their own separate business while ordering about the daemonettes that served as their administrative staff and shock troops.

Great, hulking Kraygorn was busy berating a daemonette for cowardice and dismembering it, extremity by extremity, while its former companions watched and absorbed the bloody lesson. Vhaengoth, his artillator, beat sense into the Chaos-tainted slaves that served him, constantly polishing and shaping new arrow and spear shafts for his own and his troops' collective use. Ghorgovaar, ever in his own mind, sat bent over a makeshift workstation composed of a broad, flat board balanced between two kegs of Slaaneshi soul ale, fiddling with some small, deadly implement from his cache of lethal treasures, while his own daemonette servants sat in small circles, oiling and polishing the gears, springs, casements and chains that he bore along with him in the hopes of building some new vile device. Finally there was Orryseth, his mage, alone in a shady glade just a stone's throw distant, perusing a magical grimoire of his own on a vast crimson drop cloth while he fussed and fiddled with a number of tinctures, powders and glowing vials before him.

So much talent. So much cunning. So many eager, corrupted souls vying for his attention and his favour. Surely with such servants as these he could not be beaten, could he? His victory was not only imminent but assured, was it not?

Nothing is assured, he thought grimly. *Remember the rout at the foot of the mountain. You set the whole of your army loose upon that Vanari warhost – all an elaborate ruse to draw their attentions away from this little expedition into the highlands – but your servants failed you. Your force should have swept through the Lumineth lines and carried on across the plains. Instead, they were smashed and scattered. For all you know, at this very moment they've already broken into separate bands and defected to the camps of Astoriss or Meigant, or been slaughtered by another Vanari host.*

No. I gave commands. My lieutenants assured me they would rally at the agreed-upon place of rendezvous and drive them towards the nearest populated centre to wreak more havoc. They knew what I required. They knew the part they played – a loud, violent distraction from my furtive expedition into these peaks. They need only fulfil that duty...

Would they dare defy him? *Could* they?

Your worry is pointless, he told himself. *You have the Eidolith. You have this smaller, more dependable force. You go now to claim your prize – your destiny. When your army sees what you've accomplished, when Astoriss' pious godseekers and Meigant's bloodthirsty invaders see that you wield more power than their masters ever hoped to–*

He sensed a dark, brooding presence moments before he heard her voice.

'Master,' that low, rasping voice said at his elbow.

Ezarhad calmly turned. There, kneeling upon the ground at his feet, was Tyrirra, his spy, her lithe-limbed form wrapped tightly in black silks and a latticework of leather belts and straps, all supporting an array of small, silent, deadly weaponry, from blowguns with poison-tipped darts to long, slender dirks to a rolled-up length of serrated silver chain capable of sawing through the trunk of a sapling – or a mortal throat and spine – in moments. Her sudden appearances like this – silent and wholly undetected right up until the moment she announced herself – had the twin effects of filling him with admiration for her skills and stirring within him the faint spectre of paranoia. What if someone managed to over-whelm her adoration and convince her that she would be better served elsewhere? Could Ezarhad himself, or anyone in his employ, actually curb Tyrirra's lethality if she put her sights upon him?

Stop it. Those thoughts will not serve you in this moment.

He forced his doubts and suspicions deep into the bowels of his being and stood tall above her. 'Report.'

'We are being tracked,' Tyrirra said in that breathy, half-dead voice of hers. 'They are, most likely, watching us as we speak.'

She raised her mostly covered face so that her eyes could meet his. Ezarhad knew well what her face looked like – pale blue skin, smooth and childlike, with a narrow, bowed mouth full of needle-sharp teeth, a gently upturned nose that almost wasn't there and two massive, sparkling black eyes like orbs of onyx – but at present he could only see her startling black eyes, for she usually kept herself swaddled inside a tight-fitting black cowl, the lower portion of her face obscured by a black mask.

Ezarhad struggled to keep his eyes focused upon her, the urge to raise them and search the rocky, forested landscape around them strong.

'As we speak, you say?'

She nodded. 'I did my best to lead their scouts to the overlook directly behind you, then slipped away from them and retreated down the hillside behind them. I thought it best to direct their attentions, if those attentions were going to be applied.'

Ezarhad understood immediately. 'Do we have an egress obscured from their vantage?'

'The gully beyond the treeline, on my right,' Tyrirra said quietly.

'How many?'

'Two scouts. No more than seven in the primary group.'

'You are certain we can encircle them?'

Tyrirra nodded subtly. 'Leave the bulk of the force milling about here in the glade. Direct a hand-picked unit to disperse, one by one, with great patience, into the trees and down the track of that gully. While we surround them, they will continue to watch our position, wondering what we plan to do or where we are headed.'

Ezarhad dared a slight smile. 'Most effective, my ever-subtle retainer.'

'I live to serve,' Tyrirra whispered, voice dry as a newly dug grave. 'I shall wait at the foot of the hill.'

Slowly, seeming neither eager to be away nor directed in any fashion, Tyrirra rose from where she knelt, gave her master one more nod of her swaddled head then turned and sauntered away. In moments, she had concealed herself in a milling throng of daemonettes, wholly indistinguishable from the jerking, brawling creatures as she used their bold movements to slip quietly away undetected.

Ezarhad crossed the great clearing towards Kraygorn, his hulking, formidable lieutenant. The enormous champion of Chaos stood over the constituent parts of that daemonette he'd been meting out bloody punishment to, watching with sneering satisfaction as the slain creature's former comrades picked over its remains in search of tasty morsels to fill their bellies.

The moment Ezarhad came up beside Kraygorn, the enormous soldier knelt and lowered his helmeted head.

'I await your command,' Kraygorn said.

You await my carelessness, Ezarhad thought mordantly, *you scheming, ambitious traitor. Oh, you may not be hatching any plans at this very moment, but that does not mean you won't, given time. I know your sort. Strong, courageous, always eager to be the best, the most powerful...*

'My most trusted servant,' Ezarhad said silkily. 'I have a task for you.'

He unfolded the plan presented to him by Tyrirra – offered wholly as his own inspiration, of course, for were not the mental workings of all his servants his own property? His *own* thoughts, for all intents and purposes? When the plan was explained, Ezarhad retreated to once more repose upon his carven throne.

He waited. Patience was not one of his many virtues – at least, not in the short term. Eventually, after some seemingly great interval of time, a daemonette with a bristling stripe of bright crimson hair and skin the colour of a dying man suffering jaundice presented itself at his elbow.

'Oh, Lord of Magnificence and Glory,' the sharp-toothed creature spat, 'our enemies are subdued.'

Ezarhad smiled in spite of himself. 'Survivors?'

'Only one,' the daemonette said with relish.

Ezarhad rose from his lordly chair. 'Excellent,' he said. 'Show me.'

They were servants of Chaos – not so unlike the murderers and miscreants that served him – faceless, anonymous invaders who had plotted, only an hour before the present, to fall upon his unit and destroy them. Or, alternatively, to retreat and summon a larger force to achieve such an end. Now they were the charnel leavings of a slaughterhouse – dead, dismembered, their foul blood staining stone, tree and soil, the marks of their death struggle evident in a broad circle all around the little glade where they'd sought to secrete themselves.

Ezarhad's servants still had the battle fever upon them, every muscle and limb trembling with anticipatory ecstasy, all eyes wide and staring, all mouths spread into vile rictus grins that could have just as easily been snarls. As he strode through the glade, examining the aftermath of their ambush, they all fell to their knees, spoke his name and declared their undying fealty, indicating that the dead now strewn about were offerings to his holy and glorious endurance.

Most of the enemy troops were daemonettes, lithe of limb and once as deadly as they were delicate, but he counted two fiends among the slain, legs cut right out from under them. At least one of those fiends seemed to have choked on the black ichor from its own torn-out tongue. The only survivor was a daemonette of unusual size and beguiling aspect. She was female, her skin tinged a sickly pale green, her hair a long, tangled purple mass now thickened with gobbets of rent flesh and the blood of both her enemies and her comrades. Kraygorn held her high off the ground, one enormous fist clamped hard around her slender throat. Despite his strong grip, still the daemonette fought, refusing to give in, even though she had to know her end was nigh upon her.

Ezarhad stood, studying the last survivor. She had four arms, but only two still functioned. One, bearing a crustacean-like pincer, had been broken and hung at a hideous angle, white splinters of fractured bone showing through her torn flesh. Another arm had been all but hacked off and now hung limp against her torso, dripping blue-black blood upon the thirsty soil of the mountainside. Of her two still-functioning arms, one beat at Kraygorn's massive, muscular forearm while the other tore at his exposed flesh with razor-sharp talons.

Such spirit, Ezarhad thought. *Perhaps I could convince her...*

'I like you,' he said, meeting her fevered gaze.

The daemonette shrieked incoherently and redoubled her efforts, reaching out to try and land a strike upon Ezarhad. He avoided her clumsy attack easily. Kraygorn tightened his fist and she shuddered, her throat suddenly crushed, close to collapsing entirely. Still, though, she struggled, however weakly.

'This is your one and only opportunity,' Ezarhad said, leaning closer and speaking as charmingly as he could. 'I know not if you belong to Astoriss or Meigant, but I do know I will be the last one standing among the three of us. Join me now, and perhaps you can make a place for yourself.'

She continued to struggle, clearly beset by a lack of vision and incapable of recognising a bright opportunity when it presented itself.

'Very well, then,' Ezarhad said, straightening. 'At least tell me where to find your speaking stone, or your enchanted mirror – whatever device you use to communicate with your warhost. I know some such thing will be about.'

She swiped with her talons. Ezarhad easily avoided them.

'Lord Ezarhad,' a quiet voice said.

It was Tyrirra, once more having crept into his presence and knelt at his side without his knowledge. Though her head was bowed, she held up before her a smooth spherical stone of cloudy, crystalline structure. Ezarhad recognised it immediately and snatched it from her open hands. Lifting the heavy orb, gazing longingly into the swirling, colour-streaked clouds that stirred in its depths, he presented it to the prisoner.

'This,' he said triumphantly. 'This is what I sought, you fool. And do you know what it means that I now have it? Through no help of yours?'

She spat, hissed, tried to lay her filthy hands on his fine, bejewelled robes.

'Kill her,' Ezarhad said.

Kraygorn's fist flexed. Bones collapsed. A glut of tainted blood and saliva geysered from the prisoner's yawning mouth and the daemonette fell limp in the warrior's grip.

Ezarhad held the orb – the speaking stone – in two hands, directly before his face. He had used similar items before, though he was not sure if this particular object had specific enchantments upon it. He would cross that bridge when he came to it. For the moment, he simply gazed into its cloudy depths, calling fire and sparks from the whirling storms therein, willing it to reveal its secrets, to send a message across space, through the aether that wove the substratum of the Mortal Realms, towards the owner of its companion.

'Come now,' Ezarhad urged. 'Let me speak to your owner – your master. Is it Meigant? Or is it Astoriss?'

The stone grew warm in his large, lithe hands. The mists and witch-lights in its depths roiled like a summer storm on a bare horizon.

Suddenly, a face presented itself – a long, chiselled visage of pale purple sporting a well-trimmed and elaborately styled crimson beard with a curling moustache. Two wide, emerald-green eyes stared out of the depths into Ezarhad's face.

'Meigant,' Ezarhad said by way of greeting.

'Ezarhad,' Meigant answered. His voice was a whisper – amazed, frightened, disbelieving.

Ezarhad turned and held the orb out before him, presenting the carnage all around him to its all-seeing depths. 'I came across some servants of yours, Meigant. I would like to say they fought bravely, but the simple fact is, we made short work of them. Now that we've disassembled the lot, I think we will have to make something lovely and decorative from their foul remains.'

'Ezarhad, you preening, poisonous peacock,' Meigant snarled.

Ezarhad drew the stone to his face again. 'Oh, Meigant... I've angered you? Believe me, that was not my intent. What I intended, rather, was to make the hopelessness of your cause abundantly clear.'

'A few fiends and daemonettes,' Meigant snapped. 'Grind them up and devour them for all I care! I have thousands more at my command!'

'But for how long?' Ezarhad asked. 'For how long, Meigant? Look upon this little taste of the ruin I plan to visit upon you and all who serve you.'

'You cannot run away from me forever, Ezarhad!' Meigant shouted back through the seeing stone. 'I know what became of your forces when they met the Vanari! Scrying and nearby spies have shown me the ruin wrought upon your so-called servants! Sooner or later, I'll find you, and when I do–'

Ezarhad drew the stone very close to his face. 'I am not running away from you, you fool. I am running towards my destiny. And when I finally snatch that destiny into my embrace and draw it to me, all the Mortal Realms will tremble and *you* will beg for a mercy I shall never allow you!'

And with that, he threw down the seeing stone and gave a curt nod. Kraygorn, already waiting with his great, monstrous sword in hand, brought the enormous blade crashing down upon the seeing stone, shattering it into a hundred jagged fragments in an explosion of spent magical energies.

Ezarhad did not even watch the stone's destruction. He was already sauntering away, back towards the main camp. 'Do with them as you like,' he said over his shoulder. 'If there's any meat to be had, we'll feast upon it tonight.'

CHAPTER EIGHT

The pike tip was razor sharp, gleaming, seeking. In a series of deft, graceful movements, it thrust, swept, dipped, each time barely missing some exposed, unarmoured portion of Ferendir's flesh – his arm, his throat, his midsection, his thigh. Only Ferendir's own speed and grace, coupled with a number of quick, desperate parries from the diamondpick hammer he wielded, kept the pike-point from biting into him and drawing blood. Ferendir felt a surge of triumph when he finally managed to knock the pike sideways then lunge forward, well inside its optimal thrusting range, a place of relative safety. Now, the pike was not in front of him but beside him, its desperate wielder still doing her utmost to redirect her attacks and keep him from closing.

He took one long step. Another. The pike-wielder was right in front of him. He drew back for a strike with his pick hammer, planning to knock the pike high, skywards, while slipping in beneath it to deliver a stunning blow.

Then Phalcea reversed her attack, changing her strategy in an instant. The pike swept aside – well out of his range – and she brought up its back end and spiked ferule instead. Before Ferendir could even adapt to the sudden change in the warden's tack, Phalcea had lowered her body and thrust the back end of the pike shaft between Ferendir's extended legs. Ferendir knew what was about to happen, but her movements were too swift for his body to react in time. As he tried to follow through on the stride he was midway through, his legs became tangled on the pike shaft. Down he went, hitting the earth beneath him with such force that for a moment the breath was knocked out of him and his vision swam with bright white fireflies on a black scrim.

He blinked, staring up into the half-lit sky, Phalcea framed against it. His adversary had now lifted her pike. She was in the midst of spinning it round, clearly preparing to bring the point down and spear him where he lay.

Ferendir had a sudden inspiration. Using his legs, he thrust hard sideways and spun, his arched back against the ground like an overturned tortoise. One moment, his legs were close to Phalcea and his head distant; in the next instant, that position was reversed. He thrust his pick hammer forward, between Phalcea's planted feet, caught one ankle with the hammer head and yanked as hard as he could.

The warden, pike still held above her, lost her footing and hit the ground hard, also on her back. At the moment of her impact, she gave a startled *whoof* and dropped her pike.

Ferendir pushed with his legs, spun again and rolled. Once his legs were under him, he leapt back to his feet. One full step, a half step, and he was looming over the fallen Phalcea, his pick hammer's head hovering close to her chest.

'Yield,' he said, feeling an unmistakable bloom of pride.

Phalcea smiled slightly from her prone vantage and raised one eyebrow. 'Cunning, youngster. Very cunning.'

'Was it, though?' a voice said from behind Ferendir. He swung his head round and found the sharp tip of an arrow hovering right before his face. Behind the arrow was a drawn bow. Holding the drawn bow was Metorrah, Phalcea's twin sister.

'Drop your hammer,' Metorrah commanded.

Ferendir did as he was told.

Metorrah slowly relaxed her bowstring and lowered the arrow. 'Help her up,' she said.

Ferendir bent and offered a hand. Phalcea took it and allowed Ferendir to help her upright again.

The others sat nearby in a loose semicircle, all watching the sparring session and murmuring to one another regarding their admiration or criticisms of Ferendir's performance. He'd grown accustomed to it. For days they had advanced through the mountains, easily following Ezarhad Fatesbane's trail, steadily closing the distance between them. During every rest period spread throughout their days of constant movement and their nights of cursory camping, Ferendir's masters had insisted he begin practising with each of the warriors in the band – themselves included – in an effort to hone his skills and expand his understanding of different fighting styles.

This was his first session with Phalcea. He had to admit, when they began he'd felt a modicum of confidence, sure that her long, unwieldy pike would prove no match for his speed and the adaptability of his pick hammer to a number of different situations. Unfortunately, he had not realised just how good a pike-wielding warden could be with their weapon. Though the pike looked long and clumsy, Phalcea handled it with the grace and skill of a simple quarterstaff user, shifting her attacks, spinning the great weapon and deploying it for both offence and defence with exceptional poise and swiftness.

Then, of course, she'd also had her sister to back her up.

'I win,' Phalcea said, now on her feet and facing Ferendir with hands planted on her narrow hips.

'You cheated,' Ferendir said, only half-jokingly. 'I thought *we* were sparring, just the two of us.'

'Sentinels and wardens,' Metorrah said behind him, 'Iliathan twins – these are two groups that never, ever fight alone unless they have no other choice. So long as I am in her presence, I will defend my sister to the last.'

'And I you,' Phalcea said to her sister, as if Ferendir were not even standing between them.

'You lost that match at the outset,' Desriel said from his perch on a nearby boulder. Ferendir looked to his master. The Alarith's face was soft, kind, but his words had been like thorns ripping at his exposed flesh.

'How so?' Ferendir asked.

Desriel cocked his head slightly. 'You tell me. You're a supplicant no longer. Find your own answers.'

Ferendir considered, reliving the entire sparring sessions in the span of an instant, the whole match still burned into his memory in all its swift and dangerous glory. Returning at last to the moments before he began, he realised what Desriel was alluding to.

'I mounted the first attack,' Ferendir said quietly.

Desriel nodded. 'And why was that a poor decision?'

Ferendir hung his head. 'Because the Alarith do not rush towards the enemy. The Alarith stand firm and force the enemy to come to them – to break upon them like waves on a cliff face.'

'The moment you attack,' Desriel said, 'you spend your greatest advantage as a Stoneguard of the Alarith. The earth beneath your feet cries out to you, pledges its fealty to your need, if only you would embrace it. Had you centred yourself and rooted yourself to the place where you stood – had you forced the warden to come to *you* – you would have been nigh-on unstoppable.'

'Forgive me, Stoneguard,' Phalcea said, 'but I believe you are misleading your student.'

'I am no longer a student,' Ferendir said, perhaps too bitterly.

'We are *all* students,' Luverion offered from where he watched. 'Desriel is yours as much as you are his, Ferendir.'

'As that may be,' Phalcea pressed on, 'if one has the opportunity to mount an attack – if one sees an opening to exploit, a weakness to undermine – one should do so, post-haste. Victory belongs to the active, not to the passive.'

'So you have been taught,' Desriel said amiably, 'for such are your ways, and your ways support your gifts. But those are not *our* ways, nor *our* gifts.'

'I still say you cheated,' Ferendir interjected. 'Two on one? No such agreements were made at the outset.'

'Wait for terms and conditions in a battle, youngster,' Phalcea said, 'and you're likely to end up dead.'

'She's right,' Desriel said before Ferendir could offer a rebuttal. 'In a real fight, there will almost always be more than one enemy to contend with. You cannot limit your awareness – your strategy – to the body before you. You must take in *everything* and anticipate all probabilities. Understanding that some adversaries might be naturally paired – like the twins – or simply trained to support one another – like sentinels and wardens on the battlefield – is part of what you must take into account.'

Ferendir knew his teacher was right, no matter how much he hoped to continue arguing against him. Suddenly, he felt a certain sense of gratitude – not for what his teacher was trying to inculcate in him but for the fact that Serath was not present. His hard-faced, dour master had disappeared an hour or two before to scout the track ahead of them. If he had been here to see Ferendir make such a foolish mistake…

'It was a good fight,' strong Taurvalon said. The Syari champion stood beside a tall tree, enjoying its shade. 'But I agree with the twins – a true warrior goes right into the thick of it, strikes first, strikes hard.'

'And spends all the energies stored in their aetherquartz at the battle's outset?' Desriel teased.

Taurvalon gave the slightest shrug. 'The aetherquartz is mine. I will use it as I see fit – from the moment the battle is under way, if I deem it necessary.'

'That is impatient,' Desriel said, 'and wasteful.'

'Some of us do not have days on end during which to stand around like statues and let the enemy break upon us,' Taurvalon said. 'Why not end the fight when it starts, I say.'

Phalcea rested her pike on her shoulder. 'Care to put that to the test?'

The Syari considered for a moment, then nodded. 'Why not? My point shall be proven.'

He turned and moved to where his shield and spear lay in repose beside the tree he'd just been leaning against. As he turned his back, Ferendir saw a subtle look of devilish mischief pass between Phalcea and Metorrah.

Then, swift and silent, Phalcea lowered her pike and rushed towards the shining Syari champion.

For a big aelf in heavy, full-plate armour, Taurvalon's almost-instantaneous reaction was impressive. In one blinding series of movements, he snatched up his shield, grabbed his spear and spun to meet Phalcea's attack. She thrust three times in succession – high, low, centre – but Taurvalon met each thrust with quick, small movements of his shield, always ensuring that the warden's blows met the centre of the shield boss and slid away harmlessly. Then, as Phalcea drew back for another attack, the Syari champion struck.

Without warning, the great quantity of aetherquartz encrusting Taurvalon's shining armour flared and flashed. Their camp was filled with a dazzling – almost blinding – white light. In the midst of that light, through raised hands and narrowed eyes, Ferendir saw Taurvalon leap forward, thrusting with his spear over the lip of his raised shield. Phalcea was driven back by the onslaught of blows, deflecting each with increasingly more haphazard movements, the light emanating from her sparring partner and his blindingly fast movements clearly throwing her off guard.

On he came. Back she went. His spear clanged against her pike; her pike's blade rang harmlessly as she struggled to land a single blow but met the boss of his shield every time.

But there was Metorrah, as good as her word, rushing in to offer her sister aid. The archer charged straight at their adversary from his left, nocking an arrow as she advanced and finally leaping into the air with fleet assurance. Ferendir instantly saw what she intended – that leap would take her high, and from that vantage, she could fire her arrow almost straight down, over the lip of Taurvalon's raised shield.

But already the Syari champion had anticipated her attempted coup. As Metorrah rose on the air towards the highest apogee of her spring, Taurvalon simultaneously raised his shield and shifted his grip on his spear. Metorrah's loosed arrow deflected harmlessly off Taurvalon's shield, while Phalcea's next pike attack was parried by his seeking spear.

His aetherquartz flared again, making direct observation impossible. Ferendir shielded his eyes and did not open them again until a breath later, when the glare subsided.

When he next looked, he saw Taurvalon spinning round, now using the shaft of his spear as a blunt instrument. Metorrah, meanwhile, had almost reached the ground again, her feet just a short distance from final touchdown. His spear slammed hard into her side just before her toes touched earth, and the sentinel was driven with terrific force sideways – right into her advancing twin.

Metorrah and Phalcea hit the ground in a tangled heap, their weapons clattering from their hands.

Taurvalon spun around once more, letting the momentum carry him, then finally ground to a halt. He stood straight and tall, spear in one hand, shield in the other. His flashing aetherquartz subsided to a dull, warm glow. He looked eminently pleased with himself.

'And,' he said, 'the match is mine.'

The twins glanced up from where they lay. A moment later, they disentangled themselves.

'Impressive,' Metorrah said grudgingly.

Phalcea looked to Ferendir. 'For the record, youngster, *that* was cheating.'

Taurvalon almost looked offended. 'I fought with honour.'

'You did,' Phalcea answered. 'And spent every advantage to put us on our backs. Tell me, oh shining one, what happens when you've spent all your aetherquartz in the midst of a real battle?'

'I spend my advantage to win the battle,' he said. 'Swiftly. Surely. If I cannot win on those terms, perhaps I should not win.'

'Again,' Desriel suddenly said.

Ferendir looked to his master. 'What was that?'

'I said, again,' Desriel said calmly. 'Your practice for the day is not yet done.'

Ferendir looked to all present, wondering whom he should challenge. Desriel, to his great astonishment, made his decision for him.

'The three of you,' Desriel said. 'Metorrah, Phalcea and Taurvalon – all at once, in any configuration you like.'

The three challengers all looked at one another before turning their attention back to Desriel.

'Hardly fair,' Phalcea said.

'It's dangerous,' Metorrah added. 'Perhaps he's not ready.'

'It would be a shame to hurt him,' Taurvalon said, 'and profit us nothing.'

Desriel's expression – normally so lax and resigned – hardened for only an instant. In that moment, Ferendir thought he saw some hint of Serath.

'I trust your abilities to mete out non-lethal challenges,' Desriel said, 'but I do not yet trust my long-time student's ability to meet them. Consider these challenges as prologue to saving his life when we catch up to our enemies.'

Something sickening and sharp coiled in Ferendir's gut. Did not trust his ability? Had he really deserved such open, public shaming? Were his efforts really so unworthy? All of a sudden, Ferendir felt a small measure of betrayal. He would have expected such harsh words from Serath but not from Desriel. How troubling for his master to so suddenly and shamefully expose a hitherto unknown aspect of his nature.

'Fine,' Ferendir said, stepping forward. 'Join the fight if you like, Master Desriel. Call in Luverion if it suits you. I challenge any of you – *all* of you.'

Desriel did not move from his perch. 'Three will do.'

The three challengers fanned out in the glade. In moments, Ferendir was surrounded, Metorrah, Phalcea and Taurvalon having withdrawn to separate, equidistant points on all sides of him.

Ferendir adopted one of the many opening stances he'd been taught in combat drills at the mountain temple – right leg extended forward, left leg bent, his hands wide on the grip of his pick hammer, the weapon held waist-high, laterally across his body. Knowing that the match would begin at any moment, he closed his eyes, drew slow, even breaths and sought the will of the mountain.

Help me now, he prayed. *If I should stand and not rush to meet my adversaries, keep me rooted, make me strong, make me a bulwark upon which my enemies will break themselves, mighty and immovable.*

A slight tremor pulsed through the earth beneath him. He felt it through the thin soles of his boots, like a ripple moving through water. It came from behind and to his left.

That would be Phalcea. He could literally feel the small, vibratory movements that her feet sent coursing through the soil as she couched her pike and prepared to attack.

She'll attack first – I know it. That's her nature.

There. Behind and to his right. A heavier footfall. The slight, metallic rattle of armour on a strong, muscular form: Taurvalon. Ferendir heard – no, more rightly, he *sensed* – the minute emanations sent through the air as the Syari champion's aetherquartz once more stirred and began to glow, however softly. Ferendir knew, logically, that aetherquartz made no sound, radiated no heat, and yet its awakening, the forces stirring and quickening within each separate gem that encrusted Taurvalon's armour, now seemed to hum and resonate, like deep, subsonic harp strings.

His armour is a weapon, Ferendir realised, *enhancing his natural speed, his natural strength, his natural prowess. Stripped of his aetherquartz, he would be a dangerous foe – empowered by it, he's nigh-on unstoppable.*

A breath sang softly on the woodland air and an arrow notch sighed as it was couched upon a bowstring. A moment later, that same string creaked as it was drawn half-taut, in anticipation of a full draw to come, aim to be taken.

She does not want to kill me, but she'll try to distract me. Send arrows whizzing by my head to draw my attention before rushing in to join her sister in neutralising me. I mustn't think her less dangerous simply because she's not drawing her bow. She has more tricks in her arsenal than simply being a fine archer.

All of these insights, these revelations, swept over him in the span of two indrawn and exhaled breaths, communicated to him by the air surrounding him and the earth and soil beneath him. He saw nothing, but he understood everything. It was a widening and attenuation of awareness that previously he had only ever known or achieved during deep meditations in the temple, or in quiet, remote places upon a mountainside. But now, reborn by facing death upon the mountain, it was as if all of those senses – already so finely honed by his training and discipline – blossomed into a wholly new array of senses within him. He felt like a musician who'd just been handed a standing great-harp after only playing a small shepherd's lyre all his life and finding that all he'd learned in miniature could yield powerful, expansive results upon a larger and more sensitive instrument.

He felt a moment's pride – the bright surge of heat and anticipation that bespoke honour and passion. Knowing both to be potentially toxic and destructive, he decried both impulses and cast them deep into the darkest parts of himself.

Phalcea attacked.

Ferendir opened his eyes.

She took three long strides then lunged, thrusting her pike out before her, the bright, broad blade plunging right towards Ferendir's left side. In the instant before contact, Ferendir felt a strange bolt of electricity surge through him, as if the ground itself were directing his movements rather than he making a conscious choice. The pulse caused his torso to flex sideways, narrowly avoiding the seeking spear tip, and his hammer rose in his grip. The sudden upsweep of his weapon deflected the seeking pike outwards, away from his body, but Phalcea's lunging form was still a force, advancing behind the pike's long, narrow shaft. Another pulse, and Ferendir bent double, driving his left shoulder into Phalcea's charging form. The application of force was modest, precise, yet wondrously effective. The warden was thrown off balance and hit the dirt.

The air whistled. Something split the wind currents of the forest, speeding right towards him.

Ferendir tilted his head sideways and the flying arrow slipped right past his ear, the feather fletching tickling him as it went. Already he could hear the sweep and rasp of another arrow sliding from Metorrah's quiver, raised to grip the bowstring even as it still vibrated from its previous release. But before he could worry about that–

Taurvalon sent what felt – to Ferendir – like earth-quaking tremors through the ground: massive, clanking, ringing. By all rights, Taurvalon's armour should have made him clumsy and vulnerable, but it was so well wrought, so perfectly shaped to his already powerful body and its specific requirements, that both its movements and its limitations were slight and subtle.

Ferendir turned his head only slightly to the right, so that he could see the Syari's barrelling form in the periphery of his vision. The champion's aetherquartz lit the clearing with a crystalline, fast-intensifying glare.

Don't challenge him, Ferendir thought. *Withstand him.*

Taurvalon raised his shield and drew back his spear, never breaking stride as he prepared for a thrust that would – in true combat – run Ferendir straight through.

Ferendir spun, facing the Syari head on. He planted his feet wide, raised his hammer horizontally before him and reached out – within himself – to the mountain.

Taurvalon's spear struck – and buckled as it slammed into Ferendir's immovable, invulnerable form. The spear tip rang as if it had struck stone.

The spent force travelled back up the length of the spear shaft and sent Taurvalon reeling backwards. When the Syari warrior recovered, his face was a mask of incredulous shock and awe.

I am the mountain, Ferendir thought, eager to maintain his present state. *I am stone. I am immovable.*

Something bounced off Ferendir's stony form and spun away into the trees – another arrow from Metorrah.

Something struck him from behind and glanced off harmlessly – Phalcea's pike, used as a blunt instrument against Ferendir's bent back.

Taurvalon charged again, this time leaping to put even more force behind his attack. As he fell towards Ferendir, he struck, using the full face of his shield now instead of his still-trembling spear.

The shield slammed full force into Ferendir... and bounced off, yanking its owner sideways with its deflected kinetic force. Taurvalon let the unexpected momentum carry him all the way round, and he came to rest again in an on-guard stance, directly before Ferendir, shield high, spear behind him at the ready.

'Alarith sorcery,' he snarled quietly. Ferendir could not tell if the words were a frustrated curse or a grudging bit of admiration.

Now.

Ferendir broke his immobility and launched an attack of his own. He used his hammer as a leading force, whirling it round in his grip and sweeping the powerful head sideways, to the right, allowing the weapon's momentum to draw his body behind it. One foot remained rooted to the forest floor as the other rose to allow him to pivot. Taurvalon saw the strike coming and lifted his shield to catch it. Ferendir followed through, channelling all of his strength – all of the mountain's terrible force – into the blow. Hammer and shield rang. Taurvalon was thrown sideways – but a lucky shift of his shield turned the tide of the match.

The flaring head of Ferendir's pick hammer was suddenly caught on the curling lip of Taurvalon's shield. Ferendir knew what that meant – it gave Taurvalon sufficient leverage to jerk his shield sideways and yank the hammer from Ferendir's hands.

But only if Ferendir allowed it. He grounded himself again, becoming one with the mountain beneath him for only an instant. If he did not wish to move – if the mountain did not wish to release him – there he would stand, and he would not be toppled. With all the force he could muster, Ferendir yanked backwards on his pick hammer, dragging Taurvalon forward in an awkward headlong stumble. Taurvalon, sensing that he had lost his momentary advantage, let go of the shield, and the great slab of sunsteel flew free – but it was too late: the Syari champion was already falling, face first, towards the forest floor.

The gentle creak of wood stressed. Metorrah was preparing another shot.

Move, a still, small voice inside Ferendir said. *Go on the offence. Charge, right towards the sentinel. Unleash everything.*

Be the avalanche.

Mountains did not just stand strong, immovable and resolute, after all. Sometimes – at the worst of times – they tore great pieces of themselves away and hurled themselves down upon the unsuspecting.

Ferendir pivoted back towards Metorrah and charged. The force with which he launched himself, the speed with which he closed the distance between the two of them, shocked even him.

Metorrah loosed her arrow.

Never breaking stride, Ferendir tilted his head to the right and rolled his left shoulder backwards. The arrow flew harmlessly past, seeming almost slow and languid. In transit, leaning precariously sideways, he dared a wide swipe with his pick hammer. The out-turned diamond spike on the hammer's head caught Metorrah's bow just below the grip and tore it from her hands. Seeing the weapon out of her grasp, Ferendir let the bow fly free, then allowed the pick hammer's sideward momentum to draw his whole body in a long, sweeping circle. Still charging, he spun on a single foot, circling fully around and levelling the hammer for a well-placed strike. Metorrah, seeing her bow torn from her hands, reached for the knife at her belt, but she was too late. Ferendir's speed and the directness of his attack had served him well. The haft of his diamondpick hammer collided with her left leg, then her right, and sent the sentinel tumbling sideways.

Ferendir skidded to a swirling halt, kicking up a cloud of loose, dry dust as he did so. The elongated moments – so slow and languid in his own mind the instant before – suddenly returned to normal. Time once more flowed at a speed he recognised and understood. Though every movement he'd made had been carefully chosen and applied and had played out in what felt like a veritable eternity, Ferendir was keenly aware that only seconds had passed since the onset of their sparring match.

What did I just do? he wondered.

'I would call that a victory,' Luverion said. 'Three victories, in fact.'

Ferendir saw all three of his adversaries on their backs, each wearing subtle expressions of shock, awe and admiration on their otherwise stoic faces.

I beat them, he thought. *I beat them. Yet... how did I beat them? How could I?*

I learned from them, he realised. *I learned... I changed... and I won.*

Even Desriel was on his feet now, studying the fallen Lumineth around Ferendir with something akin to awe and wonder. The feeling that welled up inside Ferendir – powerful, pure, hitherto unknown and undreamed of – threatened to burst out of him in the form of joyful tears and hysterical laughter.

But of course, that would be wholly inappropriate – an invitation to Slaanesh to invade his mind and heart through pride. With all the strength he could muster, Ferendir fought his feelings of power and exultation down, down into the deepest, darkest chambers in the centre of him. Instead, he simply stood straight, turned to each of his opponents one by one and bowed to them in thanks.

'You have my gratitude,' he said to each, 'and my deepest respect.'

One by one, he helped them to their feet.

When Ferendir had finished, he was shocked to find Serath

present, standing at the periphery of their fight circle. He must have returned from his scouting expedition as Ferendir was engaged with his sparring partners. The stone-faced aelf stared at his student with inscrutable intensity, his gaze all but burning into him.

'You incorporated their methods into your own,' Serath said finally.

Ferendir cocked his head, seeking the proper response. 'I observed their methods and doled out the proper *Alarith* responses.'

'Impetuous,' Serath said. 'Haphazard improvisation, nothing more.'

'And yet,' Desriel broke in, 'remarkably effective.'

Serath turned his burning gaze upon his long-time partner. 'Foolish words,' he said, the timbre of his voice still flat and tightly controlled. 'Improvisation is weakness. Deploying every trick in one's arsenal, for every challenger great and small, is weakness. We are the last, Desriel. We have a greater responsibility than ever to preserve the wisdom passed down to us – and to pass it down to *him*.'

'The wisdom that says the student is always wrong and the master always right?' Ferendir blurted. The words were impulsive, he knew, foolish and undignified. And yet, he could not help but speak them.

Serath slowly turned to appraise Ferendir. His narrowed eyes and stone-set face hurled silent accusations and unspoken recriminations sharp as curses.

'You dare,' Serath said quietly.

Ferendir tried to adopt a position of deference, to swallow his pride, but in that moment, he found himself unequal to the task. Instead, to his own great surprise, he took a single step forward and leaned towards his master, all but challenging him.

'I dare,' he said.

'Enough,' Desriel said, his voice quiet but sharp. 'From the both of you.'

Ferendir threw a reproachful look at his master – always so supportive, so encouraging, so understanding. Here, now, even after Ferendir had passed his trial and proven himself, Desriel could not bring himself to side fully with the student against the master.

Before more words could be offered, Ferendir turned and stalked away from them. Their disagreement had never turned to shouting, not a single voice had been raised, their exchange had never unfolded above the volume of a simple, staid conversation among three comrades... and yet inside he felt as if he, himself, were a mountain, containing a storm of roiling, boiling magma seeking to burst through his cap and come coursing down his sloped sides.

Serath barked at him. Desriel called to him. One of the others – Phalcea? Metorrah? – even shouted after him and begged him not to go, but he did not listen. At that moment, in defiance of one master's unceasing criticism and another's inability to take sides, Ferendir was done with them. He needed to be away from them, if only for a little while. To think. To re-centre himself. To feel, without all their prying eyes and the weight of their individual and collective expectations upon him.

The forest swallowed him. He trekked uphill for a short distance, then cut sideways down a sloping ridgeline into a deep gully between long, slender hills. In that defile, the world was shadowy and cool, the day's waning sunlight already fading as Ulgu asserted itself and began its slow rise towards its nightly apogee.

There was a small brook trickling placidly along the floor of the gully, jouncing and tumbling over rocks and deadfalls, its waters clear and cool. Ferendir followed that brook, occasionally slaking his thirst from it. After a time, he found a small, rocky outcrop that formed a miniature waterfall of sorts at a short, steep embankment in the hillside. He chose a dry spot upon a boulder beside the stream and sat down, alone. His legs were folded under him lotus-like, his elbows planted on his knees, his hands clasped before him. There was only the sound of the falling water, the songs of a few evening birds and the insistent calls of scavengers in search of sustenance. Though there was still light in the world, it was dimming towards the twilight of night.

Ferendir stared at his pick hammer, laid before him on the rock. Were he to give in now to the storm of emotions and anger within him, he would take up that hammer and fell every tree in sight. He would obliterate their trunks, rain down splinters and wood pulp, listen with relish as the soaring conifers and gnarled birch on all sides cracked and collapsed and creaked their last as they came crashing to the earth, wholly unable to stand against his onslaught. Such wreck and ruin, offered so viciously, so bitterly, would give him a great deal of pleasure. He wanted to break things. To destroy things. To make all the world bow at his feet and acknowledge his power, his might, his ability to shape it to his will.

And yet he knew that way was a trap. The temptations of power and unchecked emotion that led down the descending path towards the taint of Chaos. His fury and frustration were checked before they could even be loosed, the inculcations of twenty years of temple training making the complete and unabated release of emotions – no matter how potent and stormy – all but an impossibility.

It was foolish, he knew. Childish. The mark of an immature soul and an unquiet mind. He was ashamed to even entertain such thoughts, let alone consider acting them out.

But even his considerable well of self-control left him wondering, probing, asking, again and again: Why? Why could Serath not be pleased? Why did his master refuse, time and again, to acknowledge anything he did in even the most cursory of manners? Was he so worthless, so misguided, that he was not deserving of a single encouraging word?

And, more to the point, why could Ferendir himself not abide the ongoing denial of such praise? Why should it matter? Why should it move him? If he were truly, deeply in mastery over his own feelings and his own outlook on the world, shouldn't Serath's reticence be of no consequence to him? Should he not be strong enough, independent enough, well trained enough to know when he did well or not, and to put no stock in Serath's ongoing disapproval?

Was it so much to ask for one of those two things – Serath's hatred or Ferendir's own need – to simply evaporate and allow him to move forward? To become all that he hoped to become?

Speak to me, a voice said.

Ferendir sat still. Waited. That voice had sounded as if it were spoken aloud, in person, whispered right into his ear.

But of course, he was alone in a deserted forest.

He waited, staring at his folded hands before him.

Come into my presence, the voice said. *Speak with me.*

It was the mountain.

Ferendir was ready to do as the mountain asked, ready to seek whatever wisdom and light it could impart to him… but as he resituated himself and set his pick hammer aside, he suddenly heard something else. An actual sound, this time, rather than words spoken in the centre of his consciousness.

Shuffling feet. Heavy, slow, haphazard footfalls.

Leaves and soil, crushed and turned by the passage of moving bodies.

Ferendir listened, homed in on the sounds, then leapt down off the rock. Taking up his diamondpick hammer, he moved slowly, cautiously down the slope. That was the source of the noises. That was where he would find answers.

There, again – scrape, crunch, thump. Drag, slide, crunch. The movements were slow, ponderous, but unmistakable.

He leapt across the little stream and ventured deeper into the woods.

In short order, he located the source of those strange sounds and froze where he stood.

He was not alone. Filling the forest before him was a pack of shambling reanimated husks, all moving in similar but eerily individuated patterns involving shuffling, dragging feet and the clumsy shift of their body weight and centres of gravity. Many wore the scraps of armour or old clothes, long shredded and torn by time and the elements. A few dragged weapons or clutched the broken hafts of hammers or axes, though Ferendir did not know if they had any idea what they were for or how to use them.

Deadwalkers.

A strange sense of wonder intertwined with fear filled Ferendir's heart. He had heard stories of these roving bands of the reanimated dead – relics of the infamous and terrible necroquake, roaming across the Hyshian landscape unimpeded and untouched unless they came into direct contact with a group that needed to cull them. From where he now stood, he could count about two dozen of them, but as he scanned the darkening forest in their wake he knew there were more. It could be a sizeable horde. It could be an enormous herd.

Wide, empty eye sockets stared blankly. Jaws gaped wide. Rags of old, desiccated flesh and shrivelled muscle and sinew still clung to some, while others were nothing but bone, scoured and wiped clean by time and the elements yet still somehow ambulating and held together by the same vile, ancient magic that animated them.

Did they have any impulses? Any will of their own? Or did they simply wander, uncaring, unseeing, until something directly challenged or threatened them?

They were drawing nearer with every moment.

Ferendir had no desire to learn the extent of their destructive impulses for himself. All at once, staring down at the broadly spaced horde now slowly approaching, he simply wanted to be away from that place, to hurry back to camp and warn the others.

But how many are there? he wondered. *They will ask. They will ask and I will say I do not know, because I did not bother to reconnoitre completely and obtain even a cursory account of them. And when I admit that I simply turned and ran, Serath will once more berate and insult me.*

Very well, then. Reconnoitre. Get some vague sense of how many there are and which way they are headed. Then – only then – can you return to camp and inform the others. Be brave. Be of use.

He turned to move from where he stood hidden behind a tree, obscured from the leading edge of the shambling mass moving slowly towards him – but found his way blocked.

Deadwalkers now filled the forest on all sides of him. While he'd been watching the advance of the great party coming slowly up the slope, still more had encircled and entrapped him. They still moved with a total absence of urgency or agency – their empty eye sockets still stared sightlessly, their jawbones still gaped, or hung askew from their skulls, and their movements were still creeping, inexorable, almost unconscious – and yet they were unmistakably converging on Ferendir.

They may have been shambling and unaware of him, but they were all shambling in *his* direction, and there was no breach in the closing cordon their shuffling, rattling bodies made around him.

'Shades of Ulgu,' he cursed, and raised his pick hammer.

CHAPTER NINE

Surviving the mudslide by the mountain's grace had been harrowing, but ultimately illuminating. Sparring, again and again, with his foreign companions on their journey had given him bruises, scrapes, cuts and aches – not to mention ample opportunities for humiliation and shame. But none of those experiences had adequately prepared Ferendir for what he now faced.

Death itself. Decay incarnate. A single, aelemental force expressed in a gaggle of lolling, half-rotted forms all pressing closer and closer around him. Skeletal faces and gaping jaws filled Ferendir's vision on all sides. The forest was now a prison of high, soaring trees, with a vast, tangled mass of grasping skeletal hands and half-decayed bodies closing like a tightening noose around him. As far as he could see: deadwalkers.

And they seemed to be reaching out for him.

Ferendir tried to compose a plan of attack, to plot an egress from the shrinking space he now found himself in, but his mind was awhirl, incapable of focusing on the problem at hand and the many variables intertwined with that problem.

Bony fingers scraped against his shoulders, his arms, his chest.

Sounds like dying breaths began to issue from some of the dead-walkers closest to him – hisses, sighs, moans, none of them backed by more than the stirring air from a mild breeze: sounds of weakness, despair and submission – the sounds of a weak and hungry abyss.

Cold, skeletal hands closed on one arm. Ferendir threw them off and began swinging his pick hammer. There was no time for a plan, no time for strategy. Back and forth the great, heavy weapon arced, its long haft and heavy hammer head ploughing into any deadwalkers in its path. Skulls were crushed or swept from their perches atop rattling neck bones. Arms were batted aside or ripped free. Ribcages imploded. Ancient, rusted mail rattled and long-corroded armour clanged dully. In moments, he had downed half a dozen of the foul dead things now closing, and still kept swinging, turning, swinging, turning.

There seemed to be no end to them.

His hammer collided hard with something solid and unyielding. His arms vibrated as the sunsteel of his weapon absorbed the shock. It was a massive broadsword, wielded by one of the deadwalkers. They had weapons! Some of them, at any rate. Here, one stood before him having just blocked his hammer blow with its blade; there, even more, brandishing notched axes and time-bent spears. Still more brandished objects that might not be weapons but that could prove just as deadly, wielded properly – heavy tree limbs, stones, old chains taken from their own bodies or dragged behind their shambling feet, even the broken, torn-off limbs of their comrades.

Ferendir redoubled his attacks. The diamondpick hammer rose and fell, parried haphazard blows from the sword-wielding wight nearby, crushed the skull of one fiend charging with a massive, blunt-headed mace, swept two grasping monsters off their skeletal feet. He struck with the spike protruding from the opposite side to the hammer head. He thrust, forward and back, knocking more undead enemies off balance or down to the ground with well-placed hits.

The sword-wielding deadwalker lurched forward, eager and haphazard, blade whistling down. Ferendir swept his hammer up to parry the blow and felt a deep satisfaction when the wight's blade shattered. Before the barely sentient creature could mount another attack, Ferendir shattered it with a crushing downward blow from his pick hammer.

And still they came.

Ferendir had to move. He could not simply stand here, surrounded, and let them overwhelm him.

Swinging the hammer in a series of fierce back-and-forth arcs before him, Ferendir pressed forward, trying to clear a path through the close-packed undead bodies that blocked his way. So many of them seemed half-formed, insubstantial – they shattered or collapsed when struck with sufficient force, lost their way if their heads were damaged or knocked free – and yet they still pressed closer. When two went down, three more took their place.

He swept. He crushed. He shattered. He fled.

Then, without warning, the twilit darkness of the benighted forest suddenly grew blindingly, unnervingly bright. Ferendir shrank from the glare for a moment before daring a look. His first realisation was that the light actually seemed to draw the attention of the deadwalkers, their dulled, unconscious senses swept inexorably towards anything that struck them as sufficiently novel or threatening.

Then, holding one hand high to shield his eyes, Ferendir managed to see the source of that new, blinding light.

It was the loremaster, Luverion, standing atop a heap of boulders some distance away. The Zaitreci towered high above the scores of amassed deadwalkers, holding his beautifully forged sword above him. That sword seemed to act as a lightning rod of sorts, calling a dancing, crackling stream of lambent energy down from the sky and focusing it into a pulsing, blinding emanation from the blade itself. That blade seemed bright as a small sun, as white-hot and eye-searing as phosphorus, but gave no heat, only a concentrated, withering illumination.

This was Ferendir's chance! They were distracted! He even saw a crooked path opening among the deadwalkers just ahead of him. If he could force his way through swiftly enough–

No! He only made it a short distance before a new obstacle presented itself: a huge, hulking deadwalker – certainly not aelven or human in its living days – lumbered out of the crowd and placed itself right in his path. Ferendir was racing straight towards the behemoth, now struggling to stop his forward momentum, to keep from crashing right into the beast.

It held a huge, spike-headed mace on a long wooden haft. The bludgeon rose. Ferendir could imagine what enormous force the creature would gather when it brought the mace crashing down.

He raised his hammer, praying for the strength to meet the blow.

Then the monster exploded.

It was sudden, loud, dazzling – a deafening, ear-splitting pop, followed by a bloom of sparks and a cloud of bright white smoke. The behemoth's component parts – ribcage, arms, pelvis, skull – were scattered every which way, a few fragments even colliding with Ferendir.

A moment later, Ferendir saw the source of his salvation – Taurvalon! The heavily armoured aelf charged right into the midst of the staring, milling deadwalkers, using his great, shining shield to plough several aside while mowing through another half a dozen with his flashing broadsword. Once again, the many shards of aetherquartz encrusting the Syari's pearlescent armour began to glimmer and glow, and the many deadwalkers swarming about the champion were bathed in the gathering white light that their angelic adversary emanated even as he smote them down.

Ferendir joined the battle, turning to his right and tearing into the nearest opponents with his pick hammer. He rent skulls, shattered ribs, decimated grasping limbs and cracked snaking spinal columns. Even as he attacked, keen on quickly supporting the efforts of his fellows, he saw arrows start to rain out of the near distance as Metorrah launched barrage after barrage into the massed ranks of the dead. Before and beside her, Phalcea cleared a path with her pike, thrusting, sweeping, slashing and spinning. One moment it was a cutting instrument, the next a bludgeon, an instant later a point to skewer shambling bodies upon.

Far across the glade, on the opposite edge of the deadwalker horde, Ferendir saw Serath standing fast as the army of the dead swarmed him, eager to overwhelm him with sheer numbers. Serath's stone mallet swept left and right in fierce, mowing arcs, downing five and six adversaries at a blow, crushing dozens of skulls beneath its hammer head. They came, armed and unarmed, striking and grasping, but Serath stood his ground, unmoving, simply heaving them aside as they closed with blow after deadly blow. He was a rock – a coastal cliff face – and the tide of deadwalkers broke upon him.

Suddenly, the ground to either side of Ferendir began to heave and tear loose. Long, narrow strips of earth and rock literally rose with sudden, inexplicable force, like tree roots that some invisible hand sought to tear from their underground nests. Looking back towards the conglomeration of boulders where Luverion still stood, Ferendir realised that the long stripes of rent earth were the doing of the loremaster, who seemed now to be conducting an invisible choir in the air. His hands rose, flexed into fists, fell with deadly swiftness, then repeated their gestures in an unending parade. Everywhere that the loremaster commanded the earth to rise in protest, it tore itself loose and leapt skywards, taking with it every deadwalker that stood upon it. One moment they would be standing, milling, eager to seek an opponent; the next they would fly into the air, upended, whirling or somersaulting, until they finally came crashing down again, their bony limbs shattered with the impact of their falls, leaving them broken and immobile on the forest floor.

Ferendir downed three more, four, five. Their ranks were thinning. They were winning!

'Ferendir!'

It was Desriel's voice. Ferendir turned towards the sound – but instead of finding the face of his master, he saw a tall, grave figure lurching towards him out of the fray, a massive undead warrior wielding a gigantic warhammer, its head twice the size of Ferendir's own skull.

Ferendir planted his feet, raised his own diamondpick hammer cross-wise, hands poised at either end of its length, and sought the mountain. To his great relief and astonishment, the mountain answered. Suddenly – miraculously – he felt as if he were made of stone, one with the great peak they now trod upon – an immanence rising from it rather than a mere, fragile mortal scurrying across it. That strength, that pure, unyielding force, seemed to transform every part of his being. The deadwalker's massive hammer fell, but when it met his own raised pick hammer, it recoiled with a loud clang.

It was as if the deadwalker had struck solid stone that refused to break.

The deadwalker struck again. Again. Each time, the blow landed. Each time, Ferendir felt its kinetic force flow through him, sudden and jarring but almost without consequence. Spent force. Mere vibrations, radiating from the haft of his own pick hammer, through his frame and into the mountain at his feet.

The deadwalker took a single step back. It turned its empty eye sockets upon its enormous hammer, as if wondering what had gone wrong with the blasted thing. Finally, it turned those same gaping, empty eyes back towards Ferendir.

Ferendir begged the mountain to give him back the force just spent upon it by the foul thing before him. The mountain answered. With cold, swift fury, Ferendir raised his pick hammer and brought it crashing down upon his hulking foe.

It raised its own weapon to block his blow. Ferendir's diamond-pick hammer shattered the haft of the great maul and kept going.

It crushed the deadwalker's desiccated skull.

It shattered the deadwalker's spine and caved in its half-armoured ribcage.

It blasted its pelvis to small, porous fragments.

Ferendir stood over a pile of pulverised bones and half-rotted, parchment-dry flesh, victorious.

He could barely believe what he had just been granted the power and might to accomplish.

Never fear to seek me, that now-familiar voice said inside him. *I am always with you, beneath your very feet.*

Satisfied that the battle was won, Ferendir fell on his knees, put his head against the cold sunsteel head of his pick hammer and said a silent prayer of thanks to his mother mountain.

It was there, kneeling upon the ground, head bowed, that the cold came upon him.

Ferendir opened his eyes. Inhaled. Exhaled. His breath was visible.

Impossible. Why was the glade suddenly so cold?

He remembered his lessons on magic and spellcraft, specifically a warning about sudden shifts of temperature or weather conditions.

Wild, surging magic leeched ambient energy from the air around it. If the glade was suddenly so cold that his breath was visible…

Something's coming – manifesting, he thought. *Something big, powerful…*

He rose, eyes darting about, seeking his companions. There – Desriel, just finishing off a clinging, bisected deadwalker still dragging itself along by one arm. Nearby – Taurvalon, searching the carnage using second-hand light from the aetherquartz on his shield so that he could more clearly assess the bodies strewn about them. Behind him – Luverion, Metorrah and Phalcea, advancing with caution as they studied the scattered dead, always on the lookout for movement, for the last accursed life still clinging in vestiges to this husk or that. A stone's throw to his left – Serath, moving among the dead and finishing off those still twitching.

Did no one notice?

Ferendir exhaled again. The cold still clung to him, heavy, palpable.

He looked to Desriel again. Now his master stared at him, his lithe body in a stance of wariness.

'Do you feel that?' Desriel asked.

Ferendir nodded.

Then Ferendir heard Serath's voice ring out through the forest. 'Downhill!'

All eyes turned towards the gentle, rolling slope beneath them. Their gazes were redirected just in time to see a massive geomantic wave come rippling up the hillside, tossing earth, stone, dead wood and cloven deadwalker corpses in its wake, like some over-imaginative child's notion of a subterranean rodent's approaching burrow.

This was no rodent though. The furrow created by the oncoming wave was at least as wide as Phalcea's pike was long and mounded the earth it upset to a height almost equal with Ferendir's eye level. And it was coming on fast.

Ferendir wasn't sure what to do, so he did what came naturally – he stood, planting his feet wide, and clutched his pick hammer in his hands. The mountain had saved him once. Perhaps it could save him once more?

But he was no longer alone. Suddenly, without warning, Serath was to his left and Desriel to his right. His masters stood shoulder to shoulder with him and grasped their own hammers before them, ready for a fight. On their flanks, the others fell into a loose formation. Luverion lowered his staff before him and once more summoned that powerful eldritch light that had served them so well when the deadwalker battle began.

The burrow rolled nearer, nearer, picking up speed even though it was climbing up the slope. Then, without warning, something rose out of it. They all shrank from the initial explosion – a massive scattering of earth and mud and damp, cold loam mingled with deadwalker parts and long-dead fallen tree limbs from the forest floor. As Ferendir and the others raised their eyes again in the explosion's wake, they saw a massive, looming form now dominating the landscape before them. At first glance, Ferendir thought of a worm – long, cylindrical, its thick, massive trunk seemingly made of the forest's rich earth, scattered, befouled stones and rotting vegetation. Then, blinking, he realised that the creature's rearing cylindrical form was only part of its horrifying nature. If it was primarily a massive worm made of earth and detritus, it also boasted a number of reaching, grasping appendages and gaping, struggling faces along its length. Those appendages, upon closer examination, proved to be bits of once-living things. There were human and aelven arms, an unmistakably squat, broad duardin skull, jawbone flexing as though it tried to speak but could find no voice, the half-broken remnant of a rotted orruk face leering out of the damp earth, kicking legs, tree roots flexing and whipping like tentacles, half-absorbed deadwalker bodies now reanimated, leaning and grasping from the great, bulky body as though either seeking to draw others in or eager to be tugged free.

The great worm reared and lowered what passed for its broad, rounded face. It was a storm of skulls – human, aelven, duardin, orruk, others that Ferendir could not even identify – all pressed into the earthen form, seemingly swirling in a concentric pattern around a central axis that now split three ways and opened like a foul, gaping mouth lined with teeth made of shattered stones and hoary tree roots.

'By Teclis, Tyrion and the Perimeter Inimical...' Taurvalon breathed. 'By Shyish, what is it?'

'Spawn of the necroquake!' Serath shouted above the strange, rumbling roar that seemed to escape the beast without actually emanating from any fixed point. 'An ancient spell construct, first created as a guardian, later tainted by death itself into something alive and unnatural!'

'What do we do?' Phalcea pressed. 'How do we stand against such a... a...'

Desriel had already broken from their line, taking three long strides forward to place himself between the worm-thing and his companions. Ferendir lunged.

'Master, no!'

Serath yanked him back. 'Stand, boy. Control yourself. Desriel knows what he is doing.'

Desriel raised his diamondpick hammer before him, but not in the manner of a weapon now. Now, it was as if the long, slender sculpture of sunsteel and tightly wound leather were a wizard's staff, a focal point for all of his accumulated willpower and knowledge of the arcane. Ferendir saw that Desriel's eyes were closed and his mouth moving, pronouncing ancient words that were not spoken aloud. Ferendir had some ken of what those words might be, what they might be trying to accomplish. Only as he forced himself to calm the terror now disordering his brain did he realise that he had learned spells in the schools of the mountain temple that could, deployed with sufficient force, subdue the monstrosity before them. Or, at the very least, hold it at bay briefly while the others created a plan of attack.

He looked to Serath. Serath was watching Desriel, eyes fixed and unmoving. Ferendir could see in the burning force of Serath's gaze and the white-knuckled strength with which he gripped his stone mallet that he, too, wished to be at Desriel's side, assisting him, empowering him... but he would not risk stepping in until the moment demanded it.

The sunsteel head of Desriel's pick hammer was glowing, emanating a strange, diaphanous luminescence that wafted from it and dissipated, almost like smoke. The rearing worm towered above the Stoneguard, undulating and drifting, side to side, still emanating that fierce, subtle roar from its horrid form, all the absorbed corpses within it grasping and reaching out towards Desriel. It was as if the thing were eager to pounce upon him, to lay its entire bulk down and absorb Desriel into its foul trunk, but that light emanating from Desriel's pick hammer held it at bay.

Then the creature shuddered and rose. It was an unmistakable gesture – preparation to attack.

Serath broke from the line and ran forward. He took up a place some distance to Desriel's left and raised his own hammer in a similar fashion. Just before the worm-beast would have fallen upon Desriel, new light burst from the sunsteel head of Serath's stone mallet and seemed to halt the beast mid-lunge. The worm recoiled, danced side to side, bent and twisted, as if seeking some egress through a solid wall.

Serath now stood as Desriel did, eyes shut, mouth moving, making no sound but clearly emanating some powerful, repellent force towards the worm-beast. Ferendir thought, opening his awareness wide, that he could almost discern the twin-but-opposite forces loosed by his guardians as they stood against the great worm: the soft, lilting deference of understanding and compassion from Desriel – an invitation of sorts, asking that the beast merely make its purpose known and forego violence – contrasted with the pure, hard, crystalline willpower and repellent force from Serath – begone, or you risk destruction; attack us, and we will defend ourselves.

Unfortunately, Ferendir noted that the beast itself seemed unconvinced. While the lights emanating from his masters' hammers seemed, at first, to give the beast pause, it was now recoiling and preparing itself for another onslaught; he could see it clearly in the way its bone-filled mouth gaped and in the manner of its hunched, rearing form shifting against the forest floor.

'We have to help them,' Metorrah said, placing an arrow in her bow and drawing.

Then Ferendir heard a voice in his head. It was as clear as the mountain, as recognisable as his own.

Come forward, Desriel said.

Ferendir blinked. 'Master?' he said aloud.

Serath: *That was an order, not a request.*

Ferendir stepped forward. The others all said his name, hissed at him, as if he were a wandering child about to put himself in harm's way, but Ferendir did his best to block them out. He was reaching out now, seeking a means of hearing the will and desires of his masters without words passing between them.

Stand between us, Desriel said. *Remember the warding words.*

Ferendir hurried forward and took his place between his masters. He raised his own pick hammer in the same fashion, then dug deep into his mind in search of the cantrips that Desriel had alluded to.

The warding words. The prayers to banish all darkness malign.

An ode to dangers seen and unseen. A combined invitation and proscription.

He closed his eyes and opened his awareness.

All at once, he began to shrink – his being, his essence. All the noise and conscious sensation of the world around him grew muffled, then receded, then disappeared entirely. In moments, Ferendir had retired from the waking, present, physical world into another realm entirely – a realm of thought and intuitions, aelemental forces and pure, unbound will.

In that place – rooted to the mountain, pinned beneath the sky, bits of him flowing away with the falling water of the nearby stream, smudged and effaced by the hitching winds – he could sense the four of them as pure, disembodied essences: himself, his masters and the worm.

He and his masters were ghosts – thin, diaphanous, given power and might by their very incorporeality. The worm, by contrast, was a storm of magical force – a living, concentrated blight of swirling, contradictory, competing powers with a childish, barely self-contained consciousness turning and bouncing about at its centre. It was angry, frightened, curious and confused. It could not decide between seeking communion with the lot of them or consuming them whole, to become tormented aspects of its own multifaceted, half-mad spirit.

Desriel had tried to appeal to the passive elements of its nature – to relate to it.

Serath had thrown up a wall of hate and recrimination – the magical, emotional equivalent of all his dismissals and criticisms aimed at Ferendir, distilled.

Desriel said, *We come in peace, we mean you no harm*, and the beast thought him weak and sought to sweep him aside.

Serath said, *We are powerful, we will destroy you*, and the beast thought him a threat and prepared to defend itself.

Their messages were as separate and confusing as the worm's own contradictory nature. It could not make up its mind because they each presented such differing tacks to communing with and dispelling it.

What must I do? Ferendir asked.

What have we *done?* Serath asked. *What* can *you do?*

We are opposing forces, Desriel said, *duelling polarities. Help the creature to see that we mean it no harm but that we will defend ourselves if attacked.*

Bridge the gap. Be the lens that focuses two separate spectrums of light.

Ferendir knew not precisely how to do as they asked, but he knew that it all began by seeking the mountain's aid. He concentrated, speaking the words of the ward, working as he did so, digging deeper, deeper into the forces that rooted him to the hillside, seeking the mountain's strength, the mountain's will and the mountain's clarity.

The deeper he went, the more clearly he could separate and discern the warring, contradictory forces within the great worm. It was alive, powerful, dangerous – and yet it was only a child in terms of its mental capacity to control its own impulses and understand its own needs. It was not evil, or malign, or mad – it was simply unable to fully grasp the complexities of its own nature, let alone control them.

There. Ferendir felt the two separate fonts of energy now spilling forth from his masters – Desriel's compassion, Serath's crystalline, opposing force. They were like a pair of streams winding down a mountainside, spilling over a single shelf of stone into the same roiling bowl. He needed to bend those two streams, to combine them into a single potent force that expressed their will as a clear, focused impulse.

He drew them nearer, each stream resisting his will. The more they resisted, the more forcefully he demanded their submission.

In his own mind, he could almost see them – plunging waters,

bright as the sun, separated by the shortest span. If he could just…
combine… those… streams…

There. All at once, the two opposing forces came crashing together
at the centre of him. They curled and knotted and intertwined and
poured out again, emanating forth towards the strange worm, seeking the nucleus of its consciousness, carrying with it their message.

Be at peace, and we shall be.

Fight, and we will fight.

What you give to us, we shall give back to you, sevenfold.

With sudden, astounding clarity, Ferendir realised that his message had been received. The worm, hearing it loudly, clearly, in
the chambers of its old soul, suddenly seemed to change its entire
aspect. All at once, its rage abated. All at once, its fear subsided.
In an instant, it seemed to emanate pure, raw feeling as a means
of communicating its own intentions.

Trespass, it said.

Then we will leave, Ferendir replied.

Go, it said.

We shall, in peace.

Grateful, it said.

And then it was silent.

Ferendir opened his eyes just in time to see the earthen worm
collapse. The force animating the soil and the corpses and the rotted vegetation had simply fled, releasing all the matter gathered
to give it body and strength. The forest was quiet, dim and still.

Ferendir looked to Serath, to Desriel.

Desriel nodded. 'You see? You were all we needed.'

He heard Serath sigh. Ferendir turned to face his master, steel-
ing himself for the criticism to come.

Serath was staring at the place where the worm had been only
moments before, his eyes skating slowly, idly over the giant pile
of detritus now mounded there.

He looked to Ferendir. Stared, fixedly.

Ferendir prayed for words of praise but prepared himself for barbed words, words of reproach, words of disappointment.

To his great surprise, his master said nothing. Serath simply turned and marched away. Ferendir stood in stunned silence, watching him recede.

CHAPTER TEN

Later, when their evening meal had been consumed and they all sat quietly round the fire, the now-eradicated threat of the deadwalker horde and the spell construct still weighing upon each of them, Ferendir removed himself. The silence, he felt, was too oppressive, too awkward, for him to countenance another moment of it. So without announcement or statement of intent, he rose and left the group, withdrawing some small distance from their camp and their cookfires, though still within sight of them. Not far away, an outcropping of rock and soil thrust out of the mountainside through the forest trees, providing a stunning view across the valleys and canyons below towards the neighbouring mountains and their snow-capped peaks. Ferendir perched himself upon this naturally formed balcony and stared out over the quiet scene, soaking in the soft purple glow of the Hyshian twilight and trying to decide how he felt about Serath's refusal, once again, to offer him any small term of endearment or encouragement.

'You should not stray far,' a voice said in the silence.

Ferendir turned. There stood Desriel, just emerging from the shadows under the trees onto the outcropping.

'I can still see the firelight,' Ferendir said, by way of assuring his master that he knew better than to wander.

Desriel took a seat beside him on the rock. For a time, the two of them drank in the glorious vista before them. It all looked so peaceful, so timeless... and yet, at that very moment, powerful forces were loose in the world that could taint it and twist it for centuries – nay, millennia – to come. The world, despite its appearance, was not at peace or in repose – it was under threat. It was always, perpetually, under threat.

'He is proud of you,' Desriel said.

Ferendir was silent for a time. 'I said nothing.'

'I can sense the storm inside you, though you hide your emotions well.'

Ferendir turned to face his master. 'Do I?'

Desriel dared a gentle, enigmatic smile. 'You are a good student, Ferendir. You have always been. You continue to be.'

'A student,' Ferendir scoffed. 'But never a peer. An equal.'

'Student is simply a role you play until such a time as a new role is adopted. And even when that new role is adopted, the student remains a part of your essence. It is the same for me. I remain a student, even though I am your teacher.'

Ferendir studied his master in the gentle, gloaming light. 'I do not understand.'

'We remain students even after we become teachers,' Desriel said, 'for there are always – *always* – lessons to be learned. No matter how wise we think we become, how strong, how enlightened, the world always seeks to teach us. If we are honest, and perceptive, we never lose sight of that fact.'

'So,' Ferendir said, 'Serath despises me because I am a better student than he? Or because I dare to make my ignorance some-times known? Which is it?'

'Neither,' Desriel said with finality. 'Serath is still trying to learn some hard lessons of his own, and you continually challenge him.'

Ferendir almost laughed, but knew that to do so would be undig-nified as well as insulting. He simply shook his head. 'I see no lessons. All I see is a Stoneguard whom I have long admired and served looking upon me as though I were a fool or a failure – or both.'

'You do not understand him.'

'He does not seek my understanding.'

Desriel nodded. 'True. But not for the reasons you believe. He loves you, Ferendir, deeply – treasures you, in fact. You do not see it – you cannot see it, because he will not show it – but Serath sees potential in you the likes of which none of his students have shown in recent memory.'

A scoffing sniff escaped Ferendir. He was ashamed of the small, incredulous expression instantly. 'How can I believe that?'

'Will you receive a story?' Desriel asked.

It was an odd question, but Ferendir immediately understood what his master meant by it. Their folk often used stories and recollections to make wider points about ethics or modes of behav-iour. To be asked if one was ready to receive a story was to be asked, *I have something to impart – are you ready, and willing, to listen?*

'I will listen,' Ferendir said, preparing himself.

'Serath and I were once closely aligned,' Desriel said. 'Many, many years ago – long before you were brought to the temple. We were equally hopeful, equally open-hearted, equally encour-aging. While other masters hardened the hearts of their students with harsh, painful lessons and by creating between themselves and their supplicants an unbridgeable gap, Serath and I made our reputations by being open. We taught, and we had high standards, but we also encouraged, and opened our hearts, and helped our students to understand that while emotion must never rule them or enslave them, it could – under the right circumstances – be just as valuable a guide and boon to them as their knowledge of geomancy or their skills with a greathammer.

'There was a young supplicant in those days named Mendoryn – female, brilliant, possessed of astonishing wells of untapped power and potential. Mendoryn, we all agreed, was special, unique. There was talk in the temple that in the fullness of time she might even become a true loreseeker the likes of which our temple had not seen in generations.'

'A loreseeker?' Ferendir asked.

'It is no accident you do not know this term,' Desriel said, and Ferendir thought he detected the barest hint of sadness in his master's voice. 'After Mendoryn, the temple thought it best to eliminate the path of loreseeker from the curriculum. If such a being developed naturally, in the fullness of time and their studies, so be it – but we would not encourage such impulses. They would arise naturally, unbidden, or they would not arise at all.'

'I still do not understand.'

'We are all torn between the Tyrionic and the Teclian,' Desriel said. 'You know this.'

Ferendir nodded. He did, indeed. It was the most basic of principles, imparted to the supplicants of the temple in their earliest lessons. The first created of their kind – Tyrion, the Lord of Lumination, and his brother, Teclis, the Master of the Arcane – embodied the opposing but equally vital forces that were contained in all Lumineth. Tyrion was the avatar of strength, brilliance, inspiration and purity, while his brother, Teclis, was the paragon of reflection, refinement and deliberation. While the former symbolised positive, aggressive forces, the latter embodied the more reflective, inquisitive and introspective sides of their natures. Neither of those principles was superior or inferior to the other, nor could either exist without the other. It was the dynamic tension created by the tug of war between those two poles that created power and purpose in an individual. The Hysha-Mhensa, one of the Lumineth's greatest and most potent symbols, was holy and revered precisely because that runic mandala literalised the struggle between those opposing impulses and suggested that they could be brought into perfect balance and alignment.

But such perfect balance, Ferendir well knew, was said to be the stuff of legend, all but impossible to encounter in everyday practice. Most individuals, they were taught, had a polarity; they skewed one way or the other along the spectrum between the Tyrionic and Teclian forces at work within their natures. Their lives were, more often than not, dedicated simply to overcoming that enforced polarity, to enforcing balance where it did not naturally exist.

'A loreseeker,' Desriel continued, 'is a being who is *naturally* in balance. Their nature may sometimes express their Tyrionic nature and sometimes the Teclian, but their default state – their true essence – is at the balance point between the two. That state of being, that condition, is exceedingly rare – and, potentially, quite powerful.'

Ferendir felt a strange chill run through him. Why did Desriel's words seem to penetrate him so deeply? Had he ever encountered such a being? Ever imagined such things were even possible?

'Mendoryn,' Desriel went on, 'was just such an individual. Though she struggled to reconcile the forces inside her, when she was centred and at ease she was in balance. She was a natural loreseeker, only requiring the right lessons and the right training to help her attain the great potential that lay before her. Unfortunately, maintaining that balance was a struggle for her – a struggle that sometimes threatened to consume her.'

'I don't understand,' Ferendir said. 'If she was a being in balance–'

'Imagine a long plank, balanced at its centre upon a fulcrum. If you place weight on one end, the plank sinks. If you place weight at the other end, the plank sinks. Most of us are such creatures – we are naturally disposed to place all our weight at one end or the other of the plank, and we are naturally disposed to find ourselves secure and at rest when the plank sinks to the ground beneath us. But true loreseekers – those who are naturally balanced – live at the centre of the plank, right atop the point of the fulcrum. Though potentially in an enviable position, they are never at rest, never grounded, always teetering back and forth between one side or the other as they struggle to maintain balance. I suppose you could say they are more powerful once mastery is attained, but less powerful – and less stable – while they are still struggling to attain it, because they are never grounded, never secure. They are not simply trying to overcome one powerful force by invoking another – they are constantly yanked between the two poles, often with disastrous consequences.'

Ferendir stared. 'What became of her?'

'Mendoryn struggled,' Desriel said. 'When her introspection and thoughtful nature threatened to bring her studies to a halt, she overcompensated and became reckless, even self-destructive. When those risk-taking, aggressive impulses threatened to alienate or endanger her or her fellow supplicants, she retreated once more into her thoughts, her own mind, and was often paralysed by self-doubt and recrimination. We all knew she was, potentially, the most powerful among us, but her nature – alternately impatient and reticent – could not resign itself to slow progress and incremental growth. Serath was especially enamoured of her – in awe of her, really. I think he was secretly eager to see what such a creature could ultimately achieve with their nature in balance, for he knew well that his own nature had never been so balanced. He did everything in his power to encourage her, to support her and to empower her. When she doubted herself, or feared failure, or saw no path to achievement and growth, he would all but drag her out of her crippling melancholy with the force of his words and his faith in her potential.

'He struggled, you see, for he loved her. He loved her as a father loves a daughter, as a keen teacher loves a brilliant student, as a frustrated zealot loves a genuine, wonder-working prophet. He sought to teach her, to give her all that she required, so that when she finally became what we all knew she would become, she could, in turn, teach him.

'But it was not to be. In her despair at her regular setbacks and her ambition to prove her worth, Mendoryn decided to undertake her final trial long before she was ready to do so. She slipped away in the night, trudged over the ridge and up the mountain to the place of trial and buried herself in a shallow grave to seek the mountain's blessings.

'Because she was not ready – and was not worthy – she expired before we located her. She came to the mountain without the proper understanding or humility. Thus, the mountain denied her its sanctity.'

Ferendir stared, suddenly unable to understand. 'How is that possible?' he asked. 'If she was all you said she was, capable of so much–'

'Potentialities, not actualities,' Desriel said. 'Mendoryn was full of potential – almost limitless potential. But she came to her moment of trial too early, without the proper mindset or intent. All her potential was spent – forever – because she sought a single, instantaneous solution to a complex problem. Serath has never forgiven himself. He believed then, and believes now, that his encouragement and excess of faith in Mendoryn's abilities sent her to that trial – and to her death. Had he been harder on her, he thinks, sterner with her, she would never have thought herself equal to that life-or-death test.'

Ferendir shook his head. 'But how... why... why did he never tell me this tale? Never make me understand?'

Desriel leaned closer. 'Because,' he said softly, 'he believes that showing you his shame, his fear – his grief – is an unfair burden. In his mind, *he* is the teacher – *he* must be strong, *he* must bear all burdens – while you, the supplicant, should only gain strength from what he bears in your name. He will not share his heart with you, Ferendir, because so far as he is concerned, to share such a thing is tantamount to showing weakness, a weakness that cannot be countenanced in a teacher who truly prizes his or her pupils.'

If Ferendir did not so implicitly trust Desriel, he might have been tempted to dismiss everything his old master was currently telling him. Serath, vulnerable? Suffering, because of a student's failure? It hardly seemed possible.

And yet, Ferendir also knew that Desriel would never lie to him, nor tell him anything that he thought might be received improperly. The very fact that he now shared this fact with Ferendir spoke volumes as to how far his master believed he had progressed. It suggested his faith in Ferendir's ability not only to accept the truth and understand its import, but also to keep it a secret – indefinitely, if need be.

For if there was anything that a strong, powerful Lumineth shunned, it was any hint of weakness... any intimation of vulnerability or unassuaged pain.

Ferendir was about to ask a question – a question designed to help him best deal with his master, Serath, in the days and weeks to come – when from the camp some distance behind them he suddenly heard a commotion – scuffling feet, shouts of warning and the rattle of weapons hastily grabbed and couched for battle.

It was so sudden that Ferendir reacted to the tumult unconsciously, leaping to his feet and whirling away from the mountainside overlook to gaze back into the forest where their companions were gathered round their cookfires. At this distance, Ferendir could see nothing clearly – only shapes and movement – but those were sufficient to make the excitement of the moment clear. Bodies darted back and forth across the glow of the fire, shadows moved among the trees and underbrush. Something was afoot, and it seemed to have their comrades in a state of excitement.

Ferendir looked to Desriel. Desriel gave him a cursory glance, then broke into a run without a single word offered. Ferendir followed.

When they broke through the trees and made the clearing that they called camp, they found a static and completely unexpected state of affairs. Their companions – Serath, Phalcea, Metorrah, Taurvalon and Luverion – all stood with their backs to the fire, facing out into the forest, weapons lowered and gazes fixed on a single point – a united front against the incursion of whoever or whatever had just found them. Only when Desriel and Ferendir fell into line and managed to see past their friends – to see what had them so excited – did the scene make any sense.

Standing just a stone's throw away in a tight, close-crowded knot of short, squat bodies, were a number of duardin. Ferendir counted five, but there might have been two or three more lost in the press. The short, thick-limbed creatures seemed to have left their place of origin hastily and under duress – their clothes were covered in dirt, grime and soot, and each bore with them a hastily tied, haphazardly packed bundle that Ferendir assumed were supplies and provisions. Two at the fore of the tight knot bore weapons – one a sharp, deadly-looking axe, another a long, heavy-headed mace studded with square spikes – but the rest huddled behind those two, all appearing unarmed. There were two males, two females and at least one youth, so marked because the youngster was slightly shorter than the rest and not bearded at all.

Ferendir studied the tense scene: the wide-eyed, frightened duardin;

his hard-faced, silent companions; the stand-off persisting between them. No one dared speak or break the momentary stalemate.

'What have we here?' Desriel asked at last.

The duardin with the spiked mace licked her thick lips. 'Just peaceful passers-by, aelf-kin. We want nothing from you but safe passage, but we'll fight if you insist.'

'Safe passage,' Serath muttered. 'What are your kind even doing in these mountains? This is *our* world, the realm bequeathed to us by *our* makers. Who let you even set foot here, let alone dare to wander freely?'

'We set our feet where we like,' the bearded duardin with the axe barked. 'Are not all the Mortal Realms for all the mortal folk?'

'We need help,' a small voice said from behind the two armed leaders.

'Shush,' the axe-wielder hissed.

Luverion stepped forward. The loremaster had held his staff before him, its bejewelled head emanating a cold, bright glow in expectation of use. In the moment that he broke from the line and lowered the staff, however, the jewel's glow subsided.

'What help do you seek?'

'Step back, loremaster!' Serath commanded.

Luverion, to Ferendir's amazement, ignored Serath entirely.

'We will not harm you,' he said softly.

'Speak for yourself,' Metorrah said, her bow drawn and ready to loose. 'I, for one, see no good in random duardin appearing so close to our camp in such remote climes as these.'

'Agreed,' Phalcea said, pike level and eager to strike.

'Perhaps,' Desriel said, 'we should hear them out.'

'We will ask questions and they will answer them,' Serath said, never taking his eyes off the strangers. 'And neither our weapons nor our instinct for self-preservation shall be relaxed until we have answers that satisfy us.'

Ferendir was not sure where to place himself among his present company. A part of him truly wanted to welcome the newcomers, to assist them in their hour of need – but what if this was a trick? What if they were followers of Slaanesh, disguised and ready to deal them all killing blows the moment their defences were lowered? True, they looked harmless enough – filthy, haggard, beaten and cowed by circumstances still unknown to the Lumineth that now faced them – but appearances could be deceiving, could they not?

And yet, something inside him still seemed to urge caution – and compassion. Caught as he was between those two opposing polls – to protect or to accept, to drive away or to welcome in – Ferendir could barely make sense of his own thoughts or feelings, let alone discern the right course of action.

Ask yourself, then, a voice within him said, *what is to be lost and gained by each course of action. What do you lose – as a group, as a race, as individuals on an important quest – by lowering your defences and giving these duardin a moment's succour and support? Likewise, what do you possibly gain by taking them into your confidence, by hearing their tale and finding if they have anything of use to share with you?*

Suddenly, as if being instructed by a calm, sure voice wholly alien to his own consciousness, Ferendir knew what to do. He, too, stepped forward as Luverion had, and stood in the space between his suspicious comrades and the huddled, frightened newcomers. His hands were empty, his diamondpick hammer left beside the fire before he had retired to the hillside for his quiet reverie, and so it was easy to offer his empty hands and display them for the duardin.

'You are safe among us,' he said.

'Get back in line,' Serath hissed from where he stood on guard.

Ferendir only half turned, finding Serath in his peripheral vision. 'Forgive me, Master Serath, but I will not. These duardin need our help.' He looked to the refugees again. 'We have little to share, but what can be spared is yours. Come, sit by the fire.'

'You have wounded among you,' Luverion said, edging closer to the group. 'Please, allow us the privilege of aiding you.'

'Supplicant–' Serath began.

'He is no longer our supplicant,' Desriel said, stepping forward. 'And he is right in this. We must aid them.' He addressed the duardin now. 'Come now, all of you. Our fire is yours.'

There were six duardin in all – two males and two females of middling age and maturity, with a male youth and a stooped old female rounding out the group. The youth had suffered a horrible spell-burn on his left arm, the boiling scars and scorched skin still pulsating with a deep and terrible purple glow that Luverion immediately set to extracting with his spellcraft. The old woman had a game leg and moved with hobbling uncertainty with the help of an improvised crutch, while the rest of the band exhibited crusted and superficial wounds of various sorts, from the angry red infection of talon strikes to clean, cross-wise cuts that could only have come from blades.

The bearded male with the axe – whose name was Jalgrim – all but sagged when he finally sat down beside the fire, his compact, muscular body losing all of its strength and vitality in an instant. Clearly, he'd been struggling mightily to maintain both strength and vigilance for the sake of his little band as they fled through the mountains. Now, given some modicum of rest and safety, his exhaustion was so apparent that it almost made Ferendir weary simply to look upon him.

Ferendir and Desriel joined Luverion in attempting to provide aid and succour. They tended the duardins' wounds, offered them some water and bread for sustenance and generally tried to make them feel at home. The others, still in an attitude of guarded aloofness, sat on the far side of the fire, watching.

After a long, lingering silence, Serath finally pressed for answers.

'Who are you?' he demanded. 'And how do you find yourselves here, in this remote and sacred place?'

'This remote and sacred place is our home,' the duardin female with the spiked mace said. 'Our people have dwelt here since the close of the Age of Chaos, unchallenged and untroubled by anyone.' Her name, by her own report, was Geralla.

'Impossible,' Taurvalon said.

'No,' Desriel corrected as he washed a seeping wound on the female's stocky leg. 'It is not.' Ferendir saw him raise his eyes to meet the duardin woman's weary gaze. 'You are the dispossessed, is that it?'

Geralla nodded.

'I do not understand,' Ferendir said.

'They are leftovers,' Serath said from his perch across the fire. 'Remnants of the world that was, cast adrift when the Mortal Realms were forged and forced to find a new home, be it a place for their kind or not.'

'Clearly we have been no burden,' Jalgrim muttered, 'seeing as we have shared a continent with you Alarith for untold generations without your knowledge. Aye, I know your folk and your ways – all of your folk, all of your ways! Why do you know nought of us, if we share the same world?'

'Because we have never had need to,' Metorrah offered flatly.

Jalgrim looked like he was about to argue, but Geralla broke in and continued her own narrative before a disagreement could begin. 'We have always dwelt in these mountains – native outcasts, you might say... settled outsiders. We kept to ourselves, working a deep vein of ore and gems in a mine we've maintained for generations, just a short distance from here. In all our years, we have dwelt in peace, untroubled, barely noticed, remaining self-sufficient and only venturing forth through the Ten Paradises from time to time with jewels and tools and the produce of our forges for sale and trade.

'Until this very day, when those dogs of Slaanesh came swarming into our vale in search of plunder and sport.'

An almost palpable shudder ran through the group. Ferendir noted the silent, barely noticeable reaction only because he knew how to read his own people and their subtle emotional indicators. The mention of Slaanesh had hit home, powerfully.

'You say dogs of Slaanesh?' Serath asked.

'Aye,' Jalgrim said, his voice barely a croak. 'Not some enormous warhost – just a few dozen. But sufficient to tear us to pieces before we could even mount a defence. We know not what they sought – our jewels and weapons, though of fine quality, seemed hardly worthy of their notice. But we six were all that escaped. The rest...'

'Clearly,' Phalcea said, 'you had allowed your defensive instincts to lie fallow too long. Relative safety softened you.'

'You were unequal to the challenge,' Serath said with finality. ''Tis a wonder you've lasted as long as you have in such an alien place... a place not your own.'

Ferendir looked to the duardin. The two leaders – the female, Geralla, and the male, Jalgrim – now glared at his companions, clearly struggling to keep their tongues still and silent lest they lose what little safety and aid they had managed to acquire. The rest, though not so visibly troubled, simply kept their eyes down and their mouths shut, sure that their leaders would – for better or worse – handle the situation.

'They surprised us,' Geralla finally said, slowly, as if explaining something to a thick-headed child.

'The vigilant are *never* surprised,' Serath said stonily. 'All possibilities are considered, hour after hour, day after day, and all eventualities planned for.'

Ferendir threw a look at Desriel, then at Luverion. The loreseeker was so deeply involved in the healing of that youthful duardin's magical wound that he could expend no energy, no attention, on the present argument. Desriel, meanwhile, was concentrating hard sewing up that long, bleeding gash on Geralla's lower leg. Were they really going to let Serath and the others speak to these poor, miserable duardin so brusquely?

'Perhaps if your weapons were of finer make,' Taurvalon offered, 'or the mettle of their users more hard-proven in the field–'

'In any case,' Serath added, 'your losses and humiliation are, no doubt, sufficient to teach you a lesson. With luck, it shall not be the last lesson you ever learn.'

'And what lessons have we learned?' Ferendir spat.

Serath rose the moment his former supplicant spoke. 'What did you say?'

Ferendir rose to meet him. He stood squarely, facing Serath unafraid, only the crackling fire between them.

'I asked what lessons *we* had learned,' Ferendir said. There was no bitterness in his voice, no reproach, no anger. It was a simple question, born out of his own sudden realisation that Serath's apparent contempt for these unfortunate duardin could just as easily apply to their own lost temple brothers and sisters. 'Were our own folk not caught unaware? Surprised? Ravaged and slaughtered to the last – save the three of us, here, who remain?'

Serath levelled a finger coldly. 'You know not of what you speak, supplicant.'

Desriel rose now. 'He knows *precisely* of what he speaks,' the Stoneguard said. 'And it is his right to speak, because he is no longer our supplicant but our comrade.'

Serath's cold gaze pivoted to Desriel. Though his fury was clear, to anyone who knew how to mark it, he stood stone-still and his voice never rose above a soft murmur.

'You dare take his side in this?' Serath asked.

'I take no sides,' Desriel said. 'There are no sides, only lessons. Days ago, when our temple still stood and our temple family still lived, I might have spoken to these duardin as you have, Serath – haughty, dismissive, sure that I, a child of Lumineth, knew so much more than they. But Ferendir is right in this. When the enemy found our people, they were unprepared for what beset them, and they paid the ultimate price. And it was not because they were weak or foolish or because they lacked vigilance – it was because the enemy was more cunning, more cruel, and driven towards their desires without the compunctions and self-imposed limitations that give *our* lives purpose and meaning. I wager these poor folk suffered just as we did, and therefore, they have more in common with us than we ever, before this moment, could have imagined.'

Serath studied his long-time friend and partner in sullen silence. After a moment, he swung his dread gaze towards Ferendir. Finally, he looked to the huddled duardin, studying each of them in turn as if they were beggars bearing alms bowls and asking for scraps. No doubt the duardin saw nothing in Serath's face but cold, implacable indifference, but Ferendir could read his master well, and he knew what impatience and irritation he felt in that moment, even if no one else did.

And strangely, it made Ferendir feel purposeful, powerful.

Finally, Serath sat back down again and leaned on the haft of his stone mallet. He lowered his eyes to the flames of the cook-fires and stared.

'Perhaps,' he said quietly, 'my judgements were too hasty, my opinions ungracious.' He sighed, raised his eyes and speared the two duardin leaders with a fell glare. 'We will help you, if we can.'

'Very well, then,' Metorrah interrupted. 'They are worthy of our help – what help have we to give?'

'We are giving it,' Luverion said, his spellcraft still struggling to burn the taint of Chaos magic from the young duardin's arm.

'No, this is not enough,' Desriel said, finally knotting the gut twine he had employed to sew up Geralla's leg wound. He raised his eyes to meet Geralla's wondering gaze. 'We need you to take us back there.'

'Take you back there?' Jalgrim breathed. 'You're mad, aelf.'

'I am inclined to agree,' Phalcea said. 'We've been right on Ezarhad's trail, Desriel – our magic and their wake of destruction make tracking them easy. Why should we be so interested in overtaking them now?'

'Because we may catch them unaware,' Desriel said. Ferendir could hear that his master was struggling to sound reasonable – almost amiable – but there was a subtle, low-key tremble in his voice that made it clear enough – to Ferendir, anyway – that Desriel himself was not entirely sure about this course of action. 'If they have stopped long enough to ruin the camp and plunder its provisions, they may not be expecting us to come upon them.'

'Or they may already be gone,' Taurvalon said.

'A possibility,' Desriel admitted. 'But it is a chance worth taking.'

'And I suppose you expect us to lead you back there?' Jalgrim asked.

Desriel looked to the gruff duardin. 'I would hope so, yes.'

Jalgrim hawked and spat. 'Do not take this wrongly, aelf, but I would sooner drink molten gold. The six of us barely got away from those fiends with our lives, and now you would ask us to return? To offer ourselves up?'

'We can protect you,' Desriel said.

'I doubt that,' Geralla said sadly. 'I mean no offence, good aelf. But you did not see them.'

'We would offer our aid and you would insult us by refusing?' Serath asked.

Jalgrim stood, swayed for a moment, then settled himself. 'Aye, that,' he said with a curt nod. 'I will not put my folk in danger. Not when there are so few of us.'

'I'll go,' the young duardin being healed by Luverion chimed in. 'I'm not afraid – not any more. Mother and father were left behind. They might still be–'

'*They are not!*' Jalgrim barked, wheeling round on his youthful companion. 'Anyone not here with us, right now, is dead and gone! That is the truth of it, and I'll not have you spreading false hopes among us!'

The young duardin, face a mask of grief and suffering, never let his gaze waver. He met Jalgrim's burning glare with quiet assurance, still holding his poisoned arm out for Luverion's ministrations.

'You may be right,' he said. 'But I will guide them, nonetheless.'

'Very well, then,' Serath said. 'It is decided.'

'Is it?' Metorrah asked. 'How did that happen? We went from refusing aid to forcing it upon them in the space of a breath.'

'Desriel speaks aright,' Serath said curtly. 'This may be our best chance to overtake them. Even if they've already gone, their sojourn at the home of these dispossessed delayed them. We are closer upon them now than we've ever been. If we can stop them here, now, in the mountains, before they ever reach their destination–'

'We can end this!' Desriel finished.

Ferendir understood the implicit message buried in his masters' sudden enthusiasm.

If we can stop them here, now, in the mountains, before they ever reach their destination, we can end this... and, just possibly, give meaning to all that we've lost, all that can never be recovered...

Luverion finally withdrew his hand from the young duardin's wound. It was still raw – pink in some places, angry red in others with ample subdermal flesh and drying blood still present. But the foul purple glow in the angry wounds beneath the dermis was gone. The youth was only nursing a physical wound now, not a magical one.

'We must wash and bandage that,' Luverion said softly, as though no conversation at all were taking place around him.

'Do it quickly, then,' Serath said. 'We depart forthwith. There's not a moment to lose!'

To Ferendir's great surprise, Jalgrim ultimately decided to be their guide, ordering the wounded youth and the rest of his charges to continue their journey westwards towards Xintil, where they could start again. The chieftain seemed to take no pleasure in sending his people away while he stayed to march back into danger, but Ferendir could also recognise in the short, stocky fellow the mark of all good leaders – the ability to sacrifice one's own best interests for the sake of a larger goal, and the related ability to undertake that sacrifice with a minimum of fuss or complaint.

In no time, the eight of them – Ferendir, his six companions and the duardin – were under way.

They marched all through the night, their path taking them up steep slopes and through dense forests before finally bending eastwards through a narrow pass between low peaks towards a hidden valley of sorts, locked behind high, stony walls in a forgotten cleft between the mountains. By the time the first tentative glow of the coming dawn began to paint the sky in more brilliant colours, they had emerged from the pass into the vale proper, and the mining camp that the duardin once called home was clearly visible beneath them, huddled against the mountainside on a wide, rocky promontory overlooking sharp hills that all declined down to the river winding across the valley floor below.

They crouched among close-packed rocks and boulders on a ledge below the pass, peering down towards the silent mining settlement, trying to tease out the present situation and its relative safety.

'I see no movement,' Taurvalon said, peering through a long, telescoping spyglass that he had produced from a satchel on his belt. He handed it to Serath. Ferendir's master peered through the implement for a time, surveying the scene below them.

'Bodies,' Serath said. 'Dozens, grimly arrayed...'

Ferendir well knew what that meant. Time and again they had seen the vile handiwork of the Slaaneshi hordes, great and small – their penchant for creating horrid, haunting works of art from those they slaughtered, arranging their corpses and hacked-off extremities in strange, unsettling patterns and poses to make of them foul trophies to their fouler appetites. Ferendir stole a glance at Jalgrim and saw that, at Serath's pronouncement, the duardin had lowered his face. If Ferendir was not mistaken, he saw the subtle glimmer of tears on the dwarf's ruddy, pockmarked cheeks.

'Taurvalon is correct, though,' Serath said. 'There is no movement. The camp is abandoned.'

'Can we be certain of that?' Phalcea asked. 'This could be a trap.'

Serath lowered the spyglass. 'Aye, it could be... but we will not know that until we spring it.' He looked to Desriel. 'Who shall it be, old friend?'

Desriel rose. 'Let it be me.'

They waited. The time required for Desriel to clamber silently down the rocky slope, make a cautious, half-hidden approach to the settlement and finally emerge into the open for all to see far below them seemed interminable to Ferendir. He kept expecting to see a flock of birds wing from one of the copses of trees that swallowed his furtive master during his approach, or suddenly hear a shout of alarm, the exultant war cry of their Slaaneshi enemies as they raced from cover to spring the attack.

But nothing came. The world remained silent, marked only by the sighing of the mountain winds and the even, steady breathing of his eager companions.

Finally, after what felt like endless hours, they saw a lone figure move slowly, cautiously, from the cover of the trees onto the bare, broad promontory. There were a number of buildings down there – small, huddled duardin dwellings, storehouses and places of artifice, all arranged in a vaguely semicircular pattern around a sort of central square before the yawning mouths of their several mine shafts sunk into the hillside. It was the square before those buildings and the broad, empty space before the yawning mineshafts that lay littered and bedecked with the bodies of the dead. It was into that space that Desriel now moved, clearly on edge and searching on all sides for signs of their enemies.

Ferendir watched, his breath catching in his throat. Desriel was alone down there, exposed, too far from the rest of them if any danger should present itself. His master gripped his diamond-pick hammer tightly and turned slowly, carefully. He seemed to be studying every building and corn-crib around him, seeking some sign of hidden dangers or lurking treachery. Ferendir realised he was holding his breath. By conscious will, he exhaled, long and slow, then gulped air like a thirsty man in a desert.

Desriel stood, still and alone, in the corpse-littered square below. Finally, he stood straight and raised his hammer cross-wise over his head.

That was the signal. All clear.

'Come,' Serath said, clambering out of hiding. 'Let us see what awaits us.'

Ferendir was shocked at how quickly they all climbed down the hillside, threaded a path through the close-cropped trees and finally arrived in the settlement's square. The bodies were, as he had feared, arrayed in the most horrible and evocative of attitudes, some in parodies of everyday activities, others as grim trophies claimed with pride, still more dismembered and rearranged into savagely beautiful geometric patterns and mandalas made all the more horrifying for the clarity of the artistry deployed to create them. There was evidence of fire and immolation – piles of wind-blown ash and the stench of smoke and charred wood – but all the fires were long extinguished. Clouds of flies buzzed above the dead, crawled over their staring eyes and licked at their coagulating blood.

It was a scene from a nightmare. The silence did nothing to assuage its horrible nature.

Jalgrim, their duardin guide, kept his eyes down, as though he were afraid to look upon the frozen, slack faces of the dead around him – family, friends, loved ones. No doubt he knew the name and history of every single corpse littering the square and the surrounding buildings.

Ferendir remembered their own walk through the ruined precincts of the temple and shuddered.

'Too late,' Taurvalon said as he studied the scene. 'Clearly, they've left us behind.'

'Thankfully,' Desriel said.

Ferendir glanced at Serath. His hard-faced master looked as close to furious as he could imagine – eyes narrowed, mouth set stonily, nostrils flaring as he struggled to control his ragged breathing.

Luverion was moving slowly, aimlessly, among the dead. He struck a strange attitude as he went, arms outstretched and hands splayed wide, as though magically dowsing or trying to sense something hiding just below the surface of what they could touch and smell and see.

'There is such a taint on this place,' he said quietly, almost to himself. 'Foul and ancient... bitter as gall and soot... and... something else.'

Desriel took notice of those words. 'What else?' he demanded.

Luverion turned fully around, raising his hands to the level of his eyes. It was as if he were reading the wind itself as it buffeted against him and whipped around him. Finally – suddenly, in fact – he lowered his hands and his eyes snapped open.

'You were right,' he said to Desriel. 'It's a trap.'

Ferendir felt a cold shudder run through him. No... impossible! It was so silent! So still!

Then he heard their war cries and saw the writhing, loping bodies all come streaming from the three open mouths of the mine shafts sunk into the hillside.

One moment, they were alone in a village full of only the dead – the next, they were swarmed and surrounded by the Hedonites of Slaanesh.

CHAPTER ELEVEN

For an instant, Ferendir recalled the feelings that rose up within him when, just days ago, he and his masters went to the secret vale that should have been the place of his trial and found instead a roving band of Slaaneshi invaders awaiting them. There had been nine of the foul daemons that day, and seeing them, knowing they surrounded and outnumbered them, had made Ferendir feel as powerless and helpless as he had ever felt. Even though his masters had protected him, and they'd won out in the end, the fear and sense of hopelessness that had assailed Ferendir in those moments, when he knew not if the next movement, the next breath, might be his last, had felt like some foul, soul-burning venom.

Now, he stood among comrades, outnumbered once again. There were dozens of them, pouring out of the mines and swarming in all directions to confuse and surround their little band. They dived and struck and briefly charged before making hasty withdrawals, but Ferendir knew they were not yet ready to attack in earnest. These were baits and taunts – a show of force and a taste of the slaughter to come, nothing more. The Hedonites took great delight in showing their strength, displaying their foul, sharp talons and their needle teeth and their lithe, slim bodies built for the twin engines of pleasure and pain.

'Back to back!' Serath ordered, planting his feet and holding his stone mallet high and ready. 'Form a circle, now!'

Though no clear leader had ever been established in their group, no chain of command agreed upon, everyone, in that instant, heeded Serath's command. The seven aelves and their duardin companion hastily formed a circle, back to back, facing outwards towards their horrifying opponents. While Ferendir and his masters took up on-guard battle stances with their lethal longhammers, Phalcea prepared her long, slender pike and Metorrah took her place at her sister's side, bow at the ready, an arrow already couched for a draw. Taurvalon stood like a Vanari warden in a phalanx – body hunched forward, spear thrusting out at eye level, resting on the upper lip of his raised shield. Even Luverion – moon-touched, fey Luverion – stood on guard, his own bronze shield and graceful sword each ready to strike or repel. To Ferendir's great surprise, the lunar runes upon the Zaitreci's armour and shield were even glowing with a faint, pale blue light. Amid the seven, wounded Jalgrim brandished his axe, face a mask of fury, eager to avenge his fallen kinfolk with as many daemonettes as he could drag into the dark with him.

There were all sorts amidst their enemies: the strange, body-altered creatures that looked vaguely human, twisted by their obsessions and appetites; a few battle mages wrapped in dark, be-gemmed robes from head to toe and brandishing sorcerer's staves already spitting foul purple luminescence; four-legged, long-snouted fiends stomping and snorting like centaurs eager for a head-to-head challenge; and, at the rear, mounted hellstriders circling slowly, easily, seemingly content to see their entire task as keeping any of the chosen sacrifices from slipping the surging, roiling cordon of bodies.

They all stamped and shook and trembled, their impatience and bloodlust palpable.

To Ferendir's right, the crowd split, making room for an enormous, hulking champion to saunter through – a towering humanoid of pure, sculpted muscle beneath a suit of finely tooled armour plate, a pair of curling ram's horns growing out of his deeply lined, misshapen head. He levelled the enormous sword in his hand at the group of encircled travellers.

'You are trespassers here,' he barked.

'Trespassers, ha!' Jalgrim spat back. 'That's rich, you foul, murderous gargant! This was *my* home – the home of *all* these slain and desecrated dead you see lying about us! The only trespassers here are you lot!'

The horned hulk sneered and shook its massive head. 'Fools,' it rumbled. 'Today, you are granted a gift unparalleled. You are all offered a chance – but one chance – to join the retinue of the highest, the holiest, the most hellishly potent and powerful Lord of Pleasure and Pain...'

As he spoke, the crowd tittered and parted. From the rear, a newcomer strode forward – taller than a human or any of the aelves, equal in stature to the Slaaneshi champion but of a wholly different build. It seemed to be male, lithe of limb, with a slender but muscularly sculpted frame, draped in a storm of fine silks and haphazardly draped bangles, bracelets and circlets of gold, silver and bronze. His four arms were all raised and outstretched, like a king presenting himself for the admiration of his subjects. And though there was a strange, haunting sort of handsomeness in his slender face, he was also clearly and certainly evil. His red-black eyes and the many piercings in his brows and ears and the mad, toothy grin on that mock-pretty face were enough to tell Ferendir that the creature they now beheld was not only malevolent but quite possibly mad.

'Ezarhad Fatesbane!' the hulking herald concluded. 'Your saviour, or your destroyer!'

The assembled horde howled and cheered in answer. Their four-armed master, Ezarhad, turned and faced them, looking down his nose and smiling with a sneering self-satisfaction that made Ferendir's deep-rooted hate for the monster intensify. Clearly, his followers worshipped him, and clearly, Ezarhad basked happily, haughtily, in that worship.

After a long, roaring series of cheers and praises, Ezarhad Fatesbane finally made a subtle sign indicating that he desired silence. Without hesitation, his followers complied. Once more, the promontory and the mountainside were silent, the only sounds the sough of the winds and the faint, eager rustling of the alpine trees. Somewhere, a raptor screeched, and its cry echoed through the mountain canyons.

Ezarhad Fatesbane turned to face the encircled party. He looked down his long, aquiline nose at them – smug, condescending.

'This is your only opportunity to serve a power divine,' he said in a forceful but melodious voice, declaiming like an actor upon a stage. 'Bend your knees and kiss my signet ring, and I shall help to reshape you – each and every one of you – into something beautiful, something one of a kind and without parallel. Refuse this generous offer, and you shall all be torn limb from limb where you stand.'

'Beautiful,' Desriel said sardonically. 'The same beauty you leave in your wake? The same beauty we see arrayed around us? Corpses laid in attitudes of jest and desecration? A nest of ugly servants, all twisted by their depravities and perversions?'

'Your mind is narrow and your vision short, my Lumineth friend. Why spend your long, dreary existence placing strictures and fetters upon yourself, when you can set free the wells of power and purpose inside you? All those appetites your people struggle so hard to contain, all those desires they work so diligently to bury and deny?'

'You stole something that belongs to us,' Serath said. 'Return it and you shall survive the day.'

For a moment, the pretender stared, as if he could not believe his ears. Then, to Ferendir's great astonishment and horror, the monster began to laugh.

In seconds, his servants had joined in.

The laughter was coarse, loud, raucous. Hearing it made Ferendir's ears ache. Worse, the sound seemed to penetrate his very being – deep within him, sending tremors through his bones and sickening vibrations through his viscera. One moment, the laughter would fill him with fear and dread, a certainty that they could not survive the day, let alone win it. In the next instant, he would be seized by a red-eyed, monstrous hunger to break from their little back-to-back formation and charge the nearest Hedonites, pick hammer high, content to die if only he could take a few of the foul monsters with him.

Eyes darting about, Ferendir caught sight of Serath. His master was looking askance at him, staring, as if waiting for him to take note of something.

Serath's gaze cut right through the storm of confusion inside him. All at once, Ferendir felt calm, clearly recognising the maddening power of their enemies' laughter.

'Stand,' Serath said quietly. 'Do not fear. Whatever comes, do not fear.'

Ferendir felt a sudden pang of shame, but it was brief. In moments, that shame was washed away and all that remained was a deep, empowering sense of purpose and pride. Perhaps he would die this day – perhaps they all would – but they would give these monsters the fight of their vile lives. And as he fought, and died, he would stand beside the two greatest Lumineth he could have ever hoped to be instructed and shaped by. Serath… Desriel… his masters… his teachers… by all practical definition, his fathers.

Ferendir met Serath's gaze. He did his best to project strength, assurance.

'I only seek to make you proud, master,' he said, the raucous laughter around them swallowing his words.

'You always have,' Serath answered, then turned to face outwards, towards their enemies.

Ezarhad Fatesbane lifted his four bejewelled arms. The braying horde fell silent in an instant. The pretender to the throne of Slaanesh let his eyes sweep over his gathered followers. Finally, he spoke.

'Kill them,' he said. 'And make them suffer.'

The Hedonites charged.

'Stand,' Serath said, and raised his stone mallet before him.

Ferendir and Desriel both knew what that command meant. They planted their feet wide, just as Serath had, and lowered their pick hammers horizontally before them. The three Alarith, side by side, formed a small, impenetrable quadrant of the circle made by the whole of their little band. When the Hedonites swarmed upon them and leapt forward to attack, they broke upon the magical barrier that the three of them had created.

The effect was so wondrous, so unexpected, that Ferendir almost lost concentration. He had tapped into the mountain's power almost without thinking about it, his terrible need and his master's simple command acting in concert to focus his will and put him into direct communion with the enduring forces at the mountain's call. He could almost feel his feet become rooted to the place where he stood, feel the density of his body change to something thick, heavy, impenetrable, feel the radiant, repellent force suddenly bleeding from his pick hammer.

When the Hedonites collided with the trio, they literally slammed into an impenetrable wall and bounced backwards, as though they had tried to climb a barrier that denied them a handhold. On they came, one after another in a broad, swarming line of vile, monstrous faces and gnashing teeth and sniping pincers and swiping talons. Again and again, they collided with the invisible, unyielding force that Ferendir and his masters radiated. Every time, they fell backwards, screaming and cursing, before more of their comrades surged forward for their own onslaught.

Behind them, Ferendir heard the others fighting their own battles – the swoop and clang of Phalcea's pike, the soft, regular hum of Metorrah's bowstring as she loosed arrow after arrow into the horde, the rasp and clang of Taurvalon's spear and shield as he repelled every attacker and struck savagely to hold their enemies at bay. Jalgrim the duardin cursed and spat and called for challengers as he hacked and struck and slashed, while Luverion called upon fell, ancient forces from the world and the aether around them and loosed those focused energies upon their attackers.

All this Ferendir heard, but he dared not turn to see. If he moved, even to glance behind him, the efficacy of the barrier he, Serath and Desriel now maintained would be broken. Only through an act of concerted will could he maintain his focus, face forward, hammer levelled, standing still, silent and immovable like a section of a curtain wall.

'Prepare,' Desriel said.

'For what?' Ferendir shouted back.

'To attack,' Serath answered.

They're going to break the barrier, Ferendir thought fearfully. *Now, at this moment, we stand here safe, protected, impenetrable. But the moment we move–*

'For the Alarith!' Serath cried, then raised his massive stone mallet and brought it crashing down upon the nearest adversary.

The daemonette's red-maned, misshapen head collapsed like a ripe melon. But before its lifeless corpse had even hit the ground, Serath was already trudging forward, sweeping his stone mallet right and left, interspersing thrusts of its ferule and deadly strikes from its head spike between broad, perfectly aimed sweeps of its heavy hammer head.

Ferendir broke formation and waded in. A strange feeling overtook him – something akin to an out-of-body experience – as the energies that only moments before had rooted and protected them now seemed to leap up through the length of his limbs and concentrate themselves in the muscles of his arms, even in the pick hammer itself. He pivoted, leapt, lunged and danced, and as he did so, the hammer led his torso through its paces, as though it were alive. He crushed skulls, impaled ribcages, broke curving sword blades and sent servants of Slaanesh sprawling.

For an instant, only an instant, Ferendir dared a glance at his masters beside him – Serath, standing strong, crushing and slaughtering every Hedonite that entered the circle of death surrounding him, while fluid, cunning Desriel surged and whirled among the enemy, an avalanche speeding downhill in aelven form, driving deep into their ranks and destroying them with perfect, unstoppable movements.

And here stood Ferendir, fighting beside them, all the lessons of his years as their supplicant now flooding back upon him – every sparring session, every lone drill, every pointed exercise – all returning to him as pure, unconscious muscle memory and instinct. Enemies charged Ferendir on all sides, slashing, snapping, stabbing and swarming – but he fought on, crushing them, breaking them, tearing them, impaling them.

Just as Ferendir downed another opponent – a black-eyed creature with a long, trailing braid of bone-white hair and pincers like some vile crustacean – another form reared up, huge and powerful, in his peripheral vision. As his first adversary fell, Ferendir spun towards the oncoming movement and raised his hammer for a strike–

But before he could even reach the apex of his swing, the charging Hedonite struck with its enormous scimitar and deflected Ferendir's sweeping pick hammer. The strike threw everything off balance. The hammer nearly leapt from Ferendir's sweating hands. As he struggled to hold the weapon, his body bent awkwardly, balance destroyed, form elongated.

He was vulnerable, exposed.

The great, gleaming scimitar rose and began to fall.

Ferendir's concentration was destroyed. For an instant – an impossible instant – he sought a remedy and could find none. Too close to retreat, too off balance to move out of reach, too exposed to parry or block.

Then something long and shining thrust into Ferendir's vision.

Phalcea's pike. The blade and long haft collided with a clang and bent the falling scimitar strike sideways, away from its intended target. The blade missed Ferendir, but the scimitar-wielder was already recovering, lifting its blade for another attack.

Phalcea moved with blinding speed and assurance. Her pike swept out in a flat arc, slamming hard into the exposed solar plexus of the Hedonite, then withdrew in the same instant, preparing for a powerful forward thrust.

Ferendir recovered, corrected his stance and prepared to deliver a killing blow of his own.

Thunk.

A single arrow slammed home in the Hedonite's bald skull, right through one of its glassy black eyes. Scimitar poised above its head, the Hedonite froze, its one remaining eye blinked, then it fell in a crumpled heap.

Ferendir turned. There stood Metorrah, bowstring still vibrating from the shot, her pike-wielding sister already redirecting her attentions towards a new knot of oncoming attackers.

Metorrah gave a single nod, suggesting something over Ferendir's shoulder.

Ferendir understood immediately. He spun on his heel, sweeping his hammer round as he did, and felt the haft of the weapon slam home in the midsection of a charging Hedonite. As his would-be murderer bent double around the haft, Ferendir yanked the weapon free and brought it round in a stunning overhead arc to crush the Hedonite's bowed head.

The world around him was a storm of flashing steel, slicing pincers, snapping teeth and gouts of foul black ichor and blood. There were almost a dozen dead Hedonites lying strewn at his and his masters' shuffling feet, but still more waited to attack where their comrades had failed.

There were too many of them. They could not maintain this defence indefinitely.

'This way!' Taurvalon shouted, and charged through a crowd of Hedonites. As he moved, his aetherquartz flared blindingly bright for an instant and seemed to actually add speed and force to his advance. Shield lowered, he ploughed right through all the adversaries in his path, clearing a swathe through which the others could follow. It was through that kinetically carved alley that Taurvalon led them, fleeing away from the cliff faces and the mine entrances towards the outer precincts of the duardin settlement. Ferendir looked to his masters for confirmation, but they were already falling back, urging him to do likewise as they went. Desriel led the way as Serath stood behind them to hold off the closing ranks of the enemy, his deft, economical movements belying his ruthless efficiency and cold-blooded readiness to slay all who threatened them.

Phalcea, as well, had taken up a defensive position, using her pike to skewer and slash any oncoming Hedonites while the rest of them fell back through the gap Taurvalon had created. To Ferendir's amazement, Luverion planted himself and called for their retreat, all the while raising his staff before him and calling upon unseen powers that he seemed to draw right out of the air and into his being. As Ferendir retreated through the gap, he saw Luverion point his sword towards an advancing wave of Hedonites and cast a massive bolt of pure white flame. That pale flame ignited the broad, seething line of closing Hedonites. As those afire fell and rolled and danced in an effort to extinguish themselves, they collided with others and spread the flames, or simply collapsed and created a crackling, incendiary barrier too hot and hungry for any of their comrades to pass through.

Ferendir ran past Metorrah, who stood at the mouth of the gap, loosing arrow after arrow to cover their retreat. Phalcea, one moment behind Ferendir, raced ahead and struck fast and loose as she passed, clearing the way of any overly bold Hedonites so that Ferendir and the others could follow through behind.

The promontory bucked and trembled beneath them. Ferendir stopped for a moment and spun to look back, not sure what was responsible for the tremor. Once more, he was astonished to find that it was Luverion, now calling upon powerful forces from the sky itself, directing lance after lance of white, crackling lightning from the sky right into the stone and regolith beneath them. With each strike, shockwaves knocked the enemy off their feet and sent them reeling into the white flames still consuming the other Hedonites.

Ferendir wanted to stand, to watch what unfolded, to bask in the wonder of Luverion's assured power – but there was no time to stand. He had to run with the others. They had to find a new site – higher ground – on which to make a last stand.

They fled. On all sides, the empty homes and trade shanties of the duardin who had once been settled upon the promontory gaped and stared. Behind them, the forces of Slaanesh charged onwards, still many scores remaining even after dozens and dozens had been struck down in battle. Serath stood to repel an attack from a charging fiend. Desriel took on a trio of invaders wielding barbed whips. Chaos wizards in the pretender's company began casting their spells about haphazardly, like Taurvalon suddenly throwing his explosives without let or hindrance. A thatched roof became a storm of screeching, biting, claw-ripping bats that swarmed about Ferendir and Phalcea as they fled. Another sprouted long, grasping tendrils seemingly composed of straw and fragments of mud brick. As the group retreated, Luverion did his best to cast counter-spells to the foul magical gambits of the Chaos wizards, meeting each challenge with a casual grace that Ferendir found all but unnatural. The loremaster turned the attacking bats into a storm of feathers and the wind drew them hastily away. He cast moisture towards the clay tendrils and they melted into mud and mire. To allow Serath and Desriel to fall back, Luverion cast wave upon wave of aelemental power towards the oncoming horde – walls of flame, slashing rain from out of nowhere, blasting wind that threw dozens of Slaaneshi to the ground in a tangle of limbs.

But still they came. They never stopped, only faltered, recovered and pressed forward again.

Ferendir suddenly skidded to a halt. They'd reached the edge of the promontory – a sheer vertical drop down a cliffside that ended in a narrow, rocky shelf far below, with trees clinging to the still-steep hillside beneath it. Far beneath them, a wide stream or shallow river – he could not tell which – wound through the long, meandering valley that sheltered the mining camp. Within sight, there was no easy way down the slope to the valley floor.

They were trapped.

'Formation!' Serath shouted as he sped into their ranks, turned and set himself to meet the oncoming enemy. 'Side by side! Backs to the cliff!'

All obeyed instinctively, knowing that Ferendir's master was – if nothing else – a warrior worthy of combat command. They arrayed themselves in a broad, curving line, backs to the drop-off, all facing the oncoming Slaaneshi horde. Ferendir, for his part, had no idea what might come next. Could they root themselves again? Call on the mountain's aid? Even so, they could not stand against the enemy indefinitely. For all the daemonettes and Hedonites they'd destroyed in the fray, there still seemed to be scores of them – maybe even a hundred. Sooner or later, their numbers and amassed strength would either overwhelm their small party's aelven magic or simply drive them – still shielded – right off the mountainside.

But as they each prepared to meet their fate, to make that last, desperate stand at the edge of the precipice, something strange occurred.

A foul, atonal horn roared through the valley, blown from behind and above them. None could see who blew the horn or what sort of horn it might be, but it seemed to be emanating from the ledges above the village, just beside the portals into the mines. The moment that strange, mournful instrument sounded, the oncoming Slaaneshi Hedonites skidded to a halt, en masse. They jostled and collided, all answering that wordless call but seeming thoroughly puzzled by it.

Ferendir watched. Waited. Stared.

They seem confused… lost, even. Clearly, someone was sounding a retreat. Why?

The Hedonites all exchanged puzzled glances, took last, vicious looks at their prey lined up before the ledge, then began, as a single mass, to edge backwards, withdrawing into the empty houses and trade sheds of the encampment.

Amidst the inhuman underlings on the front lines before them, Ferendir saw a number of new arrivals – strange, wizened forms in robes and cowls, some wearing strange masks, others with their faces hidden deep in the shadows of their hoods. There were perhaps half a dozen of them. They haunted the periphery of a fat knot of daemonettes like temple instructors trying to corral unruly children.

Wizards. They had to be. But what were they doing?

Ezarhad Fatesbane suddenly appeared on a pile of large fallen stones that used to be one of the larger structures in the duardin settlement. He stood tall and proud, gazing out over his minions towards those skulking wizards.

'If you will do the honours,' Ezarhad shouted, and suddenly, lilac globes of mystical energy crackled around his outstretched hands.

The wizards obeyed. Without warning, they all drew great serrated knives – short swords, more rightly – and tore into the pack of daemonettes before them. The daemonettes tried to fight back, to defend themselves, but the wizards worked swiftly and had the advantage of surprise. In short order, all thirteen of the daemonettes gathered had been slain and bled their vile black blood upon the ground.

And that ground, so anointed, began to shake.

'What is this?' Serath asked, almost to himself.

'It cannot be good,' Desriel said.

The rest of the horde was backing away now, as if they could feel what was about to be summoned. The wizards, rather than retreating, stood right where they'd done their foul sacrificial deeds, all throwing their hands and bloodied knives skywards and chanting in guttural ecstasy.

Ezarhad chanted as well, though they could not make out the words at the distance he stood from them. No matter. The intensifying orbs of sickly purple light that enshrouded his twisting, gesturing hands told them all they needed to know.

'It's coming,' Luverion said. 'His offering's been given. There's no stopping it.'

'*What* is coming?' Taurvalon asked.

In answer to Taurvalon's question, the broad, bald promontory before them – the great span of rock separating them from their would-be destroyers – began to glow. It began small – just a small bloom of light emanating from within the rock itself – but it soon spread far and wide over the open ground before them. As the glow intensified, the rock itself began to seethe and liquefy, as though a bloom of magma lay just below its surface and was about to melt through the regolith and burst forth.

'What is happening?' Serath demanded.

'The pretender struck down his own servants to beg aid,' Luverion said. Ferendir thought he heard a note of sadness in the loremaster's voice.

The half-molten rock began to ripple and crack. Then, without warning, it exploded upwards, sending a shower of molten lava droplets and still-glowing jagged fragments of stone rising high into the air before tumbling earthwards again. The stone shelf of the promontory had expanded and exploded like an overfilled wineskin. Now, rising to its full height out of a smoking pit gouged into the hillside, stood an enormous, towering Chaos daemon. It rose slowly, almost gingerly, as though it had been contorted and cramped for a long season and needed to spare its joints as it unfurled. Its great, muscular body was as tall as three aelves standing on one another's shoulders, its four arms each tipped in some terrifying, misshapen organic likeness of a blade or bludgeon. A terrifying fan of bone and gristle crests spread out from its inhuman skull, while purple fire and black smoke rolled upwards in waves from the open well beneath it.

Espying the eight of them there on the ledge, the great daemon roared. One hand – capped in a tooth-edged harrow – came sweeping down and whistled through the air in mock threat. Its other three hands – a thorn-encrusted horn that looked something like a leafless tree, a serrated sabre blade, a mass of knobby bone and gristle – all whipped about in a shameless display of dominance.

Ferendir's eyes skated over Serath – randomly, unbidden – but as they did so, he saw a clear change in his stoic mentor's countenance. Anger and frustration gave way to a strange sort of peace – a grim determination. Straightening his shoulders and lifting his stone mallet to touch his forehead, Serath seemed to be preparing for some course of action whose outcome would be quite definitive.

He's about to march out there, alone, to meet it, Ferendir realised.

But then, something even more astounding occurred. Serath shifted his weight to take a single step forward – but before he could do so, Luverion broke from their formation and marched out onto the promontory to meet the towering daemon where it stood.

'Get back in line,' Serath said forcefully.

'No need,' the loremaster said, only glancing back for an instant to offer an enigmatic smile. His pale grey eyes were bright – even eager. 'Allow me.'

The daemon lifted one great foot out of the pit, braced it on the lip and hauled itself upwards. It now stood to its full height on the outcropping, and it was truly enormous and terrifying.

Luverion raised his sword before him, lifting its graceful, silver-bright blade high towards the sky – towards Celennar. As they all watched, they heard the loremaster calling out in a language familiar to none of their ears, calling clearly and forcefully to powers they could not name or identify. As Luverion chanted, the lunar runes on his bronze breastplate and teardrop shield began to glow. In seconds, they were glaring, as bright and brilliant as any of Taurvalon's aetherquartz.

The daemon roared, stamped and prepared its four misshapen hand-weapons for killing blows.

Ferendir stared, amazed at what he was seeing.

One moment, the sky was blue and cloudless. The next, a small dark smudge like a bruise appeared. Moment by moment, that smudge swirled and grew. Out of it bloomed a roiling mass of storm clouds. As those clouds churned, they seemed to draw arcing branches of lightning down from Celennar's pale form in the sky. Round and round the scintillating light and thunderous clouds went, like silver and coal tumbling in a rolling barrel. Lightning flashed. Thunder pealed. Fleet, intermittent torrents of rain spat down upon the daemon lord.

The daemon felt the rain, heard the thunder, cringed in annoyance from the crackling lightning. It dipped its head slightly, then craned it sideways to look straight up into the gathering localised storm.

At that moment, Luverion swept down his sword, as though he were a lord regent giving the order for his Dawnriders to charge.

All at once, the storm struck at the daemon. Long, barbed branches of blinding lightning flashed and crackled as thunder shook the mountainside. Swirling in torrents at the centre of the stormy column was a solid pillar of battering rain driven by a concentrated, spinning wind funnel as pointed and forceful as a stake driven through a vampire's evil black heart.

The daemon bent, hissing and thrashing. It struck with its weapons in all directions, trying in vain to find the heart of the storm and destroy it. But the storm would not be cut or contained. Though it occupied a relatively narrow band of the air above and around the daemon, its intensity and force were terrible to behold. The rain literally slashed at the daemon's monstrous flesh like a storm of swirling knives, tearing and ripping, drawing blood and ichor in thick rivulets. The lightning strikes – swift, sure, like the stinging of angry hornets – seared the daemon's exposed flesh, set its hair and clothing aflame, even began to superheat and melt its infernal weaponry. One of its serrated blade-hands caught a direct strike and was set ablaze. At the heart of the maelstrom was a powerful column of hurricane wind that pressed down, down, ever down upon the massive beast. Even the ground around the daemon suffered under the torrent, the ragged rim of the well it had burst from eroding and collapsing as they watched, rock and soil blasted sideways, sent flying away under the terrible pressure of the battering rain and punishing column of wind.

All the while, Luverion stood, facing their monstrous adversary, sword and shield poised, his eyes now burning, alight with the lambent lunar energies that he'd summoned to protect them.

Something shifted beneath them. Ferendir saw that it was not just his imagination – everyone felt it. A moment later, another tremor wracked the precipice they stood upon.

Out on the promontory, huge cracks were radiating outwards from the well the daemon had risen out of. They spread towards the edges of the out-thrust ledge that they all stood upon.

It's too much, Ferendir realised. *The fury of Luverion's storm is containing the daemon, but it's also battering the already scarred hillside. At any moment–*

The ground gave way.

All at once, the world was nothing but roaring, riven stone, collapsing soil, the screams of the tortured daemon and a sense that the ground beneath them had simply disappeared. Ferendir barely had time to register what had occurred. He snatched a few rapid impressions – the affrighted faces of the Slaaneshi as they saw the hillside collapse and scrambled backwards, the convulsions of the daemon as gravity drew it down, a quick glimpse of Serath diving towards him, trying to grab him even though he was suddenly falling through empty space.

Then the world was all darkness and rapid descent.

CHAPTER TWELVE

I have been here before, Ferendir thought. *Buried alive. Helpless. Hopeless.*

He tried to move, found himself bounded.

He tried to breathe, found no air.

He tried to call out. He had no voice.

The world was soil and rock and darkness and pressure. The world was living death. The world was a tomb. A seizure of panic slithered through him, threatening to swallow his body, his mind, his spirit in monstrous despair and all-consuming insanity.

No, no, no! his mind screamed. *This cannot happen! We've come too far! Endured too much! We cannot fail now!*

Then do not, his many years of training told him.

I cannot move. I cannot breathe. I cannot speak. In moments I will probably subside into unconsciousness, then death...

Where are you? Think.

Beneath a rockslide.

A rockslide where? Where did all of this earth come from?

From a mountain… but not my mountain, my home.

But all the mountains are kith and kin, are they not? Is there not a web of interlaced ley lines that binds and communicates between the peaks, at their roots and foundations? Though our mountain was our mother, and she had a name, and a spirit, and a consciousness, can this mountain not commune with her? Connect you to her?

Ferendir paused. Struggled to snatch a small gulp of trace air from a minute pocket in the soil that surrounded him.

Calm yourself. Fear, desperation, struggle – none will avail you.

Breathe in. Breathe out. Small. Shallow. Short. There may be little left…

Calm. Serene. Subside. Contract. Go inwards…

Ferendir tried to do just that. He began the mental repetition of the meditative cantrips he had been taught during his lessons at the temple. His goal: to contract his consciousness and loose it from his body, thus setting it free. If he could venture outwards, apart from his body, just long enough to dive deep and connect with the mountain ley lines and contact his mother mountain…

Something shifted. His orientation seemed to change, as if the earthfall enclosing him had slid down the hillside and he had rolled with it. Everything was topsy-turvy now, his progress halted. Ferendir felt panic rising again but fought the urge.

There is only one opportunity. If I let it slip away…

There – glowing, diaphanous, pulsing rivers of light and telluric force, buried deep in the rock and earth beneath him. Ferendir's spirit wriggled, struggled. He felt like a fish swimming up-current against tremendous resistance. He could see – nay, sense – the ley lines, his means of communing with the mountain, but they were too far, and they seemed to radiate power that seemed to repel him more the closer he got.

Push. Death comes for you. Darkness waits to swallow you. Concentrate. Remain. Push.

His spirit swam, wriggled, reached out. It slipped backwards, then rocketed forward again with a surge of strength. The currents continued to buffet and repel him. He continued to press, to seek, to reach out.

And then, all at once, he was in the ley lines, bathing in them, secure. The light enveloped him, and he could suddenly hear – and feel – the dialogues of ancient mountains, one to another, all rumbling and mumbling and holding forth in philosophical discourses on their slow, easy subsidence, their scouring and reshaping by winds and waters, the small, eager beings that swarmed over them and paid tribute to them and sought their secrets.

Ferendir called out, *Mother! Mother! Your child is in need of you!*

The mountains seemed not to hear him, or not to care. They talked on, the low, subsonic thunder of their conclaves causing his whole disembodied essence to vibrate. He trembled and shook at such a frequency that he thought his spirit might be shaken apart, like a sculpture of sand on a quaking span of earth.

Mother Mountain! I call to you! I need you! Help me!

Who do you call to? a voice replied. It was not his Mother Mountain.

Why do you call? another asked. *Why do you disturb us?*

We are buried, he explained. *We are dying. Please–*

Many die, the mountains answered. *We endure.*

We are on a mission – a vital mission, he pressed. He could barely concentrate now. *We seek the pretender, Ezarhad Fatesbane... He stole from us... the Eidolith... Kaethraxis...*

It was that name that seemed to send a potent tremor through all the interlocking ley lines, rocking all the power they contained.

Kaethraxis, they all said at once, in a single, deafening voice.

We beg of you, Ferendir managed. *We seek only to serve. Please... my mother...*

We can provide. We are all your mother.

Again, something shifted – something physical, powerful, present.

Ferendir felt his body turned once more, end over end. But when the movement subsided, as he struggled to focus his distant, physical senses and his drifting, slowly discorporating spirit, he realised with amazement that his circumstances had changed.

He could move.

The earth around him was loose.

Ferendir's spirit leapt, suddenly, shockingly, back into his body. He moved one arm, found it immobile. He then tried the other arm and found it capable of wriggling, only slightly, against the soft, loosely packed earth around it. Ferendir began to wriggle that arm, as slowly and subtly as he could, all the while concentrating on his breathing, his focus, desperate to maintain his composure even as he raced against asphyxiation to free himself.

There. A modest cavity had been created around his movable arm. He began to reach out, to pierce, to grasp, to writhe. Little by little, he felt his whole body starting to shift under the weight of all that fallen soil and rock. His seeking hand, in one miraculous instant, broke the surface of the rockfall and felt chill, free air against it, along with small, cold droplets.

Rain.

Ferendir continued his struggle. He moved his limbs, then his body, then his limbs again, a constant back and forth, seeking to loosen the earth around him before finally shifting his position so that he could find leverage to dig himself free. Always he seemed seconds away from his last breath, from panic, from unconsciousness, but he fought through those banes at every opportunity, keeping his head, keeping his concentration, doing his best to simply concentrate on the next challenge. Bend a leg. Clear loose earth with his nose. Seek that cool, rainy air outside with his other hand.

Up, up, up, and finally... out.

Ferendir's face broke the surface. He opened his mouth and drew in a deep, satisfying draught of air sweeter and more satisfying

than any he had ever known. His arms flailed and sought pur-
chase. Once his elbows were couched, he began the slow, writhing
movements that would work his body out of its would-be grave
and onto the damp, sloping surface of the rockfall.

When at last he had finally extricated himself, Ferendir collapsed.
For a moment – only a moment, for he knew his work was not
yet done – he lay on his back, gulping the cool, moist mountain
air, feeling the soft pattering of the cold rains on his filthy face. He
opened his eyes and stared up into the great grey immensity of the
clouded sky above him, relishing its enormity, the sense of bottom-
lessness that it imbued in him, an awareness of his own smallness.

And how fortunate he, a single, small, petty creature, was at
that very moment.

Hurry now, he reminded himself, then turned over and went
searching for the others.

Ferendir found a lone hand protruding from the rockslide and
began to dig. The hand twitched and grasped at his own – good,
a survivor. Nearby, another body slowly, inexorably wriggled out
of the wreckage. Ferendir was moved to aid that person as well,
but the one before him – the one trapped save only their seeking
hand – needed him more desperately. Soon enough, he saw that
the other survivor – the one who managed to free themself – was
Serath. Without a word, Serath crawled out of the pile of stone and
earth, reeled about a few steps to get his bearings, then lurched
straight towards Ferendir to help him dig.

They freed Phalcea, then Desriel. Taurvalon dug himself out.
Metorrah was the last survivor recovered.

It took all six of them, working together, moving about like filthy,
soil-encrusted wights from the grave, to finally locate Luverion.
The loremaster had not survived. His body was lifeless within its
sheath of bronze plate. The expression on his pale, enigmatic face

was calm, serene. Whether he died in the fall itself or later, because he could no longer breathe, they could not say.

They searched for two more hours. They never managed to locate the body of Jalgrim the duardin. At last, they deemed the search fruitless.

Luverion was buried. Those Zaitreci burial rites known among them were observed, and though none of them had known the loremaster well, they did their best to express their admiration and gratitude for both his courage and his sacrifice.

'Sleep now, brother,' Taurvalon said. 'Let all the secrets of Teclis, Celennar and the Mortal Realms be laid bare to you.'

'Find all who came before you, your forebears and your family,' Metorrah said.

'Add your wisdom to their own,' Phalcea concluded.

Desriel knelt and placed his hands upon the cairn of stones they had raised over Luverion's grave – primarily to keep scavengers away and protect his body from misuse.

'You were the wisest of us,' he said quietly. 'We are less without you.'

'Rest, now,' Serath said, standing straight and austere above the grave, 'for your part in this fight is done, and your respite well earned.'

Ferendir stared at the grave. He felt a great many things, having seen their new friend – puzzle that he was – buried in that simple, shallow grave. And yet, he could not find the core of what moved him at that moment. Was it sadness or admiration? Loss or fury? Gratitude or remorse? It was all of those... and none of those.

It was a mystery, and it made finding the right words – the best words – all but impossible.

Unbidden, some of the first words Luverion had spoken to him returned to him in that moment.

It shall be my great honour to know you, Ferendir... in our brief time together.

Had he known this was how it would end for him, even then? That was impossible, wasn't it?

Again, he heard Luverion's voice in his mind.

Incidents and exigencies. The random and the requisite.

Celennar whispered to me…

Perhaps he had known… and he came anyway.

'I have lost a great many things in the days past,' Ferendir finally said. 'Things that I have long known, long cherished, long relied upon. You were new to me, Luverion, and I did not know you well. But I shall try to see knowing you, however briefly, as a great gift… and losing you as an equally great loss.'

Only then, with their dead comrade buried, did they finally withdraw from the enormous pile of fallen stone and mud to determine precisely where the rockslide had taken them.

They were at the base of the slope, near the river that wound through the duardin's hidden valley. They could see, far above them, where the ragged ledge had been dislodged from the mountainside and taken them with it. There appeared to be nothing alive left up there. Climbing back to the shattered promontory would take them many hours, if not the remainder of the day, yet no ready exit from the valley was apparent before them.

'What now, then?' Taurvalon asked. 'Clearly we were not sufficient, in skill or force, to stop this Ezarhad Fatesbane. Can we even carry on, knowing his forces so outnumber us?'

'We thinned their ranks,' Serath said. 'Considerably.'

'We could backtrack,' Metorrah suggested. 'Rejoin the Windstrider's warhost and seek reinforcements? We will lose time, but what we gain in strength–'

'No,' Serath said.

All looked to him.

Ferendir's grim-faced master sat on a nearby boulder as though it were a throne. His back was straight, his hands planted surely on his knees. His eyes were downcast, but after a moment, he raised his burning gaze to his companions and let it sweep over them.

'We cannot go back,' he said with finality. 'Ezarhad is already under way again, moving towards his destination. Our only hope is to stop him before he gets there… before he can awaken Kaethraxis.'

'But how can we do that?' Phalcea asked. 'Luverion struck the killing blow against that daemon the pretender summoned, but look at what it cost him. What it cost all of us. I say this not in fear but with the assurance of reason – we *cannot* defeat him. Not as we are.'

'But we must,' Desriel said. Ferendir's other master sat down by the stony riverbank, his legs folded under him, apart from the others. He had been facing away from them before speaking, staring off into the distance downriver as if trying to seek something, to tease out a new path for them to follow. Now, he had turned his head so they could see him in profile… yet he had not moved from where he sat.

'Your determination is admirable, Alarith,' Metorrah said, 'but we are a people dedicated to facts – hard truths, no matter how bitter. Desperate last stands fuelled by bitter vengeance are the province of humans, or the duardin, not of the Lumineth.'

'He is not speaking of a desperate last stand,' Ferendir cut in. 'Nor vengeance, nor hatred.' When all eyes turned to him, he realised that they now expected words from him that he had not fully prepared. For a moment, he sought the truth of things as he saw them, composed his thoughts, then carried on. 'I know my masters. Serath would stand fast, without giving an inch, and die where he stood if he thought it would punish the forces of Chaos and save this realm, or his people, or any of you. And Desriel, he may seem as soft as the breeze and as swift as flowing water, but there is method – purpose – in every choice he makes. If these two Alarith – whom I have known for most of my life as mentors and guides – say that we must go on, then we must go on. After what we've just endured, they would not insist upon it if there were any other way.'

'But our quarry is far ahead of us,' Taurvalon said, 'and his forces too numerous.'

'That cannot stop us,' Serath said darkly. 'The cost of failure in this is too great.'

'Just what is it, this Kaethraxis?' Phalcea asked. 'Hirva Windstrider spoke of a stolen artefact of power. You lot speak as if Ezarhad's ultimate destination is something more than just this artefact.'

'Aye,' Metorrah said. 'What is it, then? We all agreed to aid you in this because our lady regent told us this was the best use of our separate skills and strengths. Till now, we have been kind enough not to ask, but we need answers. What did the pretender take from you, and what does he intend to do with it?'

Desriel rose and turned to face them. He sighed, and began the tale.

'Once, an Alarith Stoneguard sought a means of combatting the threat of Chaos. He created – or rather, immanentised – Kaethraxis, a living, incarnate embodiment of all the creative–destructive principles at work in Hysh – the devouring correctives that this realm employs to keep its natural forces in balance. The construct overwhelmed every magical contingency meant to contain it. It became one with its well-intentioned summoner, then destroyed his companions and all who attempted to contain it. The creature – half pure spirit, half living Lumineth soul – was seized by a grief so deep that its rational mind and its rash, destructive urges overwhelmed one another – a perfect storm of ruin.'

'Impossible,' Taurvalon scoffed.

'The truth,' Serath snapped. 'All the Lumineth of the Ten Paradises beset the entity and tried to contain it. All failed.'

'Except the forebears of our temple,' Desriel continued. 'It was the Alarith – our folk – who made a last-ditch attempt to either tame Kaethraxis or imprison it. They braved the most treacherous regions of the mountains, found its lair and attempted to become one with the entity so that they could finally contain it. They thought to employ their knowledge of the soul of the mountain, of its patience, its understanding of slow change and cyclical growth, to pacify and restrain the destructive aelemental that Lariel had unleashed. Only one – the last remaining – was successful. She surrendered her life and freedom to the ongoing task of keeping Kaethraxis pacified in an aeons-long hibernation from which it could not wake to wreak its havoc upon Hysh.'

'But the gem,' Metorrah said. 'The treasure stolen from your temple–'

'The Eidolith,' Serath said. 'An aetherquartz gem containing the power necessary to either keep Kaethraxis dormant indefinitely or control it if it reawakens. Somehow, this Ezarhad Fatesbane learned not only of Kaethraxis but of the gem. He sees the gem as a ready means of awakening the entity and controlling it.'

'But he does not realise,' Desriel said, 'that even *we* do not know whether the gem is powerful enough to truly control Kaethraxis.'

'Surely divine Teclis and holy Celennar could stop this entity if it is unleashed,' Taurvalon interjected. 'If we but seek Teclis, petition him–'

'Aye, Teclis has the power,' Desriel said, 'especially with Celennar at his side. But there is war under way in this realm, Taurvalon. The archmage's strength and wisdom are needed elsewhere. If this beast is awakened and unleashed, taming or destroying it again would require vast energies and expend precious resources best utilised elsewhere. No, this burden is ours to bear. We have to stop this Ezarhad Fatesbane before the whole realm pays for his overweening ambition.'

'So,' Phalcea finished, 'it is a cataclysm either way. If the Eidolith works and Kaethraxis falls under his sway, Hysh will fall–'

'But if the Eidolith fails,' Metorrah said, 'Hysh still falls, because Kaethraxis will wake and Ezarhad will not be capable of controlling it.'

'Just so,' Desriel said.

They fell silent for a long time, each ruminating on what the two Alarith had told them. Even Ferendir now felt the terrible weight of the challenge before them. Was victory even possible, let alone probable?

Phalcea sighed. 'He has an enormous head start.'

'He does,' Desriel said, 'but there may be a way to catch him.'

Desriel stretched out his arm and pointed towards a place in the distance, where the river bent and disappeared into the woodlands that crowded the floor of the valley.

'Our way lies there,' he said. 'On the far side of the river, through a narrow, winding canyon that wends between the peaks. The mouth of that canyon is at the end of this valley. Its far end gives out right at Ezarhad's destination. If we go now, and push hard without stopping, we can overtake him.'

'A canyon…' Serath said, chewing on those words. His eyes suddenly narrowed. 'You cannot mean–?'

Desriel nodded curtly. 'I do.'

'Explain yourselves,' Metorrah said. 'These mountains are your homelands, not ours.'

'The canyon I speak of – a long, meandering crevasse, really – is called the Scar of Mythalion. It is a dark place – hungry and cold and fell in both desire and intent. Some say it is tainted by old magic, others that it is accursed and haunted by evil spirits. The truth of it is simply that Hysh is alive, and as its high places can uplift and exalt us, its low places – its dark places – can feed upon our fears, or doubts, and overwhelm us. Passing through

273

the Scar of Mythalion is neither impossible nor impractical, but it may prove a trial. Perhaps even a deadly one.'

Silence again. Ferendir could sense, however, that it was not a silence born of doubt, or fear. It was, rather, a moment of sober reflection – six individuals, each considering what lay ahead and what following the path they were currently on might cost them.

'There's no point in further delay, then,' Phalcea said. 'Let us begin.'

Metorrah nodded. Taurvalon as well.

Desriel looked to Serath, then to Ferendir. Serath nodded gravely. Ferendir squared his shoulders and gave a curt nod of his own.

'I follow where you go,' he said. 'The both of you.'

The six of them set out, following the river towards the valley's end.

CHAPTER THIRTEEN

They stopped for the night in a small, bounded pass high in the mountains, the wind around them cold and damp, full of raindrops that were moments away from coalescing into ice crystals. The newest members of the company had been sent out into the canyons and crevasses nearby to seek out food while those remaining in camp went about building fires when possible and spending valuable magical energies to kindle them through sorcerous means when necessary.

Ezarhad was worried. He knew how to read his underlings. At present, they were dissatisfied. He could tell because there was no jostling, no joking, no expectant teeth-gnashing or boasting among them. They were so comparatively subdued by their hard march, the massive loss of manpower they'd suffered and the hideous cold and wetness of the alpine weather that all the joy of slaughter and childish anticipation of carnage and mayhem had been sucked out of them. Save their clash with the Lumineth the day before, they had found little opportunity for the indulgence of their excesses, for this place – high in the mountains, bereft of most plant life and even soil, populated by neither beast nor anchorite – gave them no opportunity for indulgence. There was nothing here to kill, nothing to torture, nothing to twist or taint or poison.

A short season, Ezarhad told himself. *Soon, we will come to the valley housing the tomb of Kaethraxis. There, we will awaken the sleeping beast, and when that is done – when I have the creature under my sway via the power of the Eidolith – we can be away from this place. We can finally come down off this infernal mountain and venture into the more populated regions far below us.*

And when we descend upon them, there shall be slaughter, bloodshed and depravity the like of which this realm has never imagined, let alone seen manifested in the flesh...

Or so he hoped.

Hope, his mind scoffed. *Hope is for the weak. Hope is for those who are not strong enough to bend reality to their will. Are you such a wheedling creature, Ezarhad? Are you forced to defer to a power as fickle, as pointless, as hope? No. You are the heir to the throne of Slaanesh. You are the Prince of Depravity, the architect of a new eschaton of bloody indulgence and sinful delight. You are Ezarhad Fatesbane. You do not hope – you see, you know and you enact. Simple.*

Someone approached.

'Master,' a voice rasped.

'What is it?' Ezarhad asked.

'Dissension in the ranks,' the daemonette said quietly, tilting her head as she made the report, as if to better read his unspoken reaction to it. 'I have heard at least three – nay, four – of your allegedly loyal servants speak ill of this campaign and your plans for dominion.'

Ezarhad's eyes narrowed. Part of him was glad of the report, for at least it verified what he feared and suspected. Another part of him rankled – he hated telltales and loose tongues almost as much as he hated the disloyal or the overly ambitious. And yet, she had done him a favour in this instance, had she not?

Ezarhad turned to face the daemonette and knelt before her. He looked right into her eyes and smiled approvingly, then reached out and stroked her bony, thin-fleshed cheek. The daemonette's foul features became a strange parody of love and joy. Her long, crab-like pincers clicked and trembled in ecstasy.

'You are a good and faithful servant,' Ezarhad said, looking into her round, glassy black eyes. 'Have you any close comrades in the company?'

The daemonette nodded eagerly. 'Oh yes, dread lord. There are four of us, formed from the infernal fires on the same day, bound by affection since our very first manifestation. We are always challenging one another and sharing our spoils.'

'Well, then,' Ezarhad said, flashing a princely grin for her, 'I suggest you return to your comrades and tell them that their master – *your* master – bids you seize one or two of those grumbling, dissenting fools who've made their disloyalty known to you and slay them in any manner you deem fit. What say you to that?'

The daemonette's scaled tail swished eagerly behind her. 'Your will be done, my lord.'

'Indeed it shall,' Ezarhad said. 'Strike them down, let their disloyalty be known to all, then flay them for our supper. You are hungry, aren't you?'

She nodded, her toothy grin turning downwards for a moment. 'So hungry, my lord…'

'Well, then, now you won't be. If anyone challenges you, you tell them to look to me. I shall make my support of you abundantly clear.'

The daemonette nodded eagerly, turned and scuttled away.

Ezarhad currently stood on a high ledge above the broad, rock-strewn campsite, so he was visible to all below and had a good view of both the approach and exit from the flat parcel of land they'd chosen to haunt for the night. The daemonette went loping down the hillside, skidding over some loose scree, then redirected and hurried back into the camp to join her comrades. Seconds later, Ezarhad saw her hunched together with a pair of other daemonettes, the three sharing whispers mingled with intermittent glances towards a group of their fellow daemonettes just a stone's throw from where they crouched.

Now, he need only wait…

Ezarhad surveyed the scene, counting as he went. He totalled thirty-seven remaining in his little band of shock troops. Most were daemonettes or tainted mortals, just embarking upon their infernal paths as his servants and eager to prove themselves, but some of his hellstriders and fiends yet remained. They were the most troubling sorts, for they required more resources than the rest. Daemonettes could get by on meagre rations, needing little to sustain them, but those blasted fiends or those mounted hellstriders all seemed to be constantly hungry for this or thirsty for that. It was as if more limbs automatically meant more sustenance was required. It was tiring, and Ezarhad was growing weary appeasing them. Could they not sustain themselves on their burning desire to serve him alone? Perhaps supported by the warming assurance of their contribution to his greatness and elevation?

Surrounded by fools, lickspittles and ineffectual sycophants, he thought, almost wistfully. *Sometimes I don't even know why I try as hard as I do.*

Because victory is your only means of survival, he reminded himself. *Ever since you made that foolish wager with Astoriss and Meigant, directly pitting your forces, your powers, your cunning against theirs. It was a rash move, Ezarhad – perhaps so rash that it will cost you everything. Never, ever, ever should you have openly challenged them, with the outcome of the challenge being your victory or your destruction. Have all your centuries in the Mortal Realms not taught you that longevity arises from feigned loyalty and support followed by scheming, plotting and opportune applications of violence?*

Of course, he thought. *That philosophy always suited me and served me. But when Astoriss began all of her boasting, lending credence to her delusions of grandeur by daring to both diminish and threaten me...*

Pride, he reminded himself. *That is both your greatest gift and your most deadly shortcoming. Your pride may yet elevate you to the throne, Ezarhad... if it does not kill you first.*

He sighed. Heavy is the head that wears – or, at least, lusts after – the crown. So many things to consider. So many crystal balls to juggle and keep airborne...

Below, one of his daemonettes screamed. Another howled. Yet another snarled and spat curses. He heard the sounds of a struggle – grunts, hisses, inhuman feet or hooves shuffling on rockfall. When he finally, lazily, let his gaze drift towards the noise, he saw what he knew he would eventually see – that jabbering daemonette and her companions besetting two others. They had encircled the pair and now struggled to bring them to heel. He saw reddened talons and snapping pincers slicing and jabbing, lithe, pale daemonette bodies circling, darting and diving in amongst one another. As the five of them fought savagely, the rest of the company drew near, creating an ad hoc circle to contain and watch the proceedings.

He saw Kraygorn haunting the edge of the impromptu gathering, while Vhaengoth appraised the situation in his own, inimitable fashion. Kraygorn was, no doubt, horrified by the breakdown in discipline – no one was supposed to strike or challenge another without first reporting to him. The daemonette's direct report to

Ezarhad had been a breach of the chain of command and could cost the rumour-monger dearly. Meanwhile, Vhaengoth was no doubt weighing the odds of the contest, perpetually a student of hand-to-hand combat and its bloody outcomes, ever absorbing, weighing and measuring to arrive at new geometries of violence, new calculi of bloodshed.

The two challenged daemonettes were down now, one having had its leg torn to shreds by its attackers, the other worn down by a hundred bloody gashes perpetrated upon it, each tiny wound adding to the rest and weakening it moment by moment. As the two disloyal daemonettes lost their strength and floundered about on the cold mountain stones, the favour-seeking daemonette and her two companions looked to Ezarhad on his ledge above them. She smiled, clearly proud of what she'd done. She suggested the two downed daemonettes as gifts for her lord and master.

'For you, my dread and beautiful lord,' she said. 'Two disloyal fools, offered for your divine punishment!'

Ezarhad had to struggle not to smile. How sweet of her.

'Kraygorn?' he said, his raised voice echoing through the rocky pass.

'My lord?' his lieutenant called from below.

'I want those three troublemakers slain, along with the two they've damaged. Let the five of them feed the company. I shall tolerate neither disloyalty nor infighting! Is that understood?'

The daemonette's marble eyes were wide, staring, disbelieving. Then, before she could raise a cry or offer a plea, the remaining bodies of the company swarmed upon her and her two companions. Screams and shouts sounded out of the fray, but were silenced soon enough. Ezarhad watched, content, only turning away when he finally saw their torn and bleeding bodies fought over by all present, now dividing the spoils up amongst themselves to provide a most welcome nightly feast.

'Your sacrifice is most appreciated,' Ezarhad Fatesbane said quietly to himself. 'For the time being, you've bought me their loyalty as well as their full bellies and sustained strength.'

And yet, now his numbers were more greatly reduced. Thirty-seven less five – a mere thirty-two.

No matter. When he awakened and enslaved Kaethraxis, numbers would cease to have meaning.

Suddenly, the air changed.

It was a curious effect – like the strange, tingling sensation that preceded a fork of lightning. The cold, damp mountain air smelled different – charged, alive, even a little burnt. Down below, where his servants ripped and tore and delighted in the carnage they had wrought upon their former comrades, the winds began to hitch and swirl. Ezarhad could see from where he stood atop the ledge the way the thin, spitting rain would suddenly be drawn into churning trumpets or thrown back against itself – as if the wind were changing course and attacking itself. At first, none of his minions seemed to notice – they were too busy dismantling their former cohorts, luxuriating as they bathed in their blood, adding hastily snatched rags of silk or stolen jewels and bangles to their own collections, tearing into their torn flesh with their beastly teeth or even sitting aside, almost daintily, and using whatever razor-sharp blade was at hand to gently flay flesh and tissue from the bone.

But then they too began to sense the change. The wind moved strangely about them in bizarre, isolated patterns, clearly divorced from the slow, steady gusts that rolled down from the snowy peaks above. Suddenly, one of his fiends grunted and screamed, bucking forward, then back, as if struck by some invisible energy. There was an audible crackling, and a small gathering of daemonettes all shrieked and bolted from where they crouched, also as if struck by something painful and pointed.

Then the lightning came.

Ezarhad knew right away that what he was witnessing could only have one explanation: magic – and powerful at that. What would follow the crackling, glowing skeins of purple lightning and scintillating prismatic energy now searing the rain-wracked air and semi-darkness of the Hyshian twilight, he could not say... but it would not be good. Of that, he was certain.

'Move, you fools!' he cried, and began a quick descent of the nearest slope, waving his four slender arms as he went. 'Clear the ground! Back, I say!'

It was gathering now, more powerful than ever, finger-thin branches and wavering plasmic spheres bursting into existence and disappearing almost as quickly. No doubt his minions thought themselves about to face off against a force of Stormcast Eternals, hurled down to do battle with them by the lightning that so often bore them from place to place. But Ezarhad knew better. This lightning was unlike the stout, white-hot stuff that so often preceded a Stormcast onslaught. It was the colour of violets and lilacs, not thick and potent but thin, webby, spidery. The bolts of gathering energy sent gunfire-like echoes through the rugged mountain pass and lit up the drear gloaming like a fireworks display. As Ezarhad's servants and lieutenants scrambled and leapt and fled the centre of the stony clearing, the lightning intensified, seeming to tear at reality itself until–

A blinding flash, followed by a deafening crash and the sudden stench of brimstone. All shrank from the explosion, then looked once it had dissipated to see what remained.

A tall, lithe female with pale ochre-coloured skin, soft bone-white hair and an elaborate black headdress stood in the centre of the cleared space. She was terrible and beautiful all at once, her fiery yellow eyes all but glowing in her smiling, exultant face, two hands poised on her curving hips while two more – not hands at all but strange, misshapen claws, almost reptilian in their shape and angularity – hung at her side. A pair of large, leathery wings rose from her smooth shoulders, their dark flesh vaguely translucent if sufficient light were visible behind them.

Ezarhad, having reached the bottom of the slope, strode forward. Only when he realised his eyes were wide, his mouth gaping, did he finally summon the wherewithal to change his expression and hide his wonder and fear. Instead, he forced a disgusted grimace onto his face.

'Astoriss,' he said.

One of his nearest daemonettes tried to strike the tall, haunting woman with the draconian wings. Its talons passed right through her as though she were smoke.

'How sweet,' she said, regarding the daemonette. 'It wants to play.'

'Not you at all,' Ezarhad said, mostly to himself. 'A projection.'

'No small feat,' his bitter rival answered, smiling crookedly. 'We are, at this moment, some great distance apart.'

'How did you find me?'

'Does it matter?' she asked, raising one thin eyebrow. 'I wished to speak with you, Ezarhad, that is all. Can one friend not reach out to another, even over such a great distance?'

'Speak and go, then,' he said. 'Even your magic befouls my vision.'

Her crooked smile became a smug grin. 'So spirited, to the last.'

To the last? He did not like the sound of that…

Ezarhad stepped forward. He reached out his hand, spoke words and immediately felt the Chaotic forces that served him in times of need pulsing from their aetheric reservoirs into his body. His outstretched hand glowed with lambent and ancient energies, those energies sputtering effusively and wafting from his open palm like phosphorous dropping sparks and trailing smoke.

'I can dissipate this petty illusion of yours without the slightest effort,' Ezarhad said.

'Very well, then,' Astoriss said. 'I shall be brief. Meigant is no more.'

Ezarhad fought to keep his eyes from betraying the terrible fear and frustration he felt.

'Meigant,' he said flatly.

'Yes,' Astoriss continued. 'I am afraid he proved overconfident and underskilled. My forces overwhelmed his in pitched battle, and I am slowly, methodically disincorporating him as we speak. His flesh has already been flayed. I now have my carnamages rending each of his muscle fibres, bundle by bundle, while he remains thoroughly, horribly, *deliciously* alive and alert. I might have sent you this message in the precinct of his torture, but my magic and that of the torturers were likely to interfere with each other. More's the pity you could not see my masterpiece...'

'You lie,' he snarled.

Astoriss tilted her head. It was a deceptively girlish gesture from such a foul, misleading creature as she.

'You do not truly believe that,' she said. It was not a question.

He took another step forward. The energies pulsing in his open hand grew brighter, hissed louder. 'I will not tell you again–'

'Enough!' Astoriss roared. Her voice filled the pass as though it were being amplified through a massive brass horn. All present shrank from the sound of it. 'Meigant's last remaining forces – those that my minions did not sunder and flay in the field – have sworn their allegiance to me! Before our contest is done, Ezarhad Fatesbane, I swear that your forces shall do the same!'

'Never,' Ezarhad said... but he noted bitterly that none of his daemonettes or lieutenants offered defiant retorts of their own.

'Meigant is vanquished and his troops are mine,' Astoriss said. 'I outsmarted him, and I shall overpower you, you proud, preening little cockatrice. That means that we come now for *you*, Ezarhad. Let all who hear me know this – I am a kind and generous mistress. Abandon your master and present yourselves to me, and you shall be granted mercy as well as the singular honour of worshipping me and serving my desires. Stand with your foolish, outmatched master and see what torture and suffering might befall you!

'Beware, Ezarhad Fatesbane! The time of your reckoning – and my ascension – are both at hand!'

Then the witch threw up her four slender arms and disappeared in a loud pop and a belching cloud of stinking, sulphurous smoke. A moment later, the space she had occupied was empty, the swirling, quickly dissipating cloud of her vanishing the only evidence that she had ever been there.

Ezarhad closed his outstretched hand. The energies swirling therein disappeared. He lowered his face and let his eyes subtly, warily, search about the group gathered round him, eager to read their faces, their feelings. He saw wonder, fear, defiance, disgust. Some, no doubt, were still firmly loyal, unshakeable in their faith. More than a few, however, seemed at least intrigued by the witch's proposal. He could all but smell their gathering treachery, the quickening schemes and weighing of options in their small, cunning brains.

But it was Kraygorn who troubled him most. His enormous champion had stepped forward, broadsword in hand. The sword hung at the brute's side, true, but the look on his foul, goaty face – the curl of the lip, the narrowing of the eyes, the flaring of the nostrils – suggested an excess of aggression.

'What say you?' Kraygorn asked.

Ezarhad studied his servant. 'What say I? Who are *you* to ask me? Who are *you* – minion, lickspittle, sycophant – to ask me any question at all?'

Kraygorn shook – subtle, but apparent. There was a great, gathering rage-storm inside him, and he was preparing to set it free. Ezarhad made a quick perusal of all the faces now turned to him, all the black eyes now staring, all the bloodied talons now clicking in anticipation.

'I say you are weak,' Kraygorn answered. 'I say you are leading us nowhere, for a fairy tale, and you care not how many of us die to feed your fantasy.'

Ezarhad straightened his back and stared down his aquiline nose at his long-time companion and most trusted servant. 'Well, then,' he said with calculated indifference, 'it is a good thing that your foolish opinion is of no consequence to a personage of my stature and power.'

'*She* has power! *She* is the true heir to the throne of Slaanesh!' Kraygorn bellowed, then lifted his great, heavy sword and lunged. 'And she will reward the one who delivers your head!'

All things being equal, given all possible actions and outcomes, Ezarhad always preferred to lay down the lives of others rather than his own, risk the blood and flesh and health and sanity of others before his own, spend the precious resources that others bore rather than risk any of his own. Under most circumstances, Ezarhad would not simply avoid fighting, he would just refuse to fight – or he would find a way to wriggle out of it.

But that did not mean he *could not* fight.

And now?

Kraygorn's sword was already plunging towards him, splitting the air, seeking his skull.

Ezarhad stretched out all four hands, spoke familiar words, and the air between him and his would-be assassin came alive with purple lightning, green fire, white-hot fire and smoke. He unleashed four different spells at once, each of low power taken alone but given exponential killing force when combined and deployed simultaneously.

Kraygorn's strike was interrupted mid-slash. When the energies loosed by Ezarhad exploded before him, sought him, enveloped him, the great brute shrank and shuddered, suddenly wracked in horrible, searing pain from head to foot. Ezarhad knew Kraygorn was no fool – he would do his best to fight through the shock, the pain, and deliver the killing blow he'd intended no matter what the cost to himself. If he could not live as Ezarhad Fatesbane's slayer, he would at least die that way. Luckily, the magical attack interrupted his deadly sword strike and managed to drive him sideways, if only for a moment – just long enough for Ezarhad to withdraw a few steps and prepare for another onslaught.

Kraygorn's sword had been super-heated by the lightning Ezarhad unleashed, attracting all that cosmic power and absorbing it until the blade and grip glowed red-hot and began to sear Kraygorn's bare hand. As he shook and roared, the sword fell from his hand and hit the cold stone. Kraygorn jerked and wheeled, bits of him now roasted or charred, the tanned flesh once stretched across his plate armour now blasted away, persisting only as a few ragged, blackened chunks clinging to the edges, while small portions of his chain mail undershirt had clearly been pressed into his own flesh and been grafted there by the super heat. Tendrils of smoke rose from him in a swirling storm as he moaned and tried to regain himself. A horrid smell filled the cool mountain air, like roasting meat.

But he is not down, Ezarhad reminded himself. *He will not fall easily – that is why you made him and empowered him so, is it not?*

Finally, Kraygorn lowered his raised arms and tried to straighten. He was charred and blasted, head to foot, some of his visible flesh blistered and pulsing while other bits were burned away entirely. The half-immolated champion stood to his full height, shaking but unyielding, and offered a grim rictus in answer to Ezarhad's attack.

'Still… standing…' he growled.

Ezarhad was about to call another storm of sorcery to engulf the turncoat, but he could feel how much energy that last attack had taken out of him. Whatever he summoned now would be even less concentrated, less powerful, than what he'd already unleashed. If he spent too much of his magical energies at this point in their duel to the death…

Time for a more direct approach, then. Without hesitation, Ezarhad drew the formidable bejewelled blade that hung at his hip and prepared himself for his adversary's attack.

Roaring, Kraygorn charged again, broadsword raised.

Their blades met in the air, rang, trembled. Kraygorn was equal in height to Ezarhad but had far more bulk and muscle on him. Even half crisped and dying in increments, moment by moment, he could still physically overmatch Ezarhad, given the chance. Ezarhad's only hope was to keep him fighting for a few moments, long enough for the energies necessary to summon a magical killing blow to replenish themselves…

Kraygorn drew back his blade and brought it down in a hard, stunning arc that Ezarhad was barely able to parry. Another. The impact of Kraygorn's sword made Ezarhad tremble. Yet another. This time, the force was too great, and Ezarhad went stumbling backwards, reeling, doing his best to hold on to his weapon in case Kraygorn made another charge.

Of course, he did. The moment Ezarhad was thrown back a few steps, Kraygorn advanced, roaring as he came and drawing his blade back, one-handed, for a cross-body chop. The blade slashed the air and Ezarhad parried it. He slashed again and Ezarhad danced aside. The blade was whipped backwards, then suddenly redirected and thrust. The two movements – one after another – came too swiftly for Ezarhad to avoid them. He shrank from the seeking tip of the still-smoking blade, but it bit into his side and drew blood.

Ezarhad swiped sloppily with the great blade he held. Kraygorn had to throw himself back to avoid having the weapon cleave his face laterally in two. As he reeled and stumbled, trying to regain his balance, Ezarhad retreated, one hand gripping his bleeding flank while two others gripped the scimitar in preparation for another strike. He took that instant to study his minions, all gathered in a rough circle now, enclosing the two of them, watching and waiting but cunning enough not to cheer for one or the other.

They all knew this contest would be decided by a combination of brute force and guile, for no servant of Slaanesh would rely solely on either. If any of them voiced support for either combatant – even in a moment of pique – and that cry was remembered when the other combatant won, they would be marked for death.

Very well, then, Ezarhad thought. *You lot want strength and guile – I'll show you strength and guile.*

Kraygorn had regained himself. Only one eye remained beneath his misshapen, daemonic brows, the other having been cooked and jellied by Ezarhad's fire and lightning onslaught at the opening of their duel to the death. That single remaining eye burned in its socket, glaring, furious, just as Kraygorn's teeth gnashed in expectation, half his foul cheeks burnt away and exposing his jaws beneath. He spat upon the mountain stone, then raised his sword again.

'You are weak, Ezarhad Fatesbane,' he snarled. 'You have lied to us and used us! But no more! I will free these fools from your influence, and I shall take them all to *her*. She will reward us where you have misused us!'

Ezarhad wanted to laugh.

'Will she?' he taunted. 'Kraygorn, you brute, you have no idea how good you've had it.'

The champion charged. Ezarhad met three hard sword blows in succession with his princely blade, their steel ringing, each strike more furious, more hateful than the last. As Ezarhad drew back and prepared for a quick thrust towards Kraygorn's exposed flank, the big champion suddenly changed his tack. In an instant, lightning-quick, Kraygorn lunged, reached out one enormous hand and shoved.

Ezarhad was thrown backwards. His legs tangled beneath him. He felt himself about to fall but somehow, miraculously, managed to catch himself by overcompensating and bending forward.

Kraygorn raised his blade and took three long strides, ready to make his killing blow.

Now or never. Ezarhad threw down his sword, raised his hands and unleashed every scrap of energy and sorcerous force he could summon. His upper arms channelled fierce, crackling lightning. His lower arms belched fire in long, draconian streams. Both aelemental forces struck Kraygorn with terrible strength, throwing him backwards. The champion hit the stony ground hard, already burning, but Ezarhad gave him no reprieve. He poured out every bit of energy he could summon to make sure the lightning ravaged his one-time lieutenant, to assure that the fire burned so hot it melted his plate armour right upon his cooking, writhing form.

Kraygorn screamed, bucked, cooked. Fire and smoke enveloped him. Lightning wrapped round him, danced in and out of his convulsing form like glowing spiderwebs.

Ezarhad needed to stop. He could feel his energies dissipating. If he was not careful, the expenditure could prove costly. Another challenger might present itself only moments after he assured Kraygorn's destruction.

But this is how it has to end. They have to see. They have to know. No disloyalty will go unpunished.

Finally, he forced himself to strangle off the energies pouring out of him. Kraygorn lay there in a smoking, flaming heap, still and silent. The rest stood round in a large circle, watching, horrified and thrilled all at once.

Ezarhad Fatesbane, their master, heir to the throne of Slaanesh, stood over his slain enemy, bloodied, dishevelled and exhausted – but exalted.

CHAPTER FOURTEEN

It took them almost a full day to traverse the river valley and climb towards the mouth of the secret gorge they sought, but by nightfall upon the day following their departure they had arrived. The Scar of Mythalion yawned hungrily before them, a deep, dark cleft cut between two rising mountains, so deeply buried between their sprawling bulks that it barely seemed a feature of the realm's surface at all.

When they reached the mouth of the gorge, all stood in silence and appraised the dark gap, its high, looming walls and the eager, abiding shadows swaddling its deep recesses. No sound could be heard from the canyon, no wind felt, and no light was visible. Though Hyshian night was only a gentle twilight, the Scar of Mythalion would, they knew, prove almost as dark as a cave, and perhaps twice as deadly.

'Perhaps we should wait,' Metorrah suggested soberly.

'No,' Serath said. 'Our enemy pushes on towards his goal. We must as well.'

'Serath speaks the truth,' Desriel added. 'Our journey through the Scar will be taxing, but we cannot put it off.'

'How long will it take?' Ferendir asked. There had always been something in him that was willing to endure almost any hardship, undertake almost any dangerous endeavour, if he could simply understand how long it might take. With such temporal boundaries fixed in his mind, he could better prepare and centre himself for whatever trials awaited, because he was always capable of saying, *Endure... endure just this small period longer, and you will be done with it.*

But neither Serath nor Desriel offered a ready response.

'No one knows, in truth,' Desriel finally said. 'Some say three days end to end, some five, some two.'

'Such a place,' Taurvalon said, appraising the great, dark crack before them, 'would be perfect for an ambush.'

Serath nodded. 'Aye. It would.'

'Are we sure this is the only way?' Phalcea asked.

'It is not the only way,' Desriel said, 'simply the fastest. Likewise, given this place's reputation and the nature of the magic at work upon it, Serath and I agree that the challenges we might face here are still more manageable than the challenges of yet another attack. We must move quickly, and we cannot endure another attack before we reach our destination. With good fortune, we will reach the tomb of Kaethraxis before Ezarhad can penetrate it. If the guardian can repel him – if only for a short while – we can help her defend the inner sanctum.'

Ferendir studied the high, narrow ravine. Water trickled out of it over a long, meandering line of stones that wound through the forest they'd just traversed back towards the river. If water was flowing out of the ravine, that meant that this end was at a lower altitude than its far end. They would be travelling uphill, then, even though they appeared to be descending into some

Stygian underworld. That, at the very least, boded well – here was one sign, one alone, that this place operated by rules they could all understand.

But flowing water also meant wildlife, for the beasts of the wild would always seek water wherever and however they could. Maybe they could thread the canyon and reach the far side without encountering Ezarhad and his vile servants... but what else might they meet along the way?

'A last reminder, before we are under way,' Desriel said. 'This place was created, the spells upon it cast, for the sole purpose of testing those who pass through it. It will test our resolve, the purity of our purpose and our mental endurance. It will study us, lay bare our deepest fears and greatest shames and make each of us our own worst enemy. Our only hope of withstanding those attacks is to focus upon our goal. We go now to meet a terrible, driven enemy, in order to save this realm from a force that will leave it ravaged, weak and vulnerable. If we do not reach our destination, Hysh will pay the price – it is that simple. When your doubts, fears and ignominy assail you, that is your lodestone, your guiding principle.

'We go to do what must be done, and we are the chosen, because we were present when the call was made – when the realm presented its need and cried out for aid.'

They looked to one another, then back to Desriel and Serath, at the fore of the group. All nodded. All understood.

Ferendir felt a terrible, creeping fear inside him.

My deepest fears.

My greatest shame.

He thought he had already fought through those hungry, life-draining ghosts inside him, but now, trudging towards the high, narrow pillars of the canyon that marked its entrance, he was not so sure.

* * *

The Scar of Mythalion was just that – a scar, a cleft in the rocky tissue between soaring mountains, a slash in the realm itself. Within, its air was close and stale, and the meandering walls of the ravine loomed so precariously on either side that the sky was rarely visible above them. Every now and again, Ferendir would raise his eyes and see a small sliver of the deep, indigo-blue vault strewn with stars, or some small piece of the true moon, Celennar, hanging brightly in the heavens, but for the most part it was like moving through a cave. They sometimes heard the sawing wind whipping down from the mountain peaks that towered on either side of the wandering cleft, but they never felt it. It was as if the winds themselves avoided this place, skating over the surface of the ravine high above them, but never, ever penetrating beneath to whip through its narrow recesses or race its length. Consequently, the air around them was strangely stale, and strangely warm.

Hours passed, and they marched on in silence. From time to time, Ferendir would hear a small sound from one of his companions – a melancholy sigh, a thoughtful hum, a sudden intake of breath through gritted teeth – but by and large they said little and concentrated solely on movement. They rounded rockfalls, sometimes moved from one side of the narrow, shallow stream to the other in search of a dryer, broader path, but always they kept moving.

Most likely, that is our salvation, Ferendir thought. *Press on. Always press on. If we do not stop, we cannot be snared or tortured or overwhelmed.*

He found himself on edge, overeager, always ready for some dread to fall over him like a hunter's net, or for some unbidden, foolish thought to arise in his consciousness that would require his immediate attention... but nothing came. The night was still and unnervingly silent. Only their soft footfalls and those vague, occasional sounds they made – a sigh, an exhalation, a mumbled tune – ever pressed back against that silence or reminded Ferendir that they were awake and alive at all.

Sometime in the very middle of the night, they stopped for a short rest at a place where the stream widened and deepened. It was still little more than a seep, but here, the seep formed a broad puddle that might rise to their ankles if they stood in it. There, they paused, found boulders or flat spaces to sit upon and broke into their provisions. Desriel had warned them all that they must enter the Scar with their canteens filled and should only drink the water they brought with them, as the water of any streams or pools they found within might be tainted with the same magic laid upon the place. So as they took their short rest, they each ate of the provisions they carried and wet their throats with lone swallows of the water they bore, staring at the burbling, shallow little stream before them as though it were an idle snake waiting to strike.

'It's so quiet,' Metorrah said, speaking low as though she were afraid to break or affront that silence with anything more than a whisper.

Desriel sat cross-legged, staring down at the ground before him. Aelves had natural night vision, but here, in this dark, out of the way place, Ferendir noted that his companions and all the world around him were so dim as to be almost ghost-like – little more than shadows upon the shadows that surrounded them, forms visible primarily because of their movement, not their substance.

'Let the quiet endure,' Desriel said in a hoarse whisper of his own. 'Let this place take no notice of us, Tyrion willing.'

Ferendir studied his master, as well as Serath. After appraising the two of them, he let his gaze fall over the others in turn. He could just make out their faces, their wide, staring eyes, their frowning mouths. All were on edge. Though they said nothing, did nothing, sat silently and munched on stale bread and gulped a few drops of water from their canteens to wash down the crumbs, he could still clearly note how frightened and on edge they all were, how the silence and stillness of this place was oppressive rather than encouraging.

It was like walking through some hungry abyss. The emptiness demanded to be filled. The only question was, what might one's mind fill it *with*?

Then, suddenly, Ferendir opened his eyes. Had he been sleeping? Dozing? Had he lapsed into some self-induced, meditative reverie? The sudden sense of awakening when a moment earlier he had already thought himself wide awake brought with it a terrible sense of dislocation. His eyes darted about to the others.

Serath saw him. 'What is it, Ferendir?'

'Nothing,' Ferendir lied. 'I just… I must have dozed off for a moment.'

Desriel unfolded his legs and rose. 'We should keep moving,' he said. 'We have lingered too long.'

All took to their feet again. In moments, they were under way.

It was an hour later – perhaps a little more so – when Ferendir heard Taurvalon muttering to himself.

'Pretty things,' he said, his voice barely above a breathy, sub-audible whisper. 'That is all I do. I make pretty things. Pretty things, deadly things, tricky things… a toymaker. Nothing but a toymaker. A fool…'

Ferendir turned a little without interrupting his gait, trying to get a look at the Syari artificer without stopping to assess him fully. He wanted to be sly, furtive.

He barely managed. He saw Taurvalon, trudging alone behind him in his heavy armour, head down. His words were clearly meant for himself alone – a spoken monologue, a person wrestling with themselves. What Ferendir could not determine was whether anyone else heard him as well. Metorrah was at the rear of their little column, marching in Taurvalon's wake, so if anyone was capable of hearing him, it would be her. From where Ferendir now walked, he could see no indication that Metorrah heard the champion's words or if she was concerned by them.

Eyes forward. Phalcea walked several paces ahead of Ferendir, keeping pace with Serath and Desriel ahead of her. Ferendir listened, wondering if she might be having a conversation with herself as well. Though he could not be certain, he heard nothing.

And who are you to question them? a voice within him asked. *These seasoned warriors, these defenders of your realm, your home? They are your betters, now and eternally. Who do you think you are, counting yourself among them? How can you even walk beside them and hold your head up…*

'No,' Ferendir said aloud.

The whole column froze. Up ahead, he saw Serath, Desriel and Phalcea all turn and look back at him.

'Ferendir?' Desriel asked.

'Here, master,' Ferendir said. 'My apologies. I just… I…'

I what?

'We waste time,' Serath said, and pressed on, now taking the lead of the column from Desriel. 'Keep moving.'

Ferendir could not say when night had turned into day. They kept on, marching, trudging, mindless automatons putting one foot before another, and at some point, the sun returned. It did little to light the floor of the Scar of Mythalion, but there was, at least, a change in the quality of the light, and with it the blessed absence of the oppressive murk that had persisted through the night. He could see colours now, for instance, however tamed or muted, and make out sharp lines and distinct features both on the persons of his companions and on the stony walls and floor of the crevasse itself.

Occasionally, they heard the sound of birds in flight, or the tiny reverberations of rocks or pebbles kicked over the rim of the canyon by passing beasts high above. Once or twice, Ferendir even thought he heard the wind, moaning as it raked the surface of the deep, meandering canyon. But though he might imagine he heard the wind, he certainly never felt it. This was a dead place, a hungry place, and even the wind deigned not to tarry here.

Phalcea abruptly stumbled and fell, up ahead. The column halted automatically as Metorrah hurried forward to see to her sister. As she bent and offered an arm with which Phalcea could draw herself up, the pike-wielding warden suddenly snapped at her twin.

'I need nothing from you!' she said, her voice far more bitter and recriminating than anything Ferendir had heard from her previously. Then she shoved her sister aside and struggled back to her feet. 'I am strong in myself, complete as I am! You are just a shadow of me! A copy created to vex and taunt me!'

Metorrah, to her credit, made no effort to settle or placate her sister. Seeing her back on her feet, the archer simply turned her back and ventured once more to the rear of the column where she had been marching. Phalcea, seeing all eyes now on her, strode on.

'Stop staring,' she muttered. 'I slipped. That's all.'

On they went.

Ferendir found his gaze fixated upon the figures of his two masters, walking far ahead of him – Serath to the fore of their company, Desriel a few long paces behind him. After a time, he began to feel as if he were not controlling his limbs or walking of his own free will at all. Rather, he was simply drawn to them, bound to them, like a supplicant to an aelementor lode, and watching their movements assured his own. Likewise, he found himself paying close – almost obsessive – attention to their movements and posture, noting every subtlety and suggestion therein and expostulating upon them endlessly in his own mind.

Serath, pulling ahead, leaving us all behind, sure he knows the right path. Not a shred of doubt. Not a tiny crumb of fear. And likewise, no self-awareness – a dead mind, a construct, an automaton. Why do you seek his approval so desperately? His praise? He is incapable of giving it, incapable of understanding what being an alive, imperfect being even means...

And Desriel, swaying a little, stumbling a little on every seventh step, weighed down by his own weakness, his own shortcomings, his own imperfections. He who countenances failures and shortcomings in others because he is so rife with failures and shortcomings of his own. Why do you trust his judgement? His faith? His belief in you? What has he proven to you, except that he is weak enough to accept you at your worst?

And you... you, Ferendir, you child, you pretender... granted good fortune and fool's luck at terrible junctures in this journey, you truly believe you've proven yourself worthy... a Stoneguard... a servant and champion of the temple. You are nothing. You are the product of an unholy, instructive marriage between two self-absorbed and equally damaged masters – one a soulless machine, the other a wheedling, sentimental fool.

If they are nothing, you are less than nothing.

This place does not repel you, it attracts you, because this is your true home.

In this place, nothing is all. In this place, emptiness breeds and divides. In this place, the void sings and the abyss beckons and you can forget yourself. You have proven such a disappointment up to now, and your temple is no more, at any rate...

Just sit down.

Just stop.

Let the Scar do the rest.

'No,' Ferendir said aloud. He began to whisper to himself. 'There is a task and we are all that may complete it. I am only one but I

299

am vital. I cannot stop, because if I stop, the end will come – for everyone.'

Fool, that terrible, sardonic voice in his head answered. *Self-deluding, self-important fool. You believe you are vital? You are nothing. You are a speck. You are less than nothing. You are the fortunate, random survivor of a disaster. There is nothing special about you. How dare you even insinuate it! If you are so special, what about all those lost? All those slain? All those who failed when they were forced to face their enemies? Were they so very less than you? So very un-special that their deaths were inevitable and foretold? The arrogance–*

'No,' Ferendir said again.

The impudence–

'No.'

Nothing.

'No.'

Weak.

'No.'

Worthless. Foolish. Misguided. A waste of material, a tax upon the living cosmos–

'No!' Ferendir shouted. To his great surprise, there was no echo in the canyon. His voice, though loud, exploded from his throat but stopped within a stone's throw of its origins.

The column came to a sudden halt. All eyes turned towards him. Ferendir could feel their recriminating gazes, their assumptions, their pity long before he finally raised his eyes to meet theirs.

Desriel had taken a few steps towards him, though he was still some distance away.

'Ferendir,' he said, reaching out, 'what is it?'

'Stay away from me!' Ferendir shouted, and the sound of his own voice, raised in anger, thoroughly shook him to the core. 'All of you, stay away from me!'

Prideful.

Misguided.

Inconsequential.

Insignificant.

Ignoble.

Contemptible.

'Leave him!' Serath called from the front of the column. 'He is weak! He has always been weak! Would that the first mudslide wherein we found him had destroyed him!'

Ferendir heard Serath's words and could barely believe them. It was not simply the cruelty of them, the bitterness carried with them, but the fury expressed – a deep, abiding rancour and resentment. Why did Serath hate him so? What had he ever done to make the Stoneguard – his teacher, his guide, his model for all that was perfect and excellent and profound – so thoroughly loathe him?

The others were staring as well, though they made no move to approach him.

Green fool, Phalcea cursed. *Bloody stripling.*

Behind him, Metorrah watched him with a disdainful curl on her lip. *Child*, she whispered. *Simpleton.*

Taurvalon was shaking his head, slowly, almost imperceptibly. *You bloody novice, you unskilled dilettante...*

Even Luverion looked upon him with scorn and contempt – that puzzling, big-hearted enigma in the flesh, now staring at Ferendir with his large, pale grey eyes, eyes that registered something like grief and sadness.

Poor, deluded fool, those eyes said. *Poor, misguided wastrel. He does not realise how truly worthless and incompetent he is...*

Wait.

Ferendir blinked.

Luverion? *Impossible.*

'This is my fault,' Desriel was saying, addressing the others. 'I vouched for him. I should have known he wasn't ready.'

No. It could not be. Desriel would never say that. And Luverion? How could he even be here? Was he not–

'I said *leave him*!' Serath barked from the front of the line. 'He is a burden! An impediment! I told you a hundred times, Desriel! A thousand!'

'No,' Ferendir said.

'I am afraid so,' Desriel said, edging nearer. 'I must apologise, Ferendir. I failed you. I gave you faith in yourself – hope that you could endure. Your failure is truly mine, in the end. Here, let me help you...'

Suddenly, without warning, there was a knife in his master's hand.

'I shall make it quick. Painless. This is for the best. You should have died under the mud on that hillside. Fool's luck that you did not, really.'

Ferendir took a step back.

No. It was not fool's luck that he had survived.

It was the mountain's will. The mountain's faith in the efficacy of his service.

And Luverion – he *could not* be here. He had already died in a landslide of his own. He was lost to them, far behind them, buried on a riverbank.

And his master? Desriel? Now stalking nearer and nearer with that knife in his hand?

He could not be real. His behaviour, his voice, everything about him – not Desriel at all. Something else. Smoke and shadows. A hallucination. An illusion.

'Here,' someone said, and suddenly seized Ferendir round the throat and forced him into an ironclad, unbreakable hold. 'I shall do what you never had the courage to do, you soft fool...'

Another knife, sharp, laid with cool indifference against Ferendir's throat. The hand that held it was Serath's.

'No!' Ferendir shouted. He struggled, but Serath's grip was too tight.

Pitiful, Phalcea said. *End his suffering.*

Just, Metorrah said, *that he should no longer burden us.*

Useless, Taurvalon said, *a bauble imperfectly made. A flaw in the alloy. The failure of his maker's art.*

Ferendir felt a storm rising inside him – fury, grief, shame, loss, desire, desperation, sadness, guilt, hatred – all of it swirling and roiling and threatening to rise and subsume and overwhelm him. Though he struggled and bucked and fought, he could not break Serath's hold upon him, could not escape the dead, accusatory gaze of Desriel as he edged closer and closer, bearing a knife of his own, on a mission of mercy.

This is no way to meet your end, a voice inside him said.

Ferendir let his fight abate, if only for a moment.

They will not end me, he cried inwardly. *They will not destroy me.*

You destroy yourself, that voice said. *I would not have saved you from certain death had you been as worthless as you believe you are.*

I... You... Who are you?

Who am I, Ferendir? Who has guided you? Who has saved you, time and again? And I have done so not from pity, or from sentimentality, or even from special affection. I have done so because you are singular, unique, and positioned to do a thing that needs doing.

Perhaps it could have been someone else, but it is you.

Perhaps it could have been someone stronger, smarter, more determined, but it is you.

Ask yourself, who – what – is your real enemy in this?

Is it Serath?

Is it Desriel?

Is it even Ezarhad Fatesbane?

Ferendir thought about those words, tried desperately to identify the voice now speaking inside him – a voice so forceful, so commanding, and yet so soft, so cool and calming – even as his masters and the others continued their litany of shameful recriminations and Serath pressed that blade against his throat for the final slice that would end him.

Who is my enemy in this?

It is my fear, Ferendir finally realised. *My desire. My shame. My anger. My unbelief in myself.*

This – this storm inside me – this is not the Lumineth way. And this place we find ourselves – this Scar with its vile magic attuned to our deepest, darkest, most secret recesses, the grottoes of our hearts – this place is using our own long-suppressed feelings against us.

Let it all go now, the voice said. *Surrender, knowing that whatever the outcome may be, it is what must be…*

Ferendir stopped fighting. He closed his eyes, willing himself to let everything now roiling inside him simply flow out, like punching holes in a wineskin and watching it slowly, inexorably empty itself until it is flaccid and hollow.

'You will not even fight to save yourself,' Serath snarled in his ear.

I am already saved, Ferendir thought.

'Do it,' he said, 'if it is the will of Teclis and Tyrion – the will of the mountain. I will not fight you.'

The knife bit into his throat threateningly. 'Do not press me, boy,' his master said.

'I do not press you,' Ferendir said, eyes still closed, 'nor do I oppose you. I am the master of myself, Serath… the master of all that lives and moves inside me. I will not stain my death – if you deem it necessary – with fear and resistance.'

Ferendir waited, breathing, silent. The knife still dug at his throat but did not cut, did not bleed him. After a moment, Serath's strong, powerful arms seemed to release him. The murmurs and whispers he heard from his companions subsided. Even the voice inside him disappeared. There was only silence, the beating of his heart and the slow, easy, measured sound of his inhaling, exhaling breath.

Ferendir opened his eyes.

It was his own hand, and no other, that held the knife at his throat.

He lowered his hand. Stared at the knife. Had he really been ready to... about to...?

He dropped the knife and looked around him. High above, beyond the looming precipice of the canyon's upper rim, he saw second-hand light indicating that it was the middle of the day – bright, clear, if choked by all the rock that lay between where he sat and the sky he imagined above him.

Worse, his masters and his companions were strewn all along the floor of the canyon, each having halted, alone, to wrestle with whatever terrible force now threatened to swallow and subsume them from within. Taurvalon had stripped off his armour and seemed lost in a nightmare, dancing around in little more than a breechcloth with one of his many long, sharp knives in his hands, thrusting and slashing intermittently at an enemy that Ferendir could not see and knew was not actually there. Metorrah and Phalcea sat staring at one another, as if each were staring into a mirror, tears cutting tracks down their faces, mumbling and snarling out insults and dismissals. For a moment, Ferendir thought that they might each be torturing the other, but quickly enough, remembering his own experience, he knew that they each were, in fact, torturing themselves. Each twin looked into her sister's face, saw her own and continually recited a litany of all the things she hated about herself and saw more clearly and perfectly embodied by her twin.

Far ahead, Desriel was on his knees, head bowed, eyes downcast. He seemed to be muttering a prayer of some sort, though

Ferendir dared not move close enough to hear what he might actually be saying. All he knew, as he studied his master, was that the expression on Desriel's face was one of terrible shame and self-abjuration – as though he had found himself guilty of the most terrible of sins and now had gone diving deep into the dark centre of himself, seeking a place to find either absolution or perfect, peaceful self-destruction.

And Serath – where was Serath?

Ferendir moved past Desriel, ambling along the floor of the canyon towards a bend ahead. As he rounded that bend, he finally saw his master, also on his knees but in an attitude and state not half so silent or self-effacing as Desriel's. No, Serath seemed to have been wholly overwhelmed by something dark and monstrous inside him. He struck at the air with his stone mallet, slicing, arcing, attacking completely invisible enemies, all as he roared like a wounded animal, wet tears streaming down his twisted, sorrowful face.

'You took him!' he cried, his voice not carrying far despite its volume, due to the strange, dead acoustics of the canyon. 'You took them, but I shall be the instrument of their vengeance! Desriel! Ferendir! The temple acolytes and the temple masters! All of them! I shall avenge their slaughter with my last breath, so come upon me! Come upon me now!'

Ferendir stopped. Stared.

Desriel. Ferendir. The temple acolytes and the temple masters.

Serath was lost in a nightmare, believing that not only had every member of their temple been slaughtered, but Ferendir and Desriel as well. In his mind, he did battle with a massive army of the servants of Slaanesh... exacting a bloody vengeance for his lost comrades.

Ferendir understood Serath's impulses, Serath's need to balance a mountain of senseless murders with more pointed, perfect slaughter… but what made him most uneasy was the readily apparent emotions welling out of his master like waters loosed from a cracked dam. He saw sorrow, he saw grief, he saw fury and bitterness, he saw loss and unassuageable sadness. As Serath lunged and wheeled and struck at the air, fighting his phantom opponents, it was abundantly clear that all his internal bulwarks against the storm of emotions that each of them carried within them had burst. Not only could he no longer contain those emotions – he was not even trying to.

Because he's given up, Ferendir realised. *He thinks this is the end. He believes all of us dead, slain, and he the last survivor, facing the inevitability of being overwhelmed and destroyed. Bearing witness to our ends and facing his own, he's let everything out.*

Serath turned and struck. Ferendir had to leap away to narrowly avoid being smashed by his sweeping stone mallet. As he stumbled backwards and regained himself, he got a good, long look at Serath's twisted countenance. Something inside him seemed to break. He never, in all his worst nightmares, could have imagined seeing Serath in such a state. In truth, he had not thought Serath capable of such distress. Though Ferendir had been taught, time and again, that his people sought to control their urges and their emotions precisely because they coursed through them so strongly, so purely, he had somehow convinced himself that emotion no longer lived in Serath. That it had been purged entirely.

But no. Here, now, it was painfully apparent just how deep the wells of emotion in Serath still ran. They were powerful enough to paint an image before his waking eyes of hordes of enemies streaming in from all sides, of every person that he had ever loved, admired or protected slain and eviscerated, of his own imminent demise beckoning, looming, demanding that he finally set free the long-bound storm that raged inside him.

The dam holding Serath's emotions in check had burst. He was now a roiling, devastating font of fears and hatreds, desires and impulses. And this glimpse of the naked power of those feelings terrified Ferendir like nothing he had ever seen or even imagined.

'Serath,' he said quietly. 'Do not grieve for me. I am here.'

Serath spun towards him and struck with his hammer. 'Foul magic from foul enemies!' he shouted. 'You would taunt me with the voices of the dead?'

Ferendir fell back a few steps, but tried to remain before Serath, where he might see him if only his wide, dreaming eyes could finally see what the waking world offered, right before them.

'Serath, I live,' Ferendir said. He struggled to keep his voice even, soothing, welcoming. He did not want to feed all those emotions loosed within his master, but to help him rein them in once more. 'Lower your weapon, master, and see. See that I am right before you.'

'Liars!' Serath roared, and launched a devastating series of attacks that sent Ferendir scrambling backwards, desperate to avoid being smashed by his master's onslaught. 'Tricksters! Deceivers! I saw them slain! I saw them bleeding and dead upon the ground! My failure is with me and only avenging their loss will make it right!'

My failure is with me. That was it. Serath was not only convinced that they were all dead, but that it was his fault. His responsibility.

'Serath,' Ferendir said, beginning to circle now, just outside the striking distance of Serath's stone mallet. 'I am here. I live. This place where we find ourselves, the Scar of Mythalion, it's trying to destroy us. It's got into each of our heads, shown each of us what we most fear and most loathe about ourselves. Master, it's doing the same to you–'

The stone mallet split the air before him. Ferendir barely avoided it. He scurried back a few more steps.

'Master, I live,' he said, pleading. 'I live, and it is only because of what you gave me… what you taught me. I live through your strength, through your example, through your guidance. By your grace, I live–'

The stone mallet swept forward and back. Serath shook his head. Gnashed his teeth. Tears burst from his eyes in fresh streams. His whole body shook.

'I killed the boy,' he said. 'I killed him by not preparing him. I killed him by not teaching him. I killed him by not loving him…'

'I live,' Ferendir said, determined. 'I live because you prepared me, taught me, even loved me–'

'No!' Serath roared, and charged.

Something small in Ferendir bade him retreat – but he would not. For a larger part of him – a surer part of him – told him that this was the real test, the real moment of truth for him. So, he charged as well. He lunged forward as Serath came, raising his stone mallet, and when the hammer fell in a powerful, furious killing blow, Ferendir was ready.

He caught the stone mallet by its haft and halted its descent.

Serath struggled. Whatever he saw before him – a Slaaneshi Hedonite, the face of Ezarhad Fatesbane himself – Ferendir could not say. He only knew that it could not be his face. Serath fought, now trying to wrest his hammer away from the enemy holding it in place. He jerked left and right, tried to shift his weight and topple his adversary. Ferendir used every bit of cunning and guile and pure, concerted strength he had learned during his years under Serath's tutelage. He kept his feet, he held the stone mallet, he worked against Serath's own feints and attacks to try and wrest the hammer from his grip or send him sprawling.

They fought like that for what felt like an eternity – master and student locked hand to hand, a single weapon between them.

'Master,' Ferendir said. 'Open your eyes, I beg you. I am here. I live, and it is because of you.'

Serath swore, tore at the hammer.

'Monster!' he snarled. 'Murderer!'

'Master,' Ferendir begged. 'See me. I need you. The others need you.'

'Illusion!' Serath spat. 'Deceptions!'

Then, without warning, Serath managed to tear the hammer from Ferendir's grasp and landed a hard, repulsive kick to his gut, sending his student sprawling on the dirt floor of the canyon. Then he drew back.

Ferendir knew what came next. He would charge again, ready to strike a killing blow.

Fight him? Topple him? Beg? Plead?

No. Wait. Accept. Meet him.

Madness!

Do it, a part of him bade. *It is the only way.*

So Ferendir drew himself up to his knees, and he knelt there, head high, eyes fixed upon his master, waiting for the killing blow to fall. He did not raise his hands to beseech him, did not raise his arms to protect him or deflect the blow. He made no move that indicated he was afraid, at that moment, to die by his master's hand.

He simply knelt and waited.

Serath lunged, raising his stone mallet. His burning gaze fell on Ferendir... locked upon his eyes... held.

'Master,' Ferendir said quietly, calmly, 'do as you must. I trust you. I have always trusted you.'

The hammer hovered. Wavered.

Dawning awareness on Serath's face.

'No,' he said.

'Yes,' Ferendir answered. 'See.'

The storm of emotions long dominating Serath's face broke in an instant. All at once, the fury fled, the grief subsided, the embittered, suicidal rage evaporated and swirled away like scattered smoke.

Serath dropped the hammer and stood before his student, hands now empty.

'Ferendir,' he said. 'Tyrion and Teclis! I almost...'

'But you did not,' Ferendir said. He felt the sting of tears in his own eyes but refused to let them flow. *Do not give in now*, he reminded himself. *This place will use any and every advantage against you.*

Ferendir stood tall before his master. His master, Serath, stared back at him.

'Ferendir,' Serath said, 'you freed me.'

'No,' Ferendir said, 'I trusted you to free yourself. That is what my masters taught me.'

For a long time, they stood eye to eye, staring. Only after a long, interminable silence did Serath finally draw a deep breath, settle himself and bow his head.

CHAPTER FIFTEEN

Ezarhad Fatesbane stood before the high, carven pillars that flanked the equally high but narrow entryway before them – civilised, beautiful architecture carved into the living, rough-faced rock of the mountainside. He and his last minions stood now in a narrow, high-walled canyon that funnelled all approaching parties right towards that grand, hand-made portico and left no doubt that they had reached their destination.

This, at last, was the tomb of Kaethraxis. Here, his salvation – the ultimate embodiment of the power he sought, the power he deserved and was destined to wield – waited for him, and him alone, to stir and awaken it.

At last, he thought, taking in the chillingly austere sights of the pillars, pediments and reliefs graven into the glowering stone wall before them. *My destiny is fulfilled, my purpose realised. At last, all the world will bow before me and call me master, and for the first time, I will know peace – the peace of ultimate power, the peace of true safety, the peace of having no rivals capable of standing or plotting against me.*

As it always should have been... as it always should be.

His last remaining servants were knotted behind him, their silence pregnant and expectant as they, too, studied what lay before them. The way had been hard, in the end. After that terrible mess in the pass below, wherein he'd been forced to slay his long-time lieutenant, Kraygorn, the others had fallen in line, but the climb over the rough and savage landscape that had finally opened this small, hidden valley to them had claimed even more. He was down to just a few score now – daemonettes, fiends, a few slow, under-fed hellstriders and a handful of still eager-to-serve mages and would-be champions.

No matter, he assured himself. *If these are the servants who have survived to this point, then they are my strongest and most loyal. It is right that they should share this with me. Let them see the power their master is about to claim as his own, about to wield, godlike, to bring Hysh and all the Mortal Realms to their collective knees.*

They would be his heralds, his acolytes, the priests of the new, self-centred cult that he would establish once his godhood was secured.

For a long time, Ezarhad and the others stood studying the scene before them – the grim, blank face of the sheer cliff wall wherein the entryway was carved, the steep, climbing walls of the canyon on either side of them, sloping and narrowing as they neared the portico, a perfect bit of natural defensive architecture sure to force any invading army to narrow its lines and send only a trickle of troops through the main entrance to the tomb at any time.

It was ingenious, really. But it would not stop them.

'Sabrax? Gyman?'

Two of his most savage and fearless daemonettes strode forward on lithe feet to present themselves on their knees.

'Dread Lord,' said Sabrax.

'Oh, Prophet of Pleasure and Pain,' said Gyman.

Jockeying for supremacy even as they grovel, Ezarhad noted. *As it should be.*

'Scout the entryway,' he said calmly. 'Prepare the way for me.'

The two daemonettes looked to one another, then to their master.

'Scout,' Sabrax said.

'Prepare,' Gyman added.

'Did I not speak a tongue you are familiar with?' Ezarhad asked bitterly. 'Go on. I need my safety assured. It will not do for your master to enter the tomb of Kaethraxis only to succumb in a moment of chance to an unsprung trap, will it?'

Once again, the two daemonettes exchanged puzzled glances. Finally, they turned back to their master, shaking their heads.

'Certainly not,' Sabrax said.

'Most definitely unacceptable,' Gyman agreed.

Ezarhad made his wishes known with a simple arching of his brow, making it clear to both that he was still awaiting their compliance.

Sabrax and Gyman rose from where they knelt, turned and began a slow, easy approach to the yawning entryway of the tomb. Ezarhad watched as they advanced, allowing his eyes to scan the canyon walls and the cliff face, all the while trying to tease out just where the dangers might lie and how they were concealed. He assumed there would be traps, anti-personnel devices – he simply did not know what sort they might uncover. Were they magical counter-measures, or purely physical? Deadly, or simply designed to slow and frustrate one's progress? Were there waiting soldiers, snipers, perhaps horrifying beasts trained to guard the tomb with savage abandon, attacking all who approached?

Sabrax and Gyman would perform the necessary function of exposing whatever dangers lay before them. Their lives would be given for a higher and more righteous cause than either could even conceive or understand. He would do his very best to remember their names beyond the close of that day.

They were very close now, within a stone's throw of the open entrance. So far, not a single untoward thing had revealed itself or unfolded. More puzzlingly, the entrance seemed to sport neither door nor gate – it was just a high, narrow, open doorway carved into the rock itself, boasting a deep, receding darkness beyond. Nothing moved in that doorway, nor was there any sign of life at all in the whole of the valley. No plants grew here, not even alpine sedge or clinging moss, nor did any water flow out. To the naked eye, this was a place of desolation and death, cold, grey, composed of implacable stone weathered by millennia of ice, wind and rain and littered all about with fallen boulders and drifted banks of loose scree from long-collapsed ledges and erosion above.

And yet, there must be something guarding the tomb. There *must* be...

Gyman, who had pulled out ahead of Sabrax, had reached the steps leading up to the portico before the entrance now. The daemonette's pale feet left the rocky, scree-strewn floor of the canyon and mounted the first of the three steps climbing to the broad courtyard before the entrance.

Nothing.

The second step. The third step.

Nothing.

Sabrax bounded up the three steps and planted her feet on the portico surface, eager to be the first out front now that Gyman had proven no traps lay hidden in the three rising steps.

The moment Sabrax's dainty feet landed on the portico platform, something changed.

On the outside of each of the pillars flanking the entryway were tall, twisted columns of old stone. They seemed to be natural projections, as tall as the pillars – twice as tall as a mortal man – and protruding from the rock face of the cliff like raw ore presenting itself for carving – as if the rock desperately wanted to be shaped and bent outwards to offer itself for such a transformation.

But the moment Sabrax's foot fell upon the flat, polished marble before the entryway, those twisted stone formations shifted, lurched and pulled free of the cliff with a terrible, grinding roar. And then they began to move, standing tall and striding right towards Ezarhad's two hapless servants.

Ezarhad heard those gathered behind him give small, shocked exclamations of wonder and fear. One of the daemonettes even cried for its companions to clear out and flee at once. Ezarhad did not bother to turn and see who that might have been. He needed to watch, to determine just what was happening here, and how, and why.

Stone golems – two of them, their tall, asymmetrical frames barely offering any real sense of anthropomorphic shape or proportion, stomping and lurching forward as their long, misshapen arms stretched out and their wide hands began grasping for his servants.

Sabrax drew the serrated sword sheathed at her hip and hunkered down, ready for a battle. Gyman, meanwhile, turned, bounded down the three steps and began a hasty retreat back towards where Ezarhad and his servants all stood watching.

The golem nearest Gyman reached up to its own rocky shoulders, plucked off a single palm-sized grey stone and flung the miniature boulder as though it were skipping a rock on a pond's calm surface. The stone struck Gyman as he fled and sent the daemonette sprawling, a great glut of purple-black ichor exploding from his crested skull as it shattered.

Sabrax, meanwhile, had charged the golem before her and now engaged it, striking and thrusting with her sword, despite the big, rocky beast's hide being far too hard to suffer any more than a chip from her sparking, slicing blade.

The stone golem that had downed Gyman with that single throw descended the steps and lurched towards its prone target. Gyman was moving a little where he lay, his shattered skull still not enough to strike him dead, apparently. That was unfortunate, Ezarhad thought as he watched – he was sure that once the golem laid hands upon him, Gyman was likely to die in a most painful and hideous fashion. A crushed skull courtesy of a cast stone would seem, in retrospect, quite merciful.

Sabrax screamed. The golem before her had seized her white-maned skull. Her scream filled the valley for only a single, bare instant before the golem's hand contracted and that same skull collapsed like a ripe melon. Sabrax was silent, hanging limp in the golem's grip.

The advancing golem, meanwhile, had reached Gyman. It picked the sprawled daemonette up in both hands and lifted the half-limp, twitching body over its faceless, misshapen head. Gyman, only half lucid, made a strange moaning, beseeching sound. Then the golem tightened its grip on his upper and lower halves and tore him apart, all his bloodied entrails and viscera spilling out of his torso and slopping over the golem that had murdered him.

Up on the platform, Sabrax's killer had finished its task, crushing her body beneath its heavy stone hands, mashing it into the flagstones like a squashed bug. The daemonette was no more than a lumpy, smeared stain now. Without any concern for the stains on its stone hands or the spattered blood now painting its enormous, lumpy torso, the golem turned and strode back to where it had been waiting, dormant, against the cliff wall. Its companion – Gyman's slayer – was also lumbering back to where it had started, its bloodstained hands swinging beside it.

Only when each golem reached its previous place of guard duty did it stop, turn round and face the newcomers again. They did not fold themselves into the cliff wall this time, nor try to re-conceal themselves. Now, having been activated by some magical trip-wire attuned to footfalls on that portico platform, they stood and waited, clearly visible, clearly present and eager to meet any other approaching strangers should they dare to advance.

Watchers. Sentinels. Stone defenders immune to most common weapons and probably a number of magical ones.

Ezarhad stared. Considered. The only sound now was the wind in the narrow valley and the frightened murmurs of those behind him.

'Ghorgovaar?' Ezarhad called.

He heard footsteps, the sloshing of robes and the rattle of small chains. A moment later, his principle alchemist and engineer sidled into his vision, his twisted, unnatural face half-concealed under the shadows of a deep, dark cowl topping his long, sweeping robes.

'I stand ready to serve, master,' Ghorgovaar croaked.

'What do you think?' Ezarhad asked casually, suggesting the two golems. 'Can they be destroyed?'

Ghorgovaar's face twisted into an inhuman smile inside the deep cowl. 'There is no stone yet shaped in nature that my arts cannot pulverise. Give me the opportunity, my lord. I shall clear the way.'

Ezarhad smiled. 'Now that's the spirit. Go to it, good servant. Succeed and your reward shall be great.'

The alchemist removed himself, striding forward towards the entry to the tomb but pausing halfway across the desolate ground. He knelt alone on the scree and began a silent, solitary series of inventories, experiments and combinations. Ezarhad and his remaining troops watched, fascinated, as the kneeling alchemist – his back to them – bent over his mysterious labours. Occasionally, he might draw something from his belt, or one of the pouches slung across his torso, or from some pocket within his robes. They saw the glint of phials and small jars as they were set down gingerly beside him, taken up again and disappeared once more into the receptacles they had been drawn from. They saw his shoulders shift and his hands occasionally shake, holding in them some small beaker or phial that Ghorgovaar hastily mixed with the shaking of a wrist or the pivot of his elbow. Finally, after what seemed an interminable wait, Ghorgovaar rose to his feet. His hands stretched out on either side of him, each bearing in it a round wax-sealed jar roughly the size of a child's skull. Bearing his two deadly and mysterious weapons, Ghorgovaar advanced towards the cave entrance, slow but steady.

The troops behind Ezarhad began to hiss and murmur, all trading opinions about how far the alchemist might get before the stone golems lumbered forth to crush him as they had the two daemonettes that had preceded him. Ezarhad himself wondered, but he had faith in Ghorgovaar. He was a mortal, long dedicated to the rites of Slaanesh and twisted for centuries into something both more and less than human by his obsessions and bizarre hungers. He was no impulsive daemonette seeking sensual pleasures or feeding a ravening madness but a more pensive sort of obsessive. He suffered from the same hungry, heartwarming malady that Ezarhad did – an appetite for knowledge, that knowledge always more satisfying if it was obscure, dangerous and made all the more exclusive by the violent proclivities of its claimant. Learning a thing gave Ghorgovaar – and Ezarhad – great joy; slaying the person they had learned or extracted that knowledge from, thus making them the only steward of it, gave them an almost sensual satisfaction.

Now, there went the alchemist, edging closer and closer to the steps up to the broad portico and the entryway to the tomb beyond. He definitely seemed to be testing the waters, so to speak, moving step by step, always watching the two unmoving golems for signs of their advance. As he went, he also very carefully cradled and balanced those two mysterious globes in his hands, their contents clearly volatile and dangerous. Carrying only two of them seemed rather foolish to Ezarhad, but he was willing to assume that Ghor-govaar knew what he was doing.

Then, suddenly, there was movement. Before Ghorgovaar had even set foot on the first step, one of the stone golems lurched forward and advanced towards him. Ghorgovaar, to his credit, did not immediately retreat. Instead, he moved laterally, opening the distance between himself and the moving golem while approaching the other, still-unmoving golem to his right. As the moving golem took its first step to descend the temple steps, Ghorgovaar's nearness to the second golem seemed to finally awaken the thing. With a sudden jerk, the rocky automaton came to life and began its slow, steady march forward in the wake of its companion.

Ghorgovaar froze. Now, both were activated, both moving, both closing. For a moment, Ezarhad wondered if his alchemist had suddenly lost his nerve – Ghorgovaar just stood there, staring, watching as first the golem on the left, then the golem on the right, marched steadily towards him. The first had made the uneven floor of the valley now and was advancing towards him with slow, sure strides, while the other had just begun its uneasy descent of the steps.

Now Ghorgovaar moved, retreating steadily backwards, keeping a fixed distance between himself and the oncoming golem. Ezarhad could see what the alchemist intended now – he was trying to draw the beast out, to isolate it far away from its nest on the portico.

'Hurry up, you fool,' Ezarhad muttered under his breath. 'I cannot wait all day and night for you.'

Ghorgovaar drew back one arm and tossed the first of the two spheres he held. It rose in a high, slow arc – up, up, up into the air – then began a slow, sure drop. For a moment, Ezarhad wondered just what the alchemist was playing at. The way he lobbed the object looked like a doting parent tossing a ball, high and slow, to a clumsy child. But when the sphere finally impacted with the moving golem, Ezarhad realised that Ghorgovaar had known precisely what he was doing.

The moment the sphere shattered against the golem, it exploded. One moment, the valley was silent. The next, a massive peal of thunder seemed to split the sky and shake the earth beneath them, and a huge cloud of purple-white smoke belched forth, bringing with it a great, sharp shower of blasted stone fragments.

In spite of himself, Ezarhad recoiled from the explosion, even though it was too far away to truly harm him. Behind him, his troops did the same, screaming and shouting in excited shock as the blast rocked the world around them.

Ezarhad lowered his reflexively lifted hand and stared. The moving golem was no more, just a pile of rubble now, with two thick, unmoving legs left standing where the creature had been just moments before. Ghorgovaar had hunkered down and turned when he lobbed the sphere, to shield himself and his other piece of precious cargo. As the smoke cleared, he slowly, shakily rose to his feet and waved away the cloud now enveloping him.

Ezarhad felt a sudden clench in his belly.

The other golem. Where was it? With that swirling cloud out there, they could see nothing.

Ghorgovaar raised his empty fist.

'For Ezarhad Fatesbane!' he cried in his craggy, throaty voice. 'For the once and future inheritor of the throne of Slaanesh!'

A massive shadow advanced out of the smoke.

Ghorgovaar turned just in time to see the second golem now bearing down on him. It must have increased its speed after its mate had been destroyed, for it was lumbering and loping much faster than its previous, steady gait had suggested it could move. All at once, the great, bulky thing was looming out of the swirling smoke and shadows, reaching out, ready to seize Ghorgovaar and crush him.

Ghorgovaar saw the thing almost on top of him. He cursed and threw the other explosive sphere. It made no slow arc this time but shot towards the golem on a direct collision course. He was so close to the creature, to miss was an impossibility.

Unfortunately, that put poor Ghorgovaar right in the blast zone.

Another peal of thunder. Another belching, billowing cloud of smoke and another storm of shattered stone. And Ghorgovaar himself was torn apart, blasted into gristle and mist, by the very force that he had applied to destroy the golem. Ezarhad stood staring as his ears rang and the smoke roiled, peering into the haze for some sign of a survivor.

There was none. The golem had been pulverised... as had brave, stout Ghorgovaar.

'His sacrifice shall not be in vain,' Ezarhad said with no small amount of satisfaction. 'By his hand, I shall be victorious.'

And, of course, that was one less ambitious lieutenant to worry about eventually betraying him. Convenient, that.

Ezarhad strode forward. A few of his daemonettes and servants called out as though some danger remained, but could they not see? The way was clear now! The golems were no more than piles of ruined rubble. At last, the entryway to the tomb lay wide open. Ezarhad marched forth, ready to meet his destiny, enjoying the acrid scent of the still-swirling bomb smoke as he passed through the lingering cloud towards his ultimate destination.

It was not until he emerged on the far side, where the smoke was thinning and dispersing, that he saw his way was not clear after all.

Someone – a lone, small, thoroughly ordinary someone – stood framed in the open entryway to the tomb of Kaethraxis. Her aelven ears and lithe frame made her origins readily apparent. Ezarhad felt a slight thrill, realising whom he was about to treat with.

This would be the guardian. The *last* guardian. The very same

Lumineth left to keep Kaethraxis pacified centuries before this present moment.

Just imagine, he thought. *She has been waiting patiently through all these decades just for this moment, when she and I shall meet and speak, face to face.*

Just before I kill her with my bare hands...

Ezarhad kept advancing. He put a little swagger in his step, squared his shoulders. The aelven guardian moved slowly out from the open doorway into the dim grey midday sunshine of the cloudy valley. Like most aelves, her age was impossible to determine. Her eyes were ancient, impassive, deep as bottomless mountain lakes, while her face, though possessed of just a few lines and creases, largely refused to suggest any sort of age or maturity. She could be ten decades old or five centuries. These bloody smooth-faced, staring folk of Hysh made guessing age almost impossible.

Ezarhad was about to mount the steps up to the portico, but he thought better of it. It was possible, just possible, that some other enchantment yet lay upon the entryway, just waiting for his foot to set it off. First, he would have to confront the guardian. When the time came, he would send his minions up those steps and let one of them trip whatever magical countermeasure might remain.

Ezarhad turned and glanced over his shoulder. His servants trailed faithfully behind him, the daemonettes, fiends and last remaining hellstriders being herded along slowly, subtly, by black-cloaked Tyrirra and his far-striker, Vhaengoth. Confident that he had sufficient backing, Ezarhad turned back to the aelven guardian. He lifted his four hands openly, expansively, and presented himself.

'Greetings,' he said, smiling as he spoke. 'I am Ezarhad Fatesbane, the once and future inheritor of the throne of Slaanesh, soon to be supreme deity of excess and obsession. Whom do I speak to?'

The guardian stood, staring. She looked thoroughly, depressingly ordinary – a lithe frame draped in simple hand-woven clothing, a plain-pretty face of incalculable age under sandy hair streaked with silver and iron grey. A few beautiful aetherquartz gems adorned the guardian's person – a large pendant flanked by two stones at her throat, others encircling her wrist – but even those seemed to be simple, almost humble in their quiet elegance and simplicity.

She must be powerful, Ezarhad thought. *These foolish Lumineth prize humility and muted splendour in direct proportion to their inherent power and abilities. If this aelf woman looks so plain outwardly, she must be a mage of considerable strength...*

'This is no place for you,' the guardian said finally. Her voice carried with it no threat, no rancour. She simply stated a fact. 'I recommend you turn around and depart.'

Ezarhad's smile broadened – a normal reaction for him when faced with stubborn intractability. 'You mistake me,' he said. 'I have come a very long way. I have struggled much to find this place and to acquire a treasure suitable to aid me in my purpose.'

He decided to show her that the Eidolith was already in his possession. With two of his arms he reached into the great satchel at his side and drew out the gem – purest aetherquartz, the size of a small loaf of bread, clear for the most part, all its facets shining and glinting, even under the muted, cloud-choked sun, though there were milky clouds evident within its depths as well. Ezarhad held his prize before him, cradled in two hands, so that the guardian could clearly see it and understand what sort of powerful being she now stood in the presence of.

'It is a gem,' she said after a moment's study. 'There are many like it.'

Ezarhad felt his smile begin to fall. 'This is no mere gem, guardian,' he said. 'Do you not recognise the Eidolith? Your own people created it–'

'My people have created many things, for many purposes... and not all were successful or even useful. If that bauble you hold is the work of my folk, it was created and cut and polished without my knowledge or my expertise.'

'This,' Ezarhad said, lifting the gem, 'was created by a mountain temple of the Alarith for the sole purpose of replacing *you*... of making the task you fulfil, day after day after day, transferable to another. Would you not like to say your watch is finished? Would you not prefer to retire, and leave the keeping of the beast held prisoner in this place to another?'

'I would not,' the guardian said, unperturbed, 'for I am the only one who understands this beast, or its prisoner. I have waited here for centuries, praying for a replacement, learning a little more each day of what said replacement must be capable of – what they, or the magical implement they bear, must clearly possess to keep Kae-thraxis pacified and in hibernation. Looking at you, Fatesbane, and beholding this gem, I see none of what is required.'

Ezarhad could not help himself. He was frowning now. 'You should not mock me.'

'Small minds often see the statement of fact as mockery,' the guardian said. 'I do not mock you, Fatesbane. I pity you, for you possess little in the way of self-awareness, and less in the way of self-mastery.'

He felt a smile creep back onto his face. Many before her had told him such things. He had dealt with all of them in the same fashion.

'There is no need for self-mastery,' he said smugly, 'if one can bend the world to his or her will.'

'If one has attained self-mastery,' the guardian said, 'one sees the futility of bending the world to one's will... at least, on such a massive scale.'

'Enough,' Ezarhad muttered. 'Someone finish this aelven witch, please?'

There were murmurs and chatter behind him. Then, in answer to his summons, bodies sidled forward – a fiend and a daemonette, the four-legged beast huffing and snarling throatily as it went, the daemonette picking her way along on small, booted feet like a thief picking a path through sleeping marks. Ezarhad's two servants mounted the steps, climbing to the dais of the portico, and immediately charged the still, silent guardian.

The aelf moved quickly and surely, an iteration of some ancient martial art of her people giving her swift, sure movements culminating in a display of stunning magical force. Ezarhad barely knew what he was seeing – she fell back, narrowed her body by turning it sideways towards the oncoming enemies, then suddenly shifted her foot, stretched out her arms and bent her back to crouch into a pose that was clearly some sort of on-guard stance.

Then she stomped her foot. A single foot. And when she did so, the whole valley shook around her, a shockwave travelling with blinding speed outwards from the place where her small, lone foot fell.

The shockwave threw Ezarhad's servants backwards, the stone beneath their feet bucking like the waves of an angry sea. The daemonette leapt up and came down again in a sprawling heap. The fiend was thrown wholly off balance and fell, cursing and rolling, into the dust and strewn rock at the bottom of the portico stairs.

Ezarhad had almost been thrown off his feet as well. A hasty survey of his followers suggested several of them had fallen. It was like a single, pointed earth tremor, emanating from the place where the guardian stood. And even now, she was returning to her previous stance – tall, casual, uncaring.

'Go,' she said. 'If you remain – even if you destroy me – the outcome you attain will not be the outcome sought.'

'Kill her,' Ezarhad said, and slid sideways to allow his servants access to the aelven witch.

His soldiers charged.

The aelf did not disappoint.

She seemed to command the mountains and the stone itself. She first repelled her would-be slayers with two more of the fierce, ground-shaking tremors induced by single stampings of her small, ordinary feet. Most fell, rolled, struggled to regain their feet and balance again. Ezarhad himself was one of the few to remain upright as the churning tremors buckled the ground beneath them. Before most of his servants had recovered, the guardian stretched out her hands, as if she were reaching for invisible cables connected to the scree-strewn slopes rising to either side of her. With fierce tugs on those invisible, non-existent cables, massive rockfalls tore themselves away from the slopes and came crashing down the hillsides towards the portico and the open entryway. Ezarhad took several steps backwards, eager to put distance between himself and his servants as the rocks and scree tumbled towards them. Many managed to retreat and scramble out of the way. Several failed, and were crushed flat or bowled aside as the rock slides crashed home upon the broad, flat expanse before the portico.

One of the hellstriders had his mount circling, narrowly avoiding the falling rock, then spurred the beast to climb the newly formed pile of rubble, intent on heaving them up and over so that they could pounce upon the aelven guardian on the far side. With so much loose rock and scree in the way amid swirling clouds of dust, Ezarhad could no longer see the guardian. But he did see the hellstrider suddenly thrown bodily from behind the rock pile, still magically grafted to his mount even while both were airborne. The rider cried out. The mount screamed. Both landed in a crushed heap a great distance away after describing a long, savage arc.

Once again, Ezarhad thought, *I am the only one capable of seeing my will done to my satisfaction. I suppose I shall have to end this...*

Bright explosions of blunt, concussive force sprang from behind the screen of fallen rock. Ezarhad saw two more of his daemonette servants thrown backwards violently by those raw blasts of energy even as more swarmed up and over the rubble to reach their enemy on the far side.

Ezarhad charged, mounted the rock and scree and climbed to the apex. Once he reached a better vantage, he could see precisely what unfolded.

The guardian was holding her own mightily against his servants. Her movements were so fluid, so strong, that she seemed not even to be straining. Her eyes stared directly ahead, into the middle distance, as foe after foe assailed her and she repelled them with a strange and wondrous combination of hand-to-hand-combat movements and strategically applied magic. She repelled a charging daemonette with a single, inhumanly powerful open-handed strike, kicked another, then seemed to toss yet another of those flashing bursts of concussive force outwards from the gauntlet around her wrist – the one adorned with one of her aetherquartz gems. She deflected sword and spear blows, redirected charging adversaries, broke bones, shattered weapons. They encircled and charged her like ravening, hungry wolves around a lone sheep – but the sheep repelled each and every one that came against her.

This was Ezarhad's chance. While she was distracted.

He fell into his own favoured magician's stance, began muttering the words required to summon the energies necessary for the fatal operations he intended. Little by little, he felt the foul, chaotic energies that he called out to coursing into his body from the aether, like water welling up from an underground reservoir. It filled him, stirred him, threatened to subsume and immolate him.

But wait, he reminded himself. *Do not spend it. Let it build. Keep it locked inside you, the pressure rising, the power quickening–*

The aelf witch saw what he was doing. Without warning, she slammed two charging adversaries aside and unleashed a massive wall of concussive force – the produce of both aetherquartz gems at once – towards Ezarhad.

Fatesbane opened himself – only a little. He allowed through just enough of the energies building inside him to meet and dispel the wall of force now rushing towards him. The massive sphere of boiling, concentrated energy he sent rocketing towards the concussive wave broke upon it, and both magical attacks shattered and dissipated in a storm of thunder and lightning.

More of his minions were upon her now – and they had landed blows. Her momentary distraction, trying to strike at him directly, using the brunt of her strength, had allowed them to breach her defences. A sword pierced her side and drew blood. She used her elbow to send the wielder flying backwards. And yet, even that was too late – a javelin jabbed forward and bit deep into her flesh on the opposite side to the sword wound. The aelven guardian twisted, trying to see her attacker and strike to once more clear the ground immediately around her.

Ezarhad saw his chance. He unleashed all of the power built up inside him.

Fire and lightning, pure, destructive kinetic force – it all hit the guardian at once. In an instant, she was enveloped in amethyst flames, the fierce power of a hungry storm coursing through her small, wiry body, searing and burning her from the inside out. A few of Ezarhad's nearby minions were caught in the crossfire and writhed under the flames and loosed energies, but he cared not. He had to end her. That was all that mattered.

The guardian jerked, bent, tried to move to somehow free herself from the onslaught of energies now enveloping her. She failed. Ezarhad saw her flesh blackening, her eyes melting in her skull, her hair vaporised on her blistering, cracking crown. He poured everything out – everything that he possessed, all the power he had summoned, shouting and cursing as he did so. His fury invigorated the energies loosed. His hatred concentrated them. His need brightened their intensity.

The guardian exploded. It was sudden, apocalyptic, her whole body disappearing in an instant into a cloud of vapour and dust, all the heat and latent energy released into her too much to endure. The moment she disintegrated, Ezarhad choked off the massive storm of energy coursing out of him. Suddenly, everything was quiet. Still. Almost peaceful.

The air stank of smoke and char. Several of his minions lay dead or horribly wounded.

But the guardian? She was no more. A black, charred smudge on the rock-strewn portico.

Nothing stood in his way now. Nothing.

'Master,' a voice hissed beside him.

Tyrirra, once more at his side when he least expected it. And what was Ezarhad doing on his knees? Had he collapsed after that massive expenditure of energy and emotion? They could not see him like this... could not see him weak, spent, vulnerable...

But Tyrirra seemed to be troubled by something. She was facing outwards, towards the back end of the valley, pointing. Ezarhad, weak and confused by what had just transpired, trying to regain both his wherewithal and his strength, craned his neck around and blinked, staring out at the narrow, desolate valley in search of whatever it was that Tyrirra was so intent upon.

Newcomers. Witnesses.

Apparently, they were not alone.

CHAPTER SIXTEEN

From a distance, Ferendir, his masters and their companions watched the guardian die. Her solitary stand against Ezarhad's attacking forces was beautiful and terrible to behold, her power undeniable, her ferocity – in true Lumineth fashion – wholly unexpected. But in the end, Ezarhad Fatesbane had summoned a massive, concentrated burst of magical energies and thrown all of it at the guardian in a single, unstoppable wave of fire and lightning. Ferendir knew not if the guardian's energies had been depleted by her defence of the temple or if Ezarhad was simply that powerful, that monstrous in his abilities and determination. In either case, the outcome was the same.

They had arrived moments too late. The guardian was no more. The way to Kaethraxis was open to the enemy.

'Enough,' Serath said flatly, then strode away from his companions, straight towards the cliff wall and the entryway to the temple.

'Where is he going?' Ferendir asked Desriel.

'He goes to the enemy,' Desriel said softly. 'To end him. To end them all. Come – this is our fight too.'

Desriel fell in step behind Serath, moving briskly, deliberately, but still allowing Serath to remain in the lead. Ferendir and the others fell in behind Desriel. They advanced in swift lockstep, a small, sharp spear point aimed at the heart of Ezarhad's foul retinue.

As they advanced, Ferendir tried to count the enemy troops remaining. Twenty? Maybe more? It was hard to tell from here. Those visible were either atop the fallen earth that the guardian had torn down from the hillsides or just before it. No doubt more waited on the far side of the rockfall, wounded by their encounter with the guardian but not yet out of the fight. And, of course, there was the master himself – Ezarhad Fatesbane, tall and regal and strangely beautiful where he stood atop the mounded stones, studying his now-approaching opponents, no doubt trying to work out a plan of his own.

We can take them, Ferendir thought, determined. *We can take them all. So few remain, but we've come so far...*

But look what we've lost on the way. We are not at our best – none of us. Beaten, battered and bruised... and outnumbered.

Tyrion, Teclis, give us strength.

Mother Mountain, give us endurance.

Ferendir drew breath, exhaled, drew breath, exhaled. This moment was the one he had trained for – the one he might die in. Today, he and his masters and the rest of these heroic Lumineth would make their last stand against this beast, Ezarhad, and his devilish minions. Ferendir wanted to believe that virtue and light would win the day...

But he was no longer a child. He knew better than that.

Serath, far ahead, alone, marched up to the rockfall where Ezarhad and his surviving underlings now massed. Even at a distance, Ferendir could see something – sense something – in the Chaos pretender's frame. How he struggled to stand tall and straight, how he stretched out his four arms in exaltation and challenge, how he smiled yet also trembled ever so subtly.

He is performing for us, Ferendir realised. *Presenting himself as strong, sure, confident.*

The onslaught he unleashed upon the guardian weakened him.

If we attack him directly...

'You lot again?' Ezarhad said, with almost friendly aplomb. 'Were you all not cast to the bottom of a mountain with a few tons of rubble atop you?'

'A mountain is our patron,' Serath answered calmly. 'Our mother. Neither she nor any of her snow-capped kin would destroy us at *your* bidding.'

Ferendir saw Ezarhad Fatesbane's smile fade for a moment – only a moment. In that instant, Ferendir perceived worry and frustration on his sculpted blue face. Clearly, Serath's confidence and courage made the pretender to Slaanesh's throne uneasy.

The pretender's forces slowly fanned out along the ridgeline formed by the rockfalls that had crashed down from the hillsides above. A hasty count numbered fifty or sixty in all – clearly, a clutch of hidden, wounded daemonettes had joined the fight since the last appraisal. Assessing the lot of them, Ferendir saw evidence of broken or sprained limbs, still-bleeding wounds and sagging shoulders. A lone hellstrider kept his beastly mount pacing in the background.

We're weak and battered, Ferendir realised, *but so are they. Maybe, just maybe, we can stop him here, break his forces, end this madness once and–*

'Kill them,' Ezarhad said to his minions, almost casually.

The Hedonites charged – screaming, laughing and even singing as they surged forward.

Before Desriel could lead the charge, as Ferendir still registered a battle about to happen versus a battle joined, Serath shot forward. With savage efficiency, his stone mallet swooped and arced, and the three closest Hedonites lay crushed and lifeless at the Stoneguard's planted feet.

Desriel spun towards Ferendir and the others.

'Ferendir, with Serath and me at the centre! The rest of you, watch the wings. Make sure those monsters on the ridgelines don't encircle us!'

Then Desriel dashed forward, covering the space between himself and Serath in four long, bounding strides. Ferendir rushed into his master's wake. As he arrived at the place where Desriel and Serath had prepared their last stand, back to back, he fell into the tripartite formation and felt something strange – as if the three of them were puzzle pieces suddenly falling into place. It was as if some powerful, resonant energy lying dormant in the ground beneath them were suddenly awakened, coursing up through their feet and into their bodies, not only empowering each of them as an individual, but connecting them, turning them into a single, united front capable of holding off an entire warhost of Hedonites.

It was unlike any feeling Ferendir had ever known. For the first time in his life, he felt truly, entirely and unreservedly a part of something. He and his masters were one, and the mountain blessed their endeavours.

Serath's stone mallet crushed a daemonette skull and sent blood and ichor flying haphazardly through the chill mountain air. Desriel's diamondpick hammer flashed and whispered, doubling over a charging Hedonite and sending the adversary's body crashing backwards into the creatures just behind it. Ferendir met a frontal attack from a prancing daemonette bearing crustacean-like pincers, using his pick hammer to parry the monster's stabbing, thrusting blows but unable to get in a killing strike of his own. Calling upon the mountain's energies, the mountain's patience, Ferendir turned inwards, seeking that place where time and his awareness would subjectively slow, that place where he could read and assess and calculate the perfect, proper blocks, parries and potential strike zones of his own attacks, even in the midst of the chaos unfolding around him. Doing so was a struggle, because beyond the dipping, snarling form of the Hedonite just before him he saw a blaze of many colours and a whirl of activities – a handful of other would-be adversaries dancing about in a surging throng, awaiting their chance to charge and end him if their comrade failed.

Something warm and wet splattered on his face – fallout from a deadly strike by Serath, on his left. No matter. Ferendir ignored it. He parried half a dozen more blows from his assailant, seeking an opening, praying for carelessness.

There. Arms raised. The pincers snapping, clicking in the air, preparing for a downward blow. Ferendir brought his pick hammer around in a swift arc. If it had been a blade he wielded and not a blunt instrument, he would have bisected the foul thing that threatened him. Instead, the daemonette's lithe, thin body all but bent double at a terrible sideways angle, and the creature shrieked in inhuman agony. Ferendir's strike was powerful – backed by the force of the mountain – and the daemonette was swept aside and crashed to the rocky floor of the valley, broken and unable to move.

No time to celebrate. Already, two more were sliding in to take the foul thing's place.

In his peripheral vision, Ferendir saw their companions meeting the closing wings of Ezarhad's forces as they streamed down from the slopes, hoping to swarm their small company and crush them by encircling them. He caught momentary visions of Phalcea's sunmetal pike flashing in the dull grey daylight, slashing and repelling three enemies before skewering a fourth and burning its pinned prey from the inside out. Metorrah, meanwhile, undertook a complex pattern of sweeps and volleys, loosing arrows one by one against close-by attackers before seizing a moment's opportunity to couch three arrows at a time upon her bowstring and launch those multi-pronged assaults towards the rear ranks of their adversaries. Taurvalon glowed with a brilliant, almost blinding luminescence, the aetherquartz studding his armour and weapons all pulsing with bestirred energies, fuelling his swift, smooth, savage attacks upon the charging Hedonites. He had yet to draw his sword, preferring to use his shield for blunt force and his long, graceful spear for sweeping impacts and deadly thrusts. If Ferendir had not had deadly opponents of his own to deal with, he thought he could have stood in awe, watching Taurvalon hew down his oncoming opponents for hours.

Concentrate, you fool. There's a battle on.

There, charging, directly before him. Wide black eyes and snarling faces exploded into his vision. Once more, Ferendir turned his mind to the deadly contest that engulfed him.

One by one, little by little, their enemies fell.

Now three.

Now seven.

Now ten.

We can beat them, Ferendir dared to think. *The ranks are thinning. If we can but punch a hole through their mass towards Ezarhad… if Serath or Desriel could finally make it through…*

Twenty down. Thirty.

A dozen remained – certainly no more than fifteen or twenty – some now grabbing the bodies of their fallen comrades to use as blunt instruments or hurled missiles in a desperate effort to break the Lumineth's concerted defence and offence, to get close, to hurt them, to kill them. Ferendir ducked one of those hurled corpses, launched from a crouch and drove his pick hammer head on into an attacker's gut, the spike at the hammer's head punching right through the Hedonite's soft exposed middle.

A stillness. The caress of the breeze. Ferendir looked about. Only a few Hedonites and daemonettes remained now, and they had fallen back, each doing their best to suppress their natural inclination to frenzy and find some clever means to outsmart or outflank their aelven adversaries.

And there, clear as the sun on the Ymetrican plain – a broad, unguarded path right through the thinned ranks towards Ezarhad Fatesbane.

For an instant – only an instant – it occurred to Ferendir that he, himself, could punch through that hole and try to slay their terrible, towering adversary. But that impulse was instantly reined in – he knew it was not his place, beyond his skills and a foolish risk besides. That would have been giving in to a desire for glory, for violent, sacrificial apotheosis.

Emotion.

Weakness.

More importantly, Desriel and Serath had already seen the gap. Words were exchanged – though Ferendir could not hear them precisely – and his masters switched places. Serath slid into Desriel's place at Ferendir's back, now facing off against the last two daemonettes, each waiting for an opening to exploit, and Desriel charged forward, right through the gap in their enemy's defences.

Straight towards Ezarhad.

Ferendir sensed movement on his right. A charging daemonette, legs moving with silent swiftness as she zigzagged across the rough ground towards him. He spun just in time to meet the pair of foul curved scimitars she wielded and parry their swift blows, one after the other. She cackled and taunted him as she riposted and spun for another onslaught with the twin blades, her skills considerable, her confidence unnerving. Ferendir used his pick hammer to parry and deflect each attack, felt the bite of the razor-sharp blades more than once on his upper arm, his lower leg. Finally, responding with swift, unyielding attacks, he struck again, again and again. On the fourth swift blow, one of the scimitars was torn from the daemonette's hand and clattered onto a pile of nearby scree.

The daemonette wielded her remaining blade two-handed.

Ferendir parried another parcel of blows, then saw his opening. He swept the daemonette's goat-like legs out from under her, sent her sprawling on her ugly, inhuman face, then brought his hammer crashing down to end her. She died with an explosive convulsion.

No more enemies. They held the valley.

Desriel charged Ezarhad.

We've won, he thought. *The day is ours!*

It was then, when Ferendir was sure that the next instant would bring Desriel's one-on-one clash with Ezarhad Fatesbane – his monstrous, bejewelled sword already drawn and ready for a match – that the tide turned.

A sound like a shrieking, hurricane wind howled from the tributary ravines and canyons that encircled the valley. At first, Ferendir wondered if he was simply imagining it, or sensing something on a higher plane that did not affect the material. But no, looking to Serath, he saw that his master heard it and felt it as well, as did the others.

Then he saw them – a new mass of foul, scarred and silk-shrouded Hedonites, lithe daemonettes and mounted seekers pouring from two of the tributary canyons just off to their left, on the western side of the valley. First there were dozens, then scores, then hundreds. They poured from the cracks in the slopes like a flash flood of strangely coloured flesh and motley rainbow silks and flashing, jingling jewels, rings and piercings. They sounded high, ululating battle cries and sang aberrant, incoherent songs and came bounding down the slopes in a headlong rush towards where Ferendir, his companions and their enemy waited.

For a moment, Ferendir thought they might be Ezarhad's own minions, having waited in reserve until needed, now charging into the fray to save their master.

But no. Their charge drew Ezarhad's attention. Even at this

distance, Ferendir clearly saw the shock and dismay on the arrogant pretender's face. The terror in his wide black orb-like eyes.

These are not his followers, Ferendir realised. *He's afraid of them. As we should be. Tyrion and Teclis! How many of them are there?*

Desriel's charge on Ezarhad ceased the moment the new enemies showed themselves. Ferendir's master stood a short distance from his target, facing the oncoming horde, assessing the risks and dangers about to come swarming down upon him – upon them all.

The horde closed, filling the hillside. Moment by moment, they charged closer to where Desriel stood, alone, isolated, exposed.

A tall, broad form stepped into Ferendir's field of vision – Serath, now standing between him and Desriel, stone mallet ready for another round of slaughter.

'Ready yourself!' Serath snapped.

Ferendir took a single step to the left, to see Desriel. His master was prepared, standing on guard with his pick hammer ready. The charging horde were seconds away from him now.

'No!' Ferendir cried.

Serath rounded on him. 'Control yourself, Ferendir! The battle's not won yet!'

Then the tide overtook Desriel. Ferendir's master disappeared in an avalanche of bodies and weapons and motion. Ferendir, mind awhirl as his deep, bestirred emotions fought mightily to slip his bonds of self-control and mindfulness, forced himself to swing his gaze away from where his master had just been overtaken and look to the wall of bodies and blades now surging towards him and Serath.

Then the world was nothing but blood and thunder, slaughter and desperation.

Chaos reigned, and no amount of composure or self-control could quell it.

And so, Ferendir surrendered. He surrendered to the hate, to the fury, to the bloodlust. Rather than bolster the bastions of his self-control and demand the best of himself, he let the flood wash the dam away. All that he had fought to suppress through the whole of his life was unleashed. He struck and mowed and broke bones and spilt blood, and he was exalted by it. He sought his companions amid the chaos, caught glimpses of their own desperate battles in the midst of the onslaught, and he feared for them, but he did not care to aid them. It was now each for him or herself. Survival mattered more than victory. Vengeance mattered more than lofty goals or purposes.

And finding Desriel – saving Desriel – mattered more than even surviving the day. Ferendir waded through the blood and mire, struck down adversaries on all sides, pressed and pressed on, cutting a bloody swathe through the horde of enemies on a meandering, ever more desperate path towards where he had last seen his master. He thought he heard Serath calling out to him, but ignored his voice. Thought he heard his other companions – Taurvalon, Metorrah, Phalcea – all exhorting him to circle back, to join them once more, to stand with them – but he told himself it was his imagination.

There was only the ruin of the enemy and the salvation of his mentor. Nothing else mattered.

Without warning, bodies jostled and slammed against him. He was cut by blades, hit by bludgeons, snipped and slashed at by pincers and barbed tails and ragged claws. He struck on all sides, unable to focus on any single adversary or any finite moment. He felt bones crack, saw gouts of blood and ichor tossed this way and that, felt flesh and muscle yield to his strength and his hatred… but no matter how many he crushed or shattered or sent crashing to the rocky ground, there were always more.

Something hit his helm and his senses were dashed. A sun-bright flash of pain and delirium suddenly scrambled all his senses, and

Ferendir felt his legs buckle beneath him. In an instant, he was on the ground, crushed beneath the weight of jostling bodies, slashing talons and haphazardly swung weaponry. He swung his pick hammer single-handed but was unsure if he hit anything. He felt blood flowing, felt bones – his own – buckling, threatening to break if they took one more direct hit, one more lucky blow from his enemies. Voices taunted him. Daemonettes sang songs of bitter reproach. Inhuman throats spat laughter and heaped curses upon him.

Fool, he thought. *This is what succumbing to your emotions earns you. Here, now, you die… and for what?*

The braying laughter of a Hedonite was suddenly cut off mid-guffaw. Gasps and curses rose. Something screamed. Ferendir felt something thick and hot spatter against him and realised it was the blood of one of those above him. As he blinked, desperate to clear his vision, something heavy and strong arced through the air above him and flashed with beatific glory as another daemonette skull shattered under its weight.

A diamondpick hammer. Its wielder stood tall and mighty, slashing the air this way and that, hewing a path through the throng towards Ferendir's place beneath them.

Desriel.

Ferendir could not believe his good fortune – and all at once, felt shame.

Get up, the voice within him said.

Unworthy, he thought.

Get up, now, the voice insisted.

Gave in. Weakened. Succumbed.

Make another choice, the voice demanded. *Now. Right now. Waste no more time.*

Ferendir shot to his feet. For a moment, he reeled, unsteady, senses still scrambled… but he sought his strength now, his support, in the place where he should have when the newcomers overtook them.

Call to the mountain. Connect with the mountain. Be the mountain.

His feet felt heavy, rooted, firmly set. His body was suddenly, miraculously strong and steady, the shakes and tremors wracking him moments before vanishing in a warm, empowering wash of geomantic energies.

Desriel moved with swift, sure strokes and strong, confident strides – pure power, pure poise, an unstoppable force on a steady advance.

But what was that? A huge form now advancing out of the melee, hewing left and right with its long, terrible sword as daemonettes choked its path or tried to arrest its progress.

Ezarhad, determined, pressing right towards Desriel even as the newly arrived Hedonites attacked and harried him.

Breathe, Ferendir. Cut through your fear. Burn away the fury. Banish the frenzy. That is their way, not our way.

Not your *way, Ferendir.*

Several of the nearest Hedonites and daemonettes, their attentions drawn by Desriel's advance, now saw Ferendir on his feet again. As their comrades dealt with the master, those few who saw him preparing for his own counter-attack turned their attentions towards the student and surged towards him.

Ferendir – calm, centred, grounded – met them all. His heart beat steadily. His emotions – his wants – all slipped away into the aether, forgotten. He did not want anything – he only saw to the exigencies of the moment. Parry a strike, deflect a blow, exploit an exposed flank, punish overconfidence with deadly acumen.

He struck. They fell. Desriel, nearby, hewed his own path, nearer and nearer.

Ezarhad was still some distance away, a roiling mass of Hedonites between him and Desriel. The pretender's bejewelled broadsword flashed and glinted even as it separated daemonette heads from their lithe, smooth shoulders.

'Master, behind you!' Ferendir cried.

Desriel spun, striking down an attacking fiend as he did so. He saw Ezarhad, still wading through a storm of his newly arrived enemies, then turned his attentions to Ferendir.

'Back!' Desriel called. 'Towards the others! We cannot win the day alone, Ferendir!'

Ferendir nodded, understanding. He had been a fool – but now… now, all was right. Desriel was back at his side. His master fought. Ferendir fought. Their enemies fell. If they could but cut a path back to their companions–

A cry of ecstasy from the Hedonites at his back, followed by a chorus of cheers and celebration. Ferendir struck down the nearest charging daemonette and spun to see what had them so excited. The moment he did, he wished he had died rather than behold the sight now before him.

No! Impossible!

Desriel was down, bleeding, on his knees and barely holding his pick hammer aloft. Some foul spawn of Slaanesh had landed a lucky, deadly blow and crippled him before he could mount a defence.

Ferendir swept his pick hammer right and left, desperate to clear a path. He cried Desriel's name. *No! Not now!* Not when he had just come to his rescue!

Then the tide turned, so quickly that Ferendir could barely understand what was happening until it had already happened.

Desriel struggled, dazed and bleeding.

Hedonites swarmed and swirled around him, cackling and taunting him and swooping in to land quick, glancing blows as they were jostled back and forth against one another.

Desriel reeled to his feet and struck down three Hedonites in rapid succession.

The crowd around him retreated.

That's when Ezarhad broke through. Suddenly, there stood the towering pretender to the throne of Slaanesh, two of his four hands tightly gripping his princely blade and thrusting it mercilessly forward.

Desriel turned just in time to see what was coming for him. The blade ran him through, front to back, the sharpened point punching right through the back plate of his blood-spattered armour.

Ferendir threw himself towards his master's arched, trembling form. The sword withdrew. Hedonites leapt upon Ezarhad, seemingly enraged that he had claimed their aelven prize for himself. As Ezarhad reeled backwards, drawn into a savage fray by a dozen strong, taloned hands, Desriel hit the ground in a heap. Ferendir fell atop him, covering his body as the Hedonites all closed in and redoubled their attacks.

They will not have him, Ferendir thought, remembering all the dismembered, desecrated bodies they'd discovered between their home and their destination, all the horrible, blasphemous ways in which these monsters could turn their already slain victims into abominable trophies and depraved works of art.

All the walls Ferendir had built within himself, all the deflections he had learned, proved wholly useless. The fight went on around him. Servants of Slaanesh screamed and died as his companions – drawing nearer through the horde – slaughtered them with ruthless efficiency, while still more roiled forward and pressed their numerical superiority. Ferendir was struck, kicked, slashed, poked, but he would not move. His own armoured form remained atop Desriel's, sheltering him, protecting him, even in death. He heard his companions cry out for aid, shout curses at their attackers, rally one another to tighter formations leaving less room for the enemy.

But it was all background noise. Wind in the trees. Meaningless. Ferendir could only bend over Desriel, his fallen master, shielding his limp body, begging the mountain, begging Tyrion, Teclis and any gods that would listen, to save them from the horrible end that surely, inevitably, now presented itself.

Someone was calling his name. Ferendir heard them – heard his name – but cared little. Nothing mattered any more. *Nothing.* Their quest, their purpose, their ultimate aims. Everything had evaporated in the instant he saw Desriel fall and knew that he would not rise again.

No, a voice within him insisted, *you cannot give up. Desriel would upbraid you for this. This is not the Lumineth way. Not the Alarith way. Not what Desriel taught you. Your emotions are beasts. They buck and strain and bolt and balk. Control them and you can use their power to your advantage. Surrender that control and you surrender all your advantages... and all that you are.*

I do not care any more, Ferendir thought bitterly. *He's lost. Gone forever. How can I go on? What can I do?*

Live as he taught you to live, that insistent voice within him pressed. *Become what he always knew you to be. Earn his faith. Repay his trust. But to do that, you must let go of your grief and your anger and your pain... and you must do it now. Right now. This instant. No moment can be wasted–*

And then, almost as if to prove the point that small, still voice in his mind had been trying to make, rough hands seized Ferendir, tore Desriel's corpse from his arms and yanked him up onto his feet. Ferendir struggled, but the grip of those holding him was ironclad. He blinked. What had happened? What was happening?

He saw his companions – Serath, Phalcea, Metorrah, Taurvalon – all now disarmed and held fast, helpless, by the servants of Slaanesh. Ferendir looked to Serath, seeking guidance, perhaps even seeking forgiveness. Serath met his gaze and gave the slightest, almost imperceptible shake of his head.

No. No more. The fight is done.

For now.

His senses clearing, his awareness finally returning, Ferendir turned and surveyed the scene. The newly arrived Hedonites far outnumbered both his companions and Ezarhad's last remaining minions. Though many of the same horrible transformations and mutations were in evidence among the newcomers – the over-large eyes, the madly dilated pupils, the excess of wholly unnatural limbs and extremities, the strange piercings, scarifications and foul adornments – the newcomers were nonetheless clearly of a different tribe, followers of a different warlord. The differences were subtle – skin tones, the overall colour palette to their clothing and accoutrements, the nature of their adornments or twisted shapes – but those differences were still visible and pronounced.

There had to be more than a hundred of them. They presented a veritable horde beside Ferendir's tiny circle of friends and the dwindling, ragtag retinue that remained to serve the pretender, Ezarhad.

There, moving nearer through the crowd, towering above all and wading like a woman entering calm water – their mistress, their leader, as unnaturally tall as Ezarhad himself but presenting a far more striking, even tempting, figure. She was beautiful, for one thing – beautiful and terrible. Her clothing was scant and decadently styled, bejewelled and finely crafted, baring large swathes of her ochre-coloured skin in numerous places, exposing bizarre, seemingly haphazard piercings all up and down the length of her body. A great cloak seemingly woven of translucent silk and black cobwebs trailed behind her, billowing in the breeze like the banner of a rising god. She was crowned with a strange headpiece adorned with a number of protruding branches and horns, holding back the massive, tangled fall of her oiled, bone-white hair that trailed behind her and curled in the wind like smoke billowing from a churning bonfire.

As she advanced, her servants made way for her, parting to allow her through, some bowing, others throwing up their hands in exhortation, still more standing tall with their weapons or foul, inhuman claws and pincers displayed, as if to seek her praise for the blood they'd spilt. She acknowledged none of them. The towering sorceress simply glided through their midst, a god among insects, approaching Ferendir and his friends. Nearby, just off to Ferendir's left, Ezarhad Fatesbane stood watching the woman's approach. If Ferendir was not mistaken, he saw fear on the pretender's narrow, sculpted face.

The woman reached the makeshift clearing in the midst of the crowd where Ferendir and his companions were held captive. Up close, Ferendir thought the sight of her – and, likewise, the musky, perfumed smell of her – would drive him mad. All of his carefully cultivated self-control, mindfulness and ironclad supremacy over his emotions and his animal impulses seemed to be scrambled by her very presence. Serath himself, along with the others, seemed to be suffering the same crisis. No one broke. No one relented. But each was clearly fighting the impulses that this foul, alluring temptress aroused in them, simply with the striking figure she cut and strange aromas she exuded.

Ezarhad stretched out his four arms, as if in greeting.

'Astoriss, sister and friend,' he said with practised and wholly false magnanimity. 'How fortunate for me that you happened along when you did. These miscreants' – he indicated Ferendir and the others – 'have proven a most vexing obstacle in my quest. Take them now, as a gift, to do with as you please.'

The woman smiled a little, cold and cruel. 'I shall,' she said in a melodious voice. 'But not as a gift – as tribute, rightfully seized.'

'Seized?' Ezarhad asked.

Astoriss nodded. 'Aye, Ezarhad. Seized. From a wheedling rival who has finally, utterly, failed and surrendered.'

Ferendir saw the look of hatred that flashed across Ezarhad's normally composed features. 'I surrender nothing.'

Astoriss cocked her head. 'Wrong. You've surrendered everything.'

She gestured towards Ezarhad's minions, gathered closely and protectively around him.

'Kill them,' she said.

Her servants did as she asked. In truth, Ferendir was not ready for the suddenness and ferocity of the killing blows that overwhelmed and ended every one of Ezarhad's servants. In moments – mere moments – the pretender to the throne of Slaanesh stood alone and vulnerable, surrounded by the slain and torn corpses of the last dozen or so creatures that had come to this place and called him master.

Ezarhad looked like a child whose favourite pet had been discovered dead in the woods. He surveyed the slaughter, his losses. Ferendir thought he might even see the glimmer of tears in his large black eyes.

'You will pay for that,' Ezarhad said quietly.

Astoriss shook her head. She exuded strength, assurance, pure menace. There was no fear in her – no doubt in her – whatsoever. 'No,' she said, and Ferendir thought he heard the slightest hint of pity in her voice. 'No, Ezarhad, I will not. The payments are all yours, and the bill has come due. Now, if you please, hand it over.'

She stretched out one elegant hand.

He stared at her.

'Hand what over?'

'The Eidolith,' she said. 'I know you have it. If you do not present it to me of your own free will, I shall tear it from you after I've had my minions saw off your foul, thieving hands.'

Ezarhad fought the urge to reply. Ferendir thought he saw a storm of emotions at work in him, and was strangely moved by how human – how vulnerable and wounded – the nine-foot-tall pretender to a god's mantle now seemed.

The silence between them endured. Ezarhad made no move.

Astoriss stood before him, outstretched hand beckoning. Ferendir was silent. His companions were silent. The watching servants of Astoriss were silent. There was only the sound of the chill mountain wind raking savagely through the narrow valley.

Finally, Ezarhad reached beneath his cloak. He drew out a large gem – the very aetherquartz gem stolen from Ferendir's temple, the gem that so many of Ferendir's teachers and comrades had died for rather than surrender. Without a word or a fight, Ezarhad Fatesbane handed that gem to Astoriss.

The sorceress took it in her hands, cradling it, and stared into its glowing, multifaceted depths. For an instant, Ferendir thought he saw something like true wonder – true awe – on her cold and jaded face.

She held the gem aloft for all of her massed followers to see.

'Behold!' she proclaimed. 'The treasure promised! The treasure claimed!'

Her foul followers shouted acclamations and praise. Some howled. Some cheered. Some sang impromptu songs or made strange, ululating noises in their throats. Ferendir looked to Serath and his companions. They all bore dour expressions of dismay – a combination of muted anger and frustration.

The cheering died down. Astoriss, done basking in the animal cries of her servants, raised her hands for silence again.

'I told you we would smash the invader, Meigant! I told you we would welcome those with him who saw the truth – the truth I proclaimed – and slaughter those who resisted us! Did I lie to you?'

'No!' they all cried as one.

'I told you we would find this feeble pretender to the throne of our beloved god, Slaanesh!' She gestured towards the now solitary and humbled Ezarhad, who looked alternately ready to tear her limb from limb or to slink, as a coward might, under the nearest rock. 'I told you we would wrest the gem from his hands! Did I lie to you?'

'No!' they all answered. Several of those closest to Ezarhad dared to lay hands on him, shoving him, clawing at him, mocking him. Ferendir could see the hatred in Ezarhad's downcast eyes, the way his teeth gnashed so hard they might be ground to dust. No doubt he still possessed a great deal of power – spells, hidden weapons, even some skill as a hand-to-hand opponent – but here, now, with no one to support him and hopelessly outnumbered, forced by a powerful rival to surrender his greatest prize and his hopes of victory, he was incapable of fighting back. His ego had been shattered, and he had not, as yet, managed to pick up and account for its many scattered shards.

'And now,' Astoriss continued, holding the Eidolith aloft once more, 'I hold the key to unlocking the door of our salvation! To free the power entombed here – to awaken and unleash Kaethraxis – is to place in our hands the power to seize all the secrets of the Mortal Realms and to finally uncover the whereabouts of our beloved Lord Slaanesh! This, too, I promised you! And this, too, I have now delivered! Did I lie to you?'

'No!' they proclaimed, the whole debased host of one voice and one fervent spirit.

'Now,' she said, 'I lead you into a new age! An age when our dread lord, our beautiful, blighted, long-absent Lord Slaanesh, may be petitioned and summoned and restored incarnate, so that we may work his holy debaucheries and sublime excesses upon all the Mortal Realms once more! Our enemies' – she suggested not only Ezarhad now but also Ferendir and the other captured Lumineth – 'will bear witness to their failure and our victory! And perhaps they, too, will see the futility of their opposition! The holy righteousness of sweet surrender to our cause and to the cause of our lord and master! What say you? Is it time to awaken sleeping Kaethraxis?'

Cheers. No longer words now, but simple, barbaric yawps and

howls answering in a cacophony of affirmation. The cheer was deafening, ear-splitting, and Ferendir felt his being recoil from the immensity and hideousness of it. Worse, Astoriss did not seek to silence or control her followers. She simply stood, exultant, turning and turning for all to see and worship, holding aloft in one hand the stolen Eidolith and all but beckoning their adulation with the other. The Hedonites and daemonettes holding Ezarhad and the captive Lumineth shook them with their filthy hands, squeezed them, tore at them, shoved them. Ferendir heard words of insult and provocation, foul curses and silkily whispered taunts and temptations. The world around them was chaos, pure pandemonium, with Astoriss rising tall and alluring and evil at its centre, the eye of a churning storm.

One of her bejewelled hands suddenly shot out, pointing towards the still-yawning entryway to the tomb.

'Come now! Follow me into the sleeper's sanctum! Bear witness to my triumph and the dawn of a new day!'

Off she went with a flourish, striding and strutting proudly through the miasma of her followers on a straight path towards the waiting tomb in the mountainside.

Ferendir and his companions – much against their will – were dragged along behind her.

CHAPTER SEVENTEEN

Ferendir knew not what to expect from the interior of the tomb. The entryway was a single opening, high and arched, as one might find in a temple or reliquary, carved right into the rock of the mountainside by hands long dead and forgotten. No door barred the way, no gate or portcullis ready to fall and prevent any fool or criminal from venturing inside. One moment they were outside, under the grey, cloud-streaked alpine sky; the next, they were borne by the tide of Astoriss' churning, surging followers under the great arch and into the dark cavern beyond.

For a moment, Ferendir was jostled close to Serath. As the two of them collided – knocked about by Astoriss' clumsy minions – Ferendir's stone-faced master managed to speak to him. His words were whispered and hasty, but Ferendir heard them clearly.

'We live,' Serath said. 'This is not over.'

Then they were torn apart again by the movement of those holding and controlling them. Ferendir stared at his master as the tide of bodies separated them, meeting his narrowed, flinty eyes. He almost did not know what to think, what to feel, what to imagine. His master – the master who had for so long seemed disappointed by him, ashamed of him – now offered words of hope? Words of encouragement?

But staring into Serath's hard, unflinching gaze, Ferendir knew he had not heard those words incorrectly. His master had not given up. He might not know what would come next – none of them did – but until he had breathed his last breath and closed his eyes eternally, he would resist. He would find some way – any way – to await the right moment and do whatever he could – however small, however hopeless – to frustrate Astoriss and save the rest of them.

Ferendir, his gaze locked onto his master's, nodded in understanding.

Serath mouthed silent words then, words that Ferendir could not hear but which he instantly comprehended.

For Desriel.

Ferendir nodded in answer and mouthed the same words. *For Desriel.*

The chamber just beyond the entryway was enormous, rising some three or four storeys above them in a smooth, vaulted ceiling, spreading endlessly to either side before giving off onto a number of substratum corridors and chambers. Directly ahead of them, on the far side of the roughly circular rotunda they now passed through, was a line of tall, ornately carved columns supporting five more open archways carved into the stone of the mountain. Ferendir could see from where he bobbed and struggled among the followers of the sorceress that dark, empty spaces lay beyond those columns – another chamber, or perhaps a tributary passage – but could not tell precisely what might wait there, or how far it might extend.

Nearby, Taurvalon suddenly bucked and thrashed against his captors. Ferendir was not sure what moved the Syari champion to try and hew free at that moment, but it was quickly apparent that his struggles were for naught. Almost as soon as he'd thrown off the two daemonettes that held him and a third that beset him from behind, half a dozen more were upon him, piling on bodily and bearing him down in an instant with ferocious blows and the weight of their own lithe, squirming bodies. A nearby Hedonite bearing Taurvalon's own shield as a spoil of war stepped forward and brought the shining, teardrop-shaped slab crashing down in a quartet of savage blows upon its owner. Taurvalon tried to recover from the first blow but was knocked senseless by the next three. When next Ferendir saw him, he was entirely unconscious, being borne along by a group of daemonettes like a limp rag doll.

Ahead, Ferendir saw Ezarhad Fatesbane, held prisoner by a quintet of strong, tall Hedonites whose broad grins and evil eyes made it clear they were taunting him even as they led him along in shame in the wake of their mistress. Ferendir wagered that whatever the corrupted sorceress had in store for him would be both agonising and humiliating.

Astoriss and the trailing company poured under the five archways into the space beyond. All at once, everyone was crowded together, too close, too tight. The archways had led into a passage that seemed to extend in both directions, curving away around matching bends. Astoriss seemed to know where she was going, so her minions remained in her wake, but the bottleneck created by the sudden squeezing of all those milling bodies into that single dark passageway seemed to make the daemonettes and Hedonites of her coven more than a little crazy. Even as they jostled and pressed on down the corridor, curses were slung, haphazard strikes and attacks made, arguments fomented.

Ferendir looked around him, bounced about like a cork on a sea in the midst of all those monsters in their distemper. Briefly, he lost sight of his comrades. Serath, Phalcea, Metorrah, unconscious Taurvalon – he could see none of them. All he saw were the foul, inhuman faces of his captors as they leered at him or snarled and snapped at one another.

Then, pressed along, he once more found his friends. Serath had somehow pulled ahead, he and the daemonettes guarding him now farther down the hall ahead of Ferendir rather than behind him. Metorrah, likewise, was now almost beside Ferendir, while Phalcea and Taurvalon still trailed behind. The passage carried on, gently curving and – if Ferendir was not mistaken – sloping downwards. They were not only moving deeper into the mountain, but descending.

I will keep the faith of my masters, Ferendir thought, *the faith of my people. I will not fear. I will not despair. I will not even want. I will simply wait. I will watch.*

Some opportunity will present itself.

Some course of action will make itself manifest.

While we live, this is not over.

While we live, this is not over.

Mother Mountain, help me. Help me to believe victory is possible, if not survival.

Suddenly, the passage took a sharp turn. There seemed to be a wide, open portal into another chamber or passage, and from beyond that entryway, Ferendir saw light. It was ghostly and shimmering, like the evanescence of glow-worms reflected off gently bestirred waters, and its colour spectrum shifted as he watched, from deep, fiery red to turquoise green to a brooding, bruised violet and back again. Ferendir wondered what might be waiting for them beyond that threshold, what fierce magic might still dwell in this place, so long abandoned by all but its guardian. But he did not have long to wait.

In moments, he was borne through the portal and into the vast, iridescent space beyond. The moment they entered, the moment Ferendir's eyes fell upon the great space before them and what it contained, he knew they were at last in the presence of an entity of immense and terrible power... even when it was, ostensibly, sleeping and dreaming.

The cavern was enormous, so large that an entire warhost could have fitted inside. Its ceiling was high and vaulted, evincing both the random contours and rough edges of natural formation even as its hemispherical shape seemed impossibly exact, a thing created by will and not by the accidents of time. The bottom half of the cavern was also hemispherical, like a great, deep basin, with a number of wide, concentric tiers leading from the entryway down towards its base. The bottom, however, was not visible. Two or three tiers below the ledge they all now gathered upon, Ferendir saw what looked like a slowly rolling, placid sea, a swelling, shifting surface reminiscent of a large body of water tossed gently in slow-trundling waves by unseen tectonic forces beneath it. Myriad colours spanning the entire visible spectrum and beyond flickered and flashed beneath the undulating surface, cascades of rippling, scintillating light that lent both this chamber and the outer entryways their strange, phantasmic illumination. At intervals, pillars of sudden, silent lightning would burst into being, stretched between the surface of the calmly rolling reservoir and the high, arching stone dome far above it. The effect was haunting, wondrous... even a little terrifying.

But this was not water, nor any liquid. It was light. It was energy. It was the raw stuff of magic.

This was the tomb of Kaethraxis.

Those rising and falling waves of pure light and manifest energy were, Ferendir assumed, Kaethraxis itself – the dormant entity whose awakening could prove catastrophic for the realm they called home.

Ferendir turned, searching for Serath and the others. He saw his master some distance away, still held by his captors, staring down at the coruscating light in the great basin, just like all the servants of Astoriss around him. Serath turned, found Ferendir's wondering gaze and held it for a moment. He said nothing. His silent appraisal was enough.

This may be our last chance, that grim silence seemed to say. *If you see a chance, take it.*

Ferendir nodded. He understood. He only hoped such an opportunity presented itself. Slowly, calmly, he turned away from Serath and searched for the others. Nearby, he saw Metorrah and Phalcea, similarly held by a crowd of Hedonites, each weighing and appraising the strange sight beneath them with their own special modes of understanding. For once, Metorrah seemed the more frightened and uneasy of the two. Though she hid her true feelings admirably, Ferendir could still see the faint hint of trepidation and disbelief in her eyes. Phalcea, meanwhile, stared down into the glowing miasma as though she were looking upon some grim and horrible sight – a mass grave, or a vast slaughter on a battlefield. Beyond them, Ferendir saw Taurvalon, only now starting to awaken from unconsciousness. When he saw the deep basin before them and the churning light that occupied it, all the weight of his wounds seemed to disappear. Suddenly, miraculously, he was wide awake and trying to understand what it was that lay beneath him.

Two tiers beneath where Ferendir and his companions stood, Astoriss led her most trusted lieutenants and the humbled Ezarhad towards a lonely, out-thrust structure like a pier or quay – a pier that protruded directly over the roiling energies in the basin. Astoriss and her retinue strode along this extended outcropping, finally stopping at its abrupt end. There they stood, a short distance above the churning surface of that lambent lake of energy, bathed in its ever-shifting colours and luminescence, closer to its power and purity than any of the others now gathered on the upper tiers of the chamber.

Ferendir watched, wondering what would come next.

Astoriss stared out over the scintillating un-waters. More tongues of lightning burst into existence, first near, then far across the cavern, then near again. A few of those probing, forking strands even struck close to the pier. None seemed to move or worry Astoriss. For a long time the Chaos priestess stood there, her back to her assembled servants and prisoners, gazing out over the moving, glowing light beneath her. Then, at last, she raised the Eidolith in one hand. Even at this distance, Ferendir could see that she was staring into the gem. Whether in answer to her will or by its own volition, the Eidolith began to glow from within, its pale blue light illuminating Astoriss' half-turned face.

Finally, she held the gem aloft, like a prize being brandished for a great horde. She spoke words into the emptiness before her, her voice loud, clear and powerful, carried and reverberated by the enormity of the cavern.

'I am Astoriss,' she proclaimed. 'Servant of the dread lord Slaanesh, Mother of Calamities and conqueror of the Mortal Realms. By the power of this gem I possess – this Eidolith – I bid you, Kaethraxis, awaken! Awaken, and accept from me this sacrifice!'

She spun towards Ezarhad, and something flashed in her hand before plunging hilt-deep into Ezarhad's chest. Though Ferendir was some distance from where they stood, far below him, he saw clearly the shimmer of lilac flame and the look of surprise and agony on Ezarhad's face as the enchanted blade bit deep, stabbing towards his foul, corrupted heart.

The pretender said something to his adversary... but, of course, he was too far away for Ferendir to hear any part of it. All that Ferendir saw was a defiant sneer, moving lips and the way the tall Slaaneshi mage's silk-clad knees buckled beneath him. Astoriss wore a smug, satisfied grin as she shoved Ezarhad Fatesbane and sent him plunging over the edge into the maelstrom of searing energy and scintillating light beneath them. Ezarhad fell silently and disappeared without a sound.

The destroyer of my home, Ferendir thought. *The destroyer of my people. The architect of so much destruction and misery… dispatched with a single thrust of an enchanted blade.*

Who is this Astoriss, Mother of Calamities, that she can destroy our deadliest and most cunning enemies with barely any effort expended?

For a moment, nothing happened. Astoriss' only answer appeared to be a spectral cascade of light and colour within the bright waves heaving beneath her. Then, without warning, a great storm of the lightning that skated across the light-waves burst into being. Forks and flossy webs exploded hither and yon over the waters, some actually cracking and hissing as they came and went, and as the lightning intensified, so too did the rolling and churning of the spectral waves.

It was like watching water in a basin held still and gentle one moment, churned and tossed the next by the jerking of a powerful hand. Huge, rolling waves and breakers formed amid the roiling light storm and crashed on the lower face of the pier upon which Astoriss stood. Where the waves broke, more lightning burst upwards and skated across the vaulted ceiling of the cavern.

Ferendir could feel the energy in the great cavern changing. For one, the air was growing suddenly, impossibly cold. For another, there was a vaguely scorched scent in the air, like the smell of ozone that accompanies a lightning strike from a summer storm.

More importantly, Ferendir felt a change in the grips of the Hedonites that held him. All were loosening their holds, so amazed and enraptured by the storm of light and force playing out beneath them that they barely remembered they were holding a captive at all.

Just wait, he thought. *Be patient. Let them slip–*

'Yes!' Astoriss cried below, still holding the now-brilliant Eidolith above her. 'Awaken, child! Awaken and let me present the waiting world to you! You have slept too long! Been held captive too long! Been a slave too long! Hear me, serve me, and I shall glut all your appetites on the world beyond these mountains where your makers imprisoned you!'

A deafening, rumbling roar rose out of the roiling sea of light. That roar shook the stones beneath their feet and sifted long-untouched dust from the high cracks in the cavern's construction. For a moment, that was all they could hear – that roar, a strange, godlike moan – and then, slowly, gradually, the roar and moan rose in pitch towards a different sort of sound. An exhalation. A sigh. A keening, childlike wail.

The lightning storms on the roiling tides intensified. The crests of the waves peaked, higher and higher. The troughs between them cut deeper and deeper. The once still, once gentle sea of light was now being churned by deep, unseen forces into a raging tempest, swirling and leaping and crashing against the outstretched stone pier and the lower tiers cut into the cavern's basin.

Astoriss stood and watched, seemingly unmoved by the newly bestirred chaos now unleashed beneath and around her. Moment by moment, the scintillating storms of lightning that had once moved lazily over the tossed sea appeared with greater intensity, greater rapidity, snapping and crashing when before they had been ghostly and silent.

Ferendir half-wished he could see the servant of Slaanesh's face as she stared upon the storm she was now inciting. He wondered if he would see courage and confidence there, or simple fear and disbelief – an outmatched child suddenly realising that she had awakened forces she had no hope whatsoever of controlling.

'Awaken, Kaethraxis!' she shouted. 'Awaken, my servant, and make my will manifest! By the Eidolith, by my right as victor, by the power of Slaanesh, I command you, awake!'

The sea of light crashed against the tiers of the basin, spat lightning and phantasmal colours across the narrow, high face of the
pier on which Astoriss stood. Then, as Ferendir watched, amazed
and terrified, the awakening became a reality. What had come
before – the storming seas, the lightning, the moaning and the
wailing – was all just a prelude.

Kaethraxis awakened.

First, the storming sea of light and force collapsed inwards on
itself, turning from a seascape into a swirling, descending maelstrom. Lightning spun and danced around the seething corona
that ringed the great whirlpool. Then, impossibly, all implicit cosmic order was suddenly subverted and upended. The swirling sea
rose, the whirlpool still at its centre, solid and corporeal, a moving
tower, a dancing, whirling funnel cloud stretching from the deepest
depths of the huge circular cavern to its high, arching apex. Where
there had been a sea, there was now a tornado, a typhoon, a massive, whirling column of pure light and energy, tossing horizontal
limbs of crackling, blinding lightning in all directions as it spun.
As the tornado whirled, it roared, the sound so deep and resonant
that it seemed all the earth was trembling beneath and around it.

Then the lightning started to strike outwards, pointedly, towards
the clumps of daemonettes and fiends and mortal Hedonites lined
along the concentric tiers spiralling down towards the basin of the
cavern. Wherever that energy fell with a crash, it turned those it
touched to ash, charring them and vaporising them where they
stood, transfixed by the aelemental forces now unleashed.

Astoriss' servants began to panic. Those on the upper tiers broke
and ran for the entry they'd come through. Dozens were shoved
aside or trampled. Scores more were thrust out of the way and fell
through space to crash down on the tiers beneath them.

Down on the pier, Astoriss herself still stood, Eidolith held high,
shouting something at the entity she had so foolishly awakened.

The roar of the funnel and the searing crackle of the lightning were too loud, too chaotic, to allow Ferendir to hear anything she said. He could see, however, that her closest advisers and servants, the favoured few who had stood beside her upon the pier, were now retreating from the powers unleashed before them.

Ferendir felt his captors' grasp loosening. As many of the Hedonites around him began to break and run, his captors were wrestling with their desire for survival versus their loyalty to their queen and benefactor. When the grip of one daemonette was loosed and the creature broke for the entrance, Ferendir saw his chance.

With all the speed and assurance he could muster, Ferendir seized the daemonette that still held his left arm and thrust her sideways, right into the one that stood directly behind him. In a single moment – a single movement – he was free. Seeing the daemonettes colliding and stumbling, he followed through, using his weight and momentum to swing both back around in front of him. Then, before either could regain their balance or try to arrest their motion, he threw all his weight forward, driving them towards the sheer ledge of the tier.

Down they went, screaming and clawing at the air.

Ferendir was free. Chaos reigned around him.

Down below, the servants of Astoriss were dying in scores, vaporised by the random tongues of flame and lightning that stabbed monstrously out of the enormous whirling column of energy and light. Astoriss herself still stood out on the end of that high pier, her voice crying into the roaring of the creature's great energetic maelstrom, still holding the Eidolith high as if it could save her – could save any of them.

No matter now. He was free – he needed to stay that way. Ferendir turned and prepared himself to meet an enemy – any enemy – in the next instant. But none came. The daemonettes and Hedonites crowding the high tier around him were all screaming or shouting and rushing for the exit, pushing one another aside mercilessly, shoving any and every moving body out of their way. Several fell over the ledge to crash down to the next tier, as Ferendir's captors had, while others fell and were trampled.

There. Ferendir saw Serath, further along the ledge, grappling with his captors and trying to free himself and neutralise the lot of them. He was holding his own, but there were far too many. Unarmed as he was, he would be overcome in moments if Ferendir could not assist him.

Ferendir searched. Just steps away, a daemonette stood by, watching her companions struggle with Serath. She held in her hands Serath's long, heavy stone mallet and danced back and forth as she watched the grappling and fighting, thrilled by it and cheering it on while seemingly edging closer to intervene.

Ferendir was upon her. He charged in, laid hands upon the greathammer, then used the element of surprise and his body weight to swing the startled daemonette towards the ledge and the fall. She snarled and screamed, trying to right herself, but providence sent her flying right into a crowd of fleeing Hedonites, her grip on the hammer coming loose with little effort. As the Hedonites buckled under her weight and the daemonette fought to find her feet and attack Ferendir, Ferendir raised Serath's stone mallet and launched into a fierce, side-swinging attack. His blows crushed skulls and ribcages, pierced foul daemon skin and laid low both the one-time possessor of the hammer and the many Hedonites she was entangled with.

Then, to Serath. Ferendir charged into his master's fray with his many captors. He landed blow after stunning blow, crunching, shattering, rending, tearing. The daemonettes and Hedonites growled and snarled and tried to defend themselves, but to no avail. Ferendir, empowered by a determination to survive – to be away from this place, instantly – was too fast, too cunning and deadly to be stopped. In moments, he stood before his newly freed master, a pile of crushed and twisted Slaaneshi bodies littering the small space between them.

Serath stared, taking in the carnage. Ferendir, suddenly realising that the weapon in his hand was not his own, tossed the greathammer to his master without a single prompt. Serath caught the weapon and studied the purple-black blood now splashed along its length.

Down below, there was a sudden attenuation in Kaethraxis' roar. Now the magical beast seemed to be screaming and crying, though whether in anger or lament Ferendir could not say. As the screams rose in intensity, more lightning forked out in deadly cascades from the spinning, whirling funnel of the creature's aelemental form. Both Ferendir and Serath stared down into the basin of the great cavern and watched as a trio of massive energy bolts shot forth from the heart of the spinning beast and vaporised everyone standing on the pier. In an instant, Astoriss, Mother of Calamities, and all her attending servants burst into white-hot flame and fell into clouds of whirling, glowing ash.

The Eidolith itself simply disappeared in the light storm.

'Well,' Serath muttered, 'that answers the question of the gem's efficacy.'

'Master?' Ferendir said, his insinuation clear – it was time to go.

Serath nodded. 'Hurry now – before we die in similar fashion.'

They turned to run along the tier towards the entryway some distance ahead of them. They saw Phalcea, Metorrah and Taurvalon lurching towards them out of the surging crowd, clearly eager to rejoin them and help them find a way out.

'Turn around!' Serath commanded. 'Out! Get out!'

They did as they were told, and the five of them pressed on as one towards the exit. Just steps ahead of them, a tight knot of fleeing fiends was suddenly vaporised by a random lick of Kaethraxine lightning. The air still stank of ozone and the ash that had once been living creatures yet swirled in the air, glowing like dying embers, as the five of them barrelled through the remains and pressed towards the entryway and freedom.

Ferendir dared a single glance down into the basin.

Kaethraxis was not only awake now – it was moving. Already, its swirling columnar form had climbed up the lowest visible tiers and bent towards the entryway. Ferendir guessed the beast had no need of doors or portals – it would, no doubt, burn or power straight through any obstacle in its way.

How would they stop it?

Could they stop it?

CHAPTER EIGHTEEN

The fact that their escape came late worked in their favour. A few score among Astoriss' minions still clambered for a means of egress and rushed towards safety and salvation, but their ranks were greatly thinned now and none of them paid any attention to Ferendir and his comrades. With their queen destroyed and their imminent destruction promised, these greedy, salacious beings knew only the desire for another breath, another moment of life, to seek escape if it could be sought. They no longer cared who might be their enemies or what their mistress may have wanted from them when she lived. They only knew that if they could steal a few more moments of existence before one of those fierce, random bolts of lightning and fire took them, they must steal that time.

Serath led the way. He, Ferendir, Phalcea, Metorrah and Taurvalon fled out into the main passage and began what suddenly felt like an arduous, impossibly slow uphill climb towards the surface and the safety of the outside world. Behind them, they heard screams, shouts and exhortations, voices begging mercy or pleading for assistance. In fitful bursts, the fire and lightning pealed and cracked. Each time the sound of thunder shook the cavern, more voices, loud and potent a moment before, were instantly silenced. The passage around them and the mountain above them shook, cracks and fissures breaching the walls and ceiling, great slabs of rock and clouds of dust sheering away under the terrible vibrations.

'Faster!' Serath commanded. 'Faster, the lot of you!'

Ferendir obeyed, as did the others. They ran, threading a nimble track through the fleeing, loping hordes that had served Astoriss and were now helpless and bereft without her. Just ahead of them, a huge piece of carved masonry shattered and fell away from the curving walls, toppling right into their path. Serath, leading, stopped and spun, throwing out his arms to keep his companions from stepping any further. The masonry crashed to the floor in a giant updraught of dust, crushing a pair of fleeing daemonettes. When the dust had cleared, it became apparent that the fallen column now choked the passage, presenting a considerable yet not impassable obstacle. Serath, without hesitation, leapt and clambered up the smooth convex monument. It took him several attempts, seeking the most minute hand- and footholds, to scale the monolith. Bracing himself atop it, he offered his hands to the others. They followed, each struggling as he had with the size and relative smoothness of the fallen pillar. Their collective progress to the top of the impediment felt painfully slow.

Behind them, a huge portion of the tunnel buckled, cracked and collapsed, burying dozens of Hedonites. It belched forth an enormous, rolling cloud of smoke and dust that instantly clogged the passage, obscured their vision and made breathing terribly difficult. As Ferendir blinked and coughed, trying to clear his lungs, he saw something flashing deep within the dust cloud – a moving, scintillating glow climbing out of the dark, murky depths towards them, burning through fallen stone and scattered bodies as it went.

'It's coming,' he said.

He felt a tug. The others were already over the fallen column. Serath was trying to pull him along.

'Do not stare!' his master urged. 'Run!'

Ferendir obeyed.

Their way was largely clear. Because they were so desperate, so eager to be away, their flight seemed – to Ferendir, anyway – impossibly slow. Little by little, the passage climbed and curved, Ferendir all the while waiting for the familiar sight of the five arches that would lead out of the passage into the massive vestibule. Behind them, the mountain continued to shake and roar, belching clouds of dust and ash as Kaethraxis burned right through all the rock and rubble in its path on a steady, unyielding path towards the surface. There were more growls and screams behind them as well, as scrambling daemonettes and huffing fiends and foolish Hedonites tried to flee before Kaethraxis and were incinerated by its random, destructive power.

Finally, the five arches loomed before them. Serath poured on speed as they came into sight and the rest of them followed suit, all eager to put at least one more layer of rock and stone between themselves and the rising threat tunnelling through the mountain at their backs. When they emerged from the archways and went fleeing across the broad, open floor of the great vestibule, they saw ancient rock formations far off on their left start to shake and cough small stones and boulders onto the ground as if some massive, unstoppable force were rising beneath it.

'Keep moving!' Serath called. 'Get outside!'

Ferendir did as his master bade. It took every ounce of self-control and willpower left in him not to look back, not to search for Kaethraxis as it bore down upon them. In moments, they were through the vestibule, outside the primary entryway, clambering over the rockfall and fleeing straight ahead, along the floor of the

371

valley, putting even more space between the five of them and the aelemental beast rising beneath.

Ferendir only stopped when he realised that Serath was no longer leading the way, no longer out in front of him. Skidding to a halt and turning back, he saw his master standing alone in the centre of the long, narrow valley, staring back at the cliff face, the high arch leading into the tomb and the haphazard rockfall that nearly blocked it all from view. Ferendir called to the others, indicating that they'd lost their leader, then doubled back, hurrying to Serath's side. When he stepped up next to his master, he studied him.

Serath stood, face impassive, studying the cliff face and the entrance to the tomb – assessing, waiting, formulating a plan.

'Master,' Ferendir said. 'Is this where we stand?'

Serath shook his head slightly. 'This is where I stand. Go with the others.'

'No,' Ferendir said. 'Master, if you're to face this thing–'

'You're mad,' Phalcea said. She and the others had appeared without Ferendir realising it. 'What can you do against such a creature, Serath?'

'My sister is right,' Metorrah said. 'We have to be away from here. If we can fetch a coven of aelementiri–'

'It'll take more than a single coven to contain that thing,' Taurvalon said grimly.

'No,' Serath answered, eyes still fixed on the tomb. 'My temple sought to contain and control this beast when they created the Eidolith. That means it lives and moves and destroys with the sanction of *our* magic, *our* wills. If there is a means of stopping it, it will be one of our own – an Alarith – who succeeds in doing so. I am prepared to take the chance.'

'And if it destroys you?' Taurvalon asked.

Serath turned and looked to his one-time supplicant. 'Then it will be up to you, Ferendir.'

Ferendir stared back, stunned. 'Me, master?'

Serath nodded. 'Aye. You and you alone. Desriel is no longer here with me, young one. In life, my strength was tempered by his compassion, his flexibility of mind and spirit. I made him adamant – he made me supple. Now, standing alone, I may not be enough to contain it.'

'But, master,' Ferendir said, 'if you are not enough–'

'You are the best of us both, in one person,' Serath said, and Ferendir thought he saw something like a slight, warm smile on his master's normally implacable face. In truth, recognising that small, sad gesture sent a chill of fright through him. 'You have always thought yourself weak, unworthy, because you were not entirely like either of us, evincing my will, my strength, my determination, even as those qualities were always tempered by the mercy and empathy and suppleness of spirit that Desriel imparted in you. But you are not less than, Ferendir. You never were. You are the best of us both, incarnate. You are all that we could give you, combined and alloyed into a new material – a better material.'

The cliff face suddenly shook. All the ground and the mountainsides around them joined in. Kaethraxis was coming, rising from within the mountain, pounding right through its stony innards on a direct course towards the surface and freedom. Billowing clouds of dust and smoke were already roiling from the open archway that marked the entrance.

Ferendir shook his head. 'Let me help you, then–'

'No,' Serath said flatly. 'The two of us cannot be spent in one attempt. If I fail, you must succeed. Do you understand, Ferendir? *You cannot fail.* If you do, all of Hysh will pay the price.'

'Then let me go first,' Ferendir said. 'Let me make the attempt while you back me.'

'No,' Serath said, again without hesitation. 'I must face it. I must make the attempt. Even if I fail, I may weaken it enough for you to finish the job. This is the only way, Ferendir. Let your master go before you. Let your master take the brunt of what's to come. Then – only then – will the challenge be yours and yours alone. Do you understand?'

Ferendir's vision was blurred. Suddenly, he realised there were tears in his eyes.

'Master,' he said quietly. 'Serath…'

Then, shockingly, his master did something Ferendir would never have expected. He reached out and laid a single calloused hand on Ferendir's cheek. For a moment, Serath – hard-hearted, severe, cruel Serath – stared into Ferendir's eyes, and the storm of pure, true, unadulterated emotions pouring out of his gaze and into Ferendir's psyche was both moving and startling. It seemed as if, in that moment, all the unspoken words and long-suppressed feelings between them as master and pupil, mentor and suppli-cant, adopted father and surrogate son, came surging to the fore.

'I was only hard on you because I knew I would not always be there for you,' Serath said.

The mountain shook beneath them. Far ahead, the cliff face was beginning to crack.

'Go now,' Serath said quietly. 'I shall make my attempt… then it will be up to you.'

'Master,' Ferendir said, tears streaming down his cheeks.

'Never call me master again,' Serath said, 'for you are my equal in every way.'

Then he addressed the others.

'Take him,' Serath said to them. 'Prepare him.'

Ferendir felt their hands on him, struggling with him, drag-ging him away.

He saw Serath standing tall and strong, facing the cliff and the archway full of dust. Then the cliff cracked and split open like a rent melon. Mountains of rock and scree fell in a massive roar.

Huge clouds of dust and debris billowed forth and choked the end of the valley.

Then Kaethraxis emerged, a storm incarnate, magical energies and pure, destructive force surging and whirling and shining, casting fire and lightning in all directions, terrible and sublime at once.

Serath went to meet it. There was no fear in his stride.

He can do this, Ferendir told himself. *It will be just like the entity in the woods. He and Desriel handled it. They only included me as extra psychic muscle – another consciousness to support and back them against a less-than-reasonable personality. Serath is strong. Serath is a legend. Serath is as immovable as the mountain itself – his will is adamant, his strength unconquerable.*

Serath was well inside the range of the light cast by the creature's whirling cyclonic form, his long shadow thrown down upon the ground in his wake, shifting and dancing with each scintillation and flash of brilliance from within the living storm that was Kaethraxis. The great, towering funnel shifted and turned and danced about the broad, empty space before the now-ruined entrance to the mountain, casting its haphazard lightning about as though it were scattering seeds on eager soil. From time to time, gouts of fire stabbed outwards from the twisting, shining form and seared the air itself, changing the smell of the whole valley. More lightning sought targets. It turned a pile of scree on the nearest hillside into glowing, half-molten slag. It shattered a leaning boulder, freeing a great fall of rock to come crashing down the slope to the valley floor.

'Ferendir,' Phalcea said at his elbow. 'What does he hope to do?'

'The Alarith will is strong,' Ferendir said. 'We are taught from our first lessons under our Teclamentari masters to commune with beings as old and powerful and monstrous in their impulses and appetites as this Kaethraxis. The spirits of the mountains. The more volatile spirits of magma and molten rock that live beneath them.

Serath will try to communicate with the creature – to calm it, or to cow it into submission with the force of his will.'

'Calm it or cow it?' Taurvalon asked. 'Does he see that thing? Has he no inkling of the power it wields?'

Ferendir said nothing. *No, he knows precisely what power it wields. But this is what we do. We are the Alarith. We commune with gods and we win their admiration with deep humility and unbreakable will.*

There. Serath had halted now. He fell to his knees, perched his hands on his folded thighs and lowered his head. He was in an attitude of prayer – of supplication. He would be moving inwards, seeking the deepest, truest, most concentrated part of himself, wrapping himself in utmost confidence, armouring himself in the certainty of that self's inviolate nature, before reaching out to Kaethraxis.

'Listen to me,' Ferendir said. 'You all need to fall back.'

'We will not,' Metorrah said. 'If Serath fails–'

'If Serath fails, I shall be next,' Ferendir said, shocked by the determination in his own voice. 'And I cannot fail. But... if I do, you all have to escape from here. You have to move swiftly, to warn the world outside. Maybe, just maybe, someone else can find a way to control or contain it.'

'Foolish boy!' Taurvalon spat. 'If your master fails, what can you do against that thing? What could you possibly be capable of that he is not?'

'Anything and everything!' Ferendir answered. His response came suddenly, surely, almost unbidden. A moment later, he was ashamed, but he could not back down now. 'He is my master. He shaped me, made me all that I am. If he believes I have what is necessary to control the thing... I have to believe him. I *have* to.'

Far ahead of them, Kaethraxis shuddered. It was a sudden, violent movement that seemed to work all the way up its shape from its whirling base, as though an explosive had been unleashed in the heart of the thing. For a moment, the lightning and fire thrown by its wild whirlings all seemed to flare at once, charring the crisp mountain air, lighting up the grey day with a terrible, lambent urgency. Ferendir looked to the small, kneeling figure of Serath. His hands were high, in a warding gesture, as if telling an approaching enemy that it was their time to stop and go back to where they came from.

Miraculously, Kaethraxis seemed to respond. For a moment – just a moment – the centrifugal force of the whirling tower of air and crackling energy seemed to contract, to thin. Its scintillating lights, the storm of colours within it, actually dimmed and subsided. Then, to Ferendir's amazement, he saw the creature retreating. It was slow at first – barely perceptible – but soon enough it became clear. Kaethraxis was struggling to control itself, to control its impulses, before the adamant, insistent will of this small, fleshly creature before it.

Like a rueful child that had met its match, Kaethraxis was responding to Serath's show of strength and resolve.

Ferendir took a single step forward. 'It's working,' he said.

'Tyrion and Teclis, he's doing it,' Phalcea muttered behind him.

'Aye,' Taurvalon said, mostly to himself. 'That he is.'

Farther... farther. Kaethraxis retreated, slowly but surely, the storm within it abating, the frequency and intensity of the lightning forks and the columns of flame also shrinking as it went. It left ruined ground and slagged stone and whirling dervishes of smoke and ash in its wake, but it was going, working its way along a meandering line back towards the mountain and the tomb.

Ferendir took another step. Only then did he realise what must come next.

If Serath was successful – if he managed to drive Kaethraxis back

into the mountain – he would have to become its new keeper…
its guardian.

He would never leave this place, even if he survived the day.
Something in that revelation filled Ferendir with a terrible sadness and dread. No. It could not be. He could not leave this place
an orphan by Alarith standards – a servant with no masters, no
teachers.

Stop it! a voice within him barked. *Your feelings do not matter
in this. Your desires do not matter in this. All that matters is victory. All that matters is putting Kaethraxis back into its tomb, lulling
it back to sleep. You should sacrifice a hundred beloved masters if
that is what it takes to assure the containment of this terrible thing–*

Kaethraxis suddenly grew angry.

Ferendir could not say what triggered it, what accounted for
it, but the effect was clear and immediate. All at once, the lights
and luminescence flashing and whirling inside the living cyclone
flared and became twice as bright, twice as intense. The funnel
likewise expanded and its whirling pattern became more erratic,
its base scraping violently along the rocky, corpse-strewn ground
as its wide, high corona spat a whole spate of fire and lightning
towards the sky and the surrounding peaks. In an instant, the
whole of the valley was crackling and roaring, the lights bursting out of the funnel so bright that Ferendir could barely stare
at it with his naked eye. His hands flew up in front of his face.
Serath, standing before the bright, shining monstrosity, was little
more than a blurred shadow at its foot, his shadow so long and
sharp-edged now that it seemed to be made of obsidian.

Then Kaethraxis struck. Three jittering bolts of lightning and a
single belching column of fire arced out of its undulating lower
strata, right towards where Serath knelt before it.

Ferendir saw Serath open his arms – not a gesture to shield himself but one of challenge – and then the lightning and fire took

him. Ferendir's master was blasted by a wall of pure, super-heated energy, turned to ash in an instant, then scattered into absolute nothingness an instant later by a gust of snarling wind that rolled out of Kaethraxis.

Ferendir wanted to scream but had no voice. He could only stare, his mind roiling with fear and disbelief, his heart hammering in his chest.

He heard Serath's voice in the empty, panicked chambers of his mind, the words he had spoken only moments ago.

This is the only way, Ferendir. Let your master go before you.

CHAPTER NINETEEN

Serath's destruction seemed to energise Kaethraxis. The moment Serath was vaporised, his ashes scattered, the great, towering monster's cyclonic form swelled and spat surges of lightning and fire in all directions, slagging more scree, blasting nearby boulders to small, glowing fragments, even loosing its energies straight into the sky and churning the grey clouds swirling above. And yet, strangely, the gales twisting and buffeting all around them did not seem to be blowing outwards. Instead, they seemed to be drawn inwards, towards the locus of all the chaos – towards Kaethraxis itself.

It was hungry, trying to devour the world, eager to glut itself.

Ferendir looked to the others. 'Go,' he said.

'This is suicide, boy,' Taurvalon said. 'You will come with us.'

'I will not,' Ferendir said, 'and if you lay hands on me, you will see just what might an Alarith is capable of.'

The words fell out of his mouth before he realised what he was saying. The clear, cold intent they carried – his intention to now go to meet the beast before them, his intention to subdue it or die trying – was already planted within him, true and resolute. Strangely, Ferendir felt no fear. At least, the fear was not imminent or unmanageable. Rather than churning on the surface of his warring emotions, quickening and tossing them, it lay instead like a quiet substratum – cool, sickening, waiting behind the many forces swirling and contending inside him, a scavenger awaiting a weakened, picked-over enemy.

No, on the surface there was just a grim determination – the need to avenge his masters by succeeding where they had failed, the mandate to save this realm with what little insight and ability he possessed.

I am no one's hero, he thought. *I am not the best, not the strongest, not the fastest, not the most cunning nor the most wise.*

But I am here. I am all Hysh has in this moment.

That will have to be enough.

I will have to be enough.

'This is madness,' Taurvalon said to the sisters. 'We cannot allow this–'

'We are allowing nothing,' Phalcea said. 'The Alarith has made his choice. His masters made choices. We will honour those choices.'

Ferendir met the warden's gaze. She understood. She knew precisely what he intended and why. Perhaps most importantly, he saw hope and confidence in her eyes – a sense of some grand purpose that even he could not understand or articulate. Feeling all of those things from her in that instant – recognising her faith in him – Ferendir only nodded, silent gratitude for a silent supporter. Phalcea nodded in answer – his message had been received.

'It's coming closer,' Metorrah said, pointing back towards the tomb.

Ferendir turned. Kaethraxis was indeed coming closer. As it came it dug a deep, furrowed scar into the valley floor, bled tongues of flame and crooked limbs of lightning that melted stone into magma and the sandy, astringent earth of the valley to glass. The tug in the wind – the sense of a deep, hungry well in space and time sucking everything towards it, eager to be filled – had grown stronger.

'Go,' he urged them. 'Fall back to the far end of the valley. Watch from a high vantage. If it takes me, you've got to find the warhost and alert them.'

'You are one person,' Taurvalon said, determined. 'Alone. What can you possibly do against that thing?'

Ferendir had only one answer to give him. 'I am Ferendir of the Alarith mountain temple. I am the student of Desriel, the suppli-cant of Serath. I am the mountain's servant, and the mountain is my mother and my protector. Our hearts – our resolve – are made of stone older than the Mortal Realms. My master believed that something in me can find the heart of that thing and settle it, calm it – perhaps even reason with it. If that is what he believed, that is what I must do.' He gave them all a last, loving look. 'It has been my honour serving with you in this. Go, now – tell the world what you've seen here today.'

And with that, he turned and strode out to meet Kaethraxis… and his destiny, whatever it might be.

Kaethraxis – the living storm, incarnate destruction, offspring of Lumineth hubris – loomed tall and wide before him, filling his vision. It swirled and snaked high into the air, the funnel clouds that contained it illuminated moment by moment by flashes of bril-liant colour and pure aelemental light – hot reds, cool blues, twilit purples, oceanic greens, fiery oranges, warming golds. As Ferendir approached, fire and lightning arced from its massive undulating form, some of its effusions landing uncomfortably close to him, super-heating the stone and sand on either side of his path, fill-ing the air with smoke and burning embers and sudden bursts of pure, concussive force. Ferendir half wondered if he should make evasive manoeuvres…but no. Somehow, he felt that was not the right path.

Just like the entity in the forest, he reminded himself. *It is frightened. It is angry. It senses threats on all sides. Do not threaten it. Balance your strength with your mercy, your adamant will with the warmth of understanding–*

A bolt of lightning crashed into the ground just before him. Ferendir froze and braced himself against the sudden blast of warm air and a storm of flying scree and rock fragments. White-hot stone burned his skin as it sailed past. He stood, arms up before his face in protection, waiting. He expected to be vaporised in the next instant, for everything to simply end.

It did not.

He lowered his hands. Kaethraxis rose like a living tower, high and looming, whirling and roaring, a storm of eldritch energies and pure emotion, incarnate and inviolate, eager to destroy and tear the fabric of creation itself to pieces.

Ferendir raised his hands, open-palmed, as one might to show that they were unarmed and intended no violence.

This was the place. The time. Now or never.

Ferendir fell to his knees, still staring up into the storm of colour and light and pure kinetic force that was Kaethraxis. It would be no effort at all for the entity to destroy him. A single bolt of lightning. A spear of flame. Forward motion drawing him into its funnel and tearing him to pieces in the massive energies contained within it.

Ferendir breathed, slowly, calmly. Staring fixedly at Kaethraxis – staring into it, hoping that it could stare back into him – he closed his eyes and bowed his head.

Breathe. Breathe. Breathe.

Inwardly, he recited the warding words, followed by the prayers to banish all darkness malign, followed by an ode to dangers seen and unseen. Invitation and proscription, just as he had been taught.

I could die in the next instant. Non-existence. Ended.

No matter. Concentrate. If there is any hope, this is where it lies.

He began to shrink – his consciousness, his essence. All the noise and conscious sensation of the world around him grew muffled, then receded, then disappeared entirely. There was no more wind. No more lightning. No more fire. No more heat or cold. No more sense that a great wind was trying to press him into the bulk of Kaethraxis. In moments, Ferendir had plunged from the waking, present physical world into another realm entirely – a realm of thought and intuitions, aelemental forces and pure, unbound will.

He was rooted to the mountain, pinned beneath the sky. Bits of him were torn away and sucked into the empty void at the heart of Kaethraxis. His soul was smudged and effaced by the hungry winds lashing him from behind, driving him forward. Vaguely, distantly, he sensed his three fleeing companions as pure crystal-line essences, alight with vibrancy and desire, burning with need and desperation.

And he... he was smoke. He was black fire burning in a locked chamber. He was nothing and everything, pure spirit, pure will.

And Kaethraxis... Kaethraxis had a form. In this realm, upon this plane, the beast was not just some looming, whirling cyclone at all, but a being. The storm still surged and roiled around it, but at the heart of that maelstrom, feet firmly planted on the ground, it had a body much like Ferendir's own, a form, a sense of self.

Wrong. It did not have one body – it had two. One body was just a child – small, helpless, weak, full of raging emotions and inarticulate desires. The other was tall, mature – aelven, in fact, like one of Ferendir's own comrades or masters – and yet wholly broken. The child was all need. The adult was all trauma and scars. The child only knew impulses, emotions, hungers. The adult... it was scarred, fissured, broken. Grief, self-loathing, anger, mortal terror – they all coloured and beset the being. And as Ferendir knelt there before it, watching, the two spirits seemed to blink in and out of existence, each occupying the same space, each equally desperate to enslave and control the other.

Ferendir recalled Serath's story of the creature's genesis.

Lariel took Kaethraxis into himself, tried to contain it, to control it. It overwhelmed all the natural and magical defences arrayed against it.

Lariel was seized by grief… consumed by aelemental urges… unable to reconcile his rationality with the entity's destructive passions…

Lariel was subsumed by Kaethraxis…

Impetuous outpourings of destructive force driven by a shattered psyche…

These were the two spirits that inhabited the same entity. Kaethraxis – the embodied purge, the creative–destructive impulse of nature incarnate – was the child. All it knew was fear and want, suspicion and anger. Lariel was the adult, wholly aware of what destruction he had wrought – and it had scarred and twisted him, driven him mad.

Who? the thing demanded. It did not come to Ferendir as a word, more as a deep desire – a need to know who, or what, this small, bold creature before it might be.

Ferendir found the warmth within himself – the ghost of Desriel. He imagined his master's kind eyes, the warmth of his playful half-smile, the way his hands could enclose a wound and heal it. Ferendir conjured those memories, those images, those aching losses, and he presented them, whole and unadulterated, to Kaethraxis.

Let me help you. Let me heal you. I feel your pain, your need–

The storm intensified. Even here, on an aethereal plane, the forces churning and shifting around Ferendir were powerful, monstrous.

For an instant – only an instant – that tempest threatened to literally erase him, to simply blow away his consciousness into nothing and bar its reconstitution. But Ferendir held on. He kept himself anchored, concentrated, adamant.

His masters were his anchors.

Monster! a voice called in the darkness. *Destroyer! Abomination! It is mine! I unleashed it!*

Lariel, still traumatised by his failures, his losses, his mistakes. A master – a parent – driven mad by his own self-hatred and inability to forgive his weakness.

Ferendir imagined Serath – strong, proud, stone-faced, always seeming so distant, so disapproving… all the while haunted by his own failure, his own mistakes – or rather, his own perceptions of failure, the mistakes of others that he claimed as his own. Unable to believe. Unable to forgive.

He offered those memories to Lariel. Strong Serath. Proud Serath. Scarred Serath. Grief-haunted Serath.

Something was wrong. The two beings in one were at war again, battling, fighting for supremacy. Once more a gust of willpower and wind threatened to tear Ferendir's spirit to pieces, to scatter him into the aether and total oblivion. Before him, at the heart of the maelstrom, he saw the two spirits locked in a deadly embrace, one moment like two pugilists, grappling and rolling, the next like dancers, whirling and whirling to unheard music, the next like serpents wrapped round one another, snapping, striking, venom and hatred dripping from their bared fangs.

Ferendir anchored himself again – no small feat, their combined force was so powerful, so overwhelming.

Once more the two beings were at war with one another – two psyches vying savagely for supremacy, seemingly moved to combat by Ferendir's offerings.

I gave the frightened child Desriel's kindness and faith.

I gave the guilt-ridden adult Serath's strength and determination.

Suddenly, Ferendir felt a pang of terror.

Tyrion and Teclis, forgive me! I was a fool! A fool!

He remembered the worm in the woods.

Bridge the gap. Be the lens that focuses two separate spectrums of light.

But they are not here! he cried inwardly. *Desriel lies dead! Serath is ash and memory! How can I focus two separate spectrums of light that no longer shine?*

Kaethraxis was growing fierce now, its cyclonic form whirling with greater and greater speed, lightning and raw power bleeding outwards into the world like sloppily fired arrows – haphazard, random, indifferent to what destruction might be wrought.

Ferendir could feel panic rising in him, doubt, fear. He knew – *knew* – that if he failed to fight down those impulses, his end would come in the next instant. One of those stray bolts of lightning would disintegrate him. A pillar of fire would cook him. Great, looming Kaethraxis would consume him, draw him into its tempest and tear him to pieces.

Stop, he commanded himself. *Breathe.*

Breathe.

Seek the mountain. She has not left you. This valley is still part of a range. Within that range is a chain. And within that chain is your mountain, your mother, your home...

Death may come in the next instant... but in the present I will not fear. I will not fail because of my doubt, my panic. I will delve and seek and work this to my very last moment, as Serath did, as Desriel would have...

He went deeper. He called out along the subterranean rivers and unseen ley lines of power that connected each mountain to every other through the bowels of the realm beneath and around him. Before him, the warring souls vying for supremacy in the being known as Kaethraxis were separated, recoloured, drawn into sharper relief against one another, even as they grappled and struggled. They were not evil, not malign, nor mad – they were simply scarred, broken, deeply in need of healing and reconciliation.

Mother? Ferendir called into the dark, addressing the mountain, seeking her power and support. *Tell me, for the sake of the realm, for the sake of my masters' sacrifice – where do I find them? How do I channel their spirits, their very essences, now?*

The answer came in silence. Ferendir might have missed it for the deep, insistent prayers and petitions now echoing in the chambers of his own psyche.

They never left you, the mountain said. *They remain within you.*

He very nearly snapped out of his trance, so shocking was her answer in its simplicity.

All that they were – the parts that could be passed on – live in you now. You need not look far to find them.

He delved deeper. When the floor of his consciousness threatened to halt his dive, he shattered it, punched right through it, down into the substrata that was he, himself, the purest and most symbolic parts of him. And as though he'd uncovered a long-buried spring, Ferendir suddenly felt the separate fonts of energy that were his masters' combined legacies – Desriel's compassion, Serath's crystalline, adamant surety – exploding in raw aelemental waves from within him. With the worm in the woods, their energies had felt like a pair of streams winding down a mountainside, spilling over a single shelf of stone into the same roiling bowl. Now, there was no winding, no soft spillage. He had uncovered geysers, and he stood at the base of the massive waterfall and watched the two streams crash together, combining and churning into a roiling, powerful mélange that only he possessed the power to refine and channel.

They fall. They crash. They commingle. Two become one. I am that one. I am the bowl that receives them. I am the shelf those newly combined waters spill over. I am the river that receives them. I am the scarred landscape that channels the river.

Those two opposing forces – the spirits and legacies of his masters – crashed together at the centre of him, and he sent them hurling outwards, clear and sharp and bright.

I see your fear, the absence of mastery, your untamed impulses – I will tame them.

I see your grief, your guilt, your unresolved self-hatred and ongoing suffering. I will forgive you. I will help you heal.

The answer came as a mighty, realm-shaking roar, both within him and outside him.

No.

Lightning scarred the ground before and beside him. Molten rock glowed an angry red, growing viscous in seconds.

Ferendir was not afraid.

I will not be frightened away, he thought. *Kill me. Destroy me. I forgive you.*

No.

Pillars of fire spat from the great corporeal storm. Burning embers and whirling smoke rained down around him. But it did not touch him. It did not damage him. Still he lived.

I am here, with you, Ferendir said. *I will stay with you. So long as you need me, I will not abandon you.*

No.

I am your student–

No.

I am your teacher–

No.

I am your master.

Kaethraxis raged. The great cyclonic column stretched into the sky, tearing at the cloud, and dug deep into the scree-strewn earth beneath it, tearing up regolith and long-buried boulders. The winds around Ferendir's physical body whipped and lashed at him, lightning seared the air and bursts of angry flame filled his nostrils with the scent of sulphur and char. The whole world trembled beneath and around him. Rockslides scoured the slopes on either side, falling mercilessly towards the valley floor. His body was so shaken, so tossed about where he knelt, that he felt as if his trance might break.

But he could not let it. He had to endure. He had to remain. Kaethraxis had to know that he was true to his word.

I will be your student, your teacher, your master... and you will be mine.

You will not be alone. Not so long as I live.

And then, like a miracle, like waking from a dream, everything ceased. The buckling earth, the roaring, shaking mountains, the tempest-tossed air, the lightning, the fire, the chaos. The effect was so sudden, so unexpected, that Ferendir almost thought for a moment that his death had finally arrived. That the stillness and sense of peace he now felt were simply proof of his transition to another realm.

He opened his inward eye, seeking Kaethraxis.

The cyclone still rose and spun before him, but slowly, pensively. Seeing through his inward eye – the eye that saw all the planes at once – he could clearly discern the two warring souls that only moments before had been threatening him and vying with one another for control.

Except there were no longer two. Only one.

Reconciled. *Whole.* Not healed, but capable of healing.

Ferendir ended his trance. He drew himself up and out of his multi-planar state and opened his eyes onto the physical, present scene in the hidden valley where the tomb of Kaethraxis lay. The great column of incorporeal force and power stood before him, scintillating, bleeding an internal luminescence in a slow, easy cascade of competing colours. There was no more lightning. No more fire. No more thunder and rage.

'Show me the place where you dwell,' Ferendir said. 'The place where I shall now dwell with you.'

EPILOGUE

Ferendir felt them long before he saw them – two souls shining in the aether, venturing slowly but surely over the treacherous mountain passes that led into the valley. His awareness – strengthened and widened significantly by his daily and nightly meditations in the years since he had settled here – was now powerful enough to move into the aether above him as well as along the deep tectonic currents that flowed through and beneath the mountains. So it was that on that particular morning, deep in trance as he always was at that hour of the day, he saw those two familiar living beings hiking steadily through the pass to the west. If his calculations were correct, they would be visible on the slopes, picking their way down towards him, by mid-morning.

It had been many months since any company had joined him in his new remote home. A little conversation, some news of the world outside – both would please him immensely. He decided he would welcome them.

His calculations were correct. Phalcea and Metorrah appeared on the high ridge exactly at mid-morning and began a slow, steady descent towards the valley and the tomb. Ferendir waited patiently for them, perching himself on a large, flat boulder that had been left near the ruined entryway. He crossed his legs beneath him as Desriel often had, then straightened his back and placed his hands sturdily on his knees as Serath might have. So arrayed, he waited patiently, meditating or simply enjoying the view of his sparse, oddly beautiful little valley.

Metorrah and Phalcea did not reach the valley floor until well after midday. When they came marching down the length of the scree-strewn canyon towards the cliff and the ruined tomb, they each raised their hands in greeting. Ferendir raised his own. Though he would not embarrass them by showing excess emotion outwardly, in truth he was very happy to see them. Sitting there, waiting so patiently without going to meet them, had taken a great deal of willpower on his part, for inside he felt a vague giddiness and anticipation – a feeling wholly alien to him since his long-lost childhood.

'I told you he'd know we were coming,' Phalcea said as they approached, loudly enough that Ferendir could hear her.

'Should we be so shocked?' Metorrah answered drolly. 'A powerful and renowned Stoneguard like this one?'

'Teasing instead of a greeting,' Ferendir said. 'I missed you as well, Metorrah.'

He rose, trotted down the steps of the half-crushed, half-buried portico and marched out to meet the sisters. They gave calm, respectful salutes as greetings. Even after all they had been through together, no self-indulgent sentiment could be allowed.

'I have food,' Ferendir said, 'and I insist you partake.'

'Well, you are in luck,' Phalcea said. 'Because we assumed you would have only survival rations up here in this horrible place, and we brought fresh supplies, which *we* insist *you* partake of.'

Ferendir gave a slight smile. He felt the ghost of Desriel in it.

'I would like nothing better.'

'Three years,' Phalcea said, munching crispy twice-baked bread, 'and this place still looks like it was shattered yesterday.'

Ferendir shrugged. 'I am alone. There is only so much cleaning and reconstruction I can do as an individual.'

'Have you no visitors?' Metorrah asked, then sipped her steaming tree-bark tea.

'I do,' Ferendir assured her. 'Intermittently. Every few months, usually. Word has travelled now about what happened here, what a catastrophe we narrowly averted–'

'*You* averted,' Phalcea corrected. 'We fled, remember?'

'You fell back, on my order, so that if I failed, you could bring help. Perhaps it was only good fortune that I succeeded at all...'

'I won't hear you talking that way,' Metorrah said rather severely. 'Your masters saw power in you – purpose, strength. We all helped one another reach this place, but our efforts, in the end, were to assure *your* success. This was your destiny, Ferendir. It had been, all along.'

Ferendir nodded and thought of his masters. Not a day went by when he did not reconjure them in his imagination, to remember what they had taught him, to recall what good and singular souls they were or to simply mourn them and miss them. They haunted his dreams as well, frequently offering him insights into his nature, or the nature of Kaethraxis, that he felt he would not have stumbled upon otherwise. He often wondered whether those ghosts in his mind were them, in fact, or simply aspects of himself wearing their masks. Reason told him it was probably the latter, but he made the conscious choice to believe it was the former.

'I only wish your destiny was not such a lonely one,' Phalcea said. Ferendir heard the concern in her voice, the vague tinge of sadness.

'I am not lonely,' Ferendir said. 'Desriel and Serath are still with me. And Kaethraxis–'

'*Hush*,' Metorrah spat. 'Do not say its name.'

Ferendir shook his head. 'There is nothing to fear. It sleeps. Sometimes we commune in dreams. I will not say it is reformed, but it has changed, however slightly.'

While he told them no lies, he had not told them the whole, unadulterated truth either. But then again, what would be the point of sharing the *whole* truth? In the end, this place was his burden to bear, not theirs.

'Can it *ever* be controlled?' Metorrah asked.

'Or destroyed?' Phalcea added, almost in a whisper.

Ferendir thought about how to answer those questions. After a moment's consideration, he realised he had no answers. He shook his head.

'Perhaps,' he said. 'Someday. For now... I shall remain.'

'What of relief?' Phalcea asked. 'Another Stoneguard?'

Again, Ferendir had no answer. He could only repeat what he had already said.

'Perhaps... someday.'

They were silent for a long time then.

'The wars have not abated,' Phalcea finally said. 'It seems no matter how many minions of Chaos we slaughter and beat back, more are always waiting. The Slaaneshi Hedonites, Disciples of Tzeentch, Blades of Khorne, the Daemons of Nurgle – they are everywhere, swarming in from the darker corners of the realm, always gnawing away at its essence, its very soul.'

'That's what brought us, in fact,' Metorrah added. 'We received word from Iliatha that a new Slaaneshi warhost is tearing hither and yon across the land, reaving and plundering and murdering as they go. Given that it's home, we asked the Windstrider for leave to withdraw from her warhost and go fight with our people.'

'And you thought to invite me?' Ferendir asked.

The sisters said nothing.

Ferendir studied the two of them. They were saying less than they knew, working hard to suppress the sense of dread and portentousness that lay upon both of them, but their thoughts and impulses could not hide from his strengthened awareness and magical insight. He saw their fear as surely as he saw their mutual earnest desire to keep their unspoken fears hidden from him. He half wondered if maybe he had made an unfair assumption – maybe when he had told them there was nothing to fear from Kaethraxis they had seen through him as well?

'There is always a fight, always an enemy,' Ferendir said. 'I only wish I could join you. But for the time being, this is where I am needed. Where I belong.'

Metorrah smiled a little. 'You make us proud, young Alarith. No doubt you would make your masters proud as well. This place – this burden you've decided to bear – is what the moment demands of you, and you do not hesitate to embrace it.'

He nodded. 'Just so.'

ABOUT THE AUTHOR

Dale Lucas is a novelist, screenwriter, civil servant and armchair historian from St. Petersburg, Florida. Once described by a colleague as 'a compulsive researcher who writes fiction to store his research in,' he's the author of numerous works of fantasy, neo-pulp and horror. When not writing or working, he loves travel, great food, and amassing more books than he'll ever be able to read. His first story for Black Library, 'Blessed Oblivion', featured in the Age of Sigmar anthology *Oaths and Conquests*, and he has since penned the novel *Realm-Lords*.

A DYNASTY OF MONSTERS
by David Annandale

War makes for strange alliances – and so it is for the free city of the Colonnade, who must turn to dark forces to defend themselves against the hordes of Chaos…